SILENT SAND

SILENT SAND

Sam Stone

The Vampire Gene Series: Book 5

Published in 2015 by Telos Publishing Ltd
5A Church Road, Shortlands, Bromley, Kent, BR2 0HP

Telos Publishing values feedback if you have any comments
about this book please email feedback@telos.co.uk

ISBN: 978-1-84583-917-8

British Library Cataloguing in Publication Data. A catalogue
record for this book is available from the British Library.

For Sally-Ann Burke
Rest well brave lady.

Thanks to:

My darling David for being my harshest critic. My daughter Linzi, who has her feet firmly on the ground. Terry and Liz Martin for supporting my vision. Major Tinker for advice on weaponry and military matters. Lady Elsie for advice on costume and because she is always so utterly splendid.

'And lo we waited
Eons yet
Beneath the silent sand.
For those who came
And own'ed not
Shall perish by our hands'

Anon, from The Book of Time

Prologue
The Dead

'This is a problem,' said Hunting Buffalo to Walking Spirit.

Walking Spirit nodded. The two wise men sat by the campfire while the rest of the tribe slept. One was chief of the tribe, the other his shaman.

'The dead are rising,' explained Walking Spirit, 'and the messages I receive are that our ancestors our angry.'

'We have tried to avoid conflict,' said Hunting Buffalo. 'As chief, I must protect the interests of the living. The tribe needs to survive.'

Walking Spirit looked into the flames. 'We have let the white man drive us from our homes. The dead, if not the living, wish to take back *our* land. We have a duty to listen.'

Hunting Buffalo shook his head. 'Not at the cost of our children. Not at the cost of our souls.'

Walking Spirit considered the chief's response. He had not raised the dead; they had decided on their own that action was needed. Perhaps this was why they were so difficult to control. He looked out at the dead souls as they gathered at the outskirts of the camp. An army of deceased Indians had marched across the Nevada desert and now they waited. They were horrible to look at: some half-rotted, others little more than skeletal remains. Hunger and anger fuelled their souls, so much so, that Walking Spirit had to place a circle of power around the camp to protect the people inside.

He had also resorted to burning herbs to send out waves of calming aroma around the camp. Otherwise none of them would be resting peacefully in their tepees.

'Perhaps there is a way to control them,' he said.

'Blood is the only thing they understand,' Hunting Buffalo replied. 'It is too high a price to pay.'

Walking Spirit stood and made his way to the edge of the camp. 'Who leads you?' he asked the tribe of the dead. 'Why do you come here?'

Greedy eyes stared back at him, while broken, rotted teeth gnashed in decomposed mouths. Skin hung from the bones of some, like the remains of tattered clothing. Most were mummified corpses: the dry sand had sucked the moisture from the rotted flesh, drying it over skeletal carcases.

Walking Spirit traced the circle, looking for some sign of comprehension from the revenant souls. Blank eyes greeted him. Then, he came across his own son: newly dead, Dancing Spear still looked almost human. Almost. The eyes, red and bloodshot, held the cunning of great evil. Walking Spirit stepped back from the gathered corpses. Fear clutched at his heart.

'My son. Can you speak to me?' Walking Spirit asked.

Dancing Spear's ravenous smile chilled Walking Spirit's soul. The shaman backed away and returned to the fire. He met Hunting Buffalo's eyes and the chief saw true fear in the shaman's expression for the first time since the walking dead had arrived.

'I had hoped that we could use them to fight our enemies,' Hunting Buffalo said. 'But ...'

'The dead cannot be used in that way. I think ... it would be a mistake to try.'

Walking Spirit looked back at the line of animated corpses. They shuffled against the circle of power but made no attempt to cross.

'How long will that last?' asked Hunting Buffalo. He feared for his grandchildren. 'The white man has tried to destroy us before. Maybe this evil is their doing?'

Walking Spirit said nothing. He gazed into the flames, looking for answers from the fire spirits. When he finally looked up, he could not meet Hunting Buffalo's gaze.

'The white man knows nothing of natural power. I do not

believe he could do this.'

'Then what must we do?' Hunting Buffalo asked. 'We cannot stay behind this shield forever. The stocks of food are already diminishing. And these … these creatures frighten the children.'

Walking Spirit opened the leather pouch he kept slung around his neck and took a pinch of the herbs inside. He threw them into the fire. Smoke and sparks danced above the blaze. He stared into the billow of smoke, carefully reading the shapes as the residue rolled and expanded. Hunting Buffalo leaned forward. He too watched the smoke, but could see neither shape, nor pattern in it.

Walking Spirit bowed his head. He read and understood the message all too well. The dead could only be returned to the earth with a sacrifice, and the shaman was not prepared to offer any of his flock, for whoever gave their blood would be forced to join the creatures in their undead limbo.

'I can't,' he said.

'What is it?' asked Hunting Buffalo.

Walking Spirit stood. He looked out at the eager dead once more, sensing their hunger.

'The spirits demand a sacrifice.'

Hunting Buffalo sighed. He had feared this more than anything. Who could they offer that did not deserve to enter the spirit world? He cast his eyes around the camp, assessing each of his people by their importance to the tribe. He could not think of a single person that he would willingly sacrifice.

Suddenly, he felt the warm and gentle hand of the shaman on his shoulder. Hunting Buffalo looked up and he met his friend's eyes.

'I must do it,' Walking Spirit said. 'It must be a willing sacrifice and my blood is the magic needed to put the dead to rest.'

Hunting Buffalo stood. His heart was gripped with fear for his friend. They had both been boys together, Hunting Buffalo always destined to be chief, while Walking Spirit's skills had surfaced during puberty, talking him down the path of magic. They had been through much together. Plague, starvation, near death. Then, when times were good, the white man had stolen their land, eaten and destroyed their food sources. Even so, nothing had terrified the chief more than the arrival of their own dead. It was as though they had come back to reclaim the rest of the tribe. Hunting Buffalo knew that their survival hung in the balance more this day than any other but still he did not wish to see Walking Spirit sacrifice himself.

'After this is over, take our people to the mountains,' Walking Spirit said. 'Never return to this spot.'

'Why?' asked Hunting Buffalo.

'We cannot risk the spilling of *Wa She Shu* blood here in this place.'

Hunting Buffalo nodded but he did not fully understand what the shaman was saying. It dawned on him that Walking Spirit would not survive the night.

'My friend …' said Hunting Buffalo.

'After I have reburied the dead, take the tribe and never return,' Walking Spirit said.

Hunting Buffalo watched as Walking Spirit began to prepare for his ceremony. The shaman fetched his ceremonial robes and began to walk the edge of the circle once more. The dead became restless; it was as though they knew the time for action had come. Hunting Buffalo pulled his wolf skin tighter around himself. Despite the desert heat, he felt cold. His stomach lurched with fear and for the first time the brave chief felt like a coward. He wondered how he would face his people in the morning if he let Walking Spirit die this night.

'Do not fight this,' said Walking Spirit. 'This is my destiny.'

Walking Spirit stood by the edge of the circle and raised his arms. He began to chant and the wind rose up around the camp. It lashed at the shaman, as though trying to stop him from completing his song. The wind carried sand that was so sharp that it cut at the face and hands of Walking Spirit, and Hunting Buffalo looked on in horror as the shaman bled.

The blood was caught by the wind and it splashed out over the corpses, they stepped back from the circle, cowering as though they finally felt the fear they had inflicted. Walking Spirit stepped out of the circle of power and stood unprotected before the dead.

'No!' gasped Hunting Buffalo, even though he knew he was powerless to stop what happened next. But the dead did not fall upon Walking Spirit as the chief expected. Instead they shrank back: they were afraid of his touch.

Walking Spirit's blood dripped to the ground. The soil around his feet turned clay red and it spread before him, polluting the ground that the dead occupied. They backed away, but Walking Spirit roared a word of power. It burned his lips and tongue until they blistered, but still he used it, over and over again until the dead were unable to resist the magic and their skeletal appendages became frozen.

The blood extended around them and as it reached the decaying limbs of the first row, Hunting Buffalo saw the revenants' mouths open wide in a silent scream as they slowly broke apart and crumbled. Beneath them the ground opened up; it churned and rolled, sucking down the disintegrating remains. This pattern repeated, line by line, until all of the dead were taken back down into the sand they had somehow escaped.

Hunting Buffalo found himself propelled forward. He stared across the line as Walking Spirit, now on his knees, continued to bleed into the earth.

'Take our people and go!' Walking Spirit cried with his last breath. 'Never return to this place.'

Hunting Buffalo watched in horror as Walking Spirit fell forward onto the soil and the hungry earth opened up and swallowed the shaman down.

Then he cried.

The next day, Hunting Buffalo and the remains of his tribe packed up their camp and took to the mountains. In his lifetime no *Wa She Shu* ever lived on this part of the land again. Despite the promise he had made, Hunting Buffalo found that he could not speak of the night of the dead to anyone and after his passing, no one then knew of the warnings given by Walking Spirit.

Part One

The Castle

1
Scars

I stretch in bed, feeling the familiar and sensual ripple of my muscles as I lengthen my body, waking up all of the ligaments. Anja, my angelic beauty, sleeps beside me, undisturbed by the strange, awkward sensation that has awoken me. I feel like there is a change in the air. Something so subtle that I cannot tell from where it comes.

It is difficult to consider the brutal changes that life has brought me. Here I am relatively happy in the arms of my lover Anja. Yet sometimes the loss of Lilly is the hardest thing to bear. Lilly has become distant. More and more these days Lilly and Chez go their own way. Even so, Anja makes a good companion. Her original fragility frequently gives way to a power and strength that none of us had thought possible. She grows more like us every day. Her beauty, once like a delicate flower that always appeared to be on the cusp of bloom, flourishes. I'm in awe of her, yet feel no security in the love she seems to have for me. Love among immortals can be fleeting and fickle. Or so it seems when I think of the all-consuming passion I once shared with my darling Lilly: for this is a passion that is no longer reciprocated.

It is noon. I can feel the sun burning the world above us. I am always aware of the movement between night and day. It is as though I have some internal clock, constantly monitoring.

I test the air and notice that Lilly and Chez are not in the lair. I sense their absence almost as much as I would be aware of their presence. There is an emptiness in Rhuddlan when Lilly isn't home. Her connection with the castle sends energy rippling through the walls and foundations when she is here. She brings the ancient lady alive in a way that none of the rest of us can do. Even so, we are always safe here.

I stretch again, this time feeling that familiar twinge, and so my hand strokes the scarred skin on my spine. The old wound aches: a close call never to be repeated. It is strange that I consider our safety. We are, after all, blood sucking monsters with the strength of ten men at least. But … for a time my strength was seriously compromised. Like any mortal I was wounded and tied to a wheelchair, despite my powers to heal, and the memory of those days will always stay with me. It is like a cloak of darkness. I will always recall that death waited on the periphery and almost claimed me. I, like mortals, do not know what lies beyond that veil and fear the perpetual darkness the same as anyone. My near-death was a leveller to the invulnerability I believed was mine. I'm unsure if I will ever feel safe again.

I am Gabriele Caccini, nephew of a great musician, Giulio Caccini, the man who once devised a style of music and method of vocal training that has now led to the genre we call opera. I have a sense of my heritage still, but my belief in immortality is somewhat jaded. I no longer always feel strong and powerful, and I certainly do not believe I am invulnerable. But what we are and what we 'immortals' have, is, I believe, the closest thing to eternity that there can be.

I push aside these morbid thoughts and slip naked from the bed. Anja moans slightly and turns over but she doesn't wake.

I find myself face to face with the image of an Adonis. My nakedness reflects back in the full length mirror on the wardrobe door and I admit I like to look at, and admire, the perfection of myself even now, after all these years – or perhaps more now than ever because it was almost taken from me. I was born in the sixteenth century, but life, now that I have my family, has only recently become worth living. It is only when mortality closes in on us that we can appreciate our existence.

I love the modern world: its technology; its weapons; its consumerism. And I have embraced it completely because I think that to stay static, believing in my old values, would make me weak and unable to progress. This is not an option I am willing to consider.

'Come back to bed,' Anja murmurs. 'I'm cold.'

I reach down and pull the covers back over her, but don't comply with her request. She is lovely, but doesn't have quite the command of me that Lilly once enjoyed. Anja could one day be my equal, but for now I am enjoying my power over her. She needs me more than I need her. I don't love her, but do desire her, and being with her is convenient even if that truth seems cold and calculating.

I pull my robe from the hook on the back of the door and slip it on over my muscular frame, flicking my shoulder-length hair over the collar. I relish in the potency, the power that moves under the surface of my skin and pumps through my veins. The blood is the life after all and mine is intoxicating magic.

In the bathroom, I shower, half expecting Anja to come in – she rarely leaves me alone for long – but I finish my ablutions without interruption for a change. Afterwards, with a towel wrapped around my waist, I run a comb through my damp, slightly wavy, blond hair letting the water splash over the tiled floor. It doesn't matter though. This is a wet room and walk-in shower. The water will dissipate and feed into the waste pipes underground, or at least that is what Lilly has told me.

Returning to the bedroom I find Anja gone, but hear the ping of the microwave as she warms blood for her breakfast downstairs. The aroma stings my nostrils and makes me feel hungry. I slip into a pair of black chinos and a polo neck sweater before hurrying downstairs to be with her.

Anja is reading a magazine when I enter. The pages are full of so-called celebrities photographed at awards and events, or caught unawares when they are out shopping. She is wearing a thin robe. The lair is cool and I see the points of her nipples protruding through the thin fabric. I suddenly regret not getting back into the bed with her. She looks ruffled and sexy, but her taste in reading material puts me off slightly.

'What do you want to do today?' she asks, and it is a familiar question as we have little or no motivation to do anything most of the time.

'I think we need to go out somewhere for a drive. I'm tired of being in. Perhaps we'll go away for a few days.'

'I like the idea of going away. Will you take me to Paris, Gabi? Or Rome? Somewhere romantic.'

Excitement colours her cheeks. Blushing is a trait I find attractive in women and I soon forget about the awful magazine. I pull her to her feet, kiss her long and deep and taste the faint traces of the 'O' Positive blood she has been drinking.

'Maybe Lilly and Chez would like to come as well?' I say. 'When they get back we'll ask them.'

She freezes in my arms, withdrawing her lips and body from mine.

'I'd prefer we went alone,' she says.

I think about it. My instinct is to tell them we are going away and where we will be but I realise with a jolt that they have not told us where they are.

'Okay,' I say.

Anja is surprised, but delighted, by my sudden capitulation. Most of her requests are met with indifference but I want to please her – sometimes. Besides it will be interesting to see how Lilly reacts when she finds us gone for a while.

'Pack a bag, but don't take much. We'll fly ourselves over to Paris. I'll go online and book a hotel. There are some beautiful boutiques on the Champs-Élysées and you might want to buy what you need there. My treat.'

Anja hurries to the lounge door, excited energy coming off her in waves. She is still every bit the twenty-first century girl when she is like this. She has yet to learn that possessions mean nothing to immortals. But I don't point this out to her because I can feel her happiness bouncing around the interior of the lair as she runs upstairs to pack.

I pick my mobile phone out of its docking station and slip it into my trouser pocket. It vibrates against my thigh. I retrieve it and see a text from Lilly. She and Chez are in London. I don't reply.

A short time later we are camouflaged as I carry Anja over England and the Channel towards France. She is still too young to fly herself and so she snuggles up in my arms. She is silent but happy and I imagine that she is thinking about the shopping trip and the new clothing I'll buy for her.

'This is our first adventure together,' she says, and the thought of it scares me slightly, though I don't know why.

The air is calm. The sea a dark, deep and vibrant blue, that rolls and moves slowly below us. Above us the clear sky offers no shelter from the burning sun, but we have fed well on blood-bank ready meals and so it cannot hurt us.

As Anja rests in my arms, enjoying the feel of being carried, it crosses my mind to drop her into the ocean. She won't be expecting it and I know the fall into the sea, even though we are a mile or more above the water, won't kill her. She would, probably, suffer from some broken bones though. I envision her battered and bruised body, knowing that it would heal almost immediately: but the complaining and whining wouldn't be worth it. Anja is very annoying when she is irritable. I shelve the thought for another time but inwardly smile at the idea as it makes me feel more like my old self. I am a killer. A monster. And I have always enjoyed being that despite my old habit of only feeding once yearly. Despite all of the angst I revelled in. For some time now I have not enjoyed the restraints Lilly imposed on us all even so. Our wings are clipped, our feeding habits curtailed: we are prisoners by our own design. Yes – I admit I enjoyed my self-imposed starvation and the death that it allowed me to inflict when I broke my fast.

It feels good to fly from Rhuddlan. It feels good to make our own decisions. It feels good to leave Lilly and Chez behind instead of them leaving us.

2
Subject Five

'Mine's a coffee. Black. Two sugars,' said Private Elin as his partner, Private Parker, stood up and walked towards the percolator in the corner of the security monitor room.

'Yeah. Yeah. I know,' replied Private Parker.

Parker turned his back on the monitor-covered wall while Elin's eyes flicked over each of the screens in turn but as always were drawn back to one particular room and the young boy inside it who sat on a bed. The scientists referred to the boy as Subject Five, but unlike the first four subjects, Five showed great potential. Five had a limited understanding of language but seemed to grasp most of what they said to him. Sometimes he actually spoke.

He was a thin boy of twelve. Around his padded observation cell were various objects that might interest a normal boy: books; crayons; paper. Occasionally he used the crayons and paper, drawing obscure and strange shapes with angular corners. Or drawing what some of the scientists thought was an eye. Sometimes, it was noted, the sketches had the appearance of mouths with long, sharp, pointed teeth. Right then, though, the boy was sitting quietly, looking benign and sweet. Elin wondered if this innocent-looking child even knew why he was locked up in the bowels of the Earth like this, or if he even understood where he was at all. He barely spoke after all, and Elin had observed how the doctors drugged the kid before any of them dared go inside the room.

Right at that moment, though, Five appeared to be observing himself in the mirror on the opposite wall like any normal boy might. His dull eyes were blood-shot and held the mysteries of a mind that was much older than his appearance suggested. The face, however, was somewhat angelic. It was a pose the boy took whenever he was hungry. It was feeding time. And it was always at these times when he looked his most innocent.

Elin couldn't help but feel some sympathy for Five. He had a cousin the same age and often wondered what he would do if he discovered he was the same as Five. Would he hand him over to the Feds like Five's own relatives had done? He didn't think so. He had seen how Five was treated and it wasn't nice, no sir. But then, who knew how you would feel if you came home and found your eldest child chowing down on the youngest?

Elin blinked away the thought and glanced over his shoulder to see Parker scratching his ass as he waited for the coffee to brew. Then he looked back at the monitor as a panel opened in the door of the cell. The boy didn't stir, but watched through the mirror until the tray of food slid forward. As the panel closed, he pounced, knocking the tray onto the floor spilling the contents over the cold concrete. A red stain splashed up the wall as Five fell on the food, tearing and shredding the raw meat with a mouthful of saw-like teeth. It was one of those times when Elin wished the monitor was black and white instead of colour.

Elin pressed a button and above Five's head the cameras moved, following him as he ripped and tore at the animal carcass. The boy ignored the cameras as he ate, slowly deteriorating from the innocent looking kid, into a feral and dangerous revenant. Elin recorded the whole sorry gorging session though and he archived it with all of the others.

Elin was one of a few subordinate soldiers who had clearance to see the subjects but there were four civilian scientists that knew about the project. Three men and one woman. Doctor Cameron was in charge. He was in his early fifties with a full head of greying hair and a moustache that he stroked and smoothed as he spoke. The other two men were younger. There was Joe Carter, mid-thirties, an attractive man with mousy hair and a charming smile and Marcus Delaney, forty, almost completely bald. The woman was Lucy Collins. She was in her late twenties, blonde, with dark brown eyes. Collins was a blood specialist who had been drafted in eighteen months ago.

'The cream's off,' said Parker. 'I better go and fetch some from the mess. You okay for a while?'

'Sure,' said Elin, even though he knew the cream was fine. Parker often liked to go walkabout during their duty. He got bored watching the screens, and there was that pretty little data analyst on the floor above.

Parker pressed the door release and the door opened. Elin didn't look round as his partner left and closed the door to the room securely behind him. When he heard the click, Elin turned to the monitor covering the small room behind Five's two-way mirror and switched on the sound.

'There has been some improvement in the boy's condition,' Doctor Cameron said. 'He's learned to wait for his food instead of attacking the panel as soon as it arrives. Plus, yesterday, he started reading the books. Or at least he appeared to be reading them.'

Elin had been monitoring on the day that Joe Carter had noted Five's interest in the books. But Joe said nothing as Cameron took the bows once more for his achievements. Marcus and Joe always agreed with Cameron because he had as much power over them as he did the experimental subjects. There was a rumour that one of Cameron's previous employees disappeared: apparently the man or woman had questioned Cameron's judgement. Later, it was said, they turned up as the subject being used for their own experiment. Elin didn't believe this rumour. The detail was too general and he believed that Cameron had circulated it himself in order to keep his scientists in check.

'Therefore my report will say that the conditioning is working ...' Cameron said.

'What nonsense, doctor,' Lucy interrupted, and Elin sat forward.

Lucy was an anomaly as far as Elin could tell. She came and went on the base more than anyone else and she wasn't afraid of Cameron, despite the rumours.

'Five is little more than a semi-intelligent animal,' Lucy said. 'He's like a lion in a cage. He knows that his trainer will whip him if he steps out of line, but he is forever watching out for when that trainer has forgotten his whip. All we can conclude with the experiments so far is that Five is smart enough to realise that if he attacks the grille, he gets an electric shock and no food.'

Cameron's cheeks turned a deep purple.

Elin knew a lot about what happened on the base. He kept his eyes open, his mouth shut, and had a skill for not being noticed because of this. He knew of Cameron's nightly excursions; how the older scientist was seen frequently knocking on Lucy's door, only to be sent away, rejected. Elin wondered how long Lucy would last if she didn't put out. He felt a genuine concern for her as she continued her rant and as Joe Carter involuntarily reached out a hand to stop her talking, Elin suspected that Joe felt the same.

Elin was of American Indian heritage. The dark brown depths of his eyes had an eerie knowing look that held the knowledge of his ancestors. His skin, watered down by so many white relatives, made him appear white American. Thanks to his grandmother though, Elin could trace his mother's line all the way back to the nomadic days of his tribe and he knew, in his heart, despite his skin, that he was *Wa She Shu*. No one on the base knew this; not that it should matter at all these days. Elin knew better than to share anything about himself with the white men he was friendly with, however. He had been down that road before and the Indian jokes got a little wearing after a time.

'How dare you question my assessment, Doctor Collins,' Cameron said, spitting saliva as his flustered lips tried to form the S's in assessment.

'This isn't a challenge, Cameron. You always have to make it that, and I'm tired of it. We aren't your stooges. All of us were brought in because of our unique skills and yet you hardly let us use them. As well as his obvious skills in the lab, Joe is an excellent psychologist and you rarely listen to his opinion. Marcus is an expert in degenerative diseases, yet you throw him a few scraps to scrabble around with. And as for me …'

Elin felt the hairs rise on the back of his neck as he noticed Five looking up at the two way mirror. It was as though the boy knew he was being discussed. He dropped the half-eaten animal carcass on the floor and walked up to the glass, looking directly in at the scientists. Cameron didn't notice as he had his back to the glass while he addressed his colleagues, but Joe and Marcus instinctively backed away from the mirror even though they knew that Five couldn't possibly see or hear them.

'I think we should up the dosage of shock treatment,' Cameron said, ignoring Lucy.

'That would be a mistake, doctor,' Lucy said, pushing her small black spectacles back against her eyes. 'Five has already shown that the shock treatments aggravate him. I don't think it is helping the conditioning process, but rather hindering it.'

Cameron flushed once more at her further disagreement. 'Since you are such an expert on this subject what do you suggest then, Doctor Collins?'

'More physical contact. We try to humanise Five. We could try to give him a proper name, rather than a number.'

Elin was surprised at this show of humanity and he stared at Lucy's face, zooming in on the monitor.

Cameron threw back his head and laughed. 'Doctor, your response to Five is exactly why there are few females on this base. Humanise the beast? You can't civilise a … lion, to use your analogy, when it has lived all its life in the wild. How do you expect to tame this monster?'

'Doctor, I'll remind you that it is against company policy to discriminate against one's colleagues because of gender. I don't appreciate your remarks. I speak only as a scientist. The brutality you've inflicted on Five has achieved what exactly? You've managed to get him to eat his raw meat a little more gracefully – he's learnt this because if he doesn't it will be ripped from his hands and he'll be left to starve. We need to educate the boy if he is to be of any real use to us. He's an accident of birth but it doesn't mean he can't be improved.'

Cameron's eyes bulged. Joe and Marcus exchanged looks. And Elin, in the security booth, realised that Lucy had probably gone too far this time. Cameron was furious.

'How do you propose we … *educate* this animal?' Cameron said, his voice rising. 'Send him to school?'

'Yes. That was exactly what I was thinking. We teach him to read. Get a television in there. Talk to him.'

Cameron gave a short laugh.

'Ridiculous. He would kill anyone who went in there before they had a chance to say "hello". Delaney? Carter? Are either of you willing to go in and *educate* this creature?'

Marcus and Joe looked down simultaneously.

'I wasn't suggesting anyone but myself for the role of tutor, doctor,' Lucy said.

'No,' Joe gasped. 'You can't possibly …'

Lucy looked over the top of her glasses at Joe, 'Yes I can. I will prove to you that this … boy … can be tamed.'

Cameron folded his arms, a smile widened from a sneer on his lips.

'I'd like to see that, doctor,' he said.

'Firstly, we have to stop drugging his food. Secondly, he needs blood, not raw meat. He's not getting the nutrition he needs from the meat. Also it needs to be human blood. Animal blood doesn't kill the hunger.'

Cameron looked around the room hoping for back-up from the two men but found them staring at Lucy instead.

'As you know, I'm the one that works closest with these creatures. I'm the one who has studied them and their DNA. I suspect you will get much more sense out of Five if you follow my instructions to the letter.'

'Just who the hell do you think you are, Collins? I run this facility. I say how we play this. Delaney, Carter. Leave us.'

Joe and Marcus turned towards the door, but as Joe glanced over his shoulder he noticed that Five's face was now pressed completely against the glass.

'Doctor …' he said.

'I said leave us, Carter,' Cameron snapped.

Joe shrugged and closed the door on Cameron and Lucy.

Elin noticed the slight smile on Lucy's face. It reminded him of the leer he saw on some of the faces of the subjects just before they fed. And that was when the monitors decided to crash and Elin lost all sound and sight of both the observation booth containing Lucy and Cameron and the padded cell that held the revenant boy known as Five.

'Damn it!' Elin said slapping the side of the monitor. 'Piece of crap.'

He tweaked and jiggled the wires, turned dials, but couldn't get the monitors back on. Eventually Elin decided to reboot the digital system. Sometimes that worked, but the system was always going down like this. He shut down the main computer for a few minutes before restarting. Slowly the monitors came back to life.

As an image of the cell containing Five and the camera in the observation booth came back on, Elin began to yell. He pressed the alarm, but it was already too late. Cameron was dead and Five was eating his face. He searched the observation booth, saw that Lucy Collins was still there, staring out through the hole where the two-way mirror had once been. Elin could tell exactly what had happened.

'Get out of there!' Elin screamed at the monitor.

At that moment, as though she heard him, Lucy looked up at the camera. Elin noticed that Five had abandoned the body of Cameron and was moving rapidly towards the opening once more. The picture went black again. Elin turned, pressed the emergency release, yanked open the monitor room door and ran towards the lifts.

3

The Fixer

Darren Preacher stood at his office window and gazed down over Central Park. He hated New York. From this distance he could barely make out the pond, and the ducks swimming on the surface were little more than tiny specks. He could just about see a little boy and his mother as they sat on a bench. His mind filled in the blanks of movements that he couldn't quite make out. He speculated that the boy was throwing breadcrumbs into the water, despite the blatant sign that read PLEASE DO NOT FEED THE DUCKS. Preacher hated people who couldn't follow the simplest of rules. It made him furious. What kind of message was this stupid bitch giving her kid by ignoring an obvious sign?

His rage and frustration at society boiled up inside him, leaking out into his day job. He was aware that he sometimes took it out on his secretary, Maggie. But he detested her anyway. If he could send her home crying at least one night a week he was happy. Women, especially weak ones, infuriated Preacher more than anything. They were stupid, pathetic creatures, that served only two purposes in life and Preacher rarely allowed himself to indulge in their waning charms.

Preacher smoothed down his steel grey Armani suit and ran his hands through his neat white hair. Preacher was albinoid, which meant that his skin, hair, eyebrows and eye lashes lacked any pigment, while his eyes were a pale blue, bordering on white. He hated the paleness of his skin and so took to having regular spray tan sessions, choosing only the light tan, so that his appearance was as natural and normal as possible. He was careful of his looks and fitness, working out three or four times a week with a personal trainer, and he had his eyebrows and lashes dyed every month. He had given up trying to colour his hair though: the white, almost translucent strands threw all colorants off, failing to hold beyond the first or second wash. It had frustrated him initially, but these days he enjoyed his white hair as he had learnt that it made him attractive to both sexes. In his line of work this was useful.

Preacher sat down at his desk and began to look through the files that the agency had sent him. He was feeling wired that morning and so a new job was just what he needed. The folder contained pictures of four beautiful people that looked as though they belonged to the same family. Two women, blonde, green-eyed. One curvaceous, the other androgynous – the younger one looked like she might still be going through puberty. The two men were equally as interesting. Also blond with green eyes. One had hair that trailed down his back which he wore loose in the photograph, giving him a feminine quality but there was no mistaking the male strength around his jaw. The other wore his hair shoulder length but was equally beautiful and strong.

'Interesting,' Preacher murmured.

He felt a sexual stirring as he gazed at the men. The women didn't interest him in quite the same way, especially the curvy one. He preferred straight, slender hips in females. Boyish flanks and flatter chests were appealing because they gave the appearance of innocence. The women he slept with all looked like teenagers. The men he slept with were all pretty. Preacher understood his tastes and went with them. He felt no guilt at indulging in sex with whoever appealed to him.

The second male was the target for a reason that remained unexplained. Preacher studied his face, taking in every detail. The body was muscular and defined; he imagined the firm abs underneath the white shirt the man was wearing. The information in the file said that his name was Gabriele. The file contained no surname but a location was provided.

'Gabriele,' Preacher murmured. Even the name was female,

though he noted the phonetic description of the name which said it was pronounced Gab-ree-ell-ee.

These days he passed most jobs over to one of his lackeys, but not this kind. He always took these himself. There were so few of them and he truly enjoyed the hunt.

As he read on he saw the words, but barely registered them, 'Dangerous. Approach with extreme caution'. He had dealt with this sort before and he had dart guns which contained potent drugs that would knock out an elephant let alone a revenant.

Preacher had made a career working as a 'fixer' for the CIA. During that time the job had shown him that there were indeed strange things in the world. If the fee was high enough he would risk anything. Sometimes it had almost cost him his life. Preacher felt the old bite-wound itch. He glanced down at his wrist, pushed back the cuff of his shirt and stared down at the scar. The last one that bit him was still lying in a coffin buried deep in the ground in the basement of the building. Concrete would hold that little bastard indefinitely, but Preacher knew that containment wouldn't kill it.

He was always on the lookout for intelligent ones, the real vampires, not the drones he had so far found. He thought about the one below. Sometimes he wondered if he had been a little impulsive, but the bastard had taken a chomp out of him. Even so, what might they have learnt if he had taken this one in instead of burying it ten feet below the floor? After all there had been a great deal of intelligence. The thing had sought him out. Preacher suspected it had been of some kind of vendetta. Perhaps related to another of the creatures that he had contained and turned over to the authorities, but he couldn't be certain.

Preacher pushed away the memory of his near-death and brought himself back to the file on his desk. One million dollars. That was a lot of money and Preacher wondered why this one warranted so much more than the usual fifty thousand. He looked again at the four of them. A nest of vamps. That was new and possibly more dangerous.

Mostly the revenants lived in graveyards, or buried under soil in wastelands. Sometimes he found them living in urban settings, such as the last one. A hobo whore, fucking for blood privileges. She had a modicum of intelligence that the previous ones hadn't shown and had somehow negotiated with the other homeless people in the ghetto. Preacher didn't know if she, or any of the others, could talk though. The fact was, he shot each one with a sleep dart then rang in for a collection: that was as up close and personal as he liked to get these days. After that, military vans and helicopters arrived. The revenant was taken and he never saw them again. Not that he cared. He took his pay check and was happy to have no more involvement.

Preacher brought his attention back to the file. *Suspected of destroying Konstantin Caradien,* the brief read. *All subjects to be treated with extreme caution. Gabriele is strong but very human. He won't necessarily expose himself in a public situation. He is fiercely protective of the youngest, Anja. Put her in danger and he will be careless.*

Preacher looked at the female named Anja again. She was very different from the others. Perhaps because she was the youngest convert? He couldn't imagine the revenants he had previously captured being 'protective' of another of their kind. The thought made him both concerned and intrigued.

He picked up his phone.

'Maggie, get me on a flight to Manchester, England immediately.'

As he put down the receiver Preacher caught sight of the scar on his wrist once more. It hurt and ached some days, as if some of the poison he had sucked out was still lurking in there. Preacher still remembered the burning agony as the poison from the bite coursed through his veins. His own blood had tasted vile, not the normal taste at all and when he slashed at the wound with his penknife, holding his arm down to allow the tainted blood to drip out onto the soil, he was sure he had seen something else pouring into the sand. Like a worm, or insect that the beast had injected into him with its monstrous teeth. Of course that wasn't possible and so he knew he must have imagined it: an hallucination brought on by shock and blood loss. Even so, sometimes he dreamed that the infection was still inside him, waiting. He wondered if that was what gave him the edge over the other fixers.

4
Blood Ties

The security gate swung open and Lucrezia Borgia strode confidently passed the guard booth. Its window was mirrored, but she knew she was being watched by an armed soldier on the other side. She stopped and looked at herself in the mirror, pushing aside a stray blonde hair which she tucked behind her ear. Her hair was scraped back into a severe bun and she was wearing a pair of narrow-brimmed, black-framed spectacles, while her normally green irises were covered with brown contact lenses. As the door closed behind her she turned from the booth and walked on down the corridor, barely noticing the plain white-washed walls or the many doors on either side as her court-shoe heels clip-clopped on the black-tiled floor.

At the end of the corridor she reached another door. This one was marked with a warning sign, RESTRICTED AREA – AUTHORISED PERSONNEL ONLY. She unclipped the plastic badge from her coat and swiped it once over a scanner. Then she refastened it to the pocket as she waited for the door to open. The badge said, 'Dr Lucy Collins': a name she had often used instead of her own. Besides, she preferred to be called Lucy, and her origins as the daughter of Pope Alexander VI was now so many lifetimes ago that she rarely thought about it.

As the door opened Lucy was greeted by another soldier. This one had a semi-automatic derringer tucked into the holster belted around his waist on one side and a baton hanging from a clip on the other. He was one of the few on the base that had access to this area, and that was because the colonel trusted him implicitly. His name was Peter Elin and Lucy was familiar with him even though she rarely spoke to him or any of the other men on security. She realised that he was also the soldier who had come to her aid when Cameron was attacked by Subject Five but Lucy didn't make any reference to this. Associations were discouraged at the base, especially between scientists and soldiers and they never discussed their work.

'Doctor,' said Elin, stepping back to allow her access.

Lucy nodded but said nothing as she passed through the entrance. She heard Elin leave and as the automatic door slid back into place she pushed away that vague feeling of claustrophobia she always experienced as she entered this part of the facility. It was silly really: she could leave any time she liked, yet still she felt paranoid. But then, she supposed, she had good reason to fear being trapped here. She knew firsthand what happened to those that were.

She went into the lab. It was early and the majority of technicians would still be having their breakfast. It was the perfect time of day for Lucy to work unobserved. She walked through the white and orderly room, past the long rows of tables holding analysis equipment and then opened the glass door to her office. The office walls were transparent, but Lucy pressed a switch at the doorway and the glass went black, giving her complete privacy. Then she turned the office lights on.

Now that she was on the main floor, all the doors were open. No one without clearance would be down in this part of the base and so they were all privy to the experiments occurring. The office, however, was different. There were locked cabinets where confidential paperwork was stored. Paperwork that revealed detailed information on the subjects involved in the experiments. Not everyone had access to that and Lucy, following Cameron's attack, had only just been given full clearance herself. This was just the break she had been waiting for.

Lucy closed the door behind her and went to the desk, powering up the computer there. She checked the index files, and then went to the file cabinet indicated. She pulled a bunch of keys from her lab coat pocket and opened the top drawer, then flicked through the rows of folders until she found the one she was interested in. SUBJECT SEVENTEEN.

Sitting down at her desk Lucy opened the file and looked down at the photograph of her former lover, Gabriele. He looked good. His pale skin was smooth and beautiful. His shoulder length blond hair waved in that trade-mark Jesus-look he adopted. The picture was in black and white, but Lucy knew that Gabi's eyes were bright green, just like hers were under the disguise of glasses and lenses. Lucy turned the picture over, looking at the date on the back. It was dated several months earlier and was taken in Stockholm. This was the first time the officials she worked for had become aware of Gabi, Lilly and Caesare. All because of that big, bad mess caused by one of their operatives: Konstantin Caradien.

Lucy shook her head. Caradien had been working towards his own agenda, using their resources to further his own career or, as it turned out, to gain some bizarre revenge for a past none of them had known about. By the time the syndicate found out, it was too late. His sudden disappearance had left an opening and a different entity had taken over. It was all confused and the members weren't sure what had happened to their former leader. Lucy wasn't concerned at all about it, though she knew quite a lot about the Illuminati, even that this base was somehow connected to the cult. But if, as she suspected, they were all completely behind this, then one boss was just the same as the next to her. Ultimately they all wanted to learn the same thing from the subjects: how to use the revenants for warfare.

Lucy's agenda, of course, was something else entirely.

The door to her office opened. Lucy looked up to find her colleague, Joe Carter, standing in the doorway looking dishevelled. Joe hadn't been himself lately. He was overworked, as they all were, but he found it harder than most to cope with the constant pressure of being locked up twenty four seven.

'Morning, Joe,' said Lucy.

Joe was in his thirties, attractive, but somewhat worn around the edges due to his excessive consumption of Jack Daniels.

Lucy knew that Joe went through a bottle of the stuff every night just so he could sleep. She suspected this was because he hated his job but couldn't just walk away from it. Each of the scientists involved in the project had signed their lives away. They were paid well, but they couldn't leave the facility unless they gained special leave dispensation. This didn't bother Lucy and she rarely requested leave anymore, she had nowhere to go anyway.

Joe was another issue. Joe had joined up when life hadn't seemed worth living. He had lost his wife and child in an arson attack and when the military made him an offer, telling him he would get a clean slate and they would use their resources to bring the perpetrator to justice, Joe signed on the dotted line.

The agents at the CIA already knew that Joe had an addictive personality. Despite this, he was a good scientist and they had decided that his excess baggage would make him more pliable: they were right. Lucy had been hired to keep Joe in check, maybe even give him a love interest to hope for, but Joe had soon learnt that working on the base was like being a prisoner. Their calls were vetted. Offices and labs contained cameras recording their every move. Security was so tight that it was just as hard to get out as it was to get inside. Lucy had to change her tactics in order to keep him under control. For this reason Lucy arranged for deliveries of whiskey, cigars and cigarettes that the workers needed and she provided Joe with all the bourbon he wanted.

'I'm out of supplies,' Joe said.

'I'll have some sent over this evening to your quarters,' Lucy smiled, then made herself a note on the pad on her desk. 'There. Now I can't forget.'

'Thanks,' Joe said, turning around to leave the room.

'Joe, I'll be in the officer's club tonight. Why don't you come down and socialise for a while?'

Joe stared at her, his eyes hollow. His fingers trembling on the steel door handle.

'You sure that's okay?'

'Of course. All work and no play makes Joe a dull boy.'

Lucy stood up and came around the desk, then perched on the edge. Joe stared at her. His bleary eyes observed her with obsessive detail. He stepped back into the room.

'You need something?' she said, her lips curving upwards with a sensual smile.

'Yes … Please, Lucy.'

'Then come to the club tonight. Afterwards I'll have a reward for you. But today I need you to focus, Joe. Those samples have to be analysed and I require the level of expertise that only you can give me. You know I don't trust anyone else with this.'

'Yes … I'll get straight to work.'

He was trembling like a junkie now. Every vein and muscle was aching to touch her. A pulse throbbed in his temple and Lucy could feel the lust for her surge up from his flushed skin.

'Is there anything else?' Lucy said when she noticed his hesitation.

Joe shook his head, glancing up at the camera in the corner of the office.

'There's nothing to fear from that thing,' Lucy smiled. 'It's broken again. The engineer will be over this morning to fix it.'

Lucy grinned. Her teeth looked sharper than usual. Joe only vaguely registered this as he closed the door and ran into her arms. She held him, not like a lover, but like an indulgent parent, and she stroked his hair gently.

'There,' she smiled. 'That feels better doesn't it?'

Lucy knew full well what Joe needed, but she kept him on the edge. Controlling him was so much easier that way. She had carefully monitored his addiction to her blood, having learnt her lesson the hard way. Giving a Renfield too much was not necessarily a good thing. Once, her former Renfield, Rocco, had almost caused an Ebola meltdown that turned New York into zombie city for twenty four hours: all because he couldn't bear to be away from her. Never again would she let a relationship with a mortal get so out of hand. With the small amount of blood she was giving Joe she was certain, that after a brief cold-turkey stage, he would make a full recovery. Joe would never be normal after his contact with her, but then he wasn't what she deemed sane to begin with.

She pushed Joe back and away. The brief physical contact with her would help him get through the day, but later she would have to feed him. He was rapidly becoming unglued and she couldn't allow that to jeopardise her position at the base. Not until she had completed what she had set out to do.

'Please,' he begged again stepping towards her.

'Not here,' she whispered, kissing his forehead. 'It's too risky.' She pressed her will into his mind with each kiss and felt his grip slacken, his hunger recede and his sanity gradually return.

Joe pulled back of his own volition this time.

'I must get on with the day's work,' he said and Lucy noted that the strained expression had now fled from his brow.

'Thank you, Joe. You know I'm relying on you.'

As Joe closed the door, Lucy thought back to the other file she had found yesterday in Cameron's drawer. She unlocked the top drawer in her desk and glanced down at the thick brown folder concealed there. The name on the front said JOE CARTER. She had already committed the content to memory and she hoped that Joe would never find out how he really came to be at the base. There had been no arsonist. His wife and child had been the victims of a 'hit'. The CIA wanted Joe's skills and they had gone to extreme measures to ensure that he joined them; a decision it would have been unlikely to obtain while he still had family ties.

Lucy closed and relocked the drawer. Joe must never learn the truth. He was unstable already and without the blood tie she had created between them he would have been extremely difficult to control. This was why she had removed the file from the regular cabinet. There may be a time when Joe would have access to the information there, but no need for him to look inside her desk drawer.

She turned her attention back to the new notification and the file that had arrived a few days ago. Gabi's smiling face looked back at her. Subject Seventeen. A feeling of foreboding worked its paranoid way into her heart and mind.

Subject Sixteen had outlived her usefulness two weeks ago. Sixteen had been a vagrant kid they found living rough in an alley with three old men and a dog. The men used her body and she drank from them, but Sixteen had been unable to tell them how she became a vampire. She was, however, one of the most advanced subjects they had found since Five. Now, they were going after Gabi. He, and the other carriers of the vampire gene were the ultimate vampires. The sorry revenants that the CIA had found so far were nothing compared to them. Lucy tested her emotions. She had long ago rejected and betrayed Gabi and the others, but this would be the ultimate treachery. Lucy wasn't sure how it would feel, if indeed when face to face with her own creation she could do what she was being paid to do; or if she could fulfil her ultimate mission at the expense of her former lover.

She closed the file, lifting it off the desk and placing it back inside the cabinet. She turned the key in the lock and then placed the bunch back into her white lab coat. She shrugged. It all remained to be seen, and she could deal with her wayward emotions then. Perhaps the fixer wouldn't capture Gabi but whatever happened, nothing would stop her from completing the task she had set out to do: no matter who got hurt in the process.

5
Heritage

We fly to the top of the Eiffel Tower. It is night time and the attraction is closed so I take Anja's hand and we wander the viewing platform at the top, free of interruption. The sky is clear and the night is full of the brightest stars. I point out Orion to Anja as we stare upwards. Tonight she is shining as brightly as the stars. Our little adventure seems to agree with her.

'What would happen if we fly up there?' she asks.

'What do you mean?'

'Out into the sky, up beyond the atmosphere. Do you think it would kill us?'

'I don't know. I haven't thought of it before.'

'We don't need to breath, or eat. So how could it harm us?' Anja said.

'Perhaps the pressure of leaving the atmosphere. Maybe we would burn up. Or explode. I just don't know.'

Anja falls silent. I find her speculative mind strange at times. I wonder why she would even consider leaving the planet, or trying to, that way. I like living and enjoy all that the Earth has to offer us. What would we find beyond the atmosphere that could be better than this?

I point across the city to distract her.

'There is the Louvre,' I say. 'We can visit tomorrow. It is where they keep the Mona Lisa.'

'Yes. I know,' she says. 'I used to collect artefacts, remember.'

I'm taken aback by this momentary reference to her past. Anja had been turned, not just by a bite but by a medical process. Konstantin Caradien's doctor had perfected a method of creating the vampire gene in a non-carriers' blood through regular transfusions. We learnt from this that our blood is strong and can take hold inside others who are not of our blood line. The transfusions meant that Anja changed when she was bitten by Lilly's former companion Harry. She became one of us by default when really she should have died. After that, Caradien used her to infiltrate our small family. When she first came to us we didn't know that she was Konstantin Caradien's stooge. Caradien had picked Anja because of her ability to manipulate minds through her empathy. This extra supernatural talent, fortunately, made her the only success in Caradien's experiments. All other attempts had ended in deformity or death.

The memory of a tainted, blood-soaked bullet smashing into my spine brings a shudder to my body. Anja doesn't notice, she is thinking of something else, though I'm sure her mind is still in the past.

'Let's go to the hotel,' I say. 'I need to make love to you.'

'I never used to like sex,' she tells me as I lift her up, carrying her from the tower.

'Why?'

'Even through kissing I could feel too much emotion from my partner. It hurt. So I stopped having physical contact with others.'

This is the first time she has discussed the past with me since our adventure in Stockholm.

'When Björn … raped me, I was still a virgin. I thought I would never let another man near me after that. Then, Konstantin showed me that sex could be pleasurable. I still don't know how he blocked his emotions from me but I was able to feel my emotions, not his. It's why I thought I was in love with him I suppose.'

I tense, surprised by the revelation. 'Where is this Björn?'

'Dead. I think. At least that is what Konstantin told me and I have no reason to disbelieve him.'

I fall silent, hoping she will tell me more. The intimacy of her disclosure surprises me. It also infuriates me that she has been hurt and used so much by the men in her life. Caradien portrayed us as monsters, and true enough we are that, but we always take care of our own. All that pain for what in the end? Caradien's motive was still something I couldn't fully understand. Revenge? Insanity? Maybe it was both. It was a feeble excuse for causing so much pain. I shook away the thought. Caradien was no longer any threat to us, his time-travelling days were over and his dead carcass had been absorbed by a room that was once Chez's personal hell.

'Of course, none of that matters now,' says Anja reading my thoughts. 'We're safe. Caradien's mafia has fallen apart.'

'We don't know that for sure,' I say. 'The Illuminati wasn't created by one man over night. There may be another maniac already taking his place …'

'Let's feed,' Anja says, abruptly changing the subject.

Her manipulation is unsophisticated but for once I let her have her way. What would be the point of debating the issue without evidence? We don't know enough about the organisation and it is an area that I am happy to leave to the Knights Templar for now. In the capable hands of our kinsman, our new family member Father Anthony, I'm sure that our allies will warn us of any impending threat.

I continue to fly with Anja in my arms until I see a young couple strolling arm in arm through the park below us. There is something cynical about lovers. Their shining eyes and romantic dreams often fall by the wayside after a time. I shrug the thought away, realising that we immortals are no different from humans in this regard. At least that is how it feels to me after being cast aside so cruelly and easily by Lilly.

Lilly hasn't left us helpless though. She is not one to shirk any duty. Instead she has been training us to read the heritage lines of our victims and therefore equipping us with the ability to choose our food more carefully.

We land behind the couple and walk silently, mimicking their loving gestures as though we too are just lovers out for an evening stroll. It is July and the evening is warm. Our potential meal is dressed in light summer clothing. The man is wearing a thin short-sleeved shirt and linen trousers, the woman is bare legged and wearing a pale blue gingham summer dress. Her hair is tied up in a ponytail exposing her tanned neck.

I scan the boy for the obvious signs of our heritage. His colouring is dark and very different from ours. This is a very good sign. The girl is fairer, with red-hair, but it is hard to tell if this is a genuine colour or if it has been dyed. I glance at Anja, her fangs are out but she nods. Genuine. So far, so good.

I sniff the air behind them, pushing away the scents from the deodorants and perfumes both of them are wearing. The natural smell underneath the artifice is far more appealing than the fake odours created by the fragrance. I breathe in deeply. They smell safe at this distance.

The park is quiet, but it doesn't matter anyway as we can cloak our presence any time we chose. I look at Anja and smile. Coldness seeps in around me: the feeling of camouflage is always icy to me and I wonder for the first time if it feels the same for the others. Anja's fingers squeeze mine as she fades. Of course I can still see her. Immortals cannot hide from each other, it is one of the things that equalises us.

I slip my hand from Anja's and propel myself forward, catching hold of the man. His surprise is stifled by my hand as I sniff and lick his throat. Over his shoulder I see that Anja has the girl wrapped in her arms. The woman is already swooning under her power. I swallow the man's sweat. His lineage bursts open before me stretching out far and wide, but not anywhere connected to my own ancestry. Satisfied I bite deeply into his throat, tearing and shredding the flesh and sinew to get at the strongest flow that moves through his veins. His blood explodes into my mouth and I swallow him down gasping as his life story penetrates my mind with every gulp.

The feeding process for us has become more intense of late. I don't know why. Maybe it is the long periods of abstinence. For the most part we drink blood provided by Lilly's contacts in the blood bank and rarely feed directly from our prey. It is the best way to avoid making others by accident. Lilly is strict about that.

The man struggles briefly in my arms but his strength is no match for mine. I hold him to me, feeling his body twitch as the last of his blood is drawn out.

As I come back to myself, I see Anja laying the body of the girl down gently.

'All was well for you then?' I say.

'Yes,' she smiles. 'She was delicious and I needed that. Thank you Gabi.'

We leave the bodies dead on the pavement after making sure the wound is gouged and all sign of teeth marks are camouflaged. It should appear that an animal has attacked the lovers but for once I am not concerned if it doesn't. Sometimes I grow tired of the pretence and the hiding. I have done this so long now, that it wearies me.

We run through the park, howling like wolves. Anja's green eyes glow with vibrancy and reflect my gaze. I revel in our power, our strength and murderous intent. It is a joy and a freedom we seldom feel. Energy flows through my veins and I feel the sexual excitement that accompanies the drinking of human blood. This feeling once used to sicken me. But I don't do angst anymore. Lilly and Chez have taught me that this is futile. Instead I pander to the emotion. Grabbing Anja I push her down in the grass, ripping up her skirt, I tear away her panties and plunge into her. She squeals and gasps, her excitement matching mine as she thrusts her hips back against me. She reaches up to me, pulling my face nearer as her lips press against mine. I taste the blood that has smeared her lips. It tastes –

'Anja!'

'Don't stop …'

'The blood. It's different. It's wrong.'

'What do you mean?'

I feel the lineage float up behind my eyes and follow. The girl … the girl. The line drops, I can't see any farther but there is something different about this one.

I push harder into Anja, she cries out, wrapping her legs around me as she shivers and spasms under me. As I come inside her, my tongue explores her mouth and I can taste it again, that distant connection that may or may not be part of our heritage.

Afterwards, I straighten my clothing and I run back to the bodies but find them both gone. Surely they couldn't have been found so soon?

'Forget it,' says Anja. 'You were probably seeing my lineage mixed with the blood. I promise I tested her and it was safe.'

'I believe you. It was just …'

'We've never fucked each other covered in blood before,' Anja points out. 'All is well. It has to be.'

I lift her up and fly away back to the hotel we checked into earlier.

Anja strips, dropping her clothing on the bathroom floor. I pick up the dress, sniff the blood that has ruined it and then lick it again. The heritage bonds are defined but dying as the blood cells dry and deteriorate. There is something there, something I haven't noticed before. But Anja is right. This girl was not our descendant and I'm sure there is nothing to worry about.

6
Renfield

As Joe lay on his bunk waiting for Lucy his mind was fragmented. Over the last few months he had begun to have the strangest dreams. He imagined Lucy was one of the revenants, that she drank blood. He saw her in his mind's eye floating above the ground like the freaky vampires he had seen in horror dramas like *Salem's Lot* or crawling along the wall like the vampire in *Dracula*. It was strange because Joe wasn't given to imaginative fancies. He was a scientist. He dealt in fact, not fiction.

Joe had been working with the revenants from the beginning and had seen what they were capable of. He was there a few weeks earlier when their former boss, Doctor Cameron, was killed by one of them. Joe saw Cameron attacked and later watched him turn.

'I don't know how that happened,' Lucy had said at the time.

Joe knew what she was talking about; they had done tests before on vagrants. When they fed the poor unfortunate homeless to the revenants, all of them had died. But not Cameron, he had turned and it hadn't been a pretty sight.

'They aren't vampires,' Lucy insisted over and over after that. 'They are more like zombies.'

Sometimes he remembered how she had destroyed the subject: Five. The memory passed behind his eyes in slow motion. Lucy had been like some ninja on wires. Five had smashed through the armour-plated two-way mirror. None of them had expected that kind of strength in the boy.

Joe remembered how he and Marcus had been sent out of the room by Cameron, who hadn't liked his authority being challenged by Lucy. The argument they were having was set to continue, but as they closed the door both of the men heard the mirror give and Joe had been the first to run back inside to see what had happened. They were just in time to see Five pull Cameron into the padded cell.

Joe had never seen so much blood. Five just ripped at Cameron's jugular and a red fountain spurted up which the boy bathed in while he drank and chewed on the doctor's neck. They had all been too shocked to move at first, then Lucy ran forward looking over the broken mirror frame and down into the room. Joe and Marcus had followed her, unable to resist seeing this bizarre freak show. By then Cameron was a bloody mess. Five had his hooked claws in the man's face. He gouged at his cheeks as though he were tenderising his meat before he ate it. There was blood splattered everywhere and the once-white room looked like the work of a contemporary artist.

The three of them were in a state of paralysis, then Marcus turned and heaved up his lunch on the floor. It splashed over the shards of six inch glass and all over Joe's trainers.

'Jesus Christ …' Joe had said, stepping away from the mess.

That was when Five noticed them watching and became even more enraged. Five dropped Cameron's body and dived back through the window. Joe could do nothing but stare as the revenant headed straight for him.

He felt the monster's claws swipe for his face but at that moment Lucy threw herself against him and Joe toppled into the still heaving Marcus and they fell like dominos. For a second Joe was stunned, but he sat up, looking around and saw Lucy effortlessly fending off Five. Joe pulled himself up, turned to Marcus only to find the other man was unconscious. There was blood on his temple and Joe realised that Marcus must have knocked his head against the edge of the table or on the concrete floor as the other two fell against him.

Five screamed in rage and Joe looked back to see Lucy biting and tearing at him. She had the creature by the throat and held him up off his feet while she tried to squeeze and choke the life out of him. Five didn't faint or die though, instead his fangs gnashed at the air as he twisted and turned. *How can she hold him like that?* Joe wondered. Lucy was impossibly strong. Impossibly.

Joe felt like he was watching a movie. Lucy jumped high and seemed to float as she carried Five back through the window and into the observation cell. Joe heard the explosion of electrics, and in the reflection from the broken glass he saw the cameras in the other room sputter and die as they combusted. He stood but he didn't quite see how Lucy finished Five. By the time he reached the window the boy was dead and half of his head was missing.

'It seems we have to destroy the brain,' Lucy said matter-of-fact as she stood up and wiped her blood soaked hands on her now stained lab coat.

'Are you okay?' Joe asked.

Lucy had kept her back to him and wiped her arm over her face and mouth, when she turned her face was clean but a wet, red smear marred the sleeve of her coat.

'Yes. These cells aren't strong enough for these creatures. We need to improve on safety.'

Lucy climbed back into the room, carefully avoiding the glass like any human might, but by then Joe was beginning to believe she was anything but.

Then, Cameron sat up in the cell.

'Oh God. He's still alive,' Joe had said.

Lucy turned and they both stared at Cameron as he staggered to his feet, dazed and confused. 'He's dead,' Lucy murmured. 'Stay back.'

That was when the alarm went off. Probably someone monitoring the cameras had seen that those here had gone offline. The first soldier to arrive was Private Elin. Joe knew him to be one of the fun soldiers. He and Corporal Parker were known for their practical jokes. No one was laughing as Cameron dragged himself hungrily over the ledge that had once contained the two-way mirror. The medical soldiers were quick to arrive after that and Cameron was shot down with the anaesthetic dart guns that they used on all the subjects. He fell and slept and they rapidly moved him to another cell before the drug wore off.

Joe would never forget that day.

Now, he turned over in bed; he didn't like to recall what had happened after that. It was too awful, but his mind wouldn't let him be and he slipped into the recollection despite himself.

Cameron had been chained up in one of the concrete cells on floor minus twenty. This was where they had kept all of the most dangerous subjects. Lucy and Joe had gone down there to access the situation. Joe had been shocked to find Cameron's gouged face almost healed but for the pale pink scars that ran across his cheeks and nose. Someone had bandaged his neck wound too, but Joe had suspected that the crepe fabric was no longer needed. He imagined that Cameron's neck would be nothing more than faintly scarred too.

'He's turned,' said Lucy. 'But why?'

'Why am I here?' demanded Cameron as he came around. 'Let me out immediately.'

'I'm sorry, doctor, but that isn't possible,' Lucy had said. 'You were attacked by Five. You died. Now here you are healing and apparently alive.'

'What nonsense,' Cameron had said. 'If I'd been attacked I would …'

Cameron's face went blank, he twisted and writhed in the chains as though he was in great pain. After that he stopped speaking. The only sounds he made were whimpers.

'Feed him,' said Lucy. 'Cameron was an intelligent man. He might regain some of his previous self better than the others did.'

Joe had watched in horror as Cameron was fed the raw meat, he saw elongated teeth tear at the flesh as the guards held it out to him on sticks. There was nothing of the scientist left behind his eyes, but Joe listened as Lucy talked. All of her explanations seemed so reasonable.

'I'll deal with everything. Cameron is a subject now. Who

knows, maybe he will be the weapon that he was looking so hard to find in these pitiful creatures.'

'You have such sympathy for them. Why?' Joe had asked.

'That could be any one of us in there, Joe. Cameron turning like that has just proved that whatever this is, it is communicable to some people, if not all. What we have to do now is find out why. Who are those that are at risk? Maybe we can even find a vaccine.'

'What are we talking about here?' Joe had said. 'Plague?'

Lucy shook her head. 'I'm not sure. But it's not what I'd call vampirism.'

'The problem is, that isn't what we're being paid to do,' Joe had pointed out.

'True. But do you see any reason why we couldn't justify this change of direction on the research?'

Joe shrugged. Lucy had all the answers and he always found it difficult to disagree with her.

'What are you thinking about?' Joe came out of his memories to find Lucy standing beside his bed.

'Nothing,' he said and almost immediately the thoughts and memories that had haunted him receded. He was excited to see her and he sat up, waiting for her to make the move that would send the unrest he was feeling scurrying away like a bad dream in daylight. Somehow she always managed to sneak past the guards unobserved. Joe never understood how, nor speculated about it much either. Lucy wanted him. What she gave him made Joe feel so much stronger and made his mind razor sharp. Not for the first time he wondered what was in the substance she fed him. It was addictive for certain and was obviously some kind of drug that helped you focus. The only drawback was that his need for it seemed to be growing.

Even so, Joe was flattered that she chose to give him this gift. Lucy had been visiting Joe ever since Five broke loose. Joe frowned. He pushed the horror away. Soon he would forget it all. Soon, Lucy would make him feel as though he had finally found heaven. His mind began to float from his body as he slipped back on the bed.

Lucy stripped off her clothing. She was wearing a pair of stone-washed jeans and a checked blouse. As the blouse fell to the floor, Joe observed she wasn't wearing a bra and he knew without a doubt that she wouldn't be wearing panties either. She slipped under the covers beside him and cuddled up. Her body was unnaturally cold. It was something Joe had noticed before but always forgot about in between these moments she spent with him. He shuddered as her cold skin rested against him and never seemed to warm up. It brought him back down to Earth with a jolt.

Joe began to tremble. He needed her but was afraid to make the first move. How would she give him the blood this time he wondered? He blinked. Shocked as he recalled that this was exactly what occurred between them. She gave him her blood. Joe felt a sick, tight, knot build up in his stomach. He couldn't drink blood. It was obviously some form of sexual-fetish that was a precursor to love-making with her but Joe couldn't understand why he had forgotten this part of their relationship. Or why his mind was so confused at these times.

'Do you want me, Joe?' Lucy asked.

'Yes,' he gasped. His throat was hoarse and he could barely breathe as the anticipation of being inside her was almost choking him.

'What do you need?' she asked.

'You!'

'Now Joe, you know that isn't it at all. Don't you remember?'

Joe shook his head. Like so many times before he refused to voice the desperation that was building up inside him. He wanted to beg. He wanted to cry. But still he held back. Maybe this time it would be different, maybe she would just give him what he needed without the theatrics.

She rolled him over and began to undress him, stripping away the shorts and tee-shirt he slept in.

'You're wearing way too many clothes, Joe.' She smiled. 'Saucy boy! There is something going on down here. Now what can that be for? You *do* want me, don't you?'

Joe felt her hand on his penis, she stroked gently, her nails running lightly over his balls until he thought he would burst in her hand.

'Please,' he said.

'Please what? What do you want? What's making you so, so hot?'

Joe turned his head into the pillow. He couldn't say it. The thought of his need sickened him.

Lucy pulled on him painfully.

'Do you need to fuck me?' she asked.

'Yes! No! I don't know!'

'Of course you know. So tell me, what will get you off, Joe?'

She lay over him, her firm, full breasts pressed against his bare chest and her pubis rubbed him but wasn't quite in the right position to give him the entry he *thought* he wanted. She was taunting him as always. And Joe was panting with his desperation, sweat beaded his brow. She slid back and sat astride him then lifted up and positioned his cock against her entrance. Joe almost screamed in anguish. Lucy pushed down, her cold, dampness sucked him in and for a moment Joe felt a shock of relief. Maybe this was what he needed.

'Okay I won't make you beg this time. But I think you need to give me some pleasure first,' Lucy whispered as she moved up and down on him. 'A girl has needs that just aren't being met in this godforsaken place.'

She rode him hard and Joe's balls were bursting but he couldn't let go in her. The cold from inside her seeped into his cock and balls until they felt numb.

'Suck me,' she ordered and like a good slave Joe lay between her legs. His tongue explored and stroked, his lips suckled her clitoris and still that awful coldness froze his lips, tongue and his very soul. She came against his mouth, gasping and writhing with excitement and there was momentary warmth there. Joe lapped it up. He was starved and any sign of heat coming from her helped to bring the warmth back into his heart.

She pulled him up wrapping her legs around him. Her fingers stroked down over his body, cupped his buttocks. Joe followed his instincts, entering her hard.

When she reached her next climax she threw him aside, brought her wrist to her lips and bit deeply until the blood began to flow. Joe fell on her arm like one of the revenants. He couldn't swallow fast enough and the blood gushed down his throat and over his chin. It felt as though he was falling into a black hole. The cold coursed down into his stomach, seeping out into the rest of his body. Impossibly he felt it fill his veins, pumping around with every beat until it froze his heart. The scientific part of his brain knew that this was impossible. The blood would be absorbed and digested but no way could it infiltrate his own blood stream.

The excitement was more intense this time, as Lucy recovered, lying beside him with her eyes closed, Joe crawled over her again. This was new. This was exciting: the blood and the sex. He remembered now: usually it was *just* blood she gave him.

He forced her legs open and found her staring at him as he positioned himself against her. Fear clutched at his cold chest, but he couldn't stop himself taking command. He felt strong, invulnerable. Her eyes blazed. Not the brown he was used to seeing, but a vibrant green that glowed like emeralds in the fractured light. He pushed inside her and she rolled her hips up to meet him. Joe liked his new strength.

'Teasing bitch,' he said.

He fucked her then. Just how she deserved it for tormenting him and she lay under him, a slow, cat-like smile resting on her lips until he pounded his orgasm into her.

Afterwards, Joe lay on his back, eyes closed, while Lucy slipped away. The chill had taken all of his body and he felt as though he were frozen into a block of ice. As his mind slipped away into frosty, dreamless sleep, it occurred to him that he was more than her slave. She could use him any way she wished. But he wouldn't fight it. It was the most exciting thing that had ever happened to him in all of his dull, scientific life.

7
Decay

Where are you? Are you okay? Please answer me!

Lilly's texts have become urgent and so I let Anja respond. She tells her we are in Paris, that we felt the need to get away for a while. I have successfully put distance between us on my terms and not hers. The anger of her rejection still burns but somehow by removing myself from her world I feel I have regained control over my life again.

'Let's walk the park again,' Anja says.

Away from Lilly's influence we are like naughty children striving to partake of forbidden fruits without our parents finding out. This is a strange thought though, as Lilly is my child. I created her. The situation is insane. I am her maker; she should bow to my will. But a cruel twist of fate made her the mother of us all and therefore the strongest vampire. Once, not long ago to me, but centuries now to her, Lilly was thrown back in time and had no control over her own destiny. She made mistakes. Accidentally turning Harry, a former Viking king, was the start of it all and it set her on a path that she had to follow or risk our very extinction. Such things, I have learnt, do happen frequently in our world. Our enemies have grown strong. They have learnt a few tricks. I have the scar in my spine to prove it.

As I consider this the scar aches and my hand goes to it, rubbing as though I expect this to help. The pain, however, goes far deeper than the wound ever could.

We buy a local paper from a news stand. Anja flicks through it and reads the content to me in English. I didn't realise that she spoke French and I wonder if this is a quirk of her new found powers or whether she already knew the language. I forget to ask her though as I am more interested in whether our kills have been found in the park.

'Here it is,' she says eventually. 'Oh! That's weird. They only found the man. He was in the bushes and they are saying it looked as though he was attacked by an animal. His remains were … gnawed.'

'How strange. Sounds like a real animal found him after us,' I say.

'Possibly. But what about the woman?'

'Maybe she was still alive?' I say. 'Perhaps she staggered away.'

'No. Not with that neck wound.'

I fall quiet. I revisit my former self. Like all serial killers we delight in coverage of the murders we have committed. In the past Lilly has made us cover our tracks and so these moments of indulgence are rare. I feel a twinge of resentment even though it is unjustified. I was the one who taught her to hide who and what she was in the first place, wasn't I? It just seems unfair that now, when I'm ready to take on the world openly, she denies us the right.

Anja laughs. 'Well they got the animal attack we wanted them to find anyway.'

Her laughter pulls me from my brooding. Yes. I did promise I would angst no more, and I have forgotten what fun it was to be a blood-sucking monster. I smile. I'm going to enjoy my new freedom. Anja and I can do as we please now, can't we?

'Yes. Let's go to the park again. I'd like to find another couple. Maybe we will be *really* grotesque this evening,' I say.

Anja smiles, then throws herself in my arms. She kisses me with a passion I haven't felt from her before.

'You're so much more fun away from Lilly and Chez. All the two of them need now is a pair of fluffy slippers and a pension book.'

I laugh at her imagery. Lilly and Chez are far more serious and sedate than we are, but I would never underestimate the beast in either of them. It is just that Lilly likes a quiet life these days. She doesn't look for conflict, perhaps because in the past it has constantly looked for her. I am a hive of contradiction, I know. One moment I resent Lilly, the next I am defending her. But we vampires are complex creatures, never forget. And, sometimes, very contrary.

The park is even quieter this evening. It strikes me that the news has scared the lovers away. But then the tourists surely won't have heard of the death of the man?

'Was he identified?' I ask Anja.

'Yes, he was a business man. Karl Klondike. German I think. I guess he shouldn't have been in the park with the girl. I don't suppose she was his wife, do you?'

I shrug. He hadn't looked German, but then how could we tell when there was so much mixed blood in the world these days.

I lead us back to the site. The area is cordoned off with police tape but there is no one there.

'I suspect they have done forensics by now,' Anja whispers beside me.

I realise we are acting just as I imagine serial killers would. Revisiting the site of our kill is an obvious admission of guilt. Suddenly, I don't like the feeling. It is somewhat perverse. I accept my nature but don't always want to revel in it.

'I'm changing,' I say.

'What?'

'Come, we're leaving. We need to go back to Rhuddlan.'

'Why?' Anja asks. 'I thought we were having fun.'

'We are. We can. But not this kind, it's ...'

'Sick?'

I say nothing but taking her hand I turn her away from the site and we begin to walk back towards the path.

The woman comes out of the bushes so fast she almost runs into us.

Anja gasps and I recognise her immediately as the kill from

the night before. She is dishevelled, still covered in the blood we spilt, but her neck wound has healed.

Her eyes are bloodshot and crazed.

'My God, we turned her,' I gasp. 'She was one of ours.'

Anja shakes her head, 'No, Gabi. I'm telling you. There was no sign of our gene. Not any.'

The woman stares at us with blazing, hungry eyes. A guttural scream burbles from her lips in a burst of rabid white foam.

'What the fuck …?' says Anja.

The woman sniffs the air and us.

'Look,' I say. 'We take care of our mistakes. You probably feel a little confused now, but don't worry, we'll look after you. Show you the ropes. What's your name?'

The woman opens her mouth, and I can see she is trying to shape the words but somehow they won't come. Her mouth is unlike ours. It is full of serrated fangs. It is as though all of her teeth have been filed into perfect points.

'What is she?' Anja asks, stepping back.

'I don't know.'

She charges at us, teeth gnashing in cannibalistic hunger, and I know in that moment that we have to figure out how to destroy her. She isn't one of us. And yet, somehow, Anja created her.

'What is she?' repeats Anja.

She charges us, but we are stronger and wrestle her down to the ground. She struggles but is no match for our superior strength. She thrashes and twists, reminding me of her lover as he died in my arms the night before. She has the strength of the insane and she pulls and writhes snapping her razor teeth in our direction. I smash her head down against the ground in an attempt to daze her. Her head cracks open, blood seeps out but the struggling continues. She screams and wails so much I am sure that at any moment someone will call the police.

'Don't struggle, I'm trying to help you,' I say, looking deeply into her eyes.

I try to read beyond the surface. There is no aura to speak of, only a cold, black sheen that lies just above her skin. Her touch is alien. It is neither human nor vampire and it carries the stink of the grave. Death rides her like a parasite. I look into the black pits of eyes that have sunken back into the hollows of her skull. My attempts at hypnosis fail. She is beyond my reach in the realms of madness that lie so far in darkness that no light can penetrate it. She is a vacant shell and I feel real fear for the first time since Caradien's men shot poison bullets into my body.

Anger surges into my hands. I'm sickened by this vile parody. I smash her head down again. Hard. Once. Twice. It splits in two like an over-ripe melon. The struggling stops. Blood spurts from her mouth, nose and eyes as she finally dies. Anja squeals and jumps back but by then both of us are covered in her stink. The creature is finished, or at least almost, but I hold her down until the vicious light fades from her bloody eyes. It is only as the dullness glazes over the black orbs that I realise how much fire was truly hiding in there, and it burnt with a malevolence I have never seen in one of our kind.

Once I am sure she is at peace I release her.

'What the fuck …?' Anja says.

I stand and stare at the blood on my hands. I feel no urge to taste it; the smell alone tells me it would not be good. It smells of rotting meat, sour milk, and spoilt egg yolk. I watch the creature's body fall into decay like the special effects of an old Hammer movie. It deteriorates as though she is centuries old. Bare flesh rots before my eyes until it is nothing more than stretched, dried skin, like old crumbling parchment.

'This isn't happening,' I say. 'You killed her last night. No way could she come back from that.'

Anja shakes her head. 'She wasn't one of us. I'm sure of it.'

The woman's blood still soaks my hands as we fly back to the hotel. Anja is shaking and trembling in my arms. Her clothes are smeared with it. The stink seems to be worse as the minutes pass. It is as though the blood continues to rot, just like the body had.

I reach the hotel and pass Anja through the window first; she runs straight into the bathroom and starts the shower. I climb in behind her but I am barely in the room before the smell of decay fills the large double bedroom and so I empty my hand luggage bag and strip the reeking clothing from my skin, stuffing it inside.

In the bathroom, Anja scrubs at her skin and hair. I pick up her discarded clothing and force it into the bag. I will dispose of it later, but at least the canvas will give some protection from the smell. As Anja wraps a towel around herself I climb in the still running shower and begin to remove the stains from my hands and body. The blood has turned black and it takes effort to cleanse it from my flesh. I feel tainted. It is as though our sins have finally begun to show on our perfect skin. Unfortunately we have no portrait to banish them to in our attic.

'I don't know what happened,' Anja says. 'She … she wasn't one of us. I know it.'

'No,' I say, walking into the bedroom. 'She definitely wasn't a carrier of the vampire gene.'

Anja has opened all of the windows. The warm Parisian air wafts in and around the room but it takes time to dissipate the terrible odour.

'Then what was she?' Anja asks.

I shake my head, 'Your bite triggered a change. She was carrying something else I would guess. But I'm not big on science.'

'Lilly will know,' Anja says. 'She would be able to read the DNA.'

I'm not so sure. This is something that has never happened before and could be a new anomaly. Perhaps the long arm of the Illuminati has stretched from Stockholm to Paris?

'It can't be them,' Anja says, reading me so easily that I realise my agitation has caused all of my defences to drop. I am projecting my emotions so much that even a mortal may sense them.

'At least it can't be Caradien,' I say.

'We have to go back,' Anja says. 'I'm scared.'

She is trembling and appears every inch the fragile girl she was when first she found us in Rhuddlan. She looks like a school girl who has just been told she is pregnant. .

'What are you doing?' I ask as Anja presses buttons on her mobile phone.

'We need to tell Lilly. We need to warn her and Chez.'

I take the phone and press cancel. I know she is right. We should tell Lilly and Chez. But the thought of returning with my tail between my legs doesn't appeal to me in the slightest.

'Not yet. I want to think about this. Perhaps we should do some research of our own before we tell them anything. It might have been a complete fluke.'

'What do you mean?' Anja asks.

'Like you said, this has never happened before. It may never happen again,' I explain.

Anja listens carefully to my plan but I see the fear behind her eyes and I know she doesn't like it. Even so, I manage to persuade her to try.

'We have to find out who the woman was. We have to come in contact with others of her family,' I say.

'Why?'

'Experimentation. We need to learn more.'

'Oh my God, what are you planning to do, Gabi?'

'I'm going to turn one of them in a controlled environment. Then I want to see what happens.'

8
The Castle

The entrance to Rhuddlan Castle was tucked away in a small road just off the main high street, opposite a row of tiny cottages. Preacher turned his hired Saab into the car park and slowly swung it in between two other cars. He turned off the engine and looked over at the small, hut-like shop and the white metal barrier that blocked the way through to the castle grounds.

So, this is the place.

Preacher climbed out of the car, went around to the back and retrieved a canvas holdall which he shrugged onto one shoulder. Then he pressed the key fob to lock the doors and set up the alarm. The headlights flashed and there was a sharp, but small squeak. He turned towards the hut, but skirted around it and stood looking over the moat at the castle. Or rather, the ruins of the castle.

A dark brown wig, short and fashionably cut, hid his white hair and contact lenses disguised his pale eyes. With a darker spray tan than usual, Preacher didn't look even the slightest bit albinoid. His clothing was far from extreme, gone was the Armani, he now wore casual and inexpensive jeans and a white V-neck sweater over a pale blue shirt. He carried a leather jacket, not his normal style – God forbid he should ever be seen in a brown, hoody bomber jacket – but style was something people noticed and his own was expensive and obvious. This clothing was deliberately nothing like his own.

He entered the shop. Opposite the doorway was a rotating book rack containing paperbacks. He glanced around, noting the counter on the left and the stacks of tat jewellery, trinkets and Celtic crosses on the shelves to his right. Ironic. He smiled, then lifted his face to the girl behind the counter.

'Hi, there. I'd like to see the castle,' he said.

The girl looked at him and smiled. Her teeth were imperfect, slightly protruding but Preacher thought that they could be considered cute.

'Sure. You American?' she asked.

'Yes,' he said, then held up a booklet called *North Wales Castles*.

'On holiday are you?'

Preacher hated small talk, especially with shop girls. He nodded, trying to appear benign while all the time he wanted to slap the girl into silence.

'That way to go through to the castle,' the girl said.

The girl was pretty. No older than twenty five, and it was obvious to Preacher that she found him attractive. Most women did. He turned his best smile towards her and said 'thanks'. Then he walked away from the counter towards the turnstile that led out through the back of the shop.

Outside, Preacher strolled towards the edge of the moat and looked down. It was empty now; a green lawn filled the bottom instead of the water that once would have been there. The moat was no more than fifteen or twenty feet deep. Preacher felt disappointed. He couldn't imagine how or where the vampire's lair could possible fit in here. The ruins were small. By castle standards this one was tiny. He walked along the edge until he reached the bridge, glancing over the closed archway. No possibility of entry there either. Had the bridge been wider, and hollow underneath, then he may have suspected an entrance to a lair, or a hidden grave beneath the earth, but this was just too impossible. The stone was Welsh rock and had lain in situ for centuries. Preacher looked across at the moat wall. Moss covered the rocks and the stone steps that once would have led into the water. There were no obvious caverns, but he would have to go down there first and walk along the bottom to be really certain.

He crossed over the bridge and followed the gravel pathway up into the castle proper. Two turrets marked the entrance and beyond, Preacher found himself in the courtyard looking down into a shallow well. From the centre he looked up, turning slowly to survey what remained of the tops of the observation walkways and towers. Then he walked to each turret in turn looking up. He climbed up as far as he could go but found nothing.

In the third turret he did find what seemed to be a darkened hole in the side of the wall. There was a locked metal grille with a sign saying NO ENTRY. Preacher took a torch out of the pocket of his jacket and shone it up into the spiral stairwell. He couldn't see anything, but the thick layers of dust and grit gave the impression that no one had traversed this tower in a long time. The likelihood that it was unstable made him consider the possibility of a revenant hiding there and he decided that it was improbable. The revenants he had met were clumsy and graceless. The tower would have tumbled, the beast revealed. Plus, he had long since realised that most of them liked to be underground and rarely hid above it.

He left the tower and crossed over the broken ruins to the back of the castle. Here the grass was well maintained and Preacher found his gaze falling once more down towards the moat. He followed the edge looking at all of the crumbling stairwells until he found one that looked almost safe enough to use. Preacher descended the stairs and found himself in the moat. The grass was cut, proving that the staff of the castle regularly went down there at least, though Preacher wondered how the mower was brought down over the broken and precarious steps.

He walked the lower part of the moat on the left back to the first bridge, scrutinising the walls which raised either side of him. At the bridge itself he observed nothing unusual. The rock was worn with age as it should be, but appeared to have no extra damage. He made his way back along the right side, passing the stairwell that had brought him down, and walking the entire moat around the castle until it ended at the rear bridge.

It slowly dawned on him that the information he had been given was, for once, incorrect. The vampires couldn't possibly be living here. There were no secret passages. Not even a dungeon space that he might explore that could lead him down into the ground. Then, at least, there might be a possibility of a tomb that the creature was hiding in. He walked back to the stairs and climbed them carefully. Preacher kept himself fit, but one small slip on mossy stone could cause injury that would be, to put it mildly, inconvenient.

He walked back around the castle to the back bridge which he discovered led off towards a small patch of wooded grounds. Preacher headed across it, looking down once more at the moat.

On the other side of the bridge was a small patch of land on the left, fenced off from the woods. He turned right and into the woods, which was little more than a dense patch of trees with little depth or width to it. It didn't take him long to search the area. He found nothing. Revenants weren't usually this difficult to find.

Turning back he saw a patch of earth that looked as though it had been disturbed but on close inspection, he realised that it had recently been weeded and the soil turned in preparation for planting.

Preacher left the cover of the trees and turned back towards the castle, crossing over the bridge once more. He was disappointed that he hadn't seen anything to indicate the presence of the revenant but was sure that he must be misinterpreting his instructions somehow. Near the castle again he sat down on the grass, his back pressed against the wall of the ruin. He opened his bag and pulled out his android tablet. He scrolled the screen until he found the network share for his computer. Then he opened the file and looked again at the content.

This time he read the extra notes.

Not like the others. These appear to be more advanced. They do not hide in church yards, empty graves, or ruins. They appear to be civilised. May even live in houses.

'Careless,' he murmured as he read the file once more.

Preacher shook himself mentally. He was annoyed that he hadn't noticed this small addendum.

He put away his tablet, then walked back through the ruins, back down the path and across the first bridge again to the exit. In the shop, the girl was serving another customer. Preacher put his head down and walked out: he didn't want to get into further conversation with her.

In the car park, he stowed his bag back in the boot of the car. It was a dead end. He would have to go back and say he had failed. Preacher hated the thought. It also meant he wouldn't get paid, but he did at least have a case to answer on the lack of information. 'Seen in the vicinity of Rhuddlan Castle' didn't quite give him enough to go on really. He slammed the boot back down and turned to look back at the castle again. Clearly this was why they were offering so much for retrieval. The money had been too good to be true.

'Hey!'

Preacher turned to see the girl running out of the shop towards him. He sighed. He had been hoping to avoid more contact with her. She was way too curious about him already.

'Did you like the castle then?' she asked sidling up to the car.

'Yes. But I was a little disappointed that there wasn't a dungeon to explore.'

The girl smiled. 'Most people say that. There is one you know. It's just been buried under mountains of earth and rock over the years.'

'That's a shame,' Preacher said, wondering how to extract himself without being rude. Workers always remembered you if you were rude. He had to make sure the girl only remembered him in a good light. That way, if things went pear-shaped she would never think of him as being involved.

'I could get you down there,' she said. Her hand fell on his arm.

'But you said it's not accessible …'

'Not from here. But a friend of mine owns one of the houses across the road. It has the original passage into the dungeons.'

Preacher was surprised. He had felt certain there was

nothing to find at Rhuddlan, but a passage underground sounded like a strong lead. Even if it didn't work out, he would have explored every avenue and completed enough of the task to qualify for some payment.

'That would be great,' he smiled. 'Would your friend mind if I took pictures?'

'I guess not. I'm Ffion. I finish work in an hour, but my friend isn't home until later this evening. We could maybe ... go and have a drink or something.'

Preacher smiled. 'Darren,' he said. 'I'd like that. Ffion. What a *pretty* name.'

9

Cameron

'How are you feeling today, Doctor Cameron?' asked Lucy as she sat in a chair opposite the chained monster that used to be her boss. 'Can you try to say something?'
Cameron turned his head, his jaw opened and closed but nothing more than a monstrous groan escaped his lips.

'You're not trying, Cameron,' Lucy said.

Lucy looked up at the camera in the corner and spoke directly to the operator. She thought it was probably Private Elin.

'Has he been fed?'

'Yes,' came Elin's tinny voice through the speakers, and Lucy nodded without realising it. Strangely she always knew when Elin was around and watching her. Despite the fact she had barely dealt with him some sixth sense kicked in when he was around. Briefly she wondered if she should give the man a little more attention, find out more about him. Lucy shook the thought away and focused her attention back on Cameron.

'Are you still hungry, Cameron?' Lucy said standing up. She walked towards him.

Cameron fixed her with his blood-shot eyes. Dribble slipped from his gaping mouth and wet the front of his straightjacket. Around his waist he had a thick steel chain that attached him to two wide hooks that were set deep in the concrete wall.

'Please be careful, Doctor Collins,' said Elin.

Lucy ignored him. She drew closer and looked into Cameron's feverish eyes. She touched the skin on his throat and drew back rapidly, not because Cameron snapped his head round and tried to bite her, but because his skin was burning hot to the touch. She stared at her fingers as though expecting to see a blister appear there. His temperature was as abnormally high as hers was unusually low.

'Are you all right, Doctor Collins?' asked Elin.

'Yes,' she replied looking up at the camera. 'He has some kind of fever. I never noticed that on the other subjects.'

'Show me your teeth,' Lucy said and Cameron snarled at her, accidently obeying her order.

Lucy noticed the sharp points that were common to the revenants. The gums were blackened and Cameron's breath reeked of raw meat and blood.

'I want a heart monitor in here,' she said.

She continued her examination. Since he had turned, Cameron's eyes had sunk farther back into his skull. His features were changing, becoming more animalistic and less human. She even thought his forehead had broadened. He looked vaguely Neanderthal and like the other revenants his intelligence was limited to a certain cunning that at times helped him appear less dangerous. Maybe this was how the revenants started. Lucy thought back to the first subject. One was now quiet and mostly lay listless in her cell. She never spoke and they had given up examining her a long time ago. Lucy considered what she would learn from looking into this revenant again. She was old, over two hundred years for certain, but Lucy had found her lack of response unhelpful.

'We have to change your diet, Cameron,' Lucy said. 'No more meat for you, only blood.'

The door opened and the medical team came in wheeling the heart monitor. Beside them was a soldier with a dart gun.

'Knock him out,' said Lucy and the soldier aimed and fired. The dart punctured Cameron's neck and he slumped immediately. 'Let's get this jacket unfastened and get the monitor on him.'

An hour later, Cameron woke. He was strung up again but this time the machine was attached to him.

'We'll leave him like that for twenty-four hours,' Lucy said to Marcus who was the duty medic for the night. 'Remember. He's to be fed blood only. No meat.'

'I'll put it on his notes, but what good do you think that will do?' Subconsciously he rubbed the red scar on the side of his head. Fortunately for him, Marcus didn't remember anything after Cameron was attacked by Five because he had been unconscious for most of that time. Only Joe had seen Lucy in action, which was why she had been forced to take him so completely under her wing. Lucy hadn't wanted a slave again, but Joe was proving useful. He was working at full capacity and she enjoyed the sex with him.

'I don't know. It's an experiment, doctor, just like everything else,' Lucy said, explaining her motives to Marcus.

Lucy left Marcus and a team of soldiers to feed Cameron and headed to the lift that would take her upstairs and out into the main base.

Three floors up the lift halted and Joe joined her.

'How is Doctor Cameron?' he asked.

'Not good,' she said. 'I've put him on a blood only diet for now as that seemed to help the other subjects.'

Joe nodded. 'I've done some more tests on his blood. The results brought up some surprising similarities to the other subjects.'

'Such as?'

'Genetically they all appear to have similar DNA. They could all be related.'

Lucy looked down. This didn't surprise her at all. Wasn't it the same in her vampire family? Although, looking at Cameron it was hard to see any familial connection to the vampire gene. Lucy knew that her own blood-line was rare; making others had often been an exceptional accident. But now this new strain appeared to be far more common. Lucy knew this because already there had been sixteen other subjects in her care. That was more than double the amount of vampire gene turnings. At least that she knew of.

The doors of the lift opened again at laboratory level.

'You coming to see this?' Joe asked.

'I'll be back there shortly. I'm feeling the urge to go topside for some air,' Lucy said.

'I know what you mean.'

As the lift door closed Lucy pressed the button to take her up to the ground floor reception. She felt stifled by the days spent twenty floors below ground. She was sensitive to pressure, something that had occurred only in the last year. Sometimes she felt the sand and earth around the structure, pressing down on the building as though it would crush it. Of course her scientific mind knew this was impossible. The facility was strong and secure, water, sand and soil proof. But she felt, or at least imagined the pressure nonetheless. It felt as though the sand was a silent menace, waiting to crush the base if they made one false move.

Lucy smiled at her morbid thoughts as the lift continued without further stops. In reception, Lucy nodded to the soldier monitoring the door. He was young and new but had seen her before so made no comment as she pushed the release button and went outside.

She halted at the doorway, looked around, then removed her glasses and replaced them with sunglasses from her top pocket. She felt cold despite the desert heat. It was mid-day and the sun burned down on the base with its usual ferocity. Lucy left the shelter of the doorway and walked out into the fierce light. She followed the pathway around the main building and out towards the back. It wasn't so busy there, and she could observe the checkpoint casually without being seen.

Unlike most of the occupants working inside, Lucy knew exactly where she was. She was in the Nevada Desert, some fifty miles from Las Vegas and the base was a covert military facility that dealt with all kinds of unusual science. Lucy had been recruited several years before, and had undertaken various contracts with periods of leave between, but always returned as she felt infinitely curious about the blood work the agency was doing. Ever since learning of the presence of the revenants, however, Lucy had refrained from taking so much leave. Yet she had still been unable to learn how they found the revenants in the first place, or who was doing the capturing.

The revenants were interesting in a variety of ways. She wanted to see and control, where possible, how much knowledge the CIA gained about vampires through the current research. Until receiving the new file she had believed they were unaware of the vampire gene carriers, focusing only on this weird offspring that had appeared over the last few years. It had to be genetic of course. Lucy suspected that they couldn't be the only hereditary family that could become immortals. It was evolution after all. Lucy had seen those that had changed into vampires grow and become strong both mentally and physically: the revenants, of course, were quite different.

Lucy pulled out a packet of cigarettes and lit one. She gained no pleasure from smoking but it gave her a cover for standing outside like this. It was ironic that the need for fresh air had to be punctuated with a different reason, but she recognised this need anyway. Smoking wasn't permitted at all inside the buildings and so many a soldier, doctor, or administrator could be found outside on this pretext. It was the only good excuse in this paranoid place.

She glanced casually over at the checkpoint guard station. Another truck was pulling out and away from the base, probably containing germ warfare containers that had been developed on site. This didn't bother Lucy, or concern her – she didn't care if mankind infected itself with viruses, but she believed these things would always remain as a threat never to be used. She was looking out for a different kind of truck, one that would be arriving, not leaving, if past experience was anything to go by. But the desert road outside the fence was empty and in the distance Lucy could see no sign of anything coming their way.

No matter. I'll know soon enough if they do capture him, she thought. Her mind flashed back to Gabi's photograph and the file. How long did it take from notification to arrival? Lucy wasn't sure; she hadn't been in this position before as it had always been Cameron who received the confidential files. Lucy, Marcus and Joe had only ever heard about the new subjects once they were processed and in the facility. After Cameron had been attacked, Lucy had been forced to take over despite all of her efforts to remain freelance. She was the highest ranking science officer on the base now, so had no choice but to take up this new duty. That was until a permanent head could be appointed.

There were certain privileges that came along with the new job, although the freedom aspect was still the same. Lucy now had a pass that gave her full access to all areas. Once she discovered the benefits of her new role she became determined to make her position on the base permanent and to do that she had to show some tangible results. In this capacity she might finally learn what she came to discover in the first place.

Lucy ground out her cigarette with the sole of her shoe and headed back round the building to the reception just in time to see Doug Rainer come out. He was the colonel in charge of the facility but he had no say over what the scientists did. He didn't even have access to the medical experiments taking place. Doug's role was strictly security so he didn't even nod to Lucy, but lit his cigar and walked away in a different direction.

Good, she thought. She didn't care for Doug. Their paths had crossed one time too many and she thought the colonel was an idiot.

As she reached the reception door, the heat of the sun was finally working its way into her cold skin, but Lucy knew there was only one real cure for this feeling. She wouldn't get any real warmth back until she was able to feed.

She pressed the buzzer and the door sprang open.

'Thanks,' she said, smiling at the soldier on reception.

The boy blushed. He, like many others on the base, hadn't been laid in a long time and Doctor Collins was hot.

'What's your name?' she asked.

'Private Adams.'

'Your first name?'

'Jake ...'

'Thanks, Jake,' she smiled.

He looked tasty and Lucy enjoyed playing with the soldiers

on occasion. Sometimes, when one interested her enough, she did take a little taste.

'Do you smoke?' she asked.

'Yeah.'

'Maybe we'll meet again outside on your next break.'

Lucy walked away to the lift. Jake smiled as he watched her walk. She had a great wiggle and he was sure she was exaggerating it for his benefit.

10
Family

'The decomposing corpse was found close to the site of a recent animal attack. Forensic specialists are taking steps to try to discover who the woman might have been and how long she was dead.'

I listen to the excitement in her voice as Anja reads from the paper while I sip coffee from a small cup. We are sat in a café in the small square near Notre Dame and it has been several days since we came across Anja's shocking offspring.

'Maybe it is because I'm different,' Anja says, putting the paper down on the mosaic table.

Across the road a queue of tourists wait, ticket in hand, to take the long journey up the steps of the cathedral for a very brief glimpse of the city from the top. At the front, waiting beside the roped off entrance is a man with blond hair and features akin to vampire gene carriers. Now that I know what to look for the signs are almost obvious. But Anja may have a point and I mull over her origins. She is, after all, a manufactured carrier of our gene, subjected to weeks of blood transfusions before Harry turned her. Of course this had all been down to the machinations of Konstantin Caradien, head of the Illuminati, and bastard son of John the Baptist. He had used Anja to get to us. His motive: revenge on the offspring of Herod because the king murdered his father and raped his mother, Salome.

We have interesting lives.

Since our traumatic battle we have kept our feet firmly in the twenty-first century, and the thought of time travel hasn't occurred to me once. I'm not curious about the past because I have already lived through much of it in the natural way. Lilly, fortunately, has shown no inclination to experiment further, even though she can now control the portals. We have, instead, been trying to live quiet, idyllic lives in Rhuddlan.

'It's possible, I suppose. But why hasn't this happened at other times?' I ask. 'There have been other feedings.'

'Yes. But very few kills. Thanks to Lilly.'

I cannot argue with her. The truth is fact and Lilly has clipped our wings making all contact with humans scarce. It was almost as though she feared that more of us would be made. Though I cannot see how this would be such a bad thing. Except … My mind flies back to the woman in the park. She was not the kind of child we would choose to make.

'A revenant,' I say.

'What?'

'You made a revenant. It is something of a low-grade vampire in cult literature.'

'What does it mean?'

'Literal meaning? An animated corpse.'

Anja falls quiet. 'I guess we are revenants also then?'

'Not at all. We didn't die, Anja. But your victim did.'

I catch the eye of the waiter and lift my cup indicating that I would like a refill. He returns with a glass flagon of percolated coffee and a small white jug of fresh cream. I notice his eyes on Anja and ignore it when she smiles at him with flirty interest. It is part of her predatory nature to make men fall for her and I wouldn't dream of showing any form of jealousy when this is natural behaviour for us. Besides, I have more pressing concerns.

'Terrible tragedy, *mademoiselle*,' the waiter says suddenly in English, his eyes falling on the paper. 'I have heard only this morning that this is my friend's sister, Solange. She was indeed a beautiful girl.'

'What happened to her?' I ask.

'Found in the park. A few days after her fiancé was discovered chewed up as though a wolf had been feasting on him. The *Gendarmerie* are at a loss as to what 'as 'appened to either of them. She was in a terrible state I believe. Beyond recognition.'

'Your friend must be devastated,' Anja says meeting his eyes. 'What is his name? Where does he live?'

The waiter all but falls into Anja's bright green eyes. He is an easy victim. I could sense her giving him a little *push* and his eyes dilated slightly.

'His name is Luc Beauchamp, I don't know 'is address but 'e will be 'ere in 'alf an hour.'

Our waiter is confused when Anja releases him from her hypnotic gaze and he covers his embarrassment by refilling Anja's cup also.

She thanks him and returns to her scrutiny of the newspaper as he turns away.

'That was easy,' I say.

'Too easy,' says Anja. 'I'm more than a little freaked out by this happy coincidence.'

So am I. It seems too much of a coincidence that we are meeting Solange's brother but our life does seem to be full of strange twists of fate. Sometimes these are good twists but others have led us into danger. For a moment I wonder which one this will be.

'Looks like you are going to get your wish sooner, rather than later,' Anja says as she looks across the tables towards the waiter greeting a tall, dark-haired male. He fusses over the man, bringing him a large glass of red wine and I notice the red-rimmed eyes that would indicate the man has been crying. I'm certain that this is Solange's brother.

'I guess you're on again,' I say, nodding to Anja as she picks up her purse and walks straight for the man we assume is Luc Beauchamp.

As she passes the table, Anja swings her purse and clumsily knocks over the glass of wine. The red liquid spreads like spilt blood, pouring over the edge of the table and into Luc's lap. Fortunately he is wearing black jeans, but Anja squeals and twists with embarrassment in the way that I have seen her do so many times. She is an excellent actress. I shrug. This is why she fooled us so well when she first joined our small family.

The waiter rushes forward to clean up the mess and replace the glass.

'Naturally I will pay for the replacement,' Anja says.

'Only if you join me. My name is Luc, *mademoiselle*.'

Anja smiles. She is the proverbial cat with the cream. She introduces herself and sits down opposite Luc. He has long hair that falls to his shoulders and that fine unshaven down that a lot of modern men wear as a fashion statement. He calls over his waiter friend and before long Anja's coffee is going cold on my table while she sips wine instead. I pretend to read the paper as they chat, then as I finish the final dregs of my third coffee, I place some euros on the table, stand and walk over to where she is sitting.

'Are you coming Anja?' I say.

'Luc, this is my brother Gabi,' Anja says introducing us. 'Luc was just telling me some very sad news. Gabi, would you mind if I don't join you on the climb up to the top of Notre Dame? I'm inclined to stay here in the sun and talk to Luc. That is if you don't mind, Luc …'

Luc flushes, 'I don't mind at all. It will be my pleasure.'

'I don't know,' I say, feigning concern. 'Father made me promise to protect you on this trip.'

'I assure you *monsieur*, you sister will be safe here. You would honour me if you let her keep me company right now.'

'Please, brother,' Anja said smiling at me. 'Luc seems rather charming to me.'

'All right. But judging by that queue I may be some time.'

I leave them and pretend to join the Notre Dame tour but I notice that Luc is quickly engrossed with my vampire lover and slip silently away to do some more research on his family. I cloak myself and fly up into the air, looking down on Notre Dame before making a sweep of the city.

11
Tunnel

Preacher stared through the old iron gate, down the long, damp tunnel that led to the bowels of Rhuddlan Castle. He ran his finger over the dulled metal, then sniffed the orange powder that stained his finger. Iron oxide. The gate was old, but not by that many centuries. It made him wonder what had happened to the original covering and what it had been. Preacher ran his torch around the sides and over the ceiling surrounding the opening. He could make out traces of bare brick, as though at sometime or other the passage had been blocked off completely.

'Have you ever been down there?' he asked.

Ffion's friend, Geraint, shook his head. He was young, maybe eighteen or nineteen, and he wore casual loose tracksuit bottoms and a dirty-looking tee-shirt.

'We don't have a key,' Geraint said. 'Although my dad mentioned a few times that he wanted to force the grille and go and investigate.'

'I'm surprised he didn't. I would have,' Preacher said.

Preacher shone his torch into the blackness, the light fell flat just a few feet in. He could smell the cold dark dampness common in cellars and areas where there was no heat to disperse the moisture. He liked the smell. It reminded him of something from his childhood, like a coal cellar.

'No time like the present,' he said.

Geraint said. 'I don't think my dad ...'

'Maybe we should go and ask him?' Ffion suggested.

'He's not in,' Geraint said.

'Then he isn't here to object,' Preacher said.

Preacher unslung the canvas bag he was carrying from his shoulder and dropped it in front of the grille. He bent down, unzipped the bag and extracted a crowbar.

'Hang on. I don't know about this,' Geraint protested.

'Where's the harm?' asked Preacher. 'You said yourself, your dad wanted to explore the passage.'

'Yeah, but …'

'Perhaps we should wait to ask his permission?' Ffion said. 'You could come back tomorrow …?'

'Yeah,' Geraint agreed. 'I could ask him later.'

The two exchanged a glance which told Preacher a lot about their relationship and the scam they had been pulling. Preacher blinked. He didn't like to be taken for a ride.

'I can pay you,' he said his voice measured.

Ffion and Geraint smiled back. 'Maybe we could come to some arrangement. But this is bigger than what we usually do,' said Geraint. 'Seriously, we've never opened it. I'd have to think it through. Could mean a whole lot of trouble for me …'

Preacher switched the crowbar from his right hand to his left. Then he turned around and punched Geraint in the face with his right fist. The smile dropped from Geraint's lips as blood combusted from his nose, spraying the room and Preacher's face. Geraint's legs gave way under him as his hands flew to his face and his busted nose. He fell to the ground with a shocked grunt.

Ffion was too afraid to scream but her body reacted and she turned on shaking legs, running towards the cellar stairs. She was almost on the bottom step when Preacher grabbed her long hair, yanking her back. She fell to the floor, hands scrambling over his fingers as he dragged her back into the centre of the cellar room. She yelled and kicked, hands and feet trying to gain some leverage, but Preacher was just too strong.

Preacher let go of Ffion and turned on Geraint again as the man struggled to his feet to help his friend. Ffion scrambled away, pulling herself up against a stack of boxes in the corner, her eyes swayed to the stairs again, but Preacher was between her and them now and she was really afraid of what he would do.

Preacher weighed the crowbar in his hand. Then, as Geraint watched it, preparing to fend off an attack, Preacher used the distraction to pull a gun from his jacket pocket. Geraint froze.

'Tie and gag the bitch,' Preacher said.

Geraint glanced at Ffion then back at Preacher. Ffion was pressed against the boxes, her hair dishevelled, and Geraint noted that the hand with which Preacher clasped the gun had strips of her hair laced in between the fingers.

'You have two choices,' Preacher said. 'Tie her up or I just kill you both here and now.'

Geraint nodded. 'Okay. Don't do anything rash.'

'There's tape in the bag,' said Preacher and Geraint walked over to the bag, breathing heavily through his mouth as his nose was full of congealing blood. 'Slowly. Keep your hands where I can see them.'

Geraint couldn't help thinking how corny the line was and almost smiled at the irony of finding himself in this situation. He had trusted Ffion: she had brought him customers to see the passage before and it always resulted in both of them receiving a fee or bonus that they split. Last summer Geraint had bought a fifty inch flat screen television for his room with the collective proceeds. His parents thought he had just been saving up from the part time job he had at the local pizza restaurant. After paying his keep, Geraint barely had income left to pay for his journey to university, so when Ffion suggested the venture, he had jumped at the chance. So far it had been very lucrative for them both.

It was easy to arrange the visits whenever his folks were out. They both worked, and they had an active social life which meant that at least three nights a week he was alone in the house.

His mind flicked back to the phone call he had received that day from Ffion. 'This one's an easy mark. He's American and you know how they like to tip,' she had said. How wrong she had been.

'Hurry up,' said Preacher.

Preacher didn't wave the gun around like Geraint had seen

other villains do. He didn't even look like your typical bad guy. Apart from his pale blue eyes, he looked just like any other American tourist, even down to the Californian suntan.

Geraint found the duct tape in the bag and held it up.

'You,' Preacher said to Ffion, 'Sit down and hold out your hands. Wrap it tight around her wrists and ankles.'

Ffion slid down to the floor as Geraint approached. He began to search for the end of the tape.

As Geraint did as he was told wild plans ran through his head on how to escape and save the girl. All of the scenarios he devised seemed to point to one conclusion though: both he and Fi would be shot dead. He felt a deep sadness. He had always liked Fi and had hoped one day that she would finally say yes to going out with him. They had become closer since their little venture started. He glanced at her fear-filled eyes. Silent tears were rolling down her cheeks, and her chest was heaving with panic. He hoped she could see the apology he felt he owed her as he ran the tape around her ankles.

'Sorry Fi,' Geraint murmured.

'Touching,' Preacher mocked and it made Geraint angry that he had no emotion at all regarding tying them up.

'Look,' Geraint said. 'I'll help you. Just don't hurt her.'

'I have no intention of hurting her if you do exactly what I say,' Preacher said coldly. 'Now gag her. We don't need her raising the alarm while we're down that tunnel.'

Geraint couldn't hear one inch of compassion in his voice, and underneath it all he wondered what was going to happen. Would the man kill them both anyway? They had seen his face and could identify him. Geraint knew the man's image would forever be etched in his brain. Nightmares of this day would haunt his dreams.

His nose throbbed, reminding him that they weren't out of the woods yet. He pressed a piece of tape over Ffion's mouth.

'Can you breathe?' he asked.

Ffion nodded but her wild, scared eyes made him wonder. 'Try not to panic,' he told her.

'Shut up,' said Preacher. 'The bitch will be fine. You need to worry about yourself now.'

Preacher watched over Geraint as the younger man followed his instructions to use the crowbar on the lock of the gate. The iron lock was an ancient mortise, probably seventeenth century, and had seized in the box keep from lack of use and lubrication. Geraint forced the crowbar between the lock and the frame but the lock wouldn't budge. He pressed and pulled again, then fell forward as the crowbar slid, sending orange dust into the air.

'It's stuck fast,' he said glancing over his shoulder at Preacher. 'I don't think I can ...'

'Keep trying,' Preacher answered.

Geraint forced the bar in once more, this time he pulled and tugged in a back and forth motion. His arm muscles screamed. It was difficult to put all of his weight behind the effort as his breathing felt so shallow due to the state of his nose. He stopped, whipped the back of his hand over his nostrils in an attempt to clear his airways, but the pain of touching it only brought tears to his eyes.

'I can't breathe,' he explained turning to look at Preacher.

Preacher pulled a tissue from his pocket and dropped it down onto the bag, then backed away. 'Try blowing it. It's not broken, just bruised.'

Geraint didn't know what state he was in, but he took the tissue and careful dabbed, then blew, his nose. The paper tissue filled with blood and snot, and it took several blows before Geraint felt he could draw air up his nostrils and into his lungs.

'Thanks,' he said.

For the first time since this started he had a surge of hope that he and Fi would come out of it alive. Preacher's show of compassion helped him decide to put all of his effort behind opening the iron gate. A surge of adrenaline pumped into his veins. Geraint had always wanted to go down into the tunnel and could never understand why his father refused to open it.

Geraint picked up the crowbar and renewed his efforts. Within a few minutes he heard the lock pop and, with further exertion, he was able to pull the gate towards him, despite the seized hinges.

'Drop the crowbar back in the bag,' Preacher said.

Geraint felt as though he were in a trance as he stared into the gaping hole of the tunnel. His entire childhood had been spent imagining the moment when his father finally opened the gate and they would all walk inside and see if there really was a dungeon below ground. He dropped the crowbar down and began to walk into the tunnel.

'Wait!' ordered Preacher. 'Pick up the torch and lead the way.'

Geraint stopped and like a sleepwalker he turned and stared blankly at the torch in Preacher's hand. It was the large, square industrial type. A black, rubberised casing gave way to a bulb that was as wide as a tennis ball. Geraint took the torch by the hooked handle and his thumb automatically fell on the switch. The beam sprung into life as Geraint walked into the tunnel. Preacher watched the light skirt over the walls and floor, then he bent towards his bag, removing a miner's helmet which he placed quickly on his head. He didn't want to rely on Geraint and the torch, but it would be useful to have the other man walk ahead of him, lighting the way, and possibly being the target of any danger.

Preacher placed the pistol in his waistband after engaging the safety button. Then he pulled another gun from his other pocket. This one was longer and thinner. He extracted the dart cartridge from the pocket of his canvas bag, slotting it under the barrel. It contained six darts, but Preacher had never needed to use more than one before.

Geraint turned as he heard the click and he examined Preacher's strange weapon carefully. The sight of it shook him from his strange fugue. It was a long thin tube, with a thick round barrel attached underneath and was full of what Geraint could only describe as sharp needles. It looked vaguely antique, but oddly science fiction. Geraint wondered why Preacher would need a dart gun.

'I'm not going to try anything,' Geraint said. 'I'm as curious about this as you are.'

'I know. Otherwise you'd be tied up with your girlfriend now.'

Geraint glanced at Ffion, she still looked scared, but he knew she was safer there. Besides, if he kept the man down in the tunnels long enough, his parents would return and hopefully find her. Then they could raise the alarm and he would be saved. Geraint turned back to the tunnel. It held a weird fascination and he thought, strange as it may seem, that he could hear music somewhere down below.

'D'you hear that?' he asked drifting forward, the light from the torch swinging back and forth and around.

Preacher shouldered his bag and followed. He had seen this kind of reaction before and he knew then, without doubt, that somehow the revenants were close by and they were weaving their hypnotic magic to protect their lair. Fortunately, since one of them had bitten him, he was immune to it.

12
Hunger

The scientist's quarters were above ground level. It was a big square building made up of individual cubicle-like rooms which contained a regulation army bed, a bedside table, a small wardrobe and a dressing table as standard. Lucy, like all of the others, had added personal items to make the room homely. On the wall she had hung a picture of herself working on the dig at the La Brea Tar Pits in LA, taken several years ago. There was one of her in her graduation robes and hat, holding her doctorate casually in her hand. On the dressing table was a picture of a man and woman, holding a baby. Next to it was another of a girl in a white communion dress. The latter two were fakes. They represented a parentage that Lucy didn't have but she felt were essential in maintaining her cover.

Lucy lay on her bunk looking up at the stark ceiling. All the rooms were painted white. The light fittings had bulbs, but no shades. Home comforts, but for a few personal items were not considered necessary here. None of this actually bothered her and she barely noticed the blandness of the room. It was a base, a haven. Somewhere to sleep when she needed to. Nothing more.

She was hungry. The pains gnawed at her stomach and the vertigo had started earlier that day. It was a sure sign that her body needed the nutrition it craved and she had been starving for months now, rarely taking the risk of interfering with any of the soldiers. The problem was her body was starting to cannibalise itself. She was burning up all of her psychic and physical strength. It was making her weak and might, if left long enough, even kill her. She didn't know this for certain, but had coldly speculated on the possibility. Either way, starving was never a good thing. It would make her careless and she couldn't afford to take risks, especially when the soldiers were all geared up to look for revenants.

Sometimes some of the scientists would refer to the creatures as vampires. But Lucy knew that the pathetic creatures were no relation to her. *These fools don't have a clue*, she thought. *They wouldn't know a real vampire if they fell over one*. And it was true. She remained undetected among them. This was partly because their only experience of vampires was the revenants and if truth be told they were more zombie than they were vampire. Even though some of them could actually talk and communicate on a basic level they appeared to have longevity. Subject One was a perfect example of that. That was however where the similarity ended. The revenants, although they didn't appear to rot and could heal themselves, even looked human for most of the time, but they smelt very bad indeed. They stank of death, decay and evil.

Occasionally she wondered why she took the risk of being on the base. It would be easy to slip away and never return. But Lucy enjoyed the excitement of knowing more than the others, and she wanted to learn, just as much as they did, where the revenants came from: especially if they could pass on their infection to others. This interested her more than anything else.

Lucy closed her eyes. She could hear the sound of a television being switched on, the instant blare of speech and music, rapidly reduced as the watcher turned the volume down. Some of them had such amenities in their rooms as combination television and DVD players to help burn up the long, dull evenings. Lucy hadn't bothered to request one. She had little time and patience for the rubbish she had seen projected onto the television. It seemed to her that most programmes showed a false reality of life. There were shows that conveyed the perfect family life, promising the American dream of two point four children and a suburban house with a picket fence. There were science fiction programmes that talked of alien conspiracies, all of which she didn't believe in. And in recent years a fascination with series spun from popular cult horror romance novels – usually featuring vampires or some supernatural equivalent, which were all utterly ridiculous and sickening angst-ridden. The reality shows were the worst. They made celebrities out of scum. Lucy couldn't bear to watch any of it and even the sounds of screaming excitement from some sad game show floating through the wall made her want to shriek with rage.

Enough!

Lucy swung her feet off the bed and sat listening to the other sounds of movement in the building. The steady drop of a pair of court shoes slipped from stocking-covered feet. The hum of a small kettle as it reached the boil. The slosh of water as a body sank into a bath. The flush of a toilet. She pushed all of the noise back. Her senses were heightening as her need forced her to become more predatory. The hunger was becoming unbearable.

Lucy's chest heaved as she sighed. I'm going stir crazy in this place.

She stood up. She could ignore it no longer. It was time to take a chance and go out. She locked her door, turned off the bald, bright light, and opened the curtains.

The base was lit up with dull street lights to help prevent accidents as soldiers and civilian staff returned to their beds after their various shifts. The place was always working, even through the night. Lucy had resisted working the night shifts despite it being more of a natural time for her. She didn't want the others to notice how the moon energised and thrilled her. It was better to appear wan and tired, overworked. Just like everyone else. And mornings made her feel tired, the heat and sun drained her, even though it didn't burn and itch as it used to in the early days of her rebirth. There was some truth in the myths about vampires and their sensitivity to light. But mostly this legend had abounded to make the storytellers and their listeners feel secure. If they had known the truth, they might have realised that there was no safe time of day. True vampires could operate all day. They didn't even have to sleep if they didn't want to. Sleep, however, was something that most of them enjoyed nonetheless.

Lucy cloaked herself, pushed the window open, then climbed up and stood on the frame. She was on the second floor, a small leap down if she were willing to go that way, but she had no intention of walking out of the base. Around the perimeter security had set up sensors. The cameras may not see her, but the sensors would feel any movement on the ground and it would be investigated. Equally, flying also had its problems. There was the aerial radar to consider. The radar activated at just a few feet above the main structures. Even so, leaving and returning unseen was possible, it just meant that she had to fly low, while maintaining her invisibility: a task far more difficult than it seemed when your nutritional resources were low.

I have to do this, she thought. I'll end up munching on one of these tasty little soldier boys and then some real problems might occur.

There was a warm breeze floating over the desert. She breathed it in and then fell forward, swooping back up into the air just before her outstretched body hit the ground. She kept low, trying to maintain a height of ten feet from the earth. The air stirred around her, lifting her as though she were weightless and she allowed it to propel her forward over the desert and away from the guard station that marked the entrance of the base. The wind picked up, pulling her along until she reached the perimeter fence. Now was the time to take the biggest risk. She might soon become a blip on the radar.

The fence was electrified. Lucy knew this without having to read the warning signs because she could hear the steady hum of electricity working through the wire. She propelled herself up and hovered level with the fence for a few seconds, then she swiftly threw herself over the top and hung in the air on the other side. She waited subconsciously holding her breath.

When nothing happened she moved away, glancing down at the sensors as she maintained her level above ground. Behind her the base remained quiet. *Just as well. I'd have been pretty pissed if I had to return immediately for the room inspection.*

Once she was clear of the perimeter and the surrounding monitored land, Lucy flew higher and began to speed up. The movement of the air around her was no longer a danger so she flew towards Las Vegas with more confidence and at her full speed.

Before long she was floating above the town, looking down at the lights on the main stretch. She followed the brightly lit freeway into the centre and directly downtown. Here the nightlife was bustling. The pavements were covered with tourists weaving in and out of each other like bees in a hive. She passed over a hotel that had an artificial volcano in its front entrance. The volcano erupted to the gleeful cheers of a crowd. Farther along she saw a pirate ship battle with a Royal Navy ship in the manmade river at the front of another hotel. The ships sank, while their brave captains remained at the helm, only to rise again from the water a few seconds later with the captains still in situ.

Lucy sniffed the air, she felt sickened by the smells emanating from the many restaurants. The odour of burgers, hotdogs and slightly burnt onions, mingled with the spices of exotic curries then merged with the strong garlic smell of Italian food. The Las Vegas hotels were a representation of the world as well as of American culture. There was a hotel shaped like a pyramid in the heart of the action, and one shaped like the New York skyline. New York, New York sported a roller coaster ride wrapped around the top of a high rise and a replica of the Statue of Liberty.

Lucy drifted down into the car park of one of the hotels, letting her invisibility collapse as she stood hidden from the security cameras. Then she walked around the building, confident that she looked harmless and normal in her black jeans and white shirt. She would be the last person the casino's security personnel would be concerned with.

Around the front of the hotel a magnificent display of water cannons was exploding from the ground, with colour and music to emphasis its perfection. Lucy stopped and mingled with the throng as the water dance continued but she wasn't watching the display, she was assessing the people around her. She was so hungry now she felt her control slipping and her usually hidden fangs began to press against the back of her top lip. She took a deep breath then forced them back as she tried to quell the pain of her starvation.

Remind me never to wait this long again!

The street was thick with humans. It was almost too much to bear. She could smell hot blood, pumping through excited veins. She became blind to individuals as the horde became one huge, pulsating mass. She walked on pushing her way through the bodies towards one of the walkways. The desert heat was stifling and she felt a trickle of moisture leak down her back as she stepped into the nearest hotel. The icy blast coming from the air conditioning was a relief and it cooled the humidity on her skin. But she felt damp and chilled.

The blood fever calmed down with the cold atmosphere as she moved deeper into the hotel, following the wide reception area into the main casino. She halted at the door, looking out at the rows of one-arm bandits on the left. She turned right, following a line of tables, where people played craps, poker and backgammon.

It was quieter inside. Although busy, the guests were mostly engaged with their games. Lucy paused by a blackjack table. There were three people playing against the dealer. A man and two women. One of the women yawned as though she was bored. She had dark brown hair, hazel eyes and a thin pointed nose. She reminded Lucy of one of the research assistants she had seen at the base so she turned away quickly, just in case it was the same woman. The dealer looked over at Lucy and smiled. He was wearing a silk shirt and non-descript black trousers that were part of the casino uniform.

Lucy smiled back, then walked on. She sat down at the next table and placed some money on the green felt. The dealer whisked it away, pushing the notes down into a metal shoot that led somewhere below the table to a secure safe. He then placed a stack of chips before her.

Lucy glanced around. There were two men to her left and a

woman to her right. She noticed their curious glances so she nodded and smiled, taking in the dishevelled appearance of one of the men. He had a bristly beard newly sprouting from his chin and over his lip. His eyes were bloodshot and he appeared to be excessively tired. His clothes were crumpled and a thick stain marred the front of his shirt.

The other man called over to a waitress who was wearing a leopard print leotard with a cat's tale and a head band with cat's ears.

'Bloody Mary,' he said. 'Make it a double.'

'I'll have a Long Island Ice Tea,' said the woman beside Lucy.

'Miss? Can I get you anything?' asked the waitress.

Lucy looked up, her fierce green eyes glowed like a cat's eyes in the glare of the light above the table. The dealer took a step back.

'Long Island for me too,' she said.

'Cool contacts,' said the waitress. 'Drink coming right up.'

Lucy smiled cynically as the girl sashayed away. Her eyes were often being confused with the fake colour of contact lenses. It was ironic when she spent her entire day wearing lenses that made her eyes appear dull and normal.

As the game began, Lucy watched each of her companions closely. Who would be the easiest target? The woman? Or one of the men? The hunger roared again, protesting at the torturous waiting, but for once Lucy revelled in pain. She met the interested gaze of the woman. Not long now.

13
Discovery

We are in an old warehouse just outside of Paris. Around me are the remnants of broken machinery, a stack of wooden pallets and a smashed table. Luc Beauchamp sits patiently on the pile of pallets. There was no need to tie him: Anja did a great job of taking over his self-control. Her hypnotic powers grow stronger with every day and she really does enjoy using them. At heart I think she is a dominatrix and the thought of her in tight PVC or rubber suddenly flits through my imagination. It makes me smile but also arouses me on a level of fetish that I hadn't realised was in me. *Interesting*.

'What did you learn?' she asks.

'Not much. They have these strict rules about privacy. You can't find out anything about anyone until their records are over a hundred years old. But I did manage to find out that Beauchamp's family is old aristocracy.'

'He's wealthy then? He'll be missed.'

'No. The family has no wealth, but their lineage stretches back as far as the revolution and beyond. Luc here, with the exception of his heritage, is pretty much an average Joe now.'

'Do you have any more siblings?' Anja asks Luc and I'm surprised at myself for not having the common sense to ask the man for information directly. Anja has outsmarted me. She is proving to be far more intelligent than I might have imagined.

'Another sister,' Luc slurs. He is so far under her control he can barely keep his eyes open.

'Tell me about your family. Is there any history of ... longevity?' Anja asks.

Luc tries to raise his head but it lolls back onto his chest as though it is too heavy for his neck. He doesn't answer.

'You may have to release your hold a little,' I suggest.

Anja shrugs, 'Maybe there's no point in all of this. How would he know if there was anything unusual in his family heritage? I think we should probably just try your experiment and have done with this.'

I move closer to Luc. He is a handsome man. Traditionally dark in colouring. I remember his sister had the same shine to her hair, except it was red. His eyes, when open, are a deep rich brown.

'Do you like him?' I ask Anja.

'What?'

'You've spent all afternoon with him. Do you like him?'

'What are you getting at? You told me to keep him busy.'

'I'm not getting at anything. I'm asking a straight question. If I bite him, and he changes, he may become one of us. It is important to consider if we would want him in our lives.'

'Oh!' Anja says. 'I hadn't thought of that.'

'Of course, he may become monstrous, like his sister, and at least we know we can kill him if he does. If he comes back as one of us, then that may be a different matter.'

'Perhaps we should just let him go and return home to tell Lilly and Chez what's happening,' Anja says again and this time it angers me.

'I don't need Lilly and Chez to help me make decisions,' I say, fury colouring my cheeks. 'We're going to do this without them.'

I bend down and look into Luc's unfocused gaze.

I know that Anja's bite could have been the cause, but this time I will drain Luc. It is an experiment of a dangerous kind. We had both sensed something different on his sister. A taint in the blood that reminded me of the taste we experience when feeding from our own gene pool; though it was clearly not the same.

I tip Luc's head to the side and lick his neck. Below the surface I can feel the pump of his blood: the coursing of his instinctive adrenaline. His mind is dulled, but his body is intuitively afraid and quite rightly so. I swallow the perspiration and reach out in the way that Lilly has taught us, testing his genealogy. The heritage lines pan out, spreading over the surface of French history, but nowhere are they related to the vampire gene.

'Anything?' asks Anja.

'Taste him,' I say.

She crouches down beside him, licking his neck with her pointed pink tongue. A shudder passes through me as I experience some of her emotion as she swallows his sweat. Minutes pass as she scrutinises his lineage. Then she shakes her head.

'He tastes different to the girl,' she says. 'She had a tang ... Do you know what I mean because I find it hard to explain?'

I nod. I do know. I had tasted her too and she was different to Luc.

'Luc?' Anja says softly. 'Was Solange your full sister?'

Luc raises his head. 'Who told you? Who said ...?'

'What Luc? Tell me!'

'My mother had an affair ... Solange is only my half-sister.'

We leave him in the warehouse knowing he will wake from his mesmerism confused and disorientated. Perhaps he will put this lapse of memory down to the excessive wine he drank at lunchtime. Perhaps he will consider that his grief has made him mad. I don't know, nor do I care. The secret he revealed saved his life today. That is all that matters to me.

'What are we going to do?' asks Anja as we fly back to the hotel.

'I don't know. His mother is dead, and she never revealed the identity of Solange's father. Short of testing every single male in the city over fifty, this is a dead end.'

I can feel Anja's thoughts even though she says nothing and I am certain she is considering the strange scenario. What if there are more like Solange out there? Capable of changing into ... something that could threaten the anonymity of our existence? I have to think. My mind is going back through the many strains of blood I have tasted. Had I drunk from one such as she in the past? Had I turned my victims into the walking dead when I did not know what to look for? And if so, why hadn't I heard about this until now? The idea that my bastard creatures live on, inhuman and monstrous, makes bile rise into the back of my throat.

Later, when we reach the hotel, I go downstairs to settle the bill. When I return to the room, Anja is ready. She has packed the few items we have into a small bag. As I lift her in my arms and we take flight from the window, heading back over the ocean and towards Wales, I feel somewhat sad that our trip has ended. The shopping trip we planned never really materialised and Anja left with fewer possessions than she took with her. We don't talk, but my mind is a whirlwind of emotion. It feels as though our lives have somehow taken yet another dramatic turn. I don't like this new problem. Not one little bit. Why is it that since I discovered my vampire family there is very little peace now in our lives? It is strange, but I recall my loneliness of the past with something akin to nostalgia.

Despite the buffeting wind that carries us across the Channel, I feel cold sweat beading my brow. It is not the Sun that harrows me, not the wind. I am afraid again, and the old bullet wound scar aches once more as though in warning. My heart thumps in my chest so hard that Anja raises her head from its resting place on my torso. Perhaps the Illuminati are behind this after all. Maybe Caradien survived the hell room. Maybe we have always been monitored by these people.

'Caradien is dead,' Anja says.

I nuzzle her, breathing in the fresh wind scent in her hair. Her cleanliness reassures me and helps me push away the paranoia. We are not just monsters, though often I revel in my grotesque nature. We are not mindless creatures. Nor are we mythology. We can think, and evolve, and love. We are capable of so much good. Surely we are something better than humanity? For certain I know that we are superior to mankind and so much more than the creature that was born from the bite Anja placed on the throat of Solange.

Anja showers kisses on my face, her comfort is welcome but not needed as I am now calm. But I appreciate this new strength I see in her. I fly on across England to Wales, barely noticing the lights below us, or the bustle of humankind as they live their normal lives, unaware that we monsters walk among them. I only care that we reach the lair soon. Then we must tell Chez and Lilly all that has happened.

14
Under the Castle

Geraint's feet slipped in the sludge and he tumbled to the ground before Preacher could reach him. The torch fell from his fingers and splashed into a filthy puddle of water. Preacher always prepared for every eventuality and wasn't too concerned as the torch had a rubber coating that protected it from water and damage.

He focused his helmet light on Geraint as the man struggled to his feet cursing the thick black goo that covered the tunnel floor.

'This place stinks like shit,' Geraint said.

'Pick the torch up,' Preacher ordered and Geraint scrambled around in the mud.

'Fuck! What is this crap?'

Geraint wiped his dirty hands on his jeans and held the torch out but Preacher could already smell the vile mud without getting closer. The tunnel held the damp, rotting odour of a newly filled tomb. It reeked of death. Preacher gripped his dart gun more firmly. Then glanced back the way they had come. He could no longer see the light from the cellar room because the tunnel had taken a sharp turn a few feet in. As he turned back, Preacher found Geraint looking at him and he cursed himself for being so careless. What had possessed him to turn his back so casually on the other man?

'What are you expecting to find down here?' Geraint asked.

'Keep walking.'

Geraint turned back, sweeping the light out before him, particularly the floor. He didn't want to tumble in the muck again. The darkness was so thick it felt as though a fog surrounded them. Geraint experienced an intense claustrophobia. Despite the torch he suffered with the thought that he couldn't see. He had never been below ground before. Even their cellar had a small window at the top of the wall that let a modicum of light in from outside. The tunnel, he knew, had never seen any natural light. Geraint's breathing sped up and he began to imagine that something lurked beyond each sweep of the beam but somehow managed to skitter away as the light fell in the shadows.

Geraint took a sharp step back.

'Jesus!'

'What is it?' asked Preacher warily.

'I thought I saw … human remains.'

Geraint ran the light over the floor again, pausing when he found the pile of bones.

'Could be human,' Preacher said.

A half fractured skull lay a few feet away. Geraint gasped as the light fell on it.

'Looks like we're on the right track,' Preacher said.

'For what?' asked Geraint. His voice had now gone up an octave.

Preacher didn't answer but he nudged Geraint with the gun so, despite his anxiety, the younger man began his careful trek forward through the thickening mud.

A few feet onwards the tunnel twisted again. This time it took a sharp right bend. They had the sense of going downwards and it certainly appeared to be a sloping floor that led them deeper into the bowels of the earth. The damp mud disappeared and was replaced by thick stone blocks of ancient flagstone. The tunnel narrowed, the ceiling became lower.

Perhaps it was the sight of some form of civilisation but Geraint suddenly felt less scared. He paused, heaving in a gulp of breath. This area, strangely, appeared to be less dark and heavy. His heart stopped its wary pounding and he used the torch to look around more with curiosity now than fear.

On the walls he saw the remnants of old frames that he

guessed had been used to hold torches. To his left he noticed a crumbling patch of mosaic tiles.

'This is interesting,' Geraint said, pausing.

'Be quiet,' Preacher warned. 'Keep walking.'

Geraint shrugged. He wasn't surprised that the small details or evidence of history didn't interest Preacher. It was obvious he was looking for something else and again that slight prickle of fear tickled the back of his brain and sent goosebumps rippling over his neck and arms.

They descended. The atmosphere below was thick and humid but Preacher could feel a slow flow of air that seeped downwards. Probably from the tunnel and the house itself, he thought. By not bricking that hole up they have probably kept the air moving in here.

The tunnel twisted again.

'I hope we can find the way back!' Geraint said, his voice a husky whisper.

'It's all one route. No alternative twists so far. So I don't think it will be an issue,' Preacher said but the thought had crossed his mind that it might become a problem if they were faced with choices. At that moment the tunnel opened out into a huge cavern.

'Whoa!' Geraint said. 'Where did this come from?'

Preacher looked around but kept Geraint in full sight. The cavern was most definitely under the castle. It looked more like underground cold storage than a dungeon though and the temperature was considerably lower than it had been in the tunnel.

Geraint blew on his mud stained fingers and stamped his feet. His breath steamed in the icy air. Neither of the men was wearing appropriate clothing to be in such a cold place.

'I vote we go back and get some sweaters,' Geraint said, his voice echoing around the room.

'Hush,' Preacher whispered.

Preacher held his breath and listened to the darkness around them. The cold settled around his limbs but he ignored it. He was used to having to deal with extreme conditions in unusual situations. That was what happened when you were a fixer. He reached inside his canvas bag and extracted another torch.

'Go farther in,' he said to Geraint, and waited by the tunnel until the young man walked into the centre of the cavern.

Preacher switched on the new torch. This one was even stronger than the one Geraint carried and it contained an ultra violet bulb. The room lit up. Preacher could now see it was a circular space approximately fifty feet wide with a high ceiling. Around the edges of the room were several openings that led out to different areas. These interested Preacher more than the room itself.

'What is this place?' asked Geraint. He was no longer afraid, more awestruck. 'You could have some wild parties down here.'

Preacher smiled. It was typical of the mindless young to think of such a lame usage for such a magnificent room. He glanced at Geraint, observing that the man was too fascinated to make trouble, then he turned his torch around to scrutinise the walls and particularly the dark openings he could see on either side of the room.

There were ancient torches hanging in iron brackets placed a few feet apart. Preacher wondered if they would still flame. He searched his bag again, finding the box of matches he kept in there for emergencies. Preacher didn't know much about medieval lighting but he recalled that the torches were often soaked in animal fat to help them light. There were torches either side of the tunnel entrance so Preacher went to the nearest one and struck a match. He threw it at the torch then stepped back cautiously.

The match fell down into the centre of the rag and straw catching fire almost immediately. This meant the ancient materials were either resilient or had been freshly prepared. Preacher looked around. It was obvious that no one had been here for a centuries.

He found Geraint watching him.

'This place is awesome,' Geraint said.

'Yes. But unfortunately I think it's a dead end.'

'I don't suppose you're going to tell me what you are looking for? Is this like some Indiana Jones thing? We're supposed to be finding treasure?'

Preacher didn't answer. Instead he went to all of the torches in turn and lit each one. The room was fully lit now, but within a short time the torch smoke polluted the air as it streamed from the tips into the room.

'There should be a vent here somewhere,' Geraint said.

'You know about these things?'

'Hey. I'm Welsh. We have castles all over the place here. Part of our heritage.'

'But we're underground. Where would a vent possibly be?'

Geraint pointed his finger upwards. 'Usually through the roof, but it's probably blocked or covered over because the smoke just isn't going up there.'

Preacher glanced upwards. The smoke was floating above his head, rapidly filling the room.

'Let's check out the other tunnels,' Preacher said.

They took the left one first. Preacher made Geraint walk ahead of him but the tunnel just led to a complete dead end. They turned around, walking back into the cavern. The smoke was worse; Preacher now regretted his decision to light all of the torches. The light from them was consumed by the smoke and it was eating what little oxygen there was.

'Over to the other side,' Preacher said. He had given up pointing the dart gun at Geraint. He now believed the man to be so curious about the cavern that he wanted to investigate just as much as he did.

Geraint pulled his tee-shirt up over his nose, then crossed the room, disappearing into the cloud of black smoke. Preacher followed and they stumbled their way into the next tunnel. The smoke was spreading, searching for a natural vent. This tunnel was narrow, the ceiling so low that Preacher and Geraint had to stoop as they made their way, torches pointed ahead. They reached a shallow doorway. A wooden frame was built into the brick and an old door hung open on rotted hinges.

Geraint looked over at Preacher. All thought of escape, or

concerns for Ffion had fled with the excitement of the find.

'I've wanted to investigate this place my entire life. I won't tell anyone you were here or what happened. And I can promise you, neither will Fi.'

Preacher nodded. Then he waited as Geraint walked ahead of him into the other room.

15
Anastasia

Foolish mortal, allowing herself to be picked up by a complete stranger like that, thought Lucy as she lay naked in the hotel room with her victim. *It had been so easy.* Licking and slurping at the woman's throat, Lucy could barely swallow the escaping blood quick enough. *I haven't been this clumsy since my first kill*, she thought. She was bathed in blood and she felt so aroused by the hot liquid that ran over her breasts and down to the small blonde triangle between her legs that she squirmed against the bare skin of the woman.

The woman arched against her, half dead already but still feeling the pleasure of the vampire's bite, which Lucy knew acted like a narcotic. *If I could bottle our venom it would make me a fortune on the black market*, she thought.

She giggled. The whole thing was absurd. Of course she didn't need the money; she could already lay her hands on a king's ransom. She laughed again, half choking on the now cooling blood. She felt the life slip away from her victim and felt a brief moment of regret: not for the death, but that it had come about so soon. She had always enjoyed playing with her food.

As the evening wore on Lucy had grown more impatient. She left the blackjack table, a few dollars extra in her pocket. She could have cleaned up but she didn't want security to be able to pinpoint her at anytime on the cameras. That could be dangerous, especially as she was planning to feed, so she made her movements casual, deliberately trying to blend into the surroundings.

She had spotted the woman outside. She was around forty,

pretty but looking a little worn around the edges. She was wearing a short black, backless dress, with painfully high heels. Her hair was loose and salon-dressed in chestnut curls over her shoulders. From behind she appeared much younger than she actually was. Lucy suspected that she was a housewife, away for the weekend and looking for a good time: everything about her demeanour was craving attention. It only took a few words, a sensual touch on the arm, to show the woman that Lucy was exactly what she needed and desired.

'I've always wanted to do it with a woman,' she had said as they stood alone in the lift a few minutes later.

'Me too,' said Lucy. 'But that's the fun of Vegas isn't it? We can do what we want and no one will know about it.'

Lucy realised as she spoke that the statement was completely true. There was something about Las Vegas that made corruption seem so acceptable. It wasn't just the gambling, the mafia or the prostitution. It was more that the average person felt a need to behave differently when they arrived here. Lucy was sensitive to atmospheres but she had long ignored the invisible miasma that surrounded this desert oasis. Still, the smog touched her, and it felt as though it were focused somehow underground: as though an ancient evil fed on the sins of the occupants.

Lucy shook away the thought and returned her attention to the woman sharing the lift. Her imagination was always running wild and she could think about these things, inventing scenarios of Lovecraftian creatures but she knew deep down that the only monsters in this world were her kind.

On the eleventh floor Lucy noticed the cameras that tracked them back to the room. She focused her energy on them. The CCTV wouldn't record her image at all, but it would capture the woman walking alone towards her room. With what was about to happen she didn't really want anyone to see her at all.

'My name is …' the woman began to say.

'Don't tell me,' Lucy interrupted. 'Let's keep this as a mysterious encounter. Just between us.'

The woman nodded. Lucy could tell she was relieved. She clearly didn't wish to be observed either and if it all went pear-shaped, she didn't want Lucy to know who she really was either.

'I'll call you Anastasia,' Lucy said. 'I think that is a sexy and illicit name.'

The woman smiled. 'I like it. It makes me think of Russian spies.'

Lucy smiled and held her hand as Anastasia swiped the card key across the door lock. A green light illuminated and the door sprang open as Anastasia pushed the handle. They went inside. Anastasia was nervous, but Lucy knew how to solve that problem. She ran her nails lightly over the woman's bare back, sending ripples of lust through her skin. The nervous trembling soon altered to excitement. Anastasia turned back around and fell into Lucy's arms. Lucy explored her soft lips, licking and kissing her until the woman practically swooned.

Lucy peeled the black dress away to reveal still pert breasts, and a smooth flat belly.

'You look after yourself, don't you?' she said. Then she bent down and licked and sucked on one nipple until it stood up erect.

'Oh God,' Anastasia said. 'That feels wonderful.'

Anastasia's knees gave way, and Lucy picked her up then spread her on the bed. Her tongue licked a trail down the smooth skin, and Anastasia parted her legs with anticipation while little gasps came from her throat. Lucy could smell her sex, and it aroused her.

'I want you,' Lucy said as she stood, removing her jeans and tee-shirt. She placed them on a chair far away from the bed.

Anastasia squirmed, tilting her pelvis in an open invitation.

'You seem to know what to do,' Anastasia said.

'I'm a fast learner.'

Lucy lay down on the bed then pushed Anastasia back as she ran her hands over the woman. She cupped her breasts in a distinctly male way. Anastasia lay back closing her eyes, clearly being fucked by a woman was little different to going with a man. *Aside from the obvious lack of cock*, she thought.

Lucy's hand stroked downwards, her fingers, and long sharp nails, brushed the tops of her thighs until Anastasia squirmed again. She wanted to say 'Fuck me', but it felt like a weird thing to say to another female.

'Take me,' Anastasia murmured finally.

'Oh I plan to,' Lucy said.

Lucy's fingers slid gently over Anastasia's clitoris, sending shivers up her spine. She opened her legs allowing Lucy to slip her fingers in deeper. Lucy brushed and stroked, until Anastasia felt her hips moving of their own accord. Moisture leaked over Lucy's fingers, she pulled them to her lips and as Anastasia opened her eyes, Lucy sucked her fingers, enjoying the taste of the woman.

Anastasia groaned. Lucy moved over her and pressed her full breasts against Anastasia's. The sensation sent sensual ripples of lust coursing through the woman's body. She needed something, wanted to be penetrated but she wasn't sure how this was going to work or be satisfying.

Lucy reached up to the top of the bed and pulled the pillows from under Anastasia's head. She threw one of them far across the room. It landed near the door, a good ten feet away from the bed.

She now had Anastasia totally flat beneath her. Lucy's hand went down between her thighs as though she could sense what Anastasia wanted. She opened her up, slipping one long finger inside her.

'Yes!' Anastasia gasped. She turned her head side to side on the pillow; a small frown creased her brow as she moved her hips in time with Lucy's thrusts.

Lucy pulled away, then slid downwards, until she could see Anastasia's full lips. She licked around the woman's thighs, then over the flesh of her mound until Anastasia twitched and gasped.

'Please,' Anastasia said.

Lucy's mouth and tongue descended on the woman and as Anastasia came, the first bite ripped her open.

The blood ran from her body in pink soap bubbles as Lucy lathered her hair with Anastasia's expensive shampoo. The body in the other room was already forgotten and she felt full, warm, sensual and happy. She stepped out of the shower, then dried herself on the hotel towels.

Once clean and dry, she went back into the main bedroom and slipped into her underwear. The room was in total darkness, earlier she had turned off the lights and opened the curtains to look out over the lights of the city. Las Vegas was noisy but the balcony windows were triple glazed and the human ear wouldn't be able to detect much noise from outside. Lucy glanced over at the window. She could hear a helicopter flying around outside. She focused on the sound while paranoia stilled her heart for a split second. Then she hurried over to the chair and began to dress. Her skin was still slightly damp and she struggled to pull the jeans over her thighs. She took a breath, pushing back the panic that the helicopter had created. It was insane to fear something so normal in these parts, but Lucy knew what it could mean: her absence from the base may have been detected.

Her heart was pounding as she dressed and she glanced constantly at the window and the city beyond. *This is insane. No one knows I'm out.*

She began to worry about the cameras in the casino. *I should have been more careful.* Now the hunger was gone, Lucy could see all of the mistakes she had made, but hoped that no one would connect the dots when Anastasia's body was discovered.

She retrieved the pillow she had thrown at the door earlier and slipped off the pillow case. Then she began to stuff the used towels into it. Since she had taken such a huge risk feeding so close to the base the least she could do was take all evidence away from the scene.

She looked around. The light from outside fell over the bed and Anastasia stared at her with dead, accusing eyes. Lucy shrugged. *Food. You were just food. Nothing personal, love.*

The helicopter flew by again and Lucy looked out to see an advertising banner being dragged across the sky. *Hal's Chinese Banquet must have a huge budget*, Lucy thought. She let the air rush from her lungs and the panic inside immediately ceased.

She glanced back around the room, double checking herself

and the remaining evidence. She carefully wiped every surface and every handle in the bedroom and the bathroom with a clean towel, ensuring that no prints remained. Then she turned towards the window, and using a corner of her tee-shirt, Lucy opened the balcony doors. She slipped into invisibility easily this time and fell from the balcony, still holding the pillow case and towels. She would dispose of them somewhere in the desert: bury them deep now that she had her full strength back.

She floated away, quickly reaching the outskirts of the town. Lucy allowed the wind to buffet her and she rolled with it, like tumble-weed, making little or no impact on the world, but free and light for the first time in months.

16
Rags

The new tunnel led them deep into the bowels of the Earth. By now Geraint was so fascinated that he and Preacher felt like colleagues rather than captor and hostage. He had even forgotten the pain in his nose and the fact that Ffion was still tied up in his basement.

'I can feel fresh air,' said Preacher.

'There!' Geraint said pointing ahead.

Ahead of them a huge chunk of rock was missing, or at some time had been pulled free from the side of the wall. Geraint approached and looked through as Preacher shone his UV torch into the gap. He saw what appeared to be yet another large chamber.

'Is this the dungeon?' Geraint asked.

'No. There is no dungeon. At least not any more. This is the remains of a former room though, underground. That probably led up into the castle proper if I'm not mistaken.'

'How do you know that?'

'Look. There.'

Geraint peered in as the torchlight fell on the remains of a stone spiral staircase which was cut off in mid-air by a new structure. Modern brick. Or at least, modernish.; certainly dated much later than the twelfth century stone flags.

'Must be foundations for one of the houses,' Geraint said.

'I think not,' Preacher said. 'We are too far below.'

Geraint wasn't sure though. He was confused by the twists and turns they had taken on route. But it did feel as though they had gone deeper underground.

'We could be a hundred feet below ground now,' Preacher said.

Geraint shrugged. He knew a bit about castles but not how deep they went into the rock beneath them. A hundred feet was maybe four or five floors in an average building. Could they have built so far down in the twelfth century? He didn't think so.

Geraint swirled his torch around the space taking in the low ceiling, and what looked to be floor tiles on the ground. Something moved in the darkness.

'What was that?' Geraint said backing away.

Preacher scanned the space. The bottoms of the walls were stone and then they merged with brick. A rat skittered away from the light. Then the ultra violet light picked out a shape bundled in the corner. It was a pile of dirty rags. Preacher was just about to move the light away when the rags turned and he found himself face to face with a haggard old woman.

Geraint gasped and backed away from the hole as the woman staggered to her feet.

'How the hell did she get down here?'

Preacher raised the dart gun and pointed it at the slow moving figure.

'What are you doing – it's just an old tramp,' Geraint said.

Preacher ignored him.

Unlike the others Preacher had encountered the revenant was weak and worn. She looked hungrier somehow and as he scanned the area he realised that was probably why she was weak. This one had been trapped down here and was slowly starving to death. He wondered, like Geraint, how on earth she came to be here.

'Can you talk?' Preacher asked.

The woman looked into the light. Her eyes were blank, flat pools of mud. Nothing human remained in them. Then she moved, faster than any person could have, but Preacher was ready. He fired two shots in rapid succession. The first missed and smashed against the wall behind her. The second was lost in the rags and he wasn't sure it had hit home. As she reached out her hand towards him, he shot the third dart square into the middle of her palm. She didn't react, or even glance at the nuisance that dangled from her blue and rotten skin. Still she came.

By this time Geraint was yelling. Preacher couldn't make out the words because fear had distorted them in the boy's mouth. But the gist of it was that Geraint thought Preacher was attacking a defenceless old woman.

'Shut the fuck up!' Preacher yelled. He pushed Geraint roughly aside as the woman crawled out through the hole. She looked animalistic.

'Shit,' Preacher said. That was unusual. Normally they fell when the first dart went in.

She staggered. The initial spurt of strength was rapidly diminishing but Preacher still backed away. He couldn't risk her reaching him. He knew how strong the creatures were. He shot another dart. This one landed in the wrinkled flesh around her neck. She fell to her knees. Then she tipped forward, landing hard on her face, her hands too weak to catch her fall. Preacher saw the vague light go out of her blood-shot eyes as the creature fell into a drug induced oblivion.

'She was just an old woman for Christ sake,' Geraint said again.

'That wasn't …' Preacher stopped. 'There must be another way in here.'

Geraint felt strange. There was something so wrong about the body that still lay inside the room. It looked like an old woman, certainly acted like one, but he had caught a glimpse of her eyes and he hadn't liked what he saw there. She had looked hungry, and not surprising, she may have been down here for days. But it was a different kind of hunger he had seen. It was feral. Geraint felt that if she had been able to, she would have eaten him or Preacher alive. It was then he remembered Ffion and the situation he was in. A small part of his brain made him realise that Preacher wasn't the tourist he seemed. Well that was obvious, but … He couldn't put his finger on the thought properly.

Preacher was talking into a two-way radio that shouldn't even be able to work down here.

'It's had two doses but get down here before it starts to move again.'

Geraint felt something then: a sharp sting on the back of his hand. He tried to raise his hand to look, but his arm felt like lead. A cold wave swept up through his blood and he fell forward into Preacher's arms.

Later, he remembered coming round to see pairs of boots surrounding him.

'… minor dose,' he heard Preacher say. 'He'll be alright.'

He tried to wake but slipped back into half dreams. He saw the old woman. They had her strapped to some kind of metal device. Then he felt himself lifted. He didn't struggle. He knew they were taking him back upstairs. Back to Ffion. A small pain ached in his shoulder, he focused on it as a way to return to reality, but the drug got to him again and he slipped back into full darkness.

'Geraint?' he heard her voice as though it was coming from a long dark tunnel. 'Geraint?'

They carried him out into the fresh air. He opened his heavy lids, looked up to the drizzly sky and felt the spots of rain fall on his face. Then he was being pushed into the back of the ambulance. He closed his eyes again but he felt her hand holding his.

'You're going to be okay, Geraint,' Ffion said. 'What the hell happened down there?'

'Sown hair?' his voice was slurred and his lips and tongue felt swollen in his mouth.

'In the dungeon …'

Geraint tried to think. He remembered dark. He remembered torches and smoke, but after that everything was a blur.

'Son't know …'

He slipped away again. His body could no longer fight the exhaustion or whatever drug had been introduced into his body.

'There was a man. He attacked us,' Ffion said. She sounded like a news reporter on the radio. 'He wanted to get down into the dungeon under the castle ...'

The sound grew faint and a distinct roar came into his ears. Someone turned the radio off and the voice stopped but the roar continued. It sounded like the sea crashing against rocks.

17
Breached

As we draw closer to our home I become aware of the sound of helicopters. It is nightfall and I can see search lights focused on a spot at the back of the castle. The area is buzzing with human activity.

Still invisible, we land in the grassy moat of Rhuddlan Castle. The spotlights shift over the castle grounds as though they are searching for us. I take Anja's arm and pull her back against the moat wall.

'Something's wrong,' I tell her. Then I flip open the camouflaged brick that hides the entry keypad and punch in the numbers. The concealed door opens silently and we two vampires slip inside the lair and close the door behind us. I sigh but my breath does not release the tension I'm feeling.

Down in the bowels of Rhuddlan, the castle's power is twisting and churning as though it is a red alert warning. The air stings my eyes and a buzzing hum vibrates through the atmosphere like raw electricity. My ears hurt.

'What's happening?' asks Anja, but I can't answer because I don't know what is wrong.

At the bottom of the winding stairway, one thousand steps that I know by heart but this time my vampiric OCD is too distracted to count them, we enter the lair through the front door. It is dark and empty inside. Clearly Lilly and Chez are not home. I can see perfectly well, but I turn the lights on anyway out of habit. The lair brightens and affords us some comfort.

'The heating system seems to be off. That's unusual,' Anja

says, a stream of condensation drifts into the room with her breath.

'Strange.'

The heating system *is* switched off. I press the start button and hear the hiss of the boiler firing up. It is possible that Lilly has turned it off, but not that likely. Usually she leaves the heat on all the time to allay any damp that might seep into the rooms. I try to recall how we left things. Maybe, when I reached inside the cupboard to take my jacket, I accidentally knocked the switch. It's possible – we were in such a hurry to leave – but I'm not certain. I look around feeling strangely paranoid.

Anja flounders near the doorway. 'The hair is standing up on the back of my neck,' she says. 'Gabi, there's something wrong here.'

The lair *feels* empty. I use my senses to smell the cold air, and listen intently for the sound of heartbeats but I can't hear anything abnormal. We haven't been invaded: I'm sure that Rhuddlan is still safe but clearly the castle's essence is panicking about something because I have goosebumps too.

'Lilly will know what it is,' I say, but I am not confident that she will.

It is true that Lilly has an affinity with the subliminal power here that the rest of us don't. Even so, the fact that we are aware of a change in the energy implies to me that the situation may be urgent. I take my phone out of my pocket and dial Lilly but the reception is worse than normal and it won't connect.

'I'd better go up to the top and call them,' I say. 'Stay here.'

Anja nods, but she is distracted and nervy. The heating is already beginning to work and she takes off her coat and walks into the kitchen.

'A drink before you go?' she suggests.

I feel like the delay would be a bad thing though.

'Warm some for me, I won't be long.'

'Okay. Gabi? Be careful.'

I nod but for some reason her words chill me. I know I am not as invulnerable as I had once believed but this irrational fear of mine is growing. Something … somewhere is a threat to us. I just don't know what.

Upstairs I can still hear the helicopters flying around. There is a lot of bustle and noise. I stand behind the door that leads into the moat and hesitate. Are there too many people around? Fear grips me. What if I unintentionally give away the entrance to our lair?

My heart pounds in panic and anxiety. I need to go out. *Must contact Lilly.* I listen to the noise. I'm sure it isn't immediately before the entrance, and although I can hear humans around us – there were certainly some tramping across the castle grounds – I feel sure they are nowhere near the moat.

I try the phone again, but there's still no signal. This place has been built to hide and protect us from humanity, and it does its job well. Though sometimes even our technology doesn't cut through it. I open the door silently and look out. Nothing. The sound is coming mostly from the back of the castle and around by the other bridge. In fact if I walked along the moat I would see it.

I close the door, fly up above the castle, then land on the back turret to survey the scene.

It looks like some kind of rescue mission. An injured visitor perhaps? I scan the area intently. There is a group of men in black uniforms dragging something from a hole under the bridge, a hole that I have never seen before A white-haired man examines an ambulance trolley and there is a figure on it. An old woman is strapped down onto the trolley and she squirms as they inject her with something. She turns her head, snapping at the white-haired man. Then her eyes, her cold, black, empty eyes look up directly at me and I know I have seen that look before.

I find myself drawn to her. I cloak myself in the darkness, pulling the icy cold air around me as I float down to take a closer look at the proceedings. Two men strap the trolley to a hoist which I realise is being lifted up to the helicopter.

'This isn't what I was expecting to find,' the white-haired man says to what I now realise are soldiers. 'But at least I found something to interest us below.'

I fly closer. The woman on the trolley has stopped struggling. Her eyes are closed and she appears to be sleeping.

'It's gone very chilly,' says one of the soldiers and he shudders. He is American and this makes their presence here even stranger. I back away from him a little, knowing that he can probably sense me. Some humans, I've learnt, are sensitive to our presence even when we are camouflaged like this.

'Preacher?' says the soldier. 'What were you looking for?' He shudders again.

'Something more advanced than the usual,' the man called Preacher shrugs.

'What about the boy?'

'He won't remember much and I'm sure you lot know what to do if he does start to recall our little adventure. For now he is no threat.'

The soldier's teeth start chattering.

'You really are feeling the cold,' Preacher says. 'Maybe you're coming down with something.'

The soldier shrugs, 'Nah. I never get sick.'

At that moment, Preacher turns and looks directly up at me. It is as though he can see through the camouflage. I freeze mid-air, certain of his scrutiny, but then he turns back to examine the old woman.

I now know what she is and I am afraid. My heart thumps in my chest. It is a shock to discover one of the revenants so close to our home. This is important. I really have to call Lilly. At that moment the phone in my hand beeps as I receive a text. Preacher turns suddenly and before I know what is happening he is pointing a weapon directly at me. I feel the sting of something penetrate my skin. I fly backwards and up as a reaction to escape whatever it is the man is firing at me. Another sting hits my stomach and penetrates the polo neck sweater I'm wearing. A sharp needle pierces my skin. I feel myself falling, down, down, into darkness as the ground comes up to meet me.

I don't feel the inevitable thud as I hit the ground, and the last thing I see are Preacher's feet walking towards me.

18
Subject Seventeen

Lucy stood outside in the glaring sun watching the guard post as the reinforced steel van drove down the highway. She knew it would turn in and she had a deep suspicion what would be inside.

'Shit,' she muttered throwing down her cigarette and stamping it out on the sandy earth.

She walked around the building and back towards reception, but instead of going inside she waited for the truck at the entrance. There was no other way down to the holding cells and she wanted to see them bring him in.

She glanced in at the soldier on reception and caught him looking her over again. She turned her head away and smiled. The boy interested her and she was hungry for something other than blood these days. It was always enjoyable getting male attention, no matter how old you were, and Lucy had never tired of that feeling in the seven hundred years she had lived.

The truck rounded the corner and came to a sharp halt in front of her. Lucy waited as the driver got out and walked to the doors.

'I think this delivery is for me,' she said.

The driver looked her over; his eyes fell on her badge. 'I was told to deliver to Doctor Cameron.'

'Cameron isn't in charge any more. I am.'

'I need to see your clearance.'

Lucy turned her badge over and the soldier's eyes bulged slightly as he noted the clearance level. He swallowed.

'Sorry, Ma'am. Nobody told me there was a new person in

charge. Cameron retired finally then?'

'Something like that,' Lucy said smiling.

She took the paperwork from the soldier and quickly scanned it. Two subjects this time. Subject Seventeen was a blond male, six-foot two, with green eyes. *Shit!* Subject Eighteen was an old woman but Lucy barely registered the description of the revenant because she knew that this one did not interest her. It would be like the others. There really was no point in scrutinising these subjects any further but she just didn't want the military to realise that just yet.

'Bring them in,' Lucy instructed.

'Through there?' asked the soldier, 'Normally we take them in the other way.'

Lucy hid her surprise and nodded.

'Of course. I meant bring them in the usual way, reception is far too public. I'll come with you. This one, subject Seventeen, is especially dangerous.'

'Yes, Ma'am. We were told that,' the soldier said.

Lucy climbed into the front of the truck next to the soldier and they drove through the base. Lucy knew all of the buildings here, but she was surprised when the soldier turned the truck towards the food store, and then around the back of the building. She had no idea that there was another entrance and if she had suspected there was one, she wouldn't have thought it would be here.

She considered the rooms and floors she had never visited below ground. There were many, and it annoyed her now that she hadn't thought to explore more. The thing was, you couldn't just wander around the base. Every move you made was watched and if you went somewhere that you had no right to be, then you were liable to be questioned at the very least, perhaps even incarcerated at the worst. She had always played it safe, kept her head down and tried not to draw any extra attention to herself. Now, as Acting Head of Science her access was unlimited. She wondered if anyone would question her interest in the rest of the base, or if they assumed she already knew what was going on in every lab. The truth was she didn't.

She hadn't spent enough time reading up Cameron's notes, nor exploring the files on the computer she could now open. She had only been too absorbed in the project she was working on. Maybe that was foolish. Maybe not, after all she was at this time only temporarily in charge.

The truck pulled up at a door in the back of the storeroom. Immediately a soldier came out, looked at the papers and nodded to Lucy. A huge delivery door began to roll back. Lucy hid her interest in the process but took everything in. The opening revealed a warehouse that probably took up half of the huge food store building. Once again she wondered why she hadn't noticed this before. It had been naive of her to assume that this was just an ordinary building. Nothing was ordinary here.

The driver turned the truck into the warehouse and at that moment an internal door opened and several soldiers came out and surrounded the truck.

'When did they have their last dose?' Lucy asked.

'It's on auto-intravenous,' the soldier said and he looked at her as though he thought she should know this.

'Good,' Lucy said hiding her lack of knowledge. 'Let's do this.'

She climbed out of the truck and went round to the back as the soldiers opened up the doors. The two vampires were being held in cages and were strapped to ambulance trolleys. Both were hooked up to IV drips. There was also a medical soldier sat in the back of the truck monitoring them. Lucy didn't know this man, so she assumed he didn't work on the base.

They wheeled the revenant out first. Lucy checked the IV and noted the dosage was higher than normal.

'What happened here?' she asked the medical soldier. 'Why is the dose high?'

'She was resistant to the drug,' the soldier said. 'Thought it would be better for all if we kept her well under.'

'Okay. Take her to a cell.'

Next they wheeled out Subject Seventeen. This was the first time Lucy had seen Gabriele since his girlfriend, Lilly, had gone missing in the corridor of doors some years ago. In fact she had made every effort to avoid them since then. Her part in the whole affair wasn't exactly as innocent as it appeared and she didn't know how much Gabi and Lilly knew about her now. That was partly why she had taken the job in the base in the first place. *When you need to get out of Dodge, you can't beat hiding out at a secret military base.*

Of course she knew a lot about them. She checked on them from time to time. She knew, for example, that somehow Lilly had brought Caesare back from the dead. They had been living in some form of *ménage à trois* too. Lucy had been a little jealous when she realised this. One vampire lover would be good, but two …

Lucy brought her mind back to the task. Gabi looked innocent in his sleep. He was still as beautiful as she remembered and it brought a pang of nostalgia to study him while he lay so helpless. She looked at his chart. They had dosed him up too. This crowd were taking no chances.

'Let's get him settled in,' Lucy said, ignoring the looks the soldiers gave her as they wheeled Gabi into the large lift.

Lucy took her place beside the IV, and continued to read the notes. She learnt of how and where Gabi was found. She was surprised to learn that one of the revenants was also there. It was a strange thought that one of these creatures was living close to the vampires. Had they been aware of her? She glanced over at the other body in the lift. She looked emaciated and that was something she hadn't noticed in these creatures unless they were starved of their meat sources. Generally, despite their somewhat pungent smell, they could often pass for human with little difficulty.

The lift doors closed after the soldiers crowded in and their attention all remained on Gabi. It was as though they sensed that the real danger was the one that looked the most normal.

The lift halted on minus 20. They were in the very bowels of the base. As they wheeled Gabi's still body out of the lift, Lucy felt that same phobia once more. She could almost hear sand seeping into the foundations of the base. She felt a strange loss of perspective and direction. She didn't know why, or how, but there was something down here that terrified her all of a sudden.

'Doctor? Are you all right?' asked the medical soldier.

Lucy shook her head. The sickness and vertigo receded. 'Just felt a little ...'

The soldiers were staring at her. They seemed tense. It was as though they knew something she didn't. Or that they felt something of the encroaching terror which she sensed.

'I'm a little claustrophobic in elevators,' she said shrugging.

The medical soldier took the lead and pushed the trolley holding the revenant down the corridor. Lucy followed and another soldier wheeled out Gabi. The rest of the men fell in line beside the trolleys. They were in a long, bare corridor which contained only two doors. Each had a restricted sign and a security card scanner. Lucy tried not to make her glances at the doors as they passed anything other than casual.

They went through a set of heavy double doors and Lucy began to get her bearings again. She recognised the concrete holding cells. These held the strongest and most dangerous of the revenants, although all of them were housed here to begin with. Lucy rarely came down to this level because the main observation cells were higher up but she had been here on occasion. Usually it was to sign the forms to authorise the destruction of a subject. There had been a lot of those lately and there always had to be one of the doctors present when that happened. Then the carcase was burnt in the furnace. This too had to be supervised. They placed Gabi in the end cell. Carefully removing his body from the trolley and strapping him firmly onto a steel framed bed that was sunk into the wall.

The medical officer checked the IV. Then Lucy listened to his heart. The beat was slow and steady. Gabi seemed in good shape despite the high dose of the drug that kept him catatonic. A medical team wheeled in the examination trolley and Lucy gave him a quick medical check, placed on the heart monitor that would remain for twenty four hours, and took a few phials of blood.

'Okay. That's me done here. Let's go check out the other one. I want this one watched twenty-four-seven. Is that clear?' Lucy left the soldiers to finish securing Gabriele and she walked down the corridor to go through the motions of checking in the other subject. But she couldn't keep her mind on the job. She felt nauseated. Her hands were shaking and fear and panic fought to force its way through her calm exterior.

Perhaps I'm getting soft in my old age, she thought. But she knew it wasn't that. The capture of Gabi threatened all of the family that she too was part of, and she would have to be seen to be treating him the same as the others. She wasn't sure how she would do that or how she would continue to keep her secret from the soldiers when she finally let Gabi wake. Surely he would give her away on sight? And who could blame him?

19
Zombies

Lucy looked through the observation glass into the padded cell. She had warned the medical team to keep Gabriele drugged until she could decide what to do. Gabriele was tied as the others were, but she knew those bonds wouldn't be able to keep him contained if he ever regained enough consciousness to fight back.

'This one can fly and somehow camouflage himself,' said a voice behind her as though he could read her thoughts.

Lucy turned to find Darren Preacher in the doorway. Earlier that day Lucy had been informed that Preacher had arrived and that she was to give him any information he needed. The directive came from the top, via a confidential and unsigned email. The source was reliable though, and Lucy knew that her mysterious superiors seemed to know everything that occurred at the facility. They didn't tell her much about Preacher and this annoyed her. She was to tell Preacher everything without knowing who he was or where his allegiances lay. Aside from which, Lucy preferred to work alone. She didn't want to share her research with a total stranger: it was bad enough having to work with other doctors.

'We haven't met before, you'll forgive me if I don't know your rank,' Lucy said.

'I'm not army,' Preacher replied. 'But I do have clearance.'

'So I've been told. How can I help you?'

'I want to know about this one.'

'I can't tell you much at this point. He's just arrived as you know. The testing begins tomorrow. As of now, you know more than I do about this ...' Lucy looked back at Gabi through the glass. '... creature.'

'I'd like to see the files on the others then,' Preacher said.

Lucy nodded. 'I'll arrange them to be sent to you. Secure email?'

'I'll be staying on the base for the time being,' Preacher said. 'You can deliver me paper copies.'

Preacher noted the slight narrowing of Lucy's eyes behind the glasses. It was a fleeting moment but Preacher was observant and he knew that this woman had only just been promoted to her current position. He realised she felt threatened but made no effort to reassure her. Lucy, he knew, kept herself to herself on base. Rarely requested leave and worked longer hours than most in her pursuit of knowledge. He had come across her sort before: career doctor.

Lucy was watching Subject Seventeen again. Her expression blank, but Preacher suspected she was just as curious about the creature as he was. She would learn, no doubt, how different he was from the others.

'We should reduce his dosage if we want anything out of him. But I suspect he is extremely dangerous,' Lucy said.

'I heard about Doctor Cameron, I believe you were there.'

Lucy said nothing.

'How did you manage to subdue the revenant that attacked him?'

'Lucky blow to the head,' she said flatly.

Preacher nodded. 'How is the good doctor?'

Lucy glanced back at Preacher. 'He began to talk again yesterday.'

'I'd like to see him.'

'Of course you would.'

Lucy led Preacher out of the observation booth and down the grey corridor to the next cell. She slid the peephole open and glanced in, before nodding to the guard to open the cell. Then she stepped back as Preacher entered the cell alone.

Cameron's straight jacket was fastened to the bed, so that he couldn't stand when Preacher came in but his eyes burned like bloody coals as the pale man took a seat beside his bed.

'Doctor,' Preacher nodded.

Cameron turned his head and smiled, it was a hungry smile. Preacher noted the sharp teeth, the vile reek that came from the man's skin and the cunning that lay behind the eyes. He was far more alert than any of the revenants Preacher had seen before.

'Darren,' said Cameron. 'You have to get me out of here. There seems to be some sort of mistake.'

Preacher was surprised that Cameron remembered him. They had only met once before. This revelation, in light of the doctor's current state made him wonder about the advancements made since Lucy Collins had taken over. He had seen in her notes that she wanted Cameron only to be fed blood.

'Now, doctor. What seems to be the trouble?'

'It's Collins,' Cameron said. 'She did this to me. She keeps telling everyone I'm a revenant. Clearly, you can see that isn't the case.'

Preacher tried not to smile. He didn't know what to think of Cameron's rationale but it was obvious that he was indeed one of the creatures.

'Why would Doctor Collins lie about that?' Preacher asked. He knew Collins was watching and had been warned about the seemingly sane appearance of the subject.

'Why? Because she's a blood sucking monster, of course. And she wanted my job. She's always wanted to get rid of me.'

'I see. I saw the footage of the attack. You have become one of them. Albeit rather rational at the moment, doctor.'

'That may be,' Cameron said. 'But I'm not insane and I'm now in my right mind. I need to get back to work so that I can help to find a cure. This is obviously some disease.'

'I'll see what I can do,' Preacher said standing up.

'Get me out of here, Darren!' Cameron said, his voice rising with sudden panic. 'I'm not an animal. I don't want to be experimented on!'

Preacher knocked once on the door then glanced over his shoulder to look at Cameron.

'He's lucid,' he said to Lucy as they walked back to the

observation booth.

'Yes. Since we've been feeding him blood instead of meat …'

'How did you know to do that?'

'It was a gamble that paid off,' Lucy said.

'Can he be trusted?'

'No,' Lucy said. 'He's incredibly dangerous. You see the blood is helping to engage his mental faculties, but he still has this awful craving for gore. The gore turns them into complete animals but it's what they want more than anything. Given half a chance he would have eaten your face Mr Preacher.'

Preacher nodded. 'Then there is no hope that we can use these monsters?'

Lucy closed her eyes, then removed her glasses and rubbed them. 'They could be used in extreme situations. Drop one or two off in a war zone and you'd find them eating the enemy with no trouble at all. They are impervious to pain. Bullets would hit but not stop them and they have healing ability beyond any human. Their only weakness is the brain. Crush that and they are gone permanently. However, during that attack they may pass on the infection to others. You might find the enemy turning into revenants.'

'How infectious is it?' Preacher asked.

Lucy explained the blood tests they had done so far.

'So, what you're saying is that it can be passed on to those with the same basic DNA?'

'Family. Descendants. It's all in the blood Mr Preacher. We are all what our blood makes us,' Lucy continued.

'Good. Then let's get a look at the blood of our new boy.'

Lucy nodded. 'Already working on it. Will let you know if we find anything.'

Preacher turned to leave then paused. 'What do you think they are, Doctor Collins?'

'Excuse me?'

'These creatures … what do you think they are.'

'The word vampire has been bandied around a few times …' Lucy said.

'Yes. It has. But you don't really think they are that do you?'

'I have been giving this some thought as it happens, Mr Preacher. Revenant is a good word but …'

'Yes?'

'I think they aren't vampires. I think they are a devolved form of humanity. A cross between revenant and zombie.'

'Zombie? Seriously?'

'If we must name the creatures something. Let's face it they smell like the dead. To all intents and purposes they are the walking dead. They crave flesh, although blood makes them more lucid. Some of them have even been able to function in the world and have gone undetected for years. I'm just not sure how that happened, but it did. This shows a level of restraint, or some memory retention that made them cautious. Perhaps it is an instinct to help them survive.'

Preacher didn't answer. He suspected that it was the first time that Lucy had told anyone what she was really thinking and he felt strangely privileged. She wasn't like the air-head females he had met before. Preacher was intrigued.

'Interesting thoughts, doctor,' he said. 'Would you expect a zombie to be able to reason though?'

'Not the zombies we know in popular culture certainly. But that is fiction Mr Preacher, this, unfortunately, is reality. I haven't completely ruled out the idea of a vampire though. Tests have only just begun on Subject Seventeen and the reports I have on him are that he's quite different.'

'Yes,' Preacher closed the door and lowered his voice. 'You know *they* took out Caradien? That took planning.'

Lucy turned sharply to face Preacher.

'*Inlustret lumine,*' Preacher said, which was Latin for 'let the light shine'.

'*I luceat,*' Lucy replied. 'I shine' was the response and it identified her to Preacher. 'You are …?'

'Illuminati,' Preacher nodded. 'Like you. There were others with Seventeen. But they'll be alerted now and no doubt harder to find. If they are as smart as they seem, that is. I had to identify myself to you, doctor. That way we both know which team we are working for here.'

Things were beginning to make sense to Lucy now. The base, she knew, had strong connections with the Illuminati, though often it posed as the CIA. She wondered what role Preacher played in the newly structured cartel. She had been a mole amongst them for years and had fed them vague information when it suited her. She did not trust them though. They were human and at any time could learn that she *wasn't*. Fortunately for her, Caradien had never known she was a member of the vampire family he was attempting to destroy.

'I suppose the new boss sent you?'

Preacher nodded. He didn't elaborate on who the boss was. So far that wasn't common knowledge among the members. Even knowing other members was restricted to a need-to-know basis.

'Here's the file you wanted,' Lucy said pointing to the thick folder on the table beside her.

'May I use your office?'

Lucy nodded.

Preacher left and Lucy returned to Gabriele's observation booth. She didn't know what to do. She didn't trust or like Preacher and was worried about his presence on the base. This revelation that he was Illuminati, and therefore connected to her in other ways, concerned, rather than reassured her. She wondered why he was here. Had the new boss sent him to the base to spy on her? Maybe she was his next target.

Gabi's blood suddenly became hugely important. After years of analysing her own, she suspected what she would find there. She did not, however, want anyone else to learn the truth. Or to gain opportunities to restart the awful work that Caradien had begun in Stockholm.

At that moment one of the medical staff came into Gabi's room to change the bag containing the drip-suppressant. She was a military nurse in her early fifties, with fine salt and pepper coloured hair that was scraped back in a severe bun. Lucy ran from the observation room and into Gabi's cell just before the nurse injected the dose.

'Hold on!' she said. 'I want to let him wake. But before he

does, move him back to the secure room. Concrete surround only and no observation glass.'

'Yes, doctor,' the nurse said.

Lucy walked towards the bed and looked down at her former lover while the nurse left to fetch the team of soldiers that would move him. Sleeping, tied and contained, he was still beautiful. Yet, he looked so vulnerable. It hurt her to see him like this, but for now she could do nothing without revealing herself and she knew that she was dealing with extremely powerful people who would not forgive or forget any betrayal.

Four soldiers came in and she supervised as they lifted and moved Gabi to the new cell, following them down deeper via the other lift, and all the way to floor minus 20. By the time they reached the new cell, a concrete square room with a reinforced steel door, Gabi's faculties were beginning to return. She noted the twitch of his muscles and was surprised how quickly he was metabolising the sedative now that they had stopped administering it. Even so, it would be some time before he would properly wake from the drug enforced coma.

Part Two

The Captive

1
Loch Lomond

Lilly pulled Chez down into her arms. Sometimes it felt to her that she always had the responsibility of everyone else on her shoulders. She felt she needed this time away in order to really learn and appreciate her lover. The cabin was just what they needed.

Chez kissed her lips. Her mouth contained the blood of her kill. Lilly had lived dangerously that night, and had broken her own rules without any guilt. Beside them the body of the teenage girl lay on the blanket before the fake fire. She wasn't quite dead, but Lilly rarely took them all the way down, that she left to Chez and Gabi, both of whom could be deadly when the mood took them. Tonight though, Chez's hunger was only for her. He loved to see her like this; full of blood and the life energy she took from her victim.

The girl moaned. Chez rolled Lilly over and positioned himself between her legs. He wanted to feel the hot wetness of her and his urges couldn't wait, so he plunged into her until she rolled her head back, thick blonde hair merging with the dark brown, thin wisps of the teenager. Chez found this powerful and erotic.

His raised himself up, pulling her legs around him even as he knelt, and then, she let him lift her upright until her slender legs were astride him and her breasts were pressing against his bare chest.

The girl moaned again. Chez glanced at her, found that her dying eyes were watching them. Lilly was in full flow, completely oblivious, and she rode him hard until he felt the first signs of orgasm bursting from him.

He hadn't drunk from the girl, but now he wanted to taste her blood as well. His fangs slipped into Lilly's throat, this was the best way to share their meal. He felt her spasm around him in excitement and his own orgasm came into her. Lilly moaned, but didn't stop moving, her hips rocked against him until he felt that second rupture burst from his loins.

He lowered her down and Lilly turned her head, looking once more at the girl, even as her own throat wound healed.

'She's dead,' she commented without regret.

They were in a cabin on the edge of Loch Lomond. It was small but functional, one bedroom with *en suite* bathroom, an open plan lounge-diner, with a large kitchen. There was a balcony too, with table and chairs and sun loungers, looking out over the lake. Chez helped Lilly stand and she pulled on her robe, leaving the body of the girl to cool while they both went out onto the balcony.

It was a warm evening and the loch was lit up by lights positioned by the various hotels and rentals situated around it.

Lilly sat down and gazed out. She felt calm, accepting the glass of red wine that Chez held out to her before he joined her. He didn't say what he was thinking but she knew he would want to rid them of the body as quickly as possible. At least they had a ready made dumping ground before them.

Lilly sipped her wine then placed it on the table next to the lit candle.

'Who was she?' he asked.

'Does it matter?'

'I suppose not.'

'A foreign student, working illegally at the hotel over there,' Lilly said.

Chez glanced over at the lit building. 'You don't think she'll be missed then?'

Lilly shrugged. Thinking about caution irritated her right then. She lived her life by a code that protected them, but sometimes her nature would have its way.

'I'm proud of you,' Chez said.

Lilly frowned.

'You make no excuses. You refuse to be a hypocrite. You just accept that you broke the rules and move on.'

'What else must we do?' she said. 'I refuse to angst about being who I am. I love it too much to pretend.'

'I know,' he said. 'So do I.'

He leaned back in his chair and stretched out his legs before him. The robe he wore parted and Lilly could see the beautiful line of his bare thigh reflected in the small light from the candle. She wanted him again.

'We should check in with the others,' she said but made no move.

'I'll get rid of the body,' Chez said.

Lilly smiled. He was like a house-trained husband clearing up the dishes after the evening meal.

At that moment Lilly's phone began to ring.

Chez went inside and picked it up from the coffee table. The girl's body hadn't moved. He turned his back on her.

'It's Anya,' he called.

'Answer it.'

'Lilly? Oh my God. Are you there?' Anya's voice sounded tremulous as she spoke before Chez even had time to say hello.

'It's Chez. What's wrong?'

'Gabi's been taken. I don't know what's happened. Please get here as soon as possible.'

'Slow down ... you say he's been *taken*?' Chez said.

Lilly was beside him and she took the phone before Anya could say more. Then Lilly listened to Anya carefully.

'You're sure of this?' she said.

'I'm certain he wouldn't disappear on his own. Lilly, there were helicopters and police swarming the place ...'

Lilly hung up and turned to Chez.

'We need to get back to the castle,' she said.

There was a low moan behind them. Chez turned to see the girl stagger to her feet. She stumbled around blindly, tripping over the table, then crashed down again onto the floor.

'Not quite finished,' Lilly shrugged.

Chez bent down over the body. The girl looked up at him with feral blood-shot eyes. Her mouth opened and he saw a row of serrated teeth leer back at him.

'What …?'

'Just finish her,' Lilly said walking away.

Chez twisted the girl's neck, heard it snap. The strange eyes stayed open but the girl no longer moved. He picked up the body, carried her out to the balcony then took to the air.

As he dropped her down into the centre of the loch, he thought he saw her twist and move but knew it wasn't possible. Even so, he felt slightly unnerved as he turned back towards the cabin.

2
Tests

You have to play along. Pretend to be dumb.

I wake up slowly, my faculties dulled and for a while I cannot think beyond the fact that I know I am tied down. My body is weak. I tug at the bonds: metal cuffs circle my wrists and ankles. I open my eyes and look around.

I am in a plain grey room, solid concrete by the look of it and I am tied to a bed with iron shackles that are embedded into the walls. My head hurts. The soreness reminds me of my former mortality and the memory of a long drinking session in Venice. I close my eyes and there is a gritty stinging sensation behind them. The feeling intensifies for a moment and then it recedes.

Sickness. A dark, chemical taste fills my mouth. It reminds me of hospitals. I don't know why, as I have had so little experience of them. There is a tightness in my chest, pain across my shoulders and my legs ache because they are stretched out and secured to the wall at the bottom of the bed.

How did this happen? Where am I?

I can't remember anything beyond flying from France with Anja.

Anja! Where is she? Have they captured her too? My chest hurts again.

I groan. There is pain in my calves. Cramp perhaps. These are new sensations of discomfort that I haven't experienced since my mortal days. I try to think to take my mind away from the soreness. I remember … a sharp, stinging pain, the feeling of blackness consuming me. My eyes open again. Yes. I remember.

I am a prisoner. But where? I recall that I was outside

Rhuddlan castle – Anja, I think, was still inside and hopefully safe. There was noise. The awful wind-stirring motion of the rotors was so loud you could barely hear yourself think. But the soldiers didn't seem to mind them. Yes. Soldiers. In black uniforms. There were lots of them and one of the men had white hair …

I feel nausea tugging at my insides. Perhaps the thing they have poisoned me with is related to the poisonous heart that Konstantin Caradien had once used against us. It's all I can imagine that could incapacitate me so much. But I know this isn't the case. The heart, and its venom, are long gone.

I drift away. The poison, or whatever they have pumped into me, finally gets to me again.

You're safe for now. But you need to pretend to be less than you are! Please Gabriele, listen to me!

I snap awake. I fight the cramp. I fight the effects of … drugged, some kind of sedative, that must be it. We are not immune to sleeping aids, though their effects are not usually this lasting.

I think about Anja. Lilly. Chez. They will wonder where I am but this time there is no portal trail to follow. I have been taken by men in a helicopter. Far more difficult to track than something that uses magic.

They don't know you're here. Nobody knows this place exists.

The voice is not my own. It is familiar, and yet I cannot place it.

Lucrezia … Yes. It is you!

I work here Gabi. You can't recognise me. I'll help, I promise. But you mustn't acknowledge that we know each other.

I think about the many times she has tricked me and used me. Why should I believe her?

No one but me knows you are here. If I am taken, you will never escape.

As always she is thinking of herself but her reasoning sinks into my brain. It makes sense despite my muddled senses. I'll play along. For now. *But betray me again and I'll finish you.*

She laughs inside my head. *Don't be absurd. You love me. You always have. Let me help you and this time we really can be together. I've missed you Gabi.*

Lucy returned to her office to find Preacher heavily engrossed in the files she had given him. She glanced in, but didn't disturb him. Instead she turned and went into the lab to find Joe.

On the back of the door, Lucy hung up her suit jacket and reached for her white lab coat. Then she crossed the room to the sink and began to scrub her hands.

Joe was sat at one of the tables. Lucy knew he was examining the results from the blood samples.

'Anything?' Lucy asked.

'Eighteen is like all the others,' Joe said.

'Anything on Seventeen?'

Joe shook his head. 'Not yet. The analysis hasn't finished.'

She wondered how she was going to change the samples, or alter the results with Preacher around. It wouldn't do for them to learn they had a full-bloodied vampire on their hands. Preacher would be breathing down her neck as soon as he thought she had anything, which meant she had to get to Joe first.

She glanced at the office. The glass was clear. Preacher had his back to her, but Lucy knew better than to take a chance with the enemy so close.

'Let me see what you have,' Lucy said.

She slid next to Joe and took the results, then pretended to read them. This close she was certain of full control in her telepathy. She reached into Joe's mind, tweaking and changing the instructions he had been given.

'Like you said, Joe. Nothing much here so far.'

'I'll just check the other samples now,' Joe said.

Lucy continued reading the results, this time examining them closely while Joe went to the analysis machine. She heard him changing the samples around and knew that while he innocently appeared to be putting them into new tests, he was actually switching Seventeen's blood for one of the other subjects. Seventeen's real samples would soon find their way into the incinerator. The good thing about this was that Joe's finger prints would be all over any evidence, and yet he would have no recollection of having done anything wrong because he didn't know what she had told him to do.

The human mind is fascinating but so easy to fool, Lucy thought. She glanced over at Preacher again and noticed he hadn't changed position. So far he wasn't suspicious because he believed her to work for the same people as himself. She had to keep it that way.

She heard Joe open the incinerator. The phials dropped in. The door closed. All was well. Lucy sighed a little, then rubbed the back of her neck with her hand. She was tired and felt the strangest urge to feed again even though she really had no need to.

'Okay. I'm up to speed,' said Preacher.

Lucy looked up to see him standing by the door. She felt her cheeks flush a little, but it wasn't because she had anything to fear from the information in the files he had read; it was more that he had suddenly appeared at the door, sneaking up on her almost. She was concerned at his timing.

Lucy handed the results file to Preacher and began to explain the findings.

'Eighteen is just like the others, so nothing new to report there,' she said.

'I'd like to suggest some other tests,' Preacher said.

'What kind of tests?'

'Intelligence.'

'We have done intelligence measures on the other subjects and all can function at a certain level. Some talk as you know. Most don't,' Lucy explained.

'How is Seventeen doing?' Preacher asked suddenly.

'He's not come round properly yet. He was given a massive dose of the drug.'

'I know,' Preacher said.

'We can monitor brain function, especially while he is still doped a little.'

'Yes. Start there.'

Preacher left the lab and went out into the main building. She envied him. He was roaming free of the base without fear of questions. Preacher was an intimidating figure, and she doubted that anyone would even dare approach or question him. Giving orders came so easily to him and yet, when it came down to it, what power did he have here that she did not also have? The truth was Lucy had been trying to conform to the human world too long. If Gabi told them anything, for example who she was, she could find herself drugged and caged too if they believed him. Even so, having Gabi around also reminded her of who she was and what she was capable of. She had almost forgotten her own strength. Could these humans really contain either of them for long?

Lucy thought about Preacher's orders. They could monitor Gabi's brain functions, but what would it show? She was curious herself. This was one test she hadn't thought to try on herself. Why bother? She knew her brain was superior to human capacity and function. Her learning skills alone had proved that.

'Joe? Let's get G … Seventeen fitted up with a monitor,' she said.

Joe nodded and went away to fulfil her orders. Yes, she had her own power. She could control these tests and the results however she chose. All she had to do was give the order. And, if Preacher got in her way a little too much, or if she felt he was learning more than she cared to reveal, then it would be so easy to finish him. He was human after all.

3
Inside the Base

I wonder if I imagined hearing Lucrezia's voice in my drug induced sleep. She has not contacted me since, but still I heed the warning. It is hard to imagine how I have so foolishly allowed myself to be captured.

Earlier a soldier came in with a tray of food which he put down on the floor. When he left the room, I felt my bonds loosen. The chains rolled out from the walls and I could move about the cell enough to reach the tray. I stretched my limbs first of all, knowing that I was probably being watched and monitored though I couldn't see any cameras. I was hungry and thirsty so I went over to examine the tray, only to find, to my horror, that they had offered me raw meat and what smelt like pig's blood in a bowl.

I'm not sure what they expected. Perhaps they thought I would throw myself on their offerings like a savage but I refuse to perform like a circus animal for them. Besides, I would have much preferred a semi-cooked steak and a glass of Cabernet Sauvignon. It was a strange meal to offer me. They obviously don't know for certain what I am.

Back on the bed I continue to flex and stretch my limbs and in so doing examine the restraints. As I first suspected I am in shackles. They are primitive, but effective. The chains go deep into the wall and I assume that they are on some kind of pulley.

The door opens to my cell. And suddenly I am yanked down and stretched out. A male nurse and a male doctor enter the room. They wheel in a machine of some sort and I am about to ask what they are doing, when I recall the warning. Play dumb.

I lie in silence as they listen to my heart. Then the doctor places small pads with tiny wires around my forehead. I note there is some kind of monitor.

'All set, Doctor Collins,' says the doctor as he switches on the machine.

I would tear the chains off me but I'm curious to see what they are doing first.

'Good,' replies a voice and I hear Lucrezia through some speakers in the room that I cannot see.

'He hasn't touched his food,' says the nurse. 'Strange. I expected it to be all over him by now.'

They think I am some uncivilised … revenant. The penny drops. So. There have been more of them; the old woman they found near the castle was not the first. The doctor is looking into my eyes. I push my thoughts into his brain.

'Seventeen,' the doctor murmurs. I see the image of some of the other revenants flashing behind his eyes. Lurking there is one he thinks of as … Cameron. *Interesting*.

I release him before the nurse becomes suspicious.

'Yes, Doctor Johnson. He's number Seventeen. He doesn't smell like the others though. Haven't you noticed? They usually reek.'

The doctor and nurse leave and I watch the door close, taking in the sound of the mechanism that locks the door. It is, if I'm not mistaken, a form of mortise that locks in several places all at once. Deadbolts. I scrutinise the door. I must pay attention next time it opens: the hinges will undoubtedly be the weak point.

I feel the bonds slacken a little, but not enough to allow me to sit up again. I suppose they fear that I will pull away the monitor. But then, what could a few electrodes on my head tell them about me?

I listen to the sounds of the place around me. The concrete of these rooms is thick, sound does not travel through it easily, but I can pick up the resonance of feet walking down the corridor. Size six, female shoes, which tap lightly on the tiled floor. She's wearing low-heeled court shoes. Sensible in this line of work.

The footsteps end outside my cell.

A shutter opens. It is a viewing hole and my bed is in perfect line with it. Brown, bespectacled eyes look in at me but I know it is Lucrezia. I focus my vision on her eyes. Coloured contacts, I can see the slight gleam of green beneath them. The monitor beside me makes a strange sound. It beeps and begins to move. It is making some kind of pattern on perforated paper. I twist my head and try to see but I can only make out the movement of the writing arm.

Gabi. I'm going to get you out of here. You're doing well, just keep silent. Can I get you anything?

A hot bath would be nice …

She laughs inside my head. *They've never provided that for anyone in here … but I will see what I can do.*

Why have they given me raw meat?

Lucrezia doesn't answer. She stares in at me as though I am some alien reptile that has landed and is trying to take over the world.

You should drink the blood at least. It will keep you strong.

I don't drink animal blood. You know that.

'Doctor Collins,' says a voice beside her. 'What are you doing here?'

'I wanted to see the subject close up.'

I recognise the other voice from somewhere, but I'm not sure where. Lucrezia steps aside and I see the face, the white hair, and I know this man. He is my captor. The one who pumped the poison into me. I want to tear free and rip out his throat.

Shush. Lucrezia says in my head. *Keep calm.*

Where is Anja? I reply.

Lucrezia doesn't answer.

'He's very still,' says the man.

Preacher … I remember his name now. I heard one of the soldiers use it just before the bastard drugged me.

'Yes. He does appear to be very different from the others,' Lucrezia says.

'You!' Preacher yells. 'Open this cell. I want to talk to Subject Seventeen.'

I feel the bonds tighten. I pull against them this time, but I am only testing the level of resistance. I don't wish to reveal how strong I am just yet for fear that they will put me to sleep again and use something even stronger. The chains groan as I pull back. Then, before my efforts are noted, I release the tension and let them pull me taut. I know it would be hard to free myself stretched out but the moment will come when the bonds are loose and my arms and legs have movement enough so that I can use my full body strength. I must bide my time.

The door opens again. Preacher comes in. He brings a chair with him and sits beside me.

'Good morning,' he says.

I frown. I know it is not morning, even though there is no natural light here. Somehow Preacher is trying to trick me into a reaction.

He scrutinises my face. 'Can you talk?'

I say nothing but I watch him carefully, giving nothing away of who, or what, I am.

'I suppose you are wondering where you are,' he continues. 'You are in a military base at a secret location in the Nevada Desert. I brought you here because you were demonstrating some unusual behaviour. Do you know what we do here?'

I say nothing.

What we do! That's rich. He's only just arrived here. He came with you Gabi. He's very curious about you.

My eyes fall on Lucrezia as she stands by the door. So far she has remained outside. It is as though she is afraid she will be trapped in the cell with me. The monitor spikes again. Preacher doesn't seem to notice.

'We are researching into unusual creatures. So far we've found … well we can only describe them as the walking dead really. Have you ever seen anything like that?'

I don't answer.

'Up until now the beings, we could call them ex-humans I suppose, have been of a cannibalistic nature. They crave meat. Human, animal, it doesn't matter to them it seems. Their powers are limited, though they are extremely strong and seem to feel no pain.'

'Why are you telling him this?' Lucrezia says. 'This stuff is classified.'

'Oh. That doesn't matter here,' Preacher smiles. 'Who's he going to tell? Apparently he doesn't speak.'

I watch Preacher's mouth move as he tells me more about the base. It is a place of secrets. Germ warfare, poisonous antibiotics, intensive sleeping potions.

'But you know about that one. We used it on you. Like a dose of anaesthetic. The dose you had would kill a human. That's why, you see, I know you aren't one. Coupled with the fact that you seemed to be able to defy gravity. I won't say fly … that seems way too clichéd. But you were levitating in some way weren't you? And you were also invisible to the naked eye.'

Lucrezia steps over the threshold. She seems nervous, but I feel incredibly calm. Preacher, I have observed, is a total madman. He isn't in search of truth necessarily, but he is in search of something. Although I have yet to learn what, I'm sure I will be able to use his intense curiosity to my own advantage.

'It's a shame we didn't have any cameras working at the time. It was a capture mission, not an observation one you see. But I would like to see that trick again. Would you care to oblige? No? Pity.' Preacher shrugs.

He stands and picks up his chair. Then he turns his back on me and walks towards the door. Lucrezia steps back to allow him to exit.

'Check the monitor,' Preacher says as he walks away down the corridor. 'It spiked a few times while I talked. There is, I believe, exceptional intelligence behind the silence.'

Lucrezia enters the room and then I see the soldier too. He walks in behind her and he watches me as she tears off the paper from the bottom of the monitor. I glimpse the scribbles that move along horizontally along the page and I see the spikes he referred to. I don't know what this means of course, but Lucrezia glances at me and frowns.

'Are you going to behave yourself if I examine you?' she asks.

I feel the soldier shift position.

I say nothing, and don't move but I meet her eyes.

What the hell are you involved in here? I project. The machine moves again. It peaks further than when I was receiving her thoughts. Interesting.

She repeats the examination that the other doctor gave. She listens to my heart, she looks in my eyes, and when she touches my lips I allow her to open my mouth. She takes photographs on her cell phone of my teeth. My fangs aren't visible unless I wish them to be and my teeth appear as those of any human. Though they are perhaps whiter and straighter than most. I can only assume that her photograph will prove I'm not like the revenants. Of course Lucrezia knows that my fangs only come out when I am about to feed, but she is clearly playing a double-sided game.

I'm forming a plan. Go along with me for now, she thinks.

She backs away to the door, rapidly followed by the soldier, who quickly locks it behind them. The hinges look as solid as the locks, but I note that one of them has a missing screw.

I am alone now. I hear them walk away and count the steps down the corridor. Then I perceive the subtle sound of a lift call bell. My mind's eye fills in the picture to visualise the doors as they whoosh open and close, and the thirty feet to the lift which I assume will take me up and out of here. You see, ever since I awoke I have felt the pressure of the desert sand pressing down on me. I am below ground. The feeling is enough to send me mad which is strange because I have no problem at all being under Rhuddlan Castle in our lair. The sensation here is intense, however. It is like living in a vacuum. And my head aches with it. I wonder how Lucrezia has coped with it for so long.

4
Louis

Paris 1738

For some reason my mind drifts into the past. The drug they have given me swirls around in my system and I fight it with all my strength.

I drift in and out of sleep. My life passes behind my eyes as though this is my last day on this earth. Even when wounded I had not previously experienced this need to analyse my life so much.

My thoughts settle on Paris, probably because I was recently there, but the memories are old ones. I recall a King. Louis XV and how I became his companion for a while.

I arrived in the city in 1738 bringing fake papers of introduction to the King's advisor. I wanted to participate in the court and all it had to offer, and had taken on the identity of Count Caccini. Of course in those days it was so much easier to rewrite one's history. I could be anyone I wanted and with the wealth I continued to accumulate no one ever questioned my status.

The court was a shallow place. I was recovering from my latest conquest. An English countess of considerable note had recently parted company with her virginal daughter. The young girl had died in my arms, much to my disappointment, but I was well fed and satisfied and now looking for something to take my mind off this latest failure.

Louis XV was ideal for this. He was so easy to manipulate

because of his sensualist ways.

'Count Caccini is welcome in our court,' he said when we met for the first time after I had offered to sing for them.

He liked my beautiful voice, and the reaction the women of the court had towards me. But what Louis enjoyed most of all was the way I stepped back and watched him enjoy himself. I sang in his court for his private pleasure, and he treated me as a friend.

He was a very handsome man in his youth, and in 1738 he was only twenty eight years old. As a King, however, Louis wasn't very popular and his reign was discredited continuously by the debauchery of his courts. Although I was never into casual acquaintances that led to sex or blood, preferring to seduce and play with my virgin meal for a while first, Louis entertained me nonetheless with his excesses.

I remembered one particular orgy. I sang some of my uncle's music for the court and then Louis dismissed his wife and several others, while keeping back a handful of men and women that he seemed to chose at random.

'We wish to share our pleasures with you, Gabriele,' he said to me. 'Follow us into our private chambers.'

I walked with the King, followed by the remaining courtiers, into a room I had previously not had access to. It was a large chamber and the thick carpet was covered with cushions and thick furs.

At the end of the room Louis had a chaise and he lounged on it, indicating that I sit beside him on a cushioned stool.

As I turned I saw that the men and women were already beginning to disrobe. One man, the high chamberlain who I had come to dislike for his obnoxious manners, fell upon a fragile beauty and all but dragged her into the centre of the room.

I remained in my seat as this awful, obese man defiled her, much to the delight of the King, and when he was done, several other men took over. The woman, however, didn't object, nor did she seem to mind as the men took her in different positions, sometimes two at a time.

I said nothing and kept my face straight, though I had not

been into this type of behaviour I could not object to it if the King wished his courtiers to behave this way.

At the end of the evening I had seen all manner of behaviour, from women pleasuring each other for the King's pleasure to another man being sodomised while he was equally sodomising one of the women.

The evening ended with one of the women pleasuring the King with her mouth and as his majesty spilled into her, so the event was complete.

'Do not think that we will feel bad of you, whatever your pleasure, Gabriele,' said Louis to me afterwards. 'I am a man of varying taste. I see no harm in consensual relations. Life is made to be enjoyed. I want you to feel free to enjoy.'

I did not tell him that I never slept with whores and other men held no interest for me. Of course I didn't want to alienate him so I told him what he wanted to hear.

'I am a private man, but I gain great pleasure in watching others have pleasure.'

The King smiled. He thought me a voyeur and in reality this was the closest to the truth that it could be. I often felt myself on the periphery of life looking in. I saw its loves, its deaths and its pleasures, while all the time I was unable to participate fully in them. Being different – not human – I have little choice but to live this way.

The King accepted my explanation because, astute that he was, he sensed it to be true.

After that evening I was a regular visitor to his private rooms and I often encouraged Louis as he gave way to his own perversities – of which there were many – before me and the others in the court.

Sometimes Louis would be alone with a woman, except for me, and he enjoyed showing his stamina and prowess even more at these times.

For all of his debauchery though, I did like Louis. As well as his sexual pleasures I was also frequently involved in his legitimate practices: we went hunting together; I was invited to royal parties; and often I was asked to be the focus of their musical evenings.

As time went on the distraction worked for me and I believed we became friends.

My mind jerks awake again. The friendship of Louis, a much coveted thing, is now foremost on my mind and I cannot understand why. Then I hear Lucrezia talking to me inside my mind once more. The warnings drift in and out of my floating consciousness and I see the parallel in a strange way. She's not to be trusted … that's why I'm remembering Louis so vividly. Why else?

5

Potent

Lucy was naked and in Joe's bed when he returned from the nightshift. He was tired but the thought of her inspired the kind of reaction that would always wake a man up. He threw his clothing aside and as he climbed in the bed with her she frowned. He smelt of chemicals again and she had warned him that her nose was sensitive. In fact she couldn't bear strong smells at all, choosing always to wear a mask when dealing with compounds.

Strangely this little foible of hers hadn't made him notice the other peculiarities until now. The lack of tiredness, for example. She never looked or acted tired in the early days, then there was a moment, a few days ago, when she appeared in his room at night. She had energy to burn. Her body was positively glowing with it. And the heat of her body was a marked difference. Her body felt normal temperature again. Unlike before when she had been a cold, dead, thing.

Joe tried to define the oddities, but she was kissing him and her lips were intense and firm and definitely warm. *I'm just imagining things*, he thought.

Lucy's tongue slipped inside his mouth. He felt the heat of her passion and he moved his body over her.

'Fuck me, Joe,' she said and as always he was happy to oblige.

Afterwards she slipped away. Her stealth never failed to amaze him and he lay in bed wondering if it was all a dream. His mind floated. He tasted blood in his mouth and knew it was hers. He sucked on his tongue reliving the taste of her.

Joe closed his eyes and began to slip into that half-place between sleep and awake. His mind floated to the blood results. He had said what he thought she wanted to hear: there were no differences between Seventeen's blood and the other revenants. But the fact was, Joe had seen the results. He had noticed how different Seventeen was.

Later when he had been alone in the lab, he had used some of the blood to compare side by side with Cameron's and one of the other subjects. Cameron's blood deteriorated under the microscope as he inspected it. Seventeen's had multiplied: which was impossible. Joe had realised that there was something in the blood that wasn't in human blood. He tried to separate and analyse it, but once divided, the blood cells had dried up and died and so did the element he was trying to assess. It was as though each cell had needed the other in order to survive. He had cursed himself for not being able to break down the components enough to discover what it was.

Of course, before separation, he had been able to assess a similar, yet different DNA strand. Seventeen's strand was longer than a human's. Cameron's was shorter. Also, Seventeen's DNA had multiple layers, minutely woven between what was recognisable as human. Joe wasn't sure what this meant. He had never seen such alien genes before and this observation, particularly regarding Cameron and the revenants, had never been noted in any of Lucy's previous research. Joe had believed that this could only mean one thing as far as he was concerned: the blood was important.

Joe had put away the equipment and only recorded his findings in the small notebook he carried in his top pocket. He hadn't wanted anyone to know about the blood. The tests had just confirmed what he already knew, that Seventeen's blood was the same stuff Lucy fed him. It made him super-human and reliant on her for his next dose because it was addictive. Lucy, however, only gave him the stuff on her terms. Now, Joe realised, there was another source of that blood and he could get some of it anytime he wanted.

He began to drift off to sleep feeling happy and relaxed.

Lucy had relieved him in every way, but he knew there might be a time when she wasn't prepared to put out for him. At least, now, he could get his fix from Seventeen.

Joe opened his eyes, snapping awake, and looked over at the pile of clothes he had dropped so casually on the floor. He wondered if Seventeen would taste different from Lucy. He pulled himself out of the bed and reached for his lab coat. There was a phial of blood in his pocket. He knew Lucy had a sensitive nose which was why he had spilt the chemicals on himself before returning to his room. That way, he was sure the smell would drown out the vague odour of the blood he was carrying.

He opened the tube and sniffed at the contents. It was pure and untouched by chemicals. Joe had made sure the phial hadn't contained any preservatives. It would be just like Lucy's – almost as fresh as from the vein. He raised the glass rim to his lips and sipped. The blood tasted delicious, just like hers. Joe gulped it down, then used his finger to clean the inside of the tube. Licking his fingers he dropped the empty phial into the bin beside him.

His cock ached with new found vigour and he reached his hand down to stroke it, pulling and rubbing until his semen burst over his fingers and onto his belly. If Lucy had been there, he would have fucked her sore, but for now he had to contend with his own lust and he played with his cock over and over again until the tip was red and the shaft was chaffed. But still he couldn't stop himself from gushing one last time.

By dawn he was exhausted again, but he knew what the cure for such weakness would be and, when his shift began later, he had every intention of obtaining that magical liquid that made him feel so good, so strong and so potent.

6
The Knights' Network

A large waterfall appeared like a cavernous doorway outside the house of the Knights Templar in Stockholm. For a moment the water gushed soundlessly into the empty void below it and disappeared leaving no trace of its presence on the pavement. Then the water inside the portal moved. It parted like silk curtains and a figure emerged.

Lilly stepped down. It was night but she could see that the grounds and gates surrounding the Templar's stronghold hadn't changed much since her last visit. She had arrived by portal to save time, but because the large gothic house, looking like a Victorian insane asylum, was well protected by the priesthood's magic, she was unable to enter directly inside.

She walked to the security panel beside the gates and pressed the call button. Immediately the security camera turned towards her.

'I'm here to see Father Anthony,' she said.

Within seconds the gates swung open and Lilly walked in. She could have flown over them, but it had seemed impolite to do so. Plus she wanted to maintain the good friendship she had begun with Anthony and the Templars.

The house was as she remembered it. Tall, with three main turrets, and the obligatory gargoyles. It was the type of house you would expect to see in England. Perhaps the architect even based it on castles or manor houses he had seen. This building was a combination of both. It was grand. *Brideshead Revisited* but with Dracula's castle thrown in for good measure. Lilly knew that the middle turret, which was covered by a glass roof, was the library of the Templars. As she approached the steps which led up to the mahogany double front door, she admired the multitude of carved roses that framed the entrance.

She studied the design and beauty of the soaring arched frames with vampiric obsession as she began her ascent up to the door.

Before she reached the top one of the doors opened and John Noble came out to greet her.

'Lilly!' he said holding out his arms to her.

As she embraced him the anxiety she had felt receded. She remembered she was among friends and the feeling gave her some strange comfort. An emotion she had never expected to experience in her dealings with humans. She stepped back to look into the eyes of her human friend. John was a distant carrier of her gene, but unlike her, John had mousey coloured hair and grey-green eyes. His features were pleasant but not as refined as Gabi and Chez's, but Lilly knew that her bite could change all that.

'Anthony is expecting you in his office,' John said unaware of the fleeting thought that passed through Lilly's mind. He had no idea that just being around him was a temptation that Lilly found hard to bear.

They entered the impressive hallway where a two tiered centre staircase was illuminated by a chandelier that was almost as wide as the entrance hall but was raised high up to the second floor. Lilly observed the perfection of the large stained glass window that filled the frame on the first landing. It felt safe inside. Perhaps it was the magic wards that gave off this essence. Lilly wasn't sure, but her eyes wandered over the paintings and architecture as John led her down the long corridor to Anthony's office and her heart ceased its frantic thumping and began to beat with slower regularity.

'Thank you for seeing me,' Lilly said as she entered.

The office was large, with its own small library of books lining the walls and an imposing marble fireplace. There was a fire and it warmed the room.

For a moment Lilly paused in the doorway. Anthony sat

behind an expensive, highly polished desk. It spread perhaps five feet wide and three deep yet appeared small against the backdrop of wide, tall windows. There were all of the modern conveniences on his desk, a phone, a computer monitor and keyboard, an iPhone charging in a docking station, yet the desk itself looked antique.

It was difficult to be around Anthony again after all this time.

Anthony stood and came to greet her. He couldn't resist the pull of being in her arms, so the casual, friendly hug lingered. The touch of her skin and the flow of her aura sent shivers up his spine in a way he was unused to. They had not been lovers, but she was his maker, so there was an attraction that both of them felt, but tried to ignore. Even so, Anthony enjoyed the embrace far more than he wanted to and it was with reluctance that he withdrew.

Lilly felt the tension too. She knew it also meant that he had forgiven her for making him break his oath when she turned him. She stepped back from his embrace, mentally shaking herself.

Anthony was a talented mage. He manipulated time far better than Lilly had. He could pinpoint moments and return to them. This was something Lilly had yet to master. Even though she had improved her skills immensely and could move deftly through the portals, read them even, she still had a lot to learn. If anyone could help her now, it was Anthony and she was glad, despite the guilt, that she had given into her instincts to save him.

'You're alone?' Anthony asked.

'Yes. I thought it best. I was afraid for the others.'

'You have to stop mollycoddling them one day.' Anthony smiled and Lilly could tell that he meant this kindly.

'I can't help it.'

Anthony nodded. 'I know. They are your children. What brings you here now?'

'Gabi is gone. Kidnapped by some invaders that came to my castle.'

'They attacked your lair?'

'Not exactly. From what Anja tells me, they were in the grounds, searching for something. Gabi tried to call me, but his phone wouldn't work inside. So he went out and left her. He had been gone a while and she felt worried and so she returned to the top. At which point she saw the helicopter flying away. Gabi was gone.'

'Let's sit,' Anthony offered, pointing to the plush, velvet sofa before the fire.

It was cold in Stockholm and Lilly felt the chill in her body and soul. She was glad to sit before the roaring fire, and glad to pause before she continued her story. Right then she felt all of her years in age.

Anthony sat beside her and poured them both some brandy from a decanter that sat on a silver tray in the centre of a coffee table to his left. Lilly took the glass and sipped, cradling it in her hands.

'Thank you.'

'You don't have to thank me for anything, Lilly. You saved my life and I will do anything for you,' Anthony said.

A silence fell between them. Lilly had turned Anthony to save his life but even so she felt guilty that she had taken Anthony against his vows. All Knights Templars had sworn that they would never seek to become vampires, especially those that knew they were carriers of the gene. The search for immortality went against their beliefs in God and the celestial. It was an oath that Lilly found difficult to understand because had she known what she was before Gabi accidentally changed her, she would have willingly let him bite her anyway. Lilly had taken and changed Anthony for her own reasons. Even now she couldn't explain why she couldn't let him die. The urge to save him had been overwhelming. It had been the right thing to do.

'How are you coping? With your new life?' she asked after a time.

'I'm fine. And so are the Templars. My brothers and sisters have accepted me, vampire and all.'

'They are truly amazing people,' Lilly said. She was

surprised they would take the change of their most important member so lightly.

Anthony nodded. 'So, tell me. What did Anja do?'

Lilly felt a momentary confusion; she had let her mind wander from the threat. Being around Anthony, feeling his aura lap hers as they sat side by side, had the strangest calming effect on her. It was as though the one-time priest was her very own solace.

'Anja looked around for Gabi,' Lilly explained, pulling herself back to the crisis. 'Then she found a hole under the back bridge, which, she discovered, led down into another part of the ruins. Old rooms we didn't even know still existed. She ran through the caverns but there was no sign of Gabi. After she came back up into the moat she found his phone. It was dropped on the grass as though he had been caught unawares. By the time she rang me she was hysterical and wasn't making much sense. She can't fly yet ... she couldn't follow the helicopter, but she thought that's what had taken Gabi. It was the only explanation.'

Anthony nodded and Lilly sipped her drink once more before continuing.

'Chez and I had gone to an island off the coast of Scotland, but we flew back immediately. By then the trail had gone cold. Even so, I sensed violence down in the underground rooms. There was something else there too, a trace, a stench of death that I couldn't understand.'

'How can I help?' Anthony asked.

'I don't know if the Illuminati are involved in this, but I suspect they may be. The Templars know a lot about them, and I wondered if you could ask your people if they have seen any strange activity at any of the known strong-houses. It would have to be somewhere that they could be certain of holding Gabi.'

'Of course. I'll send out a memo immediately to all of our branches worldwide.'

Lilly rested her head against him. His touch made her feel happier, and she felt the waves of sensation that her contact gave to Anthony. Her eyes fell on his throat; she remembered how his mortal blood tasted but knew his immortal blood would be richer. There was something missing. *Dog collar?*

'I can't be a priest and a vampire,' he said reading her projected thought. 'It is something of a contradiction. And so I left the priesthood.'

'I'm sorry,' she said. 'I ruined your life.'

'I don't regret a thing. Besides, I'm very useful to my colleagues and they know that. Best to have a vampire as an ally than as an enemy.'

Despite his words Lilly felt sadness and she wondered if indeed the mention of his colleagues' acceptance of him was completely true. She didn't pursue it though. Anthony was where he belonged, the Templar priesthood was all he knew and this was his life. She couldn't change that and she didn't want to.

'Obviously our resources are at your disposal,' Anthony said. 'But how else can I help?'

'I'm not sure yet, but I think if we can discover where they have taken him, then your accuracy at opening portals will be invaluable,' Lilly said.

'Of course.'

'I should go now. I don't wish to leave Chez and Anja for too long. I fear the return of these men.'

'Then let's go back to your lair now,' Anthony said. 'But first I'll send out that memo.'

He stood and returned to sit at his desk and rapidly began to type a note.

'You'll come back with me?'

Anthony clicked 'Send' and the email went out to the Templar network.

Anthony nodded, 'The truth is I'm afraid for all of you. Safety in numbers … and in chainmail.'

'Chainmail?' Lilly smiled, recalling how the Templars still wore armour, albeit with modern technology.

'Yes. And we've made even more modifications. Come and see.'

Anthony walked to his desk, placed his hand underneath the top drawer. At the far side of the opposing wall the bookcase slid back revealing a tunnel that Lilly had never realised was there.

'Very James Bond …' she smiled.

Beyond the bookcase, Anthony led Lilly into a stairwell. A strip of lights, like cats eyes, lit up along either side of the wall. It wasn't bright, but enough for human eyes to negotiate the passage safely.

Lilly laughed at the absurdity of being led down the hidden passage, yet she knew that most houses of this sort had them.

A room opened up before them and Lilly tried to get her bearings in context with the house. They were in a large space that had several work benches, electrical and joinery equipment. There was a dummy wearing the type of Kevlar breast plate that she had seen and worn previously when the Illuminati had attacked.

'We're in the centre. Just behind the library,' Anthony said.

Across the room Lilly could see another bookshelf.

'I guess that opens up as well?'

Anthony smiled, 'We're very covert.'

Anthony walked over to the dummy. 'Let me show you the improvements. The Kevlar breast plate is pretty much the same as it was. We've added gloves, leggings and a head and neck covering. They are all made of the special Kevlar chain. Naturally these wouldn't be worn under normal combat circumstances but … we don't know what we're up against in this situation and so I'd advise all of you wear them whenever you're out. The armour is lightweight and can be easily worn under clothing.'

'So the new features are new pieces of the armour?'

'Yes and no. I hope you'll forgive my presumption but I had a slightly different suit made for you.'

Anthony opened a panel on the wall beside the bookcase. This contained a suit bag which he unzipped. He pulled out a vest, leggings, cowl and gloves and held them out to Lilly. It looked like a matt PVC ninja outfit except for the sword sheath that ran down the back.

'Once on, this will fit your sword. I thought you might find it useful.'

There were other additions too: a knife holster on the thigh, a pair of knee length boots that concealed daggers in the toes and a pistol and holster at the waist with a small pouch that held bullets.

'Looks like I'll have a complete armoury on my body,' Lilly said. 'Don't you think it's a little … excessive though? I mean I'm fairly invulnerable anyway.'

Anthony's eyes were serious as he met hers. 'No. I mean, yes you're strong, but we really shouldn't take any chances. Especially with you.'

His words confused her and she was about to question him further on his obvious paranoia when John came in and interrupted them.

'Oh good. You've seen the armour. I'll get these packed up for you.'

Lilly watched as John and Anthony packed three suits into their own individual cases.

'You should wear yours from now on,' Anthony said, placing the fourth case empty down beside the others.

'What about you?'

Anthony moved the collar of his black sweater aside and Lilly could see the suit underneath his clothing.

'Taking no chances. All the Templars wear them.'

'Good,' said Lilly. 'I will feel less afraid for my new friends now.'

7

Monitored

Preacher was in the main security centre, in the middle of the monitor room. He was watching Seventeen on a colour screen but so far the creature hadn't moved that day. It had been three days since they brought Seventeen in but he would neither eat nor drink anything they gave him.

Preacher was having a good time nonetheless. His access allowed him to go where he pleased and he used this power with extreme enthusiasm. So much so that no one dared to question him. It was as if he were running the base. Not the General and not Lucy Collins.

A female soldier, thirty something with sandy coloured hair cut fashionably short, was seated beside him. Preacher glanced at her name badge: Corporal Dealer. Preacher was aware of the shampoo and deodorant smells that wafted from her body. She took some pride in her appearance, but adhered to regulation. There was no make-up but Preacher thought he saw traces of mascara on what would have been blonde eyelashes. She behaved professionally though, keeping her eyes on the monitors, saying nothing. Preacher prided himself on his ability to make judgements about people and his sense of atmosphere. When he came in to the monitor room he felt no tension among the soldiers, something a flirty female presence might have created.

On the other side of him was a male soldier, a private by the name of Elin. Elin hadn't spoken to Preacher at all when he entered, but moved along silently to allow him the middle seat, closest to Seventeen's monitor. Preacher noted that Elin didn't quite have the pallor that the other soldiers had. Being locked below ground for months on end could do that. He wondered if he was of mixed race, but the slight tinge to his skin gave nothing away.

On the monitor, Preacher could see that Seventeen was stretched out on his bunk, arms folded casually behind his head. He seemed to be sleeping. They had allowed Seventeen to come fully awake and the drug was no longer in his system. Other than sipping from glasses of water the creature had refused all meat and blood. It was as though he were making a silent protest. He neither spoke nor made any attempt to escape. Instead he looked relaxed and comfortable in the concrete cell. He was, in fact, calm all of the time.

Sometimes Preacher allowed the gaolers to release the chains so that Seventeen could walk around. At these times the creature prowled the cell like a caged lion that is used to its environment. He gave off a sense of power, a feeling of waiting, but made no attempt at all to test his bonds or the door. Preacher couldn't help wondering if this meant the beast had already been domesticated in some way but without communication he couldn't know.

Preacher found Seventeen intriguing. He was quite beautiful. Especially his glowing green eyes.

By comparison, Eighteen, the old, rag-covered woman they found in the bowels of the castle, ate all of the offered meat and blood, and constantly tried to escape her containment. The woman had been little more than a bag of bones when they found her, but as she ate everything they gave her, she began to fill out. She looked less aged after a week and appeared to be a scrawny woman of around forty instead of an old hag. She wasn't very intelligent but she was loud and foul. She stank of the shit that she smeared over her cell at regular intervals and her attempts to free herself of her captors smacked of fear and desperation.

Preacher switched monitors and watched Eighteen wander around her cell. She, too, hadn't spoken. She turned and looked up at the camera as though she sensed she was being scrutinised. She gave a moronic smile. All sharp, blackened teeth, like a chain-smoker. Preacher grimaced. If she had still been human he was sure he would have found this one vile anyway. She was cougar-like in the cultural, not the animal, sense, and he was certain that as a revenant she would have used some of her old human ways to gain access to her victims. Even so, he couldn't understand anyone being attracted or drawn in by this hideous creature. He felt no sympathy for her, certainly no attraction to the nothing shape that was neither feminine nor attractively boyish. She was just – nothing.

The scientists were not interested in her either it seemed. She gave them no new information, but was merely another of a type they already had in abundance. He wondered why they even bothered to keep her at all and wondered if he should suggest extermination to Lucy.

Seventeen however was different. There was intelligence behind his eyes, and the fact that Seventeen was refusing to eat their offerings proved it. He was fussy, the blood they gave was animal, and Preacher suspected that Seventeen knew that instinctively. He didn't want it.

Preacher picked up the phone in the security office and dialled the extension for Lucy's office. The phone rang a few times and then she answered.

'Doctor Collins? I wonder if I might see you down at Seventeen's cell?'

In the lift, Lucy was fuming. Preacher was behaving as though he were in charge of the base. She hated him, and was beginning to find it difficult to hide her feelings. She was sick of him phoning her and ordering her to do things. Since his arrival Preacher had been a pain in the arse. She wanted to rip his throat out and feed him to the subjects. She smiled as she imagined the shock on his face when she revealed her fangs. She would drink her fill first, and watch the life drain from his eyes. The thought of chopping him up and putting his dismembered parts in the feeding buckets made her feel better and by the time the lift reached minus 20 she was calm and in control of her fury.

Preacher was waiting for her at Gabi's cell door.

'I'd like to talk to him again,' he said.

Like his phone conversation, Preacher didn't use the niceties. He didn't think to say 'good morning' or ask how she was. Everything he said was focused on the task. He definitely wasn't a people person.

'Why?' Lucy sighed. 'You know it's pointless.'

'I know he's intelligent. We can try to reason with him.'

Lucy shrugged and nodded to the guard at the door. He opened the peep shutter and looked in. Seventeen was still lying on the bed. He looked benign.

'Should I tighten the chains?' asked the soldier.

'No,' Lucy said. 'If you intend to reason with him then you should show some trust, Preacher.'

Preacher weighed her up. He glanced in at Seventeen. The subject's eyes were still closed and he hadn't moved, but Preacher knew that the creature was aware of them outside the room. He wondered what Lucy would gain from allowing Seventeen to kill him.

'Keep handy with the dart gun,' Lucy ordered as the soldier pressed the button to open the door.

The locking mechanism grated and clunked as the seven deadbolts pulled back one by one.

She stepped back as the door opened and she watched Gabi turn his head to study them as they entered.

'What have you learnt so far then?' he said, startling them all.

'You do speak,' Preacher was breathless as he entered the cell and he was aware of the shocked and somewhat sullen expression on Lucy's face.

'Of course,' Gabi said.

He glanced at Lucy, her eyes skittered away.

'I would advise you not to look in his eyes,' she warned.

Preacher threw back his head and laughed. 'Vampire mythos? Hypnosis? I don't believe in the possibility of those things.'

This man is such an idiot, Lucy thought.

Gabi sat up slowly and turned his legs until he was sitting upright and facing them, his feet on the cold floor.

'Is that what you believe I am?' he smiled revealing a full set of perfect straight teeth.

'I'm not sure what you are,' Preacher said.

Lucy shifted behind Preacher. He didn't look around at her. Instead he kept his full attention on Gabi.

'Bring me a chair,' Preacher ordered to no one in particular.

The soldier floundered at the door. His orders were to cover them with the dart gun and now Mr Preacher wanted a chair. He wasn't sure how important the man was, but knew he had to obey his request. He looked to Lucy for help. Impatiently she snatched the gun from his hands and trained it on Gabi.

'Chair,' she murmured. But the whole thing annoyed her again and she frowned. She turned her attention back to Gabi and found him scrutinising her. He was smiling.

'Trouble in paradise?' he observed.

'Shut up,' she hissed.

Preacher glanced at her surprised by her attitude towards the creature. He frowned then quickly turned his eyes back to Gabi.

The soldier returned with a chair.

'May I?' asked Preacher politely and again this angered Lucy. Preacher showed no respect to her or anyone else at the base and yet here he was, being nice and sociable with what he believed to be a monster. Of course, Lucy knew that Gabi was at his most dangerous when he appeared benign but she said nothing. *Kill the little bastard if you want to. It will get him out of my hair*, Lucy thought.

The soldier took back the gun. It had appeared awkward in her small hands but Gabi knew this was all an act. Lucy was capable of using the weapon to silence him whenever she wished. He sat back against the wall as the soldier trained the gun on him. He was not afraid of the soldier's reactions. Now that he knew what the dart contained he would be certain he wasn't caught out again, which was why it was important to gain Preacher's trust.

'Please sit, Mr Preacher,' Gabi said.

'You know my name?'

'The night you captured me, one of the soldiers called it.'

Preacher nodded and sat down. 'I remember. You interest me.'

'I'm sure I do.'

'You must be hungry. Is there anything we can get you?'

'I'm partial to fillet steak, cooked medium rare,' Gabi said and smiled again. 'I can't understand why you keep offering me blood and raw meat.'

Preacher crossed his arms and sat back stiffly in his chair. For a moment he seemed at a loss as to what to say.

'When we met,' Preacher said. 'you were levitating and camouflaged. What are you?'

8
Willing Subject

I find Preacher intriguing and his turn of phrase is so peculiar and stilted for an American that he is quite amusing. He is an albino I think, but I get the feeling that this is not a full mutation, only a partial one. Lucrezia probably understands this better than I since she seems to have some expertise on genetics. What is she doing here? Clearly they do not know what she is.

Preacher sits and begins to talk. I feel like indulging him, even though Lucrezia is screaming warnings directly into my mind. I have never been able to share what I am with humans – other than the Templars of course, but they were always too polite to ask me any direct questions. Plus I have had time to reflect on this situation: time to consider how I can escape. Though first I need to learn what they know and maybe then I will have to neutralise the danger here.

I have a mind to give Preacher some knowledge to make him trust me. I am curious about him. There is a level of power and violence that emanates from the man. I don't try mind control, even though he looks directly into my eyes. I would rather assuage my curiosity and learn in the normal way. After all I am in no real danger at this time and feel no specific urge to escape. As long as I am compliant they won't drug me. Call me foolish and misguided, but I believe it is not in Lucrezia's best interests for her to allow them to destroy me. If they could, that is.

So far, and it's strange now that I consider it under these circumstances, I am not really afraid. This is odd because the old scar, the near conclusion of my immortal life, had left me with a phobia of death that I had found hard to shake. But I have been listening a great deal since I arrived here several days ago and have learnt many things.

They do not know what I am. They have many of the revenants, one being the woman they found living near us. They understand the monstrosity of these creatures better than I do, and maybe this is the place that will help me discover what they are.

'You have captured other beings,' I say.

Preacher blinks. He does not get my subtlety.

'I wish to know what you know about them.'

'That is classified,' Lucy says.

'Mmm. But you wish to learn about me?' I address my comment directly to Preacher.

'You would help us to understand what you are?' he asks.

'I would do more than that,' I say. 'I would demonstrate my power. And make a solemn promise that I would harm no one here. Unless you give me reason to …'

'What reason would that be?' Preacher asks.

I smile. 'If I feel threatened I may take it personally. And believe me, your chains would not be enough to contain me should I believe myself to be in danger.'

'What are you?' he asks. This is amusing because it is obvious what I am. He merely does not wish to accept it.

'Do you agree to my terms?' I ask.

Preacher looks at Lucy, she shrugs. 'Yes.'

'I'm a vampire.'

Preacher leans forward. 'I don't appreciate your joke,' he says.

'I don't appreciate your ignorance,' I answer. Then I laugh throwing back my head, fangs full throttle and to the fore.

Preacher jumps up, knocking back his chair and it lands with a crash on the concrete floor. The soldier rushes forward the dart gun poised: his eyes meet mine.

'Wait!' says Lucrezia. 'Don't you see? He's proving what he said to you to be true.'

Preacher picks up his chair. He is angry at himself and so he turns on me with fierce and sharp eyes. I like him a little I think.

His pride is of course the thing I will use against him. It will destroy him and I will enjoy feeding on the arrogance in his blood.

'Please sit,' I say again. 'I have no intention of harming you or this lovely doctor here. Tell him to back off.' I indicate the soldier.

Lucrezia takes the soldier's arm and pulls him back. 'Wait outside,' she says. 'We don't need you.'

I see the soldier's sweat drip down his face despite the strong air conditioning. He's afraid and so he should be. If he had made any effort to use that gun on me I would, quite frankly, have shoved it up his backside.

I smile at him, my fangs have returned to their nest in my gums. This upsets the soldier more and so he willingly backs out of the cell.

'How do you do that?' Preacher asks as he regains some of his earlier composure.

'It is … a reflex. Like smiling, or arousal.'

'Arousal?' Preacher asks. He crosses his legs and then I know. He is interested in me in other ways too.

'Feeding and sex are often something I combine,' I say.

I look over his head and see Lucrezia is smiling. She is enjoying this as much as I. The feral part of her has been suppressed here and she wants to play with Preacher also.

'I should like to see that,' Preacher says.

'You are a voyeur,' I smile.

I reach towards him and place my hand on his leg. Preacher squirms but there is only a trace of fear and it is heightening his sexual fantasy of me. He wants me. I let him think that I swing both ways as I know he does. I am, it should be said, hopelessly straight. But even so, I am not above using my sexuality for my own gain. Despite the fact that I find androgynous women appealing, Lucrezia knows that sex with men would never interest. My attraction is more to do with an appearance of youth and innocence than any form of 'boyishness' on their part. I like women. I desire women. But. I will play with Preacher all the same.

You surprise me, Lucrezia thinks.

You never *surprise me*, my reply is deliberately cutting.

She withdraws from my mind. She is furious but I don't care. She asked for it, and I don't want her in my game. She has dominated my fun one time too often. Even so, I am not stupid enough to alienate her entirely. I will use her to my own advantage. She will protect my interests for my continued silence; otherwise she will find herself in the cell beside me. I send this thought to her. It is not a warning but a promise.

'If you are willing,' Lucrezia says, her composure giving nothing of our exchange away, 'we would care to learn about you.'

'Good,' I say. 'Remove the shackles.'

Preacher stares at my cuffed hands as I hold them out to him.

'This could be a trap,' he says.

'Yes,' I smile. 'It could be. But if you keep your trained monkey and his dart gun close by, you can knock me out if I try anything.'

Preacher stands. He takes the chair and backs away to the door where Lucrezia waits.

'I'll take it under advisement,' Preacher says. 'But for now you have convinced me that you are very different from the revenants.'

I find it interesting that he calls the creatures the same name Anja and I have given them. But then again, what else would you call the walking dead?

They lock the cell door and I hear them walk down the corridor. Lucrezia's steps are light but deliberately she mimics humanity. She could, I know, be completely silent should she want to be. I count the steps again. My first speculation was right and I'm now certain where the lift is.

Outside the soldier stands guard. Foolish mortal. In his moment of panic he made the mistake of looking in my eyes. They don't know it, but this one is already my creature. He will prove worthy when the time comes. I already know everything there is to know about Private Parker.

9
Cunning

They begin their experiments. I have no idea what Lucrezia said to convince Preacher but I am suddenly free of my bonds, and they walk with me to the lift. Private Parker, my soldier now, is the guard on duty and although I could easily escape it amuses me to go with them to their gymnasium. This is five floors up. I notice there are twenty to the surface which might explain that strange sense of pressure I feel in the cell. I am, after all, sensitive to such things. For example I can feel the earth sinking in Venice whenever I'm there and it gives me a strange sense of vertigo, so why not the movement of sand against the walls of the cells beneath the desert?

'A display of strength,' Preacher says.

'If you wish,' I answer, but first I make some petty demands just to keep it interesting and to give them a reason to keep believing I am a willing lab rat. 'I want a television and DVD player in my room. I want carpet on my floor and I don't like being expected to eat with my plate on my lap and so I wish for a small table and chair. These things are not hard for you to obtain and I spend much time in that room. It's boring.'

'Of course,' he nods. 'Whatever you wish.'

I smile. Flash a little fang and stroke his arm in exactly the same way that I might touch a female. Preacher all but swoons at my touch and I'm not even using the lust to attract him.

I bench press a hundred pounds without breaking a sweat and then I lift up an entire exercise machine. It is easy and I must admit I'm curious of the limit of my own strength too.

'That is amazing,' Preacher says. He is excited in many ways but there's only one I'm truly interested in.

'My muscles aren't from exercise,' I tell Preacher. 'It comes from my diet.'

'The steak?'

I laugh. 'Human blood.'

'You haven't drunk any since you were here,' Preacher notes.

'Of course not. You were offering me swine blood. I wouldn't drink that if I were starving to death. Even so, I'm not hungry at the moment.'

Preacher is curious about this and so I have to explain my feeding habits.

'A woman here, a boy there,' I say. 'But I don't need to feed very often. It's fiction that vampires bite someone every night. We could of course but we really don't need to.'

'You kill your victims?'

I feel cynical and so I wish to scare him a little. It makes that sexual attraction he's feeling for me so much more palatable.

'Sometimes.'

'I see.'

They have me running then, I run so fast that I'm almost a blur to their human eyes. That is hard to do in such a small environment though.

'You need a running track to see this properly,' I explain.

I feel like the bionic man being tested on his skills and speed. It is rather amusing that such an old television programme would bring up the comparisons in this day and age, but humans either revere or fear strength and power.

Preacher takes careful note of the results of each test and all this time Lucy says nothing even though she is the person scoring them. Even so, I feel her curiosity. Maybe this is an opportunity for her to test what we are capable of also. Maybe for some reason she cares to learn her own limits. I don't intend to give all of my secrets away though. The speed and strength I demonstrate is merely a fraction of my true capacity. I wonder if Lucy realises this.

'What have you learnt so far?' I ask, suddenly appearing

beside her.

She jumps, and for once I feel this reaction isn't feigned.

'You're faster and stronger than I expected.'

I glance around and see Preacher setting up yet another test for me.

'What do you hope to gain by all this?' I whisper so quietly that I know only she can hear me.

'Knowledge. That's the only interesting thing in this world,' she says.

'But why? What will it give you?'

'Gabi, if you don't understand the value of learning after all of these years then I can't explain it to you. You're still that spoilt little opera star, the darling of the Venetian salons, at heart aren't you? You must miss all those fawning women falling at your feet. The world has changed and we, who could conceivably live forever, will have to change with it if we wish to survive.'

I realise at that moment how little she knows me. Part of me is not surprised by this revelation. She talks of knowledge and yet understands nothing of emotion. Lucrezia seeks data. It is what drove her to research and become a doctor. I have known her in this role in many lifetimes and have always wondered about it. Now though her words tell me more than she perhaps intended them to. Her ignorance of me and my life and feelings is amusing more than it is upsetting. She expected to be cutting, to put me down, but the truth behind them is this: she has nothing else in her life. I have a family that love and care for me. She has her work. She has knowledge. She has tests.

Nonetheless, I'm given pause by her words. My petulance has perhaps brought me to this situation. Had I not decided to leave the lair without letting Lilly and Chez know, had I not alienated them, perhaps I would still be safe within their loving embrace. My jealousy and my competitive streak made it difficult to accept that Lilly and Chez belong together, and that Anja and I ... I halt here. It is too early to consider this I suppose. But Anja, sweet and deadly, a creature born of us whatever way she came into being, actually loves me. I've known it all along and have treated her like I believed she was second best.

Had Lucrezia understood my only real weakness is my family they would really have me where they wanted me. Fortunately for me she has no feelings of this nature and cannot therefore even consider it as a possibility.

'Thank you,' I say to Lucrezia.

'What for?'

'Your assessment of me has made me recognise what I am,' and her incorrect evaluation has in some ways helped me appraise my own motives. It has also helped me to understand her. The thing is I'm the one who has changed. Not her. Once, a long time ago, I would have done anything for her. How simple and stupid she seems to me now.

I walk away from her and take a seat at the table indicated by Preacher.

'This is an intelligence test,' he says and then I am plunged into the strangest and most simple of tests. It is a mere flex of my thoughts to calculate the mathematical problems they throw at me, or to quickly solve the puzzles they place down.

'The result?' I ask at the end.

'Off the chart. I guess that means you're the smartest person on the planet,' says Preacher and he shakes his head as though the enormity of this discovery is too much for him.

'I doubt it,' I say. 'There is bound to be someone smarter. Take the good doctor here. She knows much that I don't.'

Lucrezia smiles at me over Preacher's head. Flattery is something I'm very skilled at and I know her ego will enjoy it.

'Intelligence isn't necessarily judged by a particular knowledge,' Preacher says. 'But rather by the ability to learn. I suspect you could learn anything you wanted to.'

I shrug. 'Perhaps. If it interested me.'

'It is a lot to do with memory,' Lucrezia says. 'Because you are self-healing I suspect your brain cells don't die at the same rate that those of humans do.'

'How do you know he's self healing?' asked Preacher.

'I just assumed … well the others …'

She is stuttering a little and I know it is somewhat foolish that she has given herself away. I see Preacher's eyes narrow.

'Let's test this theory,' he says.

'What?'

'A little cut to see how fast it repairs.'

Lucrezia doesn't like the sound of this and neither do I.

'I'll play your games,' I say. 'But you will not subject me to those kinds of experiments.'

'Why not? If you heal, then the pain must be minimal.'

'I will not be dissected,' I say.

My old scar itches as Preacher orders the removal of the IQ test. Then Lucrezia surprises me.

'This is my subject and I won't allow such barbaric use of him,' she says.

Preacher's eyes narrow again. 'I have access here.'

'Yes. You do have access and I can't stop you going where you please. But the truth is that I'm in charge of this experiment. I have let you have your say as a courtesy, Mr Preacher. However, I checked your status and you do not out-rank me here. Furthermore, Seventeen … Gabriele … is the most advanced find we've had in years. There is no way that I will allow you to hurt him.'

I feel like applauding, but what did I expect? She has to protect herself and if that means protecting me then I know I can rely on her to continue to do so. Preacher is, however, very, very angry. He clenches his fist at his side and he almost squares up to her. I flick my eyes over to Parker. He steps forward.

'Is everything alright, Doctor Collins?' Private Parker says.

Parker is around six foot five and Preacher is around five ten. I reckon there is no contest, but I wouldn't wish to underestimate Preacher. After all he did capture me.

'Everything is fine,' says Preacher as he releases the tension from his hands and flexes his fists.

I'm not really worried about Lucrezia though. She can handle herself, but if he did attack her she would be forced to reveal her true nature. The air is tense with testosterone.

Lucrezia smiles and I realise she is enjoying baiting Preacher.

'Well I'm glad you're finally realising who is in charge around here, Preacher,' I say. 'Because clearly her balls are bigger than yours.'

Parker laughs at my comment and at that moment Preacher makes his move. He hits Parker, a sharp and hard blow to the throat that leaves the soldier gasping for air as it cuts off his laughter. Parker stumbles against the wall, holding his windpipe. Preacher, it seems, does not enjoy being the butt of a joke.

I wonder how he will feel when he learns he has become my subject for scrutiny just as much as I am now his.

10
Gatecrashers

Ffion looked up from the computer in the corner of the kiosk at the entrance to Rhuddlan Castle. From where she sat she could see the high stone turrets of the castle, and a flag atop one of them flapping listlessly in the breeze. Despite having a few days off work to recover from her ordeal, she felt tense and anxious. She squinted out of the window and tried to push all thoughts of the strange American who had tied her up in Geraint's basement but the fear still gripped her and she jumped as the bell above the door rang and someone entered.

It was an elderly couple. Ffion took careful and suspicious note of them as they looked through the books on the rack. They were wearing matching yellow and green jackets. The woman was wearing thick brown trousers, the man blue denim jeans. Both wore stout hiking boots. They were tourists for certain, but Ffion didn't trust her judgement any more.

'Two concession tickets for the castle, please,' said the man reaching into his jacket pocket to retrieve his wallet. Ffion took the proffered ten pound note, entered the fee into the till and then carefully counted out the change.

'That way,' she said indicating the turnstile on the other side of the kiosk.

Normally she would have chatted, been friendly, but she found herself feeling shy all of a sudden. The police counsellor had explained all this to her, but it didn't make her feel any better. She was afraid to trust a stranger again and rightly so. The counsellor had reassured her that she would get over what had happened, but it might take some time. Even so, Ffion felt fear. It was a ridiculous and debilitating feeling that she resented.

Before returning to her seat at the computer she watched the couple pass through the door into the castle grounds but her mind wasn't on the work and the new stock for the shop didn't order itself. Still, she let her eyes wander to the window and the castle beyond. There was something weird about this place; she had always known it, but now she felt that the ancient stones hid more secrets than the small passage that she and Geraint had used to earn some extra cash.

A lightning-like flash lit up the inside of the kiosk. Ffion jumped, then looked outside again. She squinted at the sky. There wasn't a cloud to be seen. The hum grew louder. It vibrated through and around the kiosk and as Ffion watched her head started to hurt slightly.

Ffion recalled hearing the sound before but it had never lasted this long.

She stood up and peered through the window, looking out over the grounds. Her eyes fell on the bridge that crossed the moat and led up to the castle. A fine white blur discoloured the space beside the bridge, almost on the edge on the moat itself. Ffion blinked. She could see the atmosphere shimmer. It looked something like running water and reminded her of the waterfall in nearby Dyserth. Her eyes began to water and she was forced to rub them. Then, suddenly, *there*! Her blurred vision picked out a shape. Then another one. A woman and a man, both wearing black. They seemed to appear from thin air on the small patch of grass beside the moat and bridge. Ffion rubbed her eyes, shook her head. For a moment she couldn't make sense of what she was seeing.

Obviously someone had crept under the barrier. An unreasonable flare of anger surged through her. *How dare they!* The castle was run by a charity. Every penny went towards the upkeep of the historical ruins and it was only a few pounds to come in any way! She turned back into the kiosk, snatched the keys from the till and headed outside, unsure what she would say and do but knowing that she was right.

'Hey!' she called, heading over to the bridge. 'You have to pay to come in here. We don't allow gatecrashers ...'

There was no one there.

Ffion stopped and looked at the bridge. She felt sick. *Now I'm imagining things too!* She glanced over into the moat. There was no-one there. The old couple in the matching anoraks came into view at the end of the moat, walking around the exterior of the castle. From this distance she couldn't make out what they were talking about but the man was pointing upwards and gesturing towards the towers. They were clearly enjoying the ruins. Ffion's eyes followed the curve of the turrets and the crumbling walkways that still remained in patches along the top. She walked to the edge of the moat and looked down, checking to see if anyone was hiding under the bridge. There was no-one there. But there was ... something ...

Ffion stood on the edge and watched the space under the bridge. Her eyes seemed fixed, and she felt a wash of contentment flow over her. She didn't move even when the phone began to ring in the office. The old couple passed by beneath her, and when they looked up, they saw that she was smiling gently, lost in a world of her own. They smiled at each other then and kept going. If the girl wanted to daydream, then let her.

For Ffion, it was as though the hum of the castle had lulled her to sleep where she stood, and the world around her faded into the background like a dull and distant dream.

'Show me what you've found,' said Anthony to Anja.

She was still clearly distressed by Gabi's disappearance and it was obvious to Anthony that she had been crying recently. It still surprised him that he, and all the other vampires, were capable of such heightened emotion. On instinct he placed his arm around her, offering what little comfort he could.

He had arrived about five minutes ago with Lilly. They had crossed through time and arrived outside the castle a few moments before they had even left Stockholm. Then Lilly had taken Anthony into the lair for the first time. He observed the well-hidden access device. The steps, one thousand exactly, spiralling down into the earth. He couldn't help but count them – some childhood instinct – and as they reached the bottom, Chez and Anja waited for them at the open door that led into the lair.

'How many?' Chez had asked.

'A thousand. But how did you know I would count them?'

Lilly had taken his arm and led him through the door and into a large and impressive hallway that any stately home would be proud to host.

'We can't help it,' she had told him. 'Gabi calls it his vampire OCD and I think he has something there. We are all very precise about everything like that. I take in details about things all the time. It annoys me actually, but I still can't help myself.'

Anthony had removed his coat which Chez had hung it up on an ornate, gold-plated coat stand.

'Blood?' Chez had offered, but Anthony shook his head.

He ate well at the Templars' base and he rarely craved blood. Deep down he wondered if it was because the Knights feared him ever getting hungry and feasting on one of them in the night. The idea was absurd though. One thing Anthony had learnt about his plight was that he could so easily control the vampire cravings. He even felt that he could go without blood for sustained periods if he should choose to. Vampirism, he had learnt, was as much about control and intelligence as it was about having super-human abilities. The blood craving was only a small part of it.

'Lilly tells me there are other rooms below,' Anthony had said, following them into the large and comfortable lounge.

He had been surprised to see the modern conveniences. The large flat screen television; the multimedia CD player in the corner; the laptop left open and switched on. There were large expensive sofas and a roaring fire. Anthony had wondered how and where the fire vented but didn't ask. Instead he had sunk down into the plush red and black sofa and let his eyes wander around the room.

Now, as they sat in the lounge, Anthony couldn't help observing how simple the decor was, Lilly, it seemed, preferred plain walls, but there were small tells around the place of the vampires' sentimentality. A simple and beautiful painting hung on the wall. It depicted Lilly as a warrior princess, sword in hand, a crown of daisies adorning her head and a simple and flimsy robe, hung from her shoulders and opened to reveal one perfect bare breast. Anthony eyes were captivated by the pink nipple.

'Renaissance,' he murmured.

She nodded, but said nothing.

Anthony looked away and his eyes fell on the stack of DVDs that filled a mahogany shelf in the corner of the room. He read some of the titles casually as a way to distract himself. *Dracula, Near Dark, 28 Days Later*. The list of horror movies continued.

'Gabi's,' Chez said. 'I don't care for them, or that.' He indicated the laptop.

'Yours I presume,' he said turning to Anja.

'Lilly's,' she answered. 'Gabi and I have iPads.'

Anthony blinked trying to assimilate the normality of the room. With the exception that it was many feet below ground, this could be a lounge in any average, but wealthy home, anywhere.

'I like my home comforts,' Lilly smiled.

'And why not?' Anthony agreed.

'Perhaps Anja could show you what she found below?' Chez suggested.

'Yes,' Anthony nodded. 'But first I'd prefer it if both of you changed into the Kevlar under-suits. That way, we'll all be as protected as we can be.'

He passed them the case he had brought and they headed off to their rooms.

'They're nice,' he said to Lilly, and she smiled in return.

'All my friends are nice.'

When Chez and Anja returned they made their way back upstairs.

'Wait,' said Lilly as they reached the wall leading outside to the moat. 'I can hear voices.'

The four of them waited, Anthony pressed his head against the wall and listened to a couple arguing on the other side of the wall.

'Someone is down in the moat,' he confirmed.

'That's the problem with doing these things when the castle is open and in broad daylight,' Chez said.

They waited until they heard the humans move on before they slipped outside, camouflaged. It was then that Lilly saw the girl standing on the edge of the moat. She recognised her as one of the women that worked in the castle shop, though she didn't know her name. The girl was staring at the castle as though mesmerized and fortunately she hadn't noticed the wall under the bridge silently opening to allow the immortals to exit.

'What …?' Anja gasped. Lilly touched her arm to silence her. All four vampires remained pressed against the wall even though they knew they couldn't be seen.

Lilly thought for a moment, and then left the wall and, still camouflaged, flew up to join the girl at the top.

As the others watched, Lilly turned her slightly, and put her hand under her chin, raising her head so that Lilly was looking into her eyes.

Anja smiled, she knew that Lilly was making sure that the girl would remember nothing, assuming she had seen anything in the first place.

After a minute or two of gazing into the girl's eyes, Lilly raised her hands, and gently thumbed her eyelids closed. Then she stroked the side of the girl's face.

After a moment, the girl opened her eyes once more and yawned. Without apparently seeing Lilly at all, she turned and headed back to the kiosk.

Lilly cloaked herself again, and hopped back down into the moat to join the others.

'What was that all about?' asked Chez.

Lilly shook her head, 'I don't know.'

They walked around the moat unobserved until they reached the bridge at the back.

'Down here,' Anja said.

They climbed down through the now large gap under the bridge and Anja led them down into the maze of tunnels that bent and twisted into the bowels of the castle.

'Fascinating,' Anthony said.

'There's a crack in the wall at this point. It looks as though it was once a room that was closed off, but there is enough space to climb through.' Anja said.

They examined the gap.

'Do you smell that?' Anja asked.

'Yes. Putrid.'

In the dark Anja nodded.

'Yes.'

'Anja do you have any idea what it was they took from down here?' Anthony asked.

Anja sniffed the air again but didn't answer. Instead she climbed over the broken rock and into the hole. Anthony followed while Chez and Lilly remained on guard in the first chamber.

The room wasn't as empty as it first appeared. In the corner Anthony and Anja found a pile of rags and bones. Inside the smell was worse. It stank of faeces and urine. But worst of all was the strong odour of rot.

'Human remains,' Anthony commented and Anja nodded. She could smell the decay as much as he could.

Anthony picked up one of the small bones and slipped it into his pocket. 'For examination.'

Anja said nothing but she hurried back through the hole and out towards the others.

'The strange thing is,' Lilly said, 'that this wall is directly against the wall of our lair.'

'I didn't realise that,' Anja said sharply.

'Anja. You have to tell us everything you know,' Anthony said.

Lilly frowned, 'She has …'

Anthony shook his head to show he disagreed.

'Anja?' Chez said.

Anja turned to them, her face was deathly pale. 'There is something. I think ... but I don't know for certain ... what they took from under here ...'

Anthony, Chez and Lilly waited.

'I think,' Anja continued, 'that they found a revenant.'

11
Nonna

Private Elin walked the boundaries of the base during his break. He needed to reaffirm contact with the land under the Sun. Recently Elin had begun to find it difficult to be below the earth. He couldn't quite explain why, but a vague memory lurked behind the burst of a dream. Maybe he had seen something about it on the reservation where his grandmother, Nonna, lived. Elin remembered visits before kindergarten, before the days when his white father stopped allowing him to go there because Nonna was filling his head with 'nonsense'.

Elin remembered Nonna well though. Her wrinkled brown face, always smiling, always sincere, sometimes appeared in the strangest moments in his sleep. Nonna was a good soul, and she had promised him that she would always be there for him.

Elin stopped at the electrified fence and stared out into the desert wasteland. A hot breeze brushed his face as he looked into the distance. The desert had belonged to the Washoe tribe long before the white man had appeared with their diseases and guns. The tribe were a peaceful people and instead of fighting had fled farther into the mountains, giving up their land to be destroyed by the greedy American hordes during the gold rush. The mad, glittering dreams of men who thought that they could get rich by claiming lands which did not belong to them, and then to systematically destroy them with mining and digging to try and find gold, the elusive metal that was more often than not a fool's venture. The land around them had been used up, ravished by the invaders. Nonna had explained why this was such a bad thing.

'The *Wa She Shu* hunted wisely,' she said. 'We did not abuse the land. The white man came and killed the animals without thought for the future. They cut down the trees that bore fruit. They stole the land from those that needed it to survive and they turned it into a wasteland.'

Nonna was very specific on this subject. She had said that technology was destroying the planet and Elin had believed her. Anyone could see that what she said made sense. Especially when she talked of the seasonal cycles, the passing of the *Gum Debeh*, and how the Washoe way was to always think of the future.

Elin knelt down by the barrier. He could hear the hum of the electricity, sense it in the fence. A strange symbol came into his head. He remembered seeing it daubed in homemade paint on the walls of Nonna's cabin. She didn't live in a tepee like her ancestors, but she made her small house look as authentic as she could. The walls were draped with animal skins, the shallow shelves decorated with authentic pottery. Nonna had even taken to wearing the robes of the healer but this was all just presentation for the visitors who came to the reservation and it was a way of making a living in the modern world, a world which she had little respect for.

'But really we should be living off the land and tending it with love and respect,' Nonna had said.

Elin found himself drawing the symbol in the earth where he knelt. It was shaped like an eye but with a snake in the centre. The snake was reared and ready to strike, but it wasn't like any rattler that Elin had ever seen, its jaw was bigger than its head, fangs as long as those of a sabre-tooth tiger, and its rattle was barbed like the tail of a scorpion. Elin stared at the image he had drawn and frowned.

It was no wonder he had nightmares.

Nonna had meant well though, and Elin had enjoyed her stories more than the fairytales the teacher told at kindergarten. Nonna's stories really meant something and Elin had always known they would be important one day.

Elin remembered one specific tale that had stayed with him

all of his life.

'There was a little boy,' Nonna had said. 'Who left his home and the land and his people. When he grew into a man he didn't know where he had come from. He forgot all about the way he should live his life. He became a white man, though his soul was *Wa She Shu.*'

'What happened to him, Nonna?' Elin had asked.

'Why, his spirit shrivelled. He drank liquor to kill the pain he always felt and he died in poverty in a slum in the dead heart of a city.'

'That is a horrible story!' Elin's mother had said. 'Please don't tell my son such things, Mother.'

'Alyeshya, Little Bird needs to understand the importance of being *Wa She Shu.* I only tell him this for his own good.'

'His name is Peter ...' Elin's mother had corrected.

'His white man's name is "Peter", but his soul is named "Little Bird",' Nonna had said, 'and one day he will fly back to his people. You mark my words, daughter, whether you or that white soldier you married like it or not.'

Elin's mother had clicked her tongue in annoyance but he knew that deep down she had brought him to Nonna so he could learn about his heritage. His father was a soldier. He was a white man. He didn't want Elin to talk about his distant Washoe blood. They lived on an army base where the family quarters were cold and bland and not as exciting or as interesting as the reservation. Alyeshya tried to fit in, smiled and dressed nicely like all of the white wives and wore her hair the way they did. Sometimes, when he was half asleep, Elin's imagination played tricks on him and he saw her in the garb of a squaw, but she had never worn these clothes, at least not during his life time. No matter how hard she tried to mimic the white man's ways, at these half conscious moments, Elin could see the native in her shining through. Nonna saw it too, and so she never blamed her for leaving and marrying a white man because she saw that Little Bird was a blessing nonetheless.

'He's destined for great things,' Nonna would say. 'You must give me time to prepare him for the future.'

Alyeshya would nod but say nothing as though she were merely appeasing the woman.

When Alyeshya died a few months after Elin's ninth birthday, Nonna left the reservation for the first time in her life.

Elin and his family had been living on a base in Los Angeles. By then, Elin had not seen Nonna for a few years, though he frequently received letters, presents and cards. Often, when his father was out, his mother had allowed Elin to speak to the old woman on the phone.

That all changed the day Elin came home from school to find his mother lying on the kitchen floor. Alyeshya had been in pain for days, but she didn't trust the white doctors so told no one she was feeling ill. She had died while Elin was at school and there was no one there to call for help. Later he learnt that his mother had been expecting another baby. What the doctors didn't know was that it was ectopic. Elin was told afterwards that something inside her had ruptured as the baby grew. She had died of massive internal bleeding.

Then Nonna had arrived.

'Let me take my baby's body home,' Nonna begged. 'She needs to be buried on Washoe land.'

'The Washoe's don't own that land, Nonna,' Elin's father said. 'You live on a reservation. Why don't you move to a normal place like everyone else?'

'The *Wa She Shu* need to live on the land,' Nonna had tried to explain. 'We have to return to it when we leave this life.'

Nonna had known that Elijah Elin was a bigot, but she hadn't realised the extent of it until she came to the base. Although he allowed her to stay in the house with him and the boy for a few days, Elijah banned her from letting anyone know that she was Alyeshya's mother while she was there.

'My daughter needs a burial fitting her heritage,' Nonna said.

'She's gonna be buried in the local parish church,' Elijah insisted. 'When Ally married me she converted to my faith. We've gone to church every Sunday since we married.'

Elin knew that his father wasn't telling the truth but he said nothing. Alyeshya had rarely entered the church. Nonna had known it was a lie too. As the funeral day approached, and people began to call to pay their respects, Nonna made sure that all of them knew she was Alyeshya's mother and Little Bird's grandmother.

'I want you to leave,' Elijah said eventually. 'You've ruined everything for me here. Now everyone knows my son is a half-breed and I married an Indian.'

'I know you loved Alyeshya. Let me take Peter and let me do right by my daughter.'

'No. He's my son.'

'By your own admission you are ashamed of the other half of his blood. What kind of father are you going to be to him now?'

Elijah was a mess. He had loved Alyeshya, and he wasn't coping very well with her sudden death. He didn't know what he was going to do with a nine year old boy now that his wife was gone. Nonna put forward such a good argument that eventually Elijah gave in. He let her take Alyeshya's body back to Nevada for burial and Little Bird went with her. From then on Little Bird was brought up on the reservation. It was many years before he took up his white heritage again.

12
Rhuddlan's Rooms

Anthony scanned the rooms for traces of magic but could find no evidence of any. He sensed the revenant though, and the evidence of its feeding habits was found all over the hidden chambers. The four vampires walked deeper into the darkened corridors and found themselves in the large central room.

'I know this place,' Lilly remarked as she glanced around the chamber.

A faint smell of smoke still lingered in the cavern and Chez examined the torches noting they had been recently used.

'That doorway over there,' Lilly continued, 'leads to the north turret.'

'How do you know?' asked Anja.

'The first time I came here, I was mistaken for a gypsy dancer and I was brought into this room. All of the other minstrels and acrobats were here rehearsing for the show they would put on for the king.'

Lilly closed her eyes; she could almost imagine the music floating up to the castle banquet hall. In her mind's eye she saw again the group of dancing girls, their skirts swaying as they moved. A feeling of intense nostalgia swept over her. Especially as she recalled Harry and what she had thought was her first meeting with him. Harry was dead now and it still hurt to think of him lying alone in his castle tomb back in Stockholm.

'It almost feels like our home has been violated,' Lilly said.

'I understand that. But at least it seems as though you have gone undetected despite the arrival of the special forces and then the police tramping through this place,' Anthony said.

'I'm surprised they haven't sealed it all back up, actually,' Anja remarked.

They climbed back out of the hole under the bridge and then Lilly, Chez and Anja followed Anthony as he walked the ruins. They were no longer camouflaged as there seemed to be little need while walking around the grounds just as though they were tourists. Lilly had done this many times, blending in with the people who visited to admire and wonder at the history of the place.

A man with short-cropped hair and glasses was wheeling a bike beside him; a mother watched her two children run around the old well in the centre screaming at the top of their lungs pretending to fight with plastic swords; an old couple with matching anoraks sat on a thick brown blanket in the lee of one of the walls sipping tea from a thermos and eating a picnic. As the wind picked up, the man's newspaper whipped up from beside him and blew across the grass, landing at Lilly's feet.

Lilly bent to pick it up while the man hurried towards her looking embarrassed. She held it out to him and then her eyes fell on the front cover story.

'What's that?' she said.

'Oh. A woman and a man were attacked in the house across the street from here,' he explained.

'May I?' Lilly asked politely.

The old man looked into her vibrant green eyes and found he was unable to refuse.

'P… please. Keep it,' he said. 'It's just the local free paper.'

'Thanks,' Lilly answered but she was already walking rapidly away with the other immortals.

'One other thing …' the man called after her. 'She works right here … the girl on the counter as you come in?'

Lilly paused and looked back at the man. The other three watched her, waiting to see what she would do. Anja looked around anxiously, she wasn't up for a killing spree that involved kids, but you never knew with Lilly. Anthony wasn't sure what to make of it either but he drew closer and looked over Lilly's shoulder at the newspaper.

'What does it say?' asked Chez.

Lilly looked up and exchanged a glance with Anthony. 'We have a lead,' she said.

They went back inside the lair. Lilly warmed blood for everyone while they gathered around the kitchen table. She then boiled a kettle and made coffee for herself while each of them read the article.

'I never knew there was a tunnel that led underneath the castle. Let alone that is was accessible from a house across the street,' Lilly said. 'I do remember a cave in on the underground rooms a few centuries after the original castle was built.'

'It's not something you'd automatically look for when building a lair under a castle,' Anja said.

Lilly nodded. 'Plus, I started the original building works years ago when the castle still had occupants. If there was an escape route or secret entrance at that time it was being kept pretty quiet for security reasons and I wasn't exactly on their list of people who would need to know. The residents didn't even know I existed.

'The girl from the shop is called Ffion. We need to go and talk to her,' Anthony pointed out. 'And her friend Geraint.'

'Let's go and talk to her. Right now,' Anja said, jumping out of her seat. 'I'm sick of all this hanging around. I want to find Gabi!'

Chez placed his hand on Anja's arm and she looked at him startled, 'Not yet. Let's wait until dark.'

Lilly quashed the feeling of foreboding that knotted her stomach. The coffee she swallowed only served to increase the sick feeling she was experiencing.

'There's no need,' she said.

'What do you mean?' asked Anja.

'You saw me with the girl earlier,' said Lilly, 'and I … well I thought she might be useful – you never know, do you – and so I made her mine.'

'Yours?' asked Anthony, unsure what Lilly meant.

'I put some of my will into her mind. So she is mine now. I can call her and she will come. She will do whatever I want,' said Lilly in an offhand manner.

'So get her here then,' said Chez. 'What are we waiting for.'

Lilly closed her eyes for a second, and then reopened them. 'She's coming,' she said.

Anja nodded, reaching for her mug of blood. 'Urgh. It's congealing.'

The other three vampires stared at her.

'What? I don't like it lumpy …'

Lilly began to laugh and Chez and Anthony soon joined in while Anja frowned. She didn't get why the moment was funny but found herself smiling as the tension expelled from the air with the laughter echoing up and around the lair while they waited for their visitor.

13
Little Bird's Visions

Private Elin was having the strangest visions. Sometimes, when he was taking his walk, he thought he saw Nonna strolling around the perimeter of the base. When he was looking straight ahead a flicker of movement would catch the corner of his eye. If he kept his eyes averted he could see the back of Nonna's healing robes blowing in the wind, like clothing on a washing line. When he turned his head though, he saw nothing more than the desert plants standing in place. Often he imagined that she was pacing alongside him; her walking stick held high as though to ward off evil and her white long hair falling in cascades over her frail shoulders.

In his sleep he dreamed of sand. He felt it running through the cracks and crevices of the concrete walls of the base. Elin often thought that if he had been a dream interpreter he would have said that this meant time was running too quickly, and that meant that he was wasting his life living and working in the white man's army. Elin didn't really believe that though. His mind was far too logical and for that he could thank his father's blood.

Even so, his Indian blood called out to him to listen.

'Nonna,' he said to the silent sands, 'if you're out there and you're trying to tell me something, I'm not a reader. My white blood doesn't understand such things.'

There was a warning in the dreams which Little Bird knew even when Pete Elin denied it. Being born of these two cultures meant that sometimes he felt pulled in two different directions and his joint heritage frequently indulged in a tug of war with his soul. His mind refused to believe what his heart knew to be the truth. The practical and the spiritual could not work side by side without conflict.

Now Elin turned over in his narrow bed. His mind wouldn't switch off from all he had seen that day. He tried to recall when the feeling of fear had intensified: possibly when Seventeen was brought in. There had been a change of atmosphere that day for sure because he remembered how the other remaining subjects all started acting up. It was nothing obvious, at least not to anyone else, but Elin had seen some strange things on the monitors.

Take Cameron for example. As the elevator carrying Seventeen reached minus 15 Cameron had a strange seizure. He threw himself all over the cell and began to bang his head on the wall. Then he spewed all of the blood he had consumed right back up and the medics had to knock him out for a few hours while they examined him. After that he was strapped back into the restraint chair while they cleaned up his cell. When he came round he was surprisingly lucid, but his eyes held that same animalistic cunning that lurked beneath the remnants of his sanity.

Then there was the young girl, Thirteen. Elin had deduced that this one had survived by living rough in the ghettos in Poland before she was found. She was always quiet, never appeared to be dangerous and there was even some interaction with the medical staff on occasion. She seemed to prefer one of the orderlies above the other and so he was mostly the one that handled her. Sedated for examination, Thirteen wasn't strapped down when the medics came in to check her vitals, take blood and do all of the things that Elin had seen them do many times before. But when the elevator descended, Thirteen snapped awake from her strong sedation and took a bite out of her friendly, neighbourhood orderly, leaving him with a disfiguring scar on his face.

The others had reacted in equally unusual ways. Nine, an old insane tramp by all appearances, started to eat his own fingers. Four, a fifty year old man, began to cry and moan and spoke for the first time since he had been brought in three years earlier. Elin could remember the sound from his cell coming over the monitor while all the other chaos was happening simultaneously in the other cells. He was saying 'Mama' over and over again.

All of this happened at precisely the same moment: when the elevator reached minus 15.

Despite the obvious flurry of activity, no one had even mentioned the incidents. Not even Doctor Collins, and she was the most observant one of all.

Elin's mind stumbled when he thought of Collins. She was an odd one. Sometimes when he was watching the monitors he thought he saw a glow around her. At first he thought there was a smudge on the monitor and so he had dutifully taken out the Windex and began to polish the screen. It soon became apparent that wherever Collins was, the blur followed. This was more obvious when she was examining the subjects or stood with other colleagues because they didn't have the same blur of light. Elin had pointed it out to Corporal Dealer once but she had stared long and hard at the monitor and had seen nothing. He never mentioned it again.

A shiver wracked Elin's body and he pulled the bed covers up to his chin. He had been worrying this through for hours but no conclusion was forthcoming. He couldn't sleep. His throat was dry so he pushed back the covers, stepped down onto the rug and walked over to the small fridge in the corner. He swigged juice from a carton, stretched and farted.

Elin took another swig before closing the fridge and cutting off its illumination. The base was always lit up and a yellow spotlight streamed down from above his window. All the rooms were fitted with thick drapes so, except for a slit of light that filtered through a small gap in his curtains where he had failed to close them completely, the room was in total darkness. The light fell on his bureau and across the eyes of the photo of his mother.

The light blinked as if someone had walked in front of the window and blocked out the spot. Elin knew this was impossible; he was on the third floor. He turned and looked directly at the gap. He thought he detected movement outside. He walked forward, hand reaching up as he pulled the drape open.

On the barren land below his window was a tribe of Indians.

Elin opened the curtain wider. The tribe remained. He blinked. The *Was She Shu* stared back at him like silent phantoms of his past.

'Nonna ...' he gasped, remembering the day they put her in the earth. The day he left the reservation and once again sought out his white father.

Nonna stepped forward and held up her arms. She drew the symbol of the snake inside the eye in the air and the power burned the oxygen until the sign glowed. Behind her the tribe backed away, bowing as though to a god. Elin didn't understand this at all but he watched Nonna as she danced around the flame hanging in the air. The mark burned into his eyes and into his mind like a cattle brand but still he looked on.

It burnt through his skin, into his muscles and veins and arteries. It sent agony through the synapses and neurons in his brain. His eyes were blinded by the light as it grew before him.

Elin fell backwards. He felt the fire burning through his blood and he rolled all over his room beating at the imagined flames, mouth open in a silent scream. His body slammed into the fridge; an open carton of milk tumbled out onto the floor and splashed up the sides of the bureau. He crashed into the bedside chair, knocking it over, and it fell with a loud thump.

'Hey? Elin man? You alright in there?'

Elin heard Parker in the distance as the pain subsided. He dragged himself up in the dark, a groan escaped his lips.

'Elin? Pete? You okay?'

He staggered to the door as he heard Parker try the handle.

'What the hell happened?' asked Parker noting the spilt cartons of juice and milk and the chair that was tipped over.

'Tripped and fell, man. No big deal,' Elin replied.

Parker looked Elin over. 'You don't look so good.'

'Hey. I'm fine. Nothing a good sleep won't cure. Sorry I

woke you, man.'

Parker was uncertain. 'You sure you're alright?'

Elin nodded. 'Just tripped and fell.'

Elin closed the door and stood for a moment with his back to it. Then he tentatively approached the window and looked outside. The base was quiet; everything was as it should be. The *Wa She Shu* were nowhere to be seen. Even so, the brand burned behind his eyes, as though he had looked at the sun or the filament of a bulb. When he closed his eyes he could still see the shape burning in colour.

Elin pulled the drapes closed and climbed back into bed. He lay with his eyes closed, examining the brand that his grandmother had given him. He was *Wa She Shu* and the white man's blood had been purged from his veins. Understanding came to him. He could see what it all meant. Especially what he had to do next.

14
Subject One

I sit in my room, with all of the home comforts they can fit in. I have decent food and wine, no more restrictive manacles, and a file of documents on the desk for me to read through. The file is thick, almost three inches of paper lie between its covers and inside is the information that will tell me precisely what Lucy has been involved in over the past few years.

I already know that she is a doctor here and seemingly in charge of the research side of the facility. But where 'here' is I am not completely clear. Lucy has told me we are in Nevada and although I know little about American geography I do know that Nevada is a vast area. This is the desert for certain. I hear the sand moving in the wind sometimes and the steady drip of dirt against the walls of the base. Sometimes at night I hear the tapping of something that feels like the souls of the dead against the concrete foundations. But I've always had an over-active imagination.

I open the file and begin to speed read the contents to take my mind off these morbid thoughts. At that moment Lucy enters my room and I look up.

'I thought you may need an interpreter for the medical jargon,' she says.

'It is full of words that mean nothing,' I say.

Lucy laughs. Her hair is tied back and yet a stray curl falls out over her cheek. She looks beautiful and vital. Full of recent blood. I can see the life of her meal pumping through the fine veins at her throat. This one died hard. It is almost as though the victim's soul is still in there and is fighting to get out.

'Medical phrases,' she says.

'Perhaps you need to summarise the content and then I will find the reading of it so much simpler.'

She explains her theories on the revenants. Their DNA, which I learn is similar, though different, to ours. This I understand because I have discussed our heritage many times with Lilly.

'I believe they are very different from you,' Lucy explains. 'They lack intelligence, and their strength is limited, even though their flesh is superior to humans.'

'I wish to talk to one of them,' I say.

'Why?' Lucy asks, and I can see the curiosity in her eyes. She genuinely doesn't know what I wish to learn from such an exchange.

'I want to learn how they were born and who sired them.'

Lucy blinks. It is obvious that such a question has never occurred to her. She sees them as a plague, an accident of nature, an unsuccessful abortion.

'I have to think about that. I don't know that it matters how they came into being. Anyway, it is unlikely that they will tell you anything. I've been studying them for years and have learnt nothing of value from anything they've said.'

'That is because you are the enemy,' I say. 'You are their captor.'

She frowns but doesn't disagree. She turns and leaves the room silently and I hear the click as the cell door closes and locks.

I am quiet as I think of her words. It is obvious to me that it is crucial we learn how these creatures came to exist. I wonder why it has never occurred to her that they may be our own bastard offspring or a mutation of our gene that could in some way threaten our very future. Perhaps she has considered all of these things but really doesn't care.

If Lucy were given a divine role I believe she would be Chaos. And yet, here at the base, she is the picture of stability and logic. Her work is clearly respected and valued. Yet I know she would throw all of this up in the air at a whim.

I glance down at the file. There are pages of jargon that she not only understands, but also writes with clarity. I am impressed with her knowledge yet I do not trust anything she says or does.

Her motives are always selfish.

The door opens once more and I do not need to turn to know that Preacher has entered. His heart is racing with fear and lust so I turn and smile at him in my most sensual and inviting way.

'You wish to meet one of the revenants?' he asks.

'Yes. Has Doctor Collins decided that I can?'

Preacher smiles and I glance up at the camera above his head. It looks like a tiny black spot in the wall and I admit it took me some time to find it, even though I knew there was surveillance. Preacher, I believe, has been watching Lucy and I converse.

'I can arrange it. There is one that they rarely bother with now and I'd be curious to see her reaction to you.'

'Who is she?' I ask.

'We don't know. By appearance a woman of maybe thirty. There is no record in Doctor Collins' files of her ever having spoken to anyone.'

'You have a name for these creatures though. A number. As you do for me.'

'You are far from being a number, Gabriele,' Preacher said. 'You are way too real to be a mere subject.'

I smile at his attempt at flattery. The more time he spends with me, the less afraid he becomes. He is as naive and foolish as any mortal in lust. Obviously I have done all I can to continue to appear benign. It is the only way to lull them into their own false security.

'She is number One. The organisation I work for has held her for centuries,' he tells me.

'Good. Then the first discovery may tell me the most. Where is she?'

I glance down at the table. I have seen no mention of One in the file. There were other subjects, other numbers, but not One.

Preacher is silent as he follows my gaze.

'She isn't mentioned here. Nor are there any photographs of her,' I point out.

'No. Though she is kept on this facility. Come.'

I follow Preacher out of the room. Parker is wary and stays back from us both, but still he follows, sedative gun at the ready.

He is still my slave, though he doesn't know it yet. His own thoughts are intermingled with my suggestions in such a way that he does not realise I am in there with him.

'Where are we going?' I ask as we head towards the lift.

'Another area. It's restricted and off limits to most people on this base.'

We walk down the corridor that has now become so familiar to me. This square building is ugly and featureless. It lacks character and history and yet, as we move down through a set of doors beyond the elevator that takes us into other areas of the base, the now familiar tightness takes hold of my chest. For a moment I feel I cannot breathe. The soldier stares at me as I pause, holding onto the wall.

'What is it?' Preacher asks. His expression is more curious than concerned.

'Nothing,' I say and I begin to walk again, pushing away that claustrophobic feeling even though it intensifies. 'Tell me more about One. Where did they find her?'

'She was found in Europe. A few hundred years ago,' Preacher explained. 'She's most unusual.'

'In what way?' I ask.

'You'll see.'

Parker walks behind us and I turn and glance at him over my shoulder. He half smiles. He likes me more than he likes Preacher and he is just waiting for an opportunity to see the albinoid suffer. I can hear his thoughts. He is hoping I will attack Preacher and then he thinks he will be the hero who brings me down. Stupid. *Stupid mortal. You don't know this but you are mine. You'll behave how I tell you.* And when the time comes, Parker will be doing my dirty work and he won't even know he is doing it.

I catch Preacher glancing at me. He is frowning. Not for the first time I wonder about him. He is a strange character and I have yet to learn all I wish to know about him.

Preacher uses his pass card to take us through yet another set of doors and I find myself in a dimly lit passageway. This area looks like it has been left unused for many years. It is dirty and slightly cold and damp in the way that unoccupied rooms become when no one goes in there to air them out.

'Musty here,' I point out.

Preacher nods.

'Oh but the creature is fed regularly,' he says. 'Even though sometimes these days she doesn't eat our offerings.'

I find myself outside a cell.

'Here?' I ask.

Preacher nods.

I press my hand against the door, then my ear. It is silent inside. Silent and empty. I wonder if this is some kind of trap and I have been lured here for some other reason.

Preacher reaches out to the shutter that covers the small grille in the door. I can smell his blood; his wrist brushes my cheek as he pulls the shutter back. He smells of death and sex. I step away.

The grille is open and I look inside at the bundle chained to the bunk in much the same way I was when I arrived.

The figure stirs. An odour of faeces and urine wafts out of the cell. Just as the others do, she stinks of decay. Though perhaps the smell is even worse with age or neglect. I glance around the cell, note the bareness, the half-eaten tray of gore that lies on the ground before her.

She moves again, turning to look with feral and bloodshot eyes at the grille. I see a bare arm, wasted flesh that hangs on ancient bones. She is a vile, deformed creature that bears little resemblance to humanity. I study the sagging cheeks, the thin wasted lips that draw back in a hungry grimace as she watches us. Her teeth are yellow and pointed and her mouth opens like a shark's serrated jaw ready to strike.

'Oh my God!' I fall back.

'What?' Preacher says.

I stumble away, back down the corridor and I try to push away the images that burst into my head. *I know her!*

'What is it?' Preacher asks, but his voice is distant and it is hard to hear him over the roar that emits from the cell.

'Helaine ...' I whisper. Fortunately Preacher doesn't understand that this is Subject One's real name.

15
What Ffion Knows

Ffion woke to find herself in what appeared to be an expensively furnished lounge. She felt confused and couldn't remember how she had arrived there or where she was. On one wall was a flat screen television, on another was a painting of a beautiful warrior woman with long blonde hair, holding aloft a magnificent Viking sword. Beneath that was a plush velvet sofa with red and black scatter cushions. It was the type of sofa her mother had always wanted but could never afford. To her right was a small desk with a red-cased laptop open, facing away from her. None of her surroundings made sense or were familiar.

Ffion tried to shake away the confusion, thinking back to being in the shop at the castle but only remembered using the computer to order some stock, and nothing more. She felt dizzy, scared. Her mind flashed to the man who had captured them. Fear flooded back into her veins and her heart pounded in her chest.

'You have nothing to fear here,' said a quiet voice beside her.

Ffion turned her head and found the woman in the painting sitting beside her. She was even more stunning in person. She wasn't dressed as a warrior nor was there a sword in her hand. She just looked like an ordinary girl, one who was similar in age to Ffion, and she was wearing snug blue jeans and a plain black tee-shirt. As she met her eyes though, Ffion realised that the woman was far from ordinary. There was age and wisdom in her gaze. It reminded Ffion of her old gypsy grandmother who used to sell tarot readings when Rhyl was a more affluent seaside resort. Ffion knew then that she was dreaming.

'I'm Lilly.'

Ffion stared at the sensual lips as they moved. The voice was rich and beautiful in a musical way. It was hypnotic. Ffion knew that she would do anything for Lilly. She wanted to.

'I need your help,' said Lilly.

'My help?' Ffion murmured. Her tongue felt swollen, her words muffled to her own ears. It was as though she had taken some kind of drug that dulled all of her senses. She closed her eyes and tried to drift back into the dream she thought she was having. Her heart filled with immeasurable joy.

'You have to remember some details for me. I need you to help me find someone.'

Ffion sank back into the sofa and listened to the beautiful sing-song voice whisper questions to her.

'Tell me about what happened to you. Tell me about the tunnel under the castle.'

Ffion shook her head. *Not that! I don't want to think about that!* It was all too horrible. She felt the gentle touch of satin flesh brush her wrist, and warmth flooded her body. The terror drifted away into the distance and she began to relate the story as though reading from a book. She felt nothing but a rolling sea of calm and happiness. Ffion wondered if Lilly was an angel sent to purge her of the guilt and fear the assault had left her with.

'What did this man look like?' Lilly asked as Ffion described their meeting.

'Brown hair, modern cut. The palest blue eyes I've ever seen. He told me his name was Darren.'

'Think Ffion. Imagine you are a zoom lens camera. What do you see up close?'

Ffion's mind obeyed the command. She felt the touch of Lilly's hand on hers. She felt as though she were standing beside her in those moments, but she knew that Lilly hadn't been there when she first saw Darren, or at the pub and certainly not in Geraint's basement. But yet, she could feel her presence and so she walked with her through the scene. Ffion felt like a distant observer in her own past. She pulled up the image of Darren in the shop as he casually browsed the books and jewellery.

'Did he wear jewellery?' Lilly asked.

Ffion thought he hadn't been wearing any but her virtual eyes fell on the neckline of the V-neck sweater. Blue shirt peeking out. His neck interested her. He was tanned, too tanned really, and it made the lines in his face look a little more obvious: just as though he was wearing make-up or something. Ffion's eyes shifted around the shirt collar. It's fake tan! I thought he looked a little orange! Then her eyes noted the gold chain. Yes. He had been wearing something.

'Show me the necklace,' Lilly whispered.

Ffion's mind skipped onwards. At the bar, as she had a glass of wine with Darren. He had paid. He seemed genuine, nice, generous. She had liked him a lot. As they had talked she remembered that he had played with the links in a very feminine way.

'I thought he might be gay,' she murmured. 'But he was so flirty …'

It was a belcher chain. She remembered that because she had one like it herself only longer and hers was silver. Darren's was white gold. Expensive. The chain belied the cheap clothing.

'Never mind the clothing for now,' Lilly said. 'Describe the chain.'

Ffion's mind moved in. She tried to look at the chain but became distracted by the hand that held it. He had long fingers. They were sensual, sexy hands. Darren turned his hand and that was when Ffion noticed the scar on his wrist. It was white and puckered as though it hadn't been treated properly. The fake tan sat on his skin like a dirty stain but didn't really cover the mark.

'Interesting. You are very observant Ffion.'

Ffion smiled at the compliment and then she saw Darren tugging at an ornament on the chain. She had thought it could be a Saint Christopher medal, but no. The flat disc had an image but it didn't make any sense to her at the time and so she had forgotten about it.

'Look at it now,' Lilly said.

She focused on the chain, saw Darren drop his fingers away and the charm, or symbol, that hung from there showed an old fashioned lamp. Like something out of the bible. There were grooves around the top of the lamp that indicated rays of light coming from the centre.

'Illuminati,' Lilly murmured. 'Not surprising really. But what else do you see Ffion?'

Ffion scrutinised Darren's face again. He was handsome, with high cheek bones that reminded her of the actor Richard Chamberlin. Beautiful he was. There was no stubble on his smooth cheeks either. Darren smelt so good. She didn't recognise the aftershave but it was an expensive brand.

'Forget that,' Lilly snapped. 'I don't care how much you fancied him ... details are what I'm after. I know you can sense he's different, Ffion. What is it you see?'

Ffion frowned. She wasn't sure what Lilly meant but she didn't like to offend her somehow. The angel needed to know something, Ffion had to show her.

Her eyes roved over Darren in a more clinical way now. They noted moles, and the pierced ear that didn't have an earring in any more. But there was something not quite right about the hair ...

Zoom in.

Ffion drew closer. She scrutinised the man's hair-line, the parting. 'Oh my God. It's a wig. Why didn't I notice that?'

'You did. You just didn't realise it at the time,' Lilly said.

'His own hair colour. His real hair ...'

Ffion saw it then. She was in the basement tied up. Geraint had just broken through the iron gate and he and Darren were walking into the tunnel. Geraint had gone on ahead. Darren was holding some kind of gun, and he glanced back at Ffion. It was then that she noticed how the wig had slipped during the tussle. Around his ear, a strand of pure white hair had worked its way free.

'Thank you,' Lilly said.

Ffion opened her eyes and looked at Lilly. The woman was smiling and this made Ffion smile too.

'Now my dear,' said Lilly. 'Just one more thing ...'

As Ffion slipped back into a deep hypnotic trance, Lilly wiped her mind of all memory of the conversation and the interior of the lair. She had seen all that the girl had seen. She now knew Darren's face and of his strange affliction. He was an albino and he had made a massive effort to disguise that fact. That detail alone would make it somewhat easier to find him. And ... he was Illuminati.

Chez lifted Ffion and took her out of the room and back up the stairs to the castle grounds.

'What will happen to her?' Anthony asked.

'She'll feel better when she wakes. I took away the anxiety she had been experiencing,' Lilly said.

'But why?' asked Anthony.

'She was suffering. Post traumatic stress syndrome is the clinical term for it.'

'I know,' Anthony said. 'But why did you help her?'

'Because it was the human thing to do.'

Anthony said nothing but he watched as Lilly plumped up the cushions on the sofa, behaving like she was human. He found it strange and comforting that she retained so much of her former compassion. After all the years she had been immortal, this was a revelation. Anthony knew that he wanted to keep this feeling within him also. How hard had it been for Lilly to keep so much of her soul intact? He had seen her kill. At such moments he would never make the mistake of believing she was anything but supernatural. Yet he loved both her violence and her empathy.

'Are we any closer to finding Gabi?' Anja asked as she came into the room.

She was holding two mugs of warmed blood. She passed one to Anthony and offered the second to Lilly. Lilly shook her head.

'You must,' said Anja. 'You haven't eaten in days.'

Lilly took the mug to please Anja and sat down on the sofa,

'Okay. Just to stop you worrying. But I don't need this as much these days.'

Anja sat down beside her and waited while Lilly explained what she had learnt.

'Albino?' Anja said thoughtfully. 'I remember something about an albino. Actually Konstantin called him something else … it was like albino but …'

'Albinoid?' Anthony said.

'Yes,' Anja nodded. 'That was it. I said "what's the difference?" and Konstantin got really annoyed with me. He said, "It makes a difference to Preacher".'

'Preacher?'

'Yes that was his name I think. Konstantin said he was a "fixer". I think that meant he did some of his dirty work for him.'

Lilly nodded thoughtfully. 'Anthony, can your contacts trace this Preacher? If I see a picture of him I'll know if it's the same guy. I got a pretty good image of him from Ffion's mind.'

Anthony stood and went over to the desk and the laptop. 'I'll get on it right away.'

'I miss Gabi so much,' Anja said.

'Me too. But we're going to find him.'

They sat in silence. All they could hear was the tapping of Anthony's rapid fingers as he typed his email.

'Done,' he said a few minutes later. 'It's a waiting game now. Declan and John will search the archive and get back to me as soon as they can.'

'Let's hope it's soon. I'm worried that time might be running out for Gabi,' said Lilly.

16
Helaine

Paris 1739

Helaine Pélissier's pale blue gaze met mine across the crowded opera house and I knew a dangerous dalliance was about to begin.

She was performing on stage a beautiful aria from a new opera, *Dardanus*, by Jean-Philippe Rameau. The opera itself was rather silly; full of plot inconsistencies and poor performances. There was even the most bizarre scene with a sea monster that turned out to be funny rather than frightening as I suspected the director had planned. Helaine was singing the lead soprano, playing Iphise, daughter of Teucer, and she was the most outstanding talent on display the entire evening.

Louis XV, King of France, had invited me to join him in his private box. I had been in the King's company for a several months by then. When Louis suggested we take the box at the *Académie de Musique* I was more than willing to join him. I had heard tell of Helaine Pélissier. Her beauty and her voice were renowned and I had seen a painting of her hanging in the King's private collection. It showed her naked, with only a piece of satin draped around her waist. I expected to see this curvaceous, wanton whore and perhaps thought that Louis would wish to spend time with her after the performance, but Helaine was nothing like her painting. The artist had exaggerated both her curves and the appearance of sexuality which had been somewhat predatory on the face of the painting. Helaine was in fact a fragile and sweet-faced beauty of no more than five feet tall, with a figure as slender as a boy's. I was completely enamoured with her from the moment she stepped out onto the stage.

Helaine was no virgin, as the painting in the King's gallery attested – she had been one of his many conquests – but for once this fact did not overly concern me. She was every bit as wonderful on stage as she was rumoured to be and I fell in love with her talent as well as with her appearance. I knew I had to make her acquaintance even though she wasn't my usual type.

After the performance the King and his entourage, myself included, went backstage to Helaine's dressing room where the lady greeted us. She was absolutely stunning and not at all embarrassed to be in her undergarments; white pantaloons, chemise and corset. She had removed the powdered wig she wore on stage and I found that the lady was a red-head. Her wild hair was tumbling over her perfect shoulders and I became besotted with the stray curl that caressed her half exposed small right breast.

'Count Caccini,' Louis said, 'may I present La Belle Helaine.'

Helaine offered her hand and I bent to skim my lips over her fingers.

'You are even more appealing close up,' said Helaine with the suggestion of a smile.

I was surprised by her words. I had thought it a mere coincidence that she looked up at me from the stage to sing her love song. I felt myself flush with pleasure and I pressed my lips firmly against the back of her hand, sending an involuntary slither of lust into her hand. Helaine shuddered and turned her open, lust filled eyes back up to me as I stepped back from her.

Louis observed this with interest and as he perceived our mutual infatuation he laughed and began patting me heartily on the back.

'Well this is splendid!' he told me in the carriage as we returned to the palace. 'I shall arrange everything for you. You shall have Helaine, my friend, with my blessing.'

As we arrived back at the palace, Louis went straight to his office and penned a letter to Helaine on my behalf.

'Please Sire. There is no need. I wish to woo the lady and sometimes the fun in that is the time it takes,' I said.

'Nonsense my boy. Time is wasting. Why wait for pleasure when it can be yours immediately.'

It was difficult to refuse Louis anything. He was the King after all, and to insult him could have meant I would have to leave Paris, and the beautiful Helaine would never be mine. So I let him send his letter singing my praises and I believe the King expressed his wish that Helaine receive me the next day.

By morning Louis had a reply.

'Your majesty, I would be most honoured to supper with the Count at his earliest convenience. I would be most pleased to see him after my performance this evening,' Louis read.

I didn't know what to say, but fortunately I didn't need to reply. The assignation was arranged and Louis had finalised all the details. He wanted me to have Helaine, and though it irritated me somewhat to be chasing the King's cast-offs it also thrilled me that I would be alone with this beautiful and vibrant creature. Of course she was nothing like my usual type – which was tall, slim and brunette, rather than this tiny girl's figure and the vibrant red hair that Helaine was famous for – but my desire for her rose every time I envisioned her in her dressing room, scantily clad.

'I feel such pleasure for you my friend,' Louis continued. 'Ah romance is a fine thing. I hope she gives you many days of fulfilment.'

Helaine was expecting me when I arrived in my carriage. It was almost midnight and I had waited all day with the strangest sensation of nervous energy and excitement. I felt like a boy again, anticipating his first sexual experience.

Helaine lived in a small, yet lavish house, but I barely had time to enjoy the furnishings as I was taken by a young servant girl directly into her boudoir.

It was an attractive, but cluttered room, and was decorated in all shades of lilac and purple, which appeared to be her favourite colour.

Helaine lay lasciviously on her bed. She was wearing a sheer nightdress of pale lilac, covered with an equally fragile robe. Her luscious red hair was long and wavy. It spread over her pillow like a coat of glossy fur.

'Count Caccini.' Helaine greeted me, holding out her hand.

I kissed her fingertips. Then, backing away, I took a seat on a chaise that stretched against the wall at the side of the bed.

'Mademoiselle. You are indeed looking incredibly beautiful this evening.'

Helaine smiled. She had unusually straight white teeth and a dimple on her chin that I found utterly charming.

'His majesty tells me you are a fine tenor,' Helaine said.

'His majesty is indeed gracious.'

'Perhaps we will sing together sometime.'

I smiled. 'I would enjoy that.'

Helaine got out of the bed, pulling her robe together and went to a small table, where she poured wine into two glasses from a crystal decanter.

'Maybe this will relax you,' she said.

'I'm perfectly relaxed, Mademoiselle Helaine,' I said taking the wine. 'But thank you. The wine is welcome.'

Helaine frowned. She was confused by the fact that I hadn't immediately climbed into bed with her.

'His majesty said you … wished to get to know me.'

'I do. I want to know everything about you.'

'I am hungry,' she said.

'Well I had come to take you to supper,' I smiled. 'So whenever you are ready.'

Helaine was perplexed. She put down her glass and went behind her dressing screen. When she came back she had slipped on a lovely deep purple satin dress that flared out over her hips. Her waist was tiny as were her perfect breasts. I could tell she wasn't wearing a corset underneath the clothing and I felt a huge surge of lust for her.

'You look beautiful,' I said.

We ate in a small restaurant that fed the theatre goers and performers in the district. It was a public place, but I asked for an alcove and we were rewarded with a small room to ourselves.

'Champagne,' I ordered.

Helaine raised her eyebrows at this. She was confused by it, expecting that the King's friend would merely use her a few times and then get bored, but I did not want to treat her like a whore. I had meant it when I said I want to know her. Of course Helaine was surprised that I sat and talked with her all night and that I made no move to seduce her. When I took her home that evening, I left her at the door, kissing her hand chastely.

A week later I sent Helaine flowers, cheeses and wine with an invitation to meet again. I offered a picnic in the park. I was trying to make certain that she knew I had no intention of pressing my advantage as the King's friend. It was early December but the weather was uncommonly mild and I felt a stroll would be nice.

I arrived in my carriage just before lunchtime. Helaine's servant girl opened the door and led me inside, but instead of taking me upstairs to the boudoir she took me into the drawing room. I found Helaine dressed demurely and appropriately for the outdoors. I was pleased. She had realised my intentions and read them well. She was the perfect mistress. You see, while I was studying her, she had been studying me. Helaine had soon realised that I was not a man of ordinary tastes.

17
Guilt

Lilly felt helpless and she didn't enjoy the feeling. The guilt was the worst though. She believed she was responsible for Gabi's disappearance. *My fault for alienating him.* She regretted the distance she had placed between them. It had been childish to run off with Chez every chance she got, just because she felt uncomfortable around Anja and Gabi. She had forced them together, after rejecting him more and more for Chez, and yet she had felt jealous when she saw displays of affection between them. It was insane. She should have been happy for him. Anja adored Gabi and followed him everywhere. She made a great companion, a wonderful lover, and when it came down to it, she was more his type.

Lilly had always known that since her travels in time, her personality had overshadowed Gabi's. He couldn't compete with her strength and knowledge and he hated it that she was now technically older than him. Even so, she had tried to maintain the equilibrium within her family. Anja's arrival had given her a way out though and she had been happy to pass Gabi onto the new vampire believing that it resolved the awkwardness of their previous *ménage a trios.*

It was obvious to Lilly that when Gabi and Anja were together, Gabi became the mentor that he had always wanted to be. Anja was more what he needed, yet Lilly had found it so hard to accept. She loved Chez. Wanted to be with him more than anything else, and had felt such relief when the new boundaries were set. She was no longer tearing herself between the two men. Even so, it didn't stop the adjustment from being difficult to make and maintain.

Chez came out of the *en suite* bathroom and removed his robe. He lay across the bed and watched as Lilly brushed her hair vigorously. In the past few months she had let it grow even longer and it was now past her bottom. Lilly knew Chez loved her hair so she slowed down the brushing and pushed aside the guilty thoughts that skittered around her head. She didn't want him to know how hard it was for her. How she was missing Gabi just as much as Anja was.

She turned the light off and climbed into bed and Chez slid over to her side, spooning her as he always did. He made no attempt to take the cuddle in any direction other than comfort.

'It's okay if you miss him,' he said. 'I miss him too.'

'Really?' She felt him nod. 'We seem to be waiting around so much for the Templars to provide information. And yet I almost feel that there is something I could do.'

'What?' said Chez. 'We are doing everything we can. The Templars are pooling their research. Sometimes these things take time.'

Lilly pulled away and sat up in the dark. 'There is something I *could* do of course. I could go back in time. Open a portal at the moment that this guy took Gabi. I could kill his abductors.'

'Yes. You could. But you've spent the last few months telling me how we shouldn't use that power again.'

'I know Chez. But this is an emergency.' Lilly sighed. 'I've tried to resist it, but I'm concerned we're running out of time.'

Chez threw back the cover and reached for the lamp beside the bed. 'Come on then. What are we waiting for?'

'I never told you this. But before we left the Templars. After we had killed Caradien, Anthony and I had a long talk about the future. He said I shouldn't rely on the portals. That I shouldn't use time as a reset button. I knew what he really meant of course. He was warning me not to play God. That it could be dangerous and may have a detrimental impact on our past, present and future.'

'I can see why he thought that. The Templars are afraid of you. You have the power to do so much harm ... if you wanted to, that is.'

'I'm always torn between using the power and not using it. I try to pretend that I'm a normal woman. But the truth is I'm fooling myself and no one else. I'm a monster and I could just go off the rails at anytime. That's the really scary part and … the power is seductive. It excites me to use it.'

'I know, but you've controlled it before and you will again. You're strong Lilly. Besides, I'll always be there to help keep you grounded.'

'You'll do this with me?'

Chez smiled. 'Lilly I will do anything with you and for you. You know that don't you?'

'But what about …?'

'What? The power? The way you use me as a channel sometimes?'

'Yes.'

Chez shrugged. 'It doesn't hurt and maybe that's partly why you can wield so much with no ill effects.'

Lilly was thoughtful. 'I love you, Chez. You do keep me grounded. Come on. Let's do this.'

They dressed in the Kevlar armour, then Lilly opened her wardrobe and removed her sword. It was a beautiful short sword that had been made especially for her some centuries ago in Paris, and it held a unique piece of amber crystal as the centre in the round pommel. The Templars of old had given her the weapon to replace one that had been broken but also to pass onto her the magic amber stone. The amber gave anyone who looked through it the ability to recognise carriers of the vampire gene. But *now we have DNA testing for that,* Lilly thought as she placed the sword in the scabbard on the back of her armour. It fit perfectly.

The moon was bright and full above the castle as Lilly and Chez made their way up to the surface and into the moat. The air was vibrating with magic. Lilly could feel the energy: the criss-cross of ley lines beneath the castle's surface were glowing as she examined the ground.

'The portal point will be the time that Gabi and Anja arrived back in the lair. Let's get to him before that bastard albinoid does.'

'Okay. What then?' Chez asked.

'Then I'm going to kill that son of a bitch.'

Lilly and Chez stood back to back as Lilly focused on the ley line energy. She raised it up around them, creating a magic circle in a way that Chez hadn't seen before. It seemed to go up so easily that both of them were uncertain how strong it was. Lilly tested it. Her hand reached out and touched the barrier until she could feel the energy running back into her hand and up through her arm.

'It's perfect,' she said and Chez heard the surprise in her voice.

You don't realise how powerful you are, Chez thought but he didn't project this observation to Lilly.

Lilly raised the energy higher. Chez heard the power source zing like static electricity and all sound outside of the circle receded.

Lilly lifted her arms and Chez turned, wrapping his arms around her again, in a reflex. He knew she needed to have her hands free and yet she also needed to touch him and so he made the contact for her.

She pulled on time and both she and Chez saw it bend before them. Portals cramped the circle, popped up around them and Lilly dismissed a dozen of them immediately. She forced her mind to think of the right date, the exact time and place but the portal refused to open and be found.

A portal to the day after the event was the closest she could find. There was nothing immediately before, not even the day prior to Gabi's disappearance. Eventually she dropped the circle, choosing instead to walk the grounds, feeling her way around the channels of magic and ley energy.

'What's wrong?' asked Chez eventually.

'Something is blocking me. I can get to any time but the one I want.'

'Why?'

'Because it doesn't seem to exist,' Lilly signed. 'And neither does any other point around that day. It's as though the entire week has been erased from time.'

'That's not possible,' Chez said.

'What are you doing out here?' Father Anthony called.

Lilly and Chez turned to find the priest hurrying up to them. He was still wearing his pyjamas and he had a thin checked robe over them.

'What is it?' Lilly asked.

'Father Declan just phoned. They think they know who this guy is. They have someone called Darren Preacher, who fits the description of our albinoid perfectly. He's emailing over photos and sightings now.'

'Good,' said Lilly. 'One door closes and another one opens.'

As the file downloaded onto her laptop Lilly told Anthony about their attempt to open a portal.

'Are you sure? That sounds impossible,' Anthony said.

'I'm certain. It was as though there was a gap in time.'

Anthony shook his head. 'I don't understand what can do that. No magic can remove or alter spaces in time. If those days didn't occur, then clearly Gabi would still be here.'

'The file is here,' said Lilly moving her mouse until the cursor was level with the file. She double clicked and a picture of Darren Preacher came up on the screen. Lilly stared at him and rage filled her heart, pumping blood into her face.

'He's the guy that Ffion saw. Even with a fake tan and wig I would recognise him anywhere,' she said. 'He has Gabi. I know it.'

'Where was the last sighting?' asked Chez.

'Las Vegas,' Anthony said. 'He flew in a few days ago.'

'That doesn't tell us much,' Lilly said. 'So, what … he likes to gamble?'

Anthony shrugged. 'His movements have been pretty erratic up until then. He's based in New York, then flew to Manchester. Fits in with the timescale. Customs has no record of him leaving the UK though.'

'So he left by means that weren't ordinary?'

Anthony nodded, 'Definitely. Forty eight hours after Gabi disappeared, Preacher briefly turned up at his offices in New York. According to our source in his work-force, he received an email that sent him into a rage. He sacked his secretary and then got the next plane out to Vegas.'

'That doesn't prove he has Gabi though,' Chez said.

'He would'd have needed help to get Gabi out of the country and through border control. Now what services are able to come and go out of the country unchecked?'

'Military?' Chez asked.

'Yes,' Anthony said. 'That's the most likely scenario.'

'It fits into the eye-witness reports we've heard as well. A military presence in the grounds and the helicopters,' Lilly said.

'Lilly …' said Anja coming into the lounge. They had left her sleeping because she had barely rested since Gabi's disappearance. 'I had a terrible dream.'

Lilly turned to Anja and the young girl ran into her arms.

'I dreamed that an army of revenants pulled Gabi's body down into the ground. All around him was sand. It was suffocating and choking him. We have to find him soon Lilly. I think he's in terrible danger.'

18
Seduction

Paris 1740

The seduction of Helaine was simple. I wanted her to pretend to be coy: she complied. She was the perfect whore that way. My plan was that eventually I would enjoy her charms. I would make love to her and I would feed from her. After which I would take my token lock of hair and dispose of her dead body. Then I would have to get out of Paris as quickly as possible. This was the pattern I lived my life by after all.

That was the plan, like I said, but days and weeks of the game became months. I grew to love Helaine in such a way that I pushed my sexual desire back into the darkest recesses of my lustful mind. I liked her. I didn't want to just fuck and feed. I wanted to savour every moment of her passionate life, her talent and her youth. Time was not on my side though and youth is something too quickly spent. Helaine would grow old and die eventually and I found myself wondering what that would feel like. Could I watch her life drip away never having satisfied my sexual attraction to her? I believed that I could; for to sleep with her meant to destroy her. So as the winter months stretched into spring, and with summer rapidly approaching, I decided I would never hurt Helaine. The only issue would come if she were unsatisfied with our arrangement.

I treated Helaine as any man in my position might treat his mistress. I provided her with jewels, clothing, food, and money. She wanted for nothing. In return I enjoyed her company. We ate out together, took walks in the park and occasionally went riding. In return this meant that Helaine was mine and therefore off limits to all other men, otherwise she would lose those privileges. We had grown into such a comfortable state of companionship that I didn't realise that this would be so difficult for her. I knew she was a passionate woman but expected her to be happy to remain celibate if that was what I wanted. It was a little naive of me to assume, given the fact that she was a woman of experience, and as our relationship grew I didn't take into consideration Helaine's feelings for me. I accepted she loved me, but never considered that she may need me to show that love to her in a physical way.

'Let us eat here this evening,' Helaine said as we returned to her small house following a walk in the park. It had been a very warm day, and as the afternoon stretched into evening Helaine's house was far cooler than the streets outside.

'That would be nice,' I said. 'The restaurant would be a trial in this heat.'

'Do you mind if I change?' she asked, removing her gloves and hat and handing them to her servant.

'Not at all. I'll wait in the drawing room.'

I went into the room and sat by the open window. It was still light outside and the sun was high in the sky. In the distance, I could hear the happy chatter of revellers outside the tavern. I heard the servant girl clattering around in the kitchen below, preparing food for our meal. I hoped it would be something simple. A repast of cooked meats, cheeses, fruit and wine appealed to me more than the fancy garlic infused foods that the restaurants favoured.

Helaine came down wearing a thin robe and her favourite sheer nightdress. I was a little taken aback by this, because since the first day she had always dressed modestly around me. I assumed that the heat had made her tired of the heavy clothing. As she walked into the room her lovely legs were revealed almost all the way up to her thighs. She posed for me, twirled and giggled. I smiled and dutifully admired her.

'What do you think?' she asked.

'You look stunning.'

She moved in towards me but I used the distraction of pouring her a glass of champagne. Her fingers caressed me as she took it. I smiled at her and placed a quick kiss on her lips so that she wouldn't feel rejected. I was used to these moments of attempted seduction even though she had never been quite been this blatant.

'Dinner is ready,' she said. 'I had Alice take up a tray to my room. I thought we might relax there. It's lovely and cool with the balcony windows open.'

'Sounds idyllic,' I said, even though I feared where this was leading.

Carrying the champagne bottle I followed her upstairs. The room was as I had remembered it, only today it was still lit by natural light. True to her word the drapes were open and the balcony windows let in a breeze that had picked up throughout the afternoon. It was the coolest room in the house.

I went out onto the balcony. Helaine's house was on a hill just off the main stretch of Montmartre but I could see the evening revellers enjoying the mild weather as they drank outside of the taverns.

'You must be so warm in that coat,' Helaine said, coming up behind me.

She took my hand, led me back inside and stripped my red brocade coat away. Placing her hand on my chest Helaine pushed me down until I was sitting on the edge of the bed. She knelt before me and removed my stockings and shoes. From her kneeling position Helaine looked up at me. Her beautiful blue eyes were wide, and they held a query that I had seen there before but had found hard to interpret. She nodded as though she had completed an internal dialogue with herself and had come to a decision then she stood and loosened my white frock shirt and lifted it over my head.

All that remained was my breeches. I watched Helaine place my clothes neatly over the chaise before she turned back to me. Then she lay back on the bed and patted the mattress beside her.

I paused for a second, feeling awkward. I didn't want to

reject her, but still had no intention of slaking my lust for fear that my passion would kill her. I just wasn't ready to lose her. Even so, I hadn't fully decided that this scenario would be forever.

I was curious about my own willpower when it came to sex though and so I sat on the bed beside her. I knew I could control my lust for blood in any situation except that I had never tried to hold back my nature during sex. As it was I lay beside her, partially naked, letting the cool breeze waft over me I pondered the question of sex without blood. It seemed somewhat perverse to deny myself either satisfaction if the possibility was that I could at least indulge in one.

We ate from the tray between us and drank more champagne and afterwards Helaine opened her robe and stretched out. The nightdress was sheer and I could see her small breasts pushing against the fabric, her nipples erect despite the heat.

'Gabi? Don't you want me?' she asked.

'Of course I do.'

'Then why aren't you touching me? Why aren't you making me yours after all this time?'

'I'm not like other men who would use and discard you Helaine. I love you. I want to care for you.'

'Then show me that you love me,' she said.

Her hand stroked my body and her warm skin sent ripples of pleasure into my blood. This close the smell of her blood tantalised my desire. When her hand found me I was already erect. I shivered. Love and lust and hunger all surged to the fore as she slid her body over me.

'Don't be afraid,' she murmured.

'I'm no virgin, Helaine.'

Helaine laughed and I realised then that she didn't believe me.

'I want you. I need you,' she said.

Her lips found mine and they were soft and smooth. She tasted better than any meal I had sampled in months. Her tongue slipped into my mouth and I enjoyed it even though my fangs were burning in my gums. I wanted to thrust them down and make the first incision in the meaty flesh that caressed my lips. I flipped her over onto her back, using this as an excuse to pull away from her mouth. Plus it gave me ultimate control.

I pulled her robe away throwing it across the chaise. Then I removed the nightdress. She looked so beautiful. Her body was naturally slender and boyish and her stomach so flat it was almost concave as she lay beneath me. Her skin was beautiful; soft and pale. I smoothed my hand down over her collar bone, pushing back the abundance of red hair. Then I kissed her shoulder, letting my tongue and mouth trail down her forearm. My eyes came level with her pale nipple. I turned my head, licked it and Helaine moaned in my arms. I found myself sucking, licking and cupping her gorgeous, small breast. It was delightful. She wriggled under me. *Why not?* I thought. *A small taste of her, through sex alone.* Could I do it and still resist the urge to feed?

'Please Gabi. Please.'

I wanted her so much my cock ached and I found myself unable to resist her charms. I stepped back and removed my breeches, dropping them casually to the floor. In the back of my mind I believed I could just make love to her without consequence. I just had to keep my blood libido under control. I lay over her. Helaine spread her legs and let me slide between them. Her confidence made me feel strange, but less afraid. Normally I was the only one in control at these moments. Normally a poor unsuspecting virgin, destined to bleed in more ways than one, would be tentatively opening up to me like a flower blossoming for the first and final time.

I buried my face in her breast, raised my body up and positioned myself between her legs. I could feel her dampness. Her anticipation was already rising and I wasn't using any of my lust power to corrupt her. She genuinely wanted me with no coercion. This was intensely exciting for me. I entered her in one hard stroke.

Helaine sighed and her pleasure flooded over me.

'Thank you,' she whispered.

I thrust into her harder, she shuddered and her legs wrapped around me. I was aware of how small she was compared to my height and build. Helaine was tiny beneath me, but I didn't find her to be fragile. I raised myself up so that I could see her face as the pleasure coloured her cheeks. It made me more aroused to see her flushed with passion like this and so, as Helaine's orgasm flooded over me, I came inside her and my fangs burst forth from my gums.

Her eyes were closed as she recovered. Her neck was thrown back and exposed to tempt me into further fulfilment. I saw blood flowing through her pale skin. I pulled back quickly as though I were merely relieving her of my weight. Then lay down at her side as I focused all my strength on forcing my blood lust back.

'That was wonderful,' Helaine said.

Her face was relaxed and I marvelled at how relieved she looked. I realised that I had never seen a woman alive after I had taken her. I had always gone all the way and killed them at that moment when their passion was pumping their blood through their delicious veins. This was a new experience. A new pleasure that I realised I could enjoy.

Helaine opened her eyes and looked over at me. Rolling onto her side she threw her arm over my stomach and began to kiss my bare chest. I was damp with perspiration and not from the sexual exertion but the sheer effort it had taken to stop myself from ripping her throat out.

'Did I hurt you?' I asked.

Helaine laughed. 'After all of these months of no contact Gabi, I think you should know your passion was incredibly exciting even though it was a little … rough.'

'I'm sorry. I didn't mean to.'

Helaine silenced me as her talented mouth found my nipple. Her tongue rolled over and around it and I felt myself harden again as her hand reached down and stroked me.

'No … I need to … I need a moment,' I gasped pulling away from her.

I slipped from the bed and poured us more wine. Helaine

lay on her side and I felt her eyes admiring me.

'I didn't know you would be ...'

'What?' I asked.

'So talented,' she laughed gazing at my cock.

I wanted her again. I ached for her, but I just didn't trust the other urge to stay down and so I sat on the chaise and drank champagne until I felt more in control.

Later I made love to her again slowly, and sensually with my blood lust held in check. My lusting heart had discovered a new way to live with Helaine and it was one that could make me happy for a very long time. Now we were lovers I had learnt that our relationship could progress in a normal way. She need never become my victim.

How foolish and naive I was.

19
Private Elin's Trail

Nonna left a trail for Elin to follow that only he could see. It went all around the perimeter. Elin had begun to remember things and he recalled why Nonna had always called him Little Bird. He felt like a bird now, following the trail of bread crumbs that led to the secret hidden in the earth. He recalled his dream of seeing the tribe the night before and it was a beautiful and special moment in which he had ultimately understood his heritage for the very first time. Elin – *no, Little Bird* – knew that he had a destiny to fulfil and his ancestors had returned to remind him.

Ancestry was a peculiar thing. Little Bird recalled watching the doctor work sometimes in her lab. That was whenever Doctor Collins' cameras worked. They had an odd way of breaking down around her and only he seemed to have noticed that. Even so, Collins knew a lot about heritage and ancestry, in a way that Little Bird would never understand, but what he did know was that your blood, your DNA, made you who you were and in *Wa She Shu* terms that meant a lot more than in white man's terms. This wasn't just about blood, though blood played a huge part. Little Bird believed that this was more to do with his soul.

'Do white men go to a different heaven?' he once asked Nonna and she had laughed at his query.

'Little Bird you worry about the strangest things. We are part of nature in life and return to the earth in death, but our spirit remains in the blood of our descendents. That's why family is so important to us.'

'I don't understand,' Little Bird said. 'Why is family so important?'

'One day, when you need it most, the souls of your ancestors will be there to help you,' Nonna had said.

Little Bird now knew this was true. His ancestors, including his beloved Nonna, had returned because something very important was happening in the desert. The sand was moving. Little Bird could feel it and he was beginning to understand why.

He walked the perimeter now with more purpose. Grains of golden sand twinkled at him through the sparse and barren grass. It took him an hour to walk the whole circle, and it spread all around the perimeter taking in the entirety of the base, including the sleeping quarters and the food warehouse.

'Hey!' said a voice.

Little Bird turned to see Parker behind him.

'You're gonna wear the ground out Elin,' Parker said.

'What do you mean?' Little Bird answered.

'All this walking round. It's kicking up the dust.'

Little Bird looked around him and he saw that a wind had indeed picked up.

'Just joshing with ya,' Parker said. 'This place gets you stir crazy doesn't it? I spend half my free time outside.'

'Yep. Underground. No natural light,' Little Bird confirmed.

'Anyway, better go. On my shift again soon.'

'You still looking after the latest freak?' Little Bird asked because that was what he knew Parker would expect him to call Seventeen. Little Bird didn't think Seventeen was a freak though. Not like the other subjects.'

'Yeah. He seems okay though. I reckon they are gonna have themselves a weapon if they can fully domesticate that one.'

'He looks pretty domesticated already.' Little Bird smiled.

'Can I tell you something, Pete? I don't think they even know what they have their hands on. For now, he's playing their game, but God help us all when he gets bored of it.'

'What you sayin'?' Little Bird asked. 'That he's just gonna bug out on us at anytime?'

'Yeah. No. I dunno, Pete. I'm tired. I've been feeling really …
weird. Just like something is gonna go down and I won't be able
to do anything about it.'

Little Bird nodded. 'Do you know much about ancestry?'

'Not much. Why?'

'I was just wondering if you had some Indian blood in you.'

'Nah!' laughed Parker. 'But my mother used to say my dad's
mom was a witch.'

'Maybe she wasn't kidding …' Little Bird let the thought
hang between them while Parker grew serious.

'I'm just fooling,' said Little Bird, but Parker noted that his
smile was crooked, and his Mom always said a crooked smile
hid a lie.

Parker backed away, 'Yeah. Well. I gotta get to work.'

Little Bird watched Parker go. Private Elin had always liked
Parker but Little Bird was learning to sever all of his feelings
towards the white soldiers he worked with. He had to.

He walked the perimeter one more time. The golden sand
twinkled brighter now and Little Bird whispered the words of
his sacred language under his breath. The *Wa She Shu* tongue
was all but extinct, but somehow Little Bird remembered it and
he chanted a prayer to his ancestors. They would eradicate the
evil of the white man. They would destroy the base and Little
Bird would see the graveyard of his ancestors free of the curse
placed on it. In his mind's eye he saw the circle of power rise up
around the base. For now though, he left it open and ready.
Ready to be activated when the time came.

20
Betrayal

I run back to my room but the smell of Helaine follows me down the corridors. In those moments when I looked into her revenant eyes I remembered her life and her death. I imagine in my terror that I can see some recognition of me in her black stare.

Helaine is not my bastard offspring. At least I don't think she is. I recall all of the times we spent together. Sex and love were something we had shared but never blood. I was sure of that, so how had this happened?

I throw myself back into my cell and sit on the bed staring at the door as Parker locks it behind me. Preacher stands looking through the hatch. He is confused, but I have no intention of revealing my past relationship with Helaine.

'But what is it, Gabriele? Why do you run away?'

'She's hideous,' I murmur and then I tell them nothing more as the memories come flooding back to me again. I cross my hands over my face and hope that none of them can see my turmoil.

I remember Helaine's hair, flowing over my stomach, as she brought me to orgasm with her mouth. I remember the smell of her lust and of her blood, both of which became so familiar that resisting that final fatal taste became easy. I channelled my lust into the sexual side only and fed elsewhere to slate my hunger to ensure it remained that way. A dock worker here, a pauper there. Sometimes I even fed on an occasional whore. My meals came from those who would not be missed. This kept Helaine safe. Or so I thought.

We had been happy for almost a year before the King saw what we had and his greed made him envious of the love we felt for each other. He began to probe me about details of our love-making, the time we spent together and of Helaine's career in the Opera.

'Are you seeing Helaine this evening?' Louis asked frequently and it seemed an innocent enough question but when I said yes, the King's face would redden a little and he would begin to find excuses why he needed me in court that evening instead.

'You displease us,' Louis said. 'I find your abandonment of our court and fun somewhat distasteful.'

Of course, I would have been at court more, but for the fact that Helaine was not welcome there. Her lack of title, more than her reputation, made her even more outcast in the eyes of the debauched aristocracy that frequented the King's salons. I was rapidly becoming bored with the court, preferring Helaine's company instead to the foppish marquises and whorish countesses. Where once I had enjoyed a voyeuristic pleasure, spying on the adulterous liaisons that took place in the curtained alcoves of the ballroom, now I found these seedy, desperate relationships a bore. Still, I knew it was never wise to displease the King of the land you inhabited and if it hadn't been for Louis I knew that I wouldn't have met Helaine in the first place.

I tried to work my time between the two of them. My evenings sometimes spent with the King, entertaining him with my voice, or merely joining him at one of his orgies, which I merely observed and never participated in. Louis didn't mind that of course, he liked an audience while he showed off his prowess. After the entertainment I would retire to Helaine's small house and we would spend the evening together making love, drinking wine and finally sleeping until late in the morning. I thought this balance worked and it did seem to appease the King for a while.

Helaine was happy and never questioned any of my absences because she understood the pressures of courtiers more than most. Louis, however, was never happy. He wanted my presence more and more at court and I couldn't understand why.

Then one morning, the servant girl, Alice, came into the bedroom with breakfast and an urgent message from the King. The letter was not addressed to me, but to Helaine. Louis wanted her to come to him that night. Helaine was distraught.

'I can't Gabi,' she cried. 'I'm no whore. I love you and I cannot give myself to the King again.'

'Maybe that isn't what he wants,' I said. 'Only yesterday we discussed you and he said my difficulty with dividing my time so much between you and the court could so easily be resolved if you had a title. I think that maybe Louis wants to give you a title.'

'Do you really think that this could be it?' she asked.

'Yes. I'm certain of it.'

How wrong I was.

Helaine had serious misgivings but it would have been impossible for someone in her position to refuse the invitation. So I agreed to accompany her to see the King that night. The meeting was taking place in his office and so I believed that this was proof that it was a formal occasion.

Helaine dressed discreetly but expensively in a dark blue silk dress that had a low neckline but her breasts were covered by a piece of sheer lace. I could see she was nervous but I took her hand and led her to my carriage anyway. I wasn't really concerned because I knew that whatever situation arouse, I could always get Helaine out of it by my mere presence.

We waited in the anti-chamber outside Louis' office. Court was quiet that evening because there was no planned entertainment and so the usual hangers-on weren't on hand. Helaine was nervous. She squeezed her gloved hands in her lap and I have to admit this whole situation also made me feel strange. I didn't know Louis' motives, but I thought I did. I thought that the King valued me. I thought that Louis cared about my feelings. The truth was, Louis was avaricious. He wanted everything for himself in a way that I have never understood. But my arrogance knew no bounds.

Eventually Louis' assistant came to fetch us. He was surprised to find me there as well, but didn't stop me from following him and Helaine into the office.

'Helaine,' Louis said, standing up and coming around his desk to take her hand.

Helaine fell into a curtsey. I bowed and the King indicated that we should both sit before him.

'I must admit I'm surprised to find you here as well,' Louis said to me. 'After all, I did request to see Helaine.'

'Forgive me,' I said. 'But we were together when Helaine received your note. I wanted to come with her.'

Louis sat down again behind his desk and he studied us both.

'I have a favour to ask of Helaine, for which she will be rewarded with the title of Countess.'

Helaine gasped and clasped her hands with excitement but I remained silent and waited. I was pleased that he was doing this but caution made me keep my reaction in check. You see, by then I knew Louis had a perverse humour and I didn't altogether trust that this 'favour' would be anything simple.

'What do you want her to do?' I asked.

'I have an ambassador coming from Spain. He is the King of Spain's nephew and I believe he is a man of certain tastes. I wish Helaine to entertain him.'

I sat forward in my seat. Helaine had been a courtesan when I met her and the life she had before me was something that I accepted and didn't think about too much. We were happy together, and I believed her to be mine. This request from the King was not only insulting to me but to Helaine. The King was treating our personal feelings for each other as though they meant nothing, as if he believed they could be purchased for the price of a title.

Helaine stared at her hands and I could feel the excited energy drain away. She was silent and so was I. We waited for

Louis to say more and when he didn't I had to break the silence.

'What do you mean by "entertain"?' I asked finally.

'Don't be naive, Gabriele,' Louis said. 'You know exactly what I mean. She will pleasure him in any way he sees fit while he is here. After the Ambassador leaves then you are both free to continue the … commitment you have to each other.'

'Why me, Sire?' asked Helaine softly. 'There are many other ladies who would be willing to do this task for you.'

'Because you are an exceptional whore and I believe he likes petite women. You fit his requirements and you need to change your status if you are to have a long career in court. What we are offering is a solution to your current problem. Of course the title would come with land and associated wealth. You will be a woman of substance and respect. You could then pick any husband in our court.'

I shook my head, fury bubbled into my face. I couldn't allow this. I just couldn't.

Helaine's hand fell on my thigh and then she spoke again. 'Your majesty is most kind. I feel honoured that you picked me and trusted me with this assignment. When will the ambassador arrive?'

Louis smiled. It was a cruel smile and I had to look away. I was tempted to rip his throat out and end his reign there and then. I knew he was a debauched and selfish bastard but this was too much, even for him.

'We knew we could rely on you,' Louis said. 'The Spaniard will be here in a few days. And so the two of you will have time to make your temporary goodbyes. We are expecting him to remain with us for three months. In which time my dear you will keep him happy.'

Helaine nodded. 'Of course, Sire.'

She stood then and curtsied taking her leave as quickly as possible. I sat for a moment and stared at Louis. I think he saw my hatred because his eyes narrowed. Instead of making any kind of apology he smiled again. He had won. He had me at his beck and call now for the next three months. That is, if I cared to stay in Paris and, without Helaine, I wasn't sure that I did.

I stood slowly and bowed but I knew my expression gave away my fury.

I followed Helaine out and back to my carriage where we sat in silence all the way back to her house. She was so still and quiet that at one point I wondered if she had fallen asleep. As the carriage pulled up I considered not going back inside with her, but returning to my rooms instead but I knew I couldn't end our love there.

I followed her inside silently and we made our way up to the bedroom and began to disrobe. The bed covers were still in disarray from our earlier indulgences that afternoon and so Helaine straightened them before turning back the sheets and slipping inside.

'I can't let this happen. I love you and you're mine Helaine. I don't know how you can even consider doing this for a title. If you want a title then I'll marry you. Give you my title.'

'Gabi this isn't about the title or the money. It is about refusing the King's request. If you married me now and thwarted Louis he would throw us both in the Bastille. Would you rather me whore to a Spaniard for a few months or whore to the prison guard for years?'.

She lay back in the bed and I had never seen her so bereft. I finally understood her silence. She felt powerless.

'I don't want to do this. I want only you. You know that, don't you? But if I do this thing, then the King will have to keep his promise and he may not claim this kind of service from me again.'

'You aren't a whore, Helaine. I can't allow this to happen. I can't share you.'

'There is something you should know. Louis made a deal with me before. He helped my career in the Opera and when he told me to entertain you I did so because he ordered it.'

I sat down on the chaise and stared at her.

'You are saying you never loved me?'

'No,' Helaine sighed. 'I do love you Gabi. I love you more than I do my own life and that is why I will do as Louis says this final time. You came to me and I expected ...'

'You expected me to use you …'

'Yes. But you didn't Gabi. You respected and loved me and now, I feel like I am your wife.'

'Then be my wife and together we'll stand up to Louis.'

'We can't fight this, Gabi. Louis is the King. His word is law,' she said. 'To disobey him is treason.'

I stood up and paced the room. My fury made me grasp and tear at my hair.

'I should have known this was going to happen. We'll leave here. We will go to a country that Louis has no power in. Helaine, pack all of your essential things. I'll go back to my house and gather money and jewels. We'll leave Paris in the morning.'

Helaine sat up in the bed. 'You mean that? You would take me away with you?'

'Yes,' I said. 'We could live anywhere in the world. Louis cannot command anything if we leave for England.'

'You do love me then …' Helaine smiled.

'Did you doubt it?' I fell onto the bed and into her arms.

'We have a few days, but we should act quickly. Louis thinks he has my acceptance and your silence will make him have confidence in your obedience. Gabi. Are you sure about this?'

'Yes. I'm returning now to my house. Get ready. You can bring Alice too if you like.'

I kissed her and took my leave quickly returning to my house. When I arrived there I discovered the King's men waiting for me.

21
Arrival

The four vampires moved forward as a black male customs officer called, 'Next.'

Lilly felt troubled the minute the plane landed at Las Vegas. She felt a dull, sick ache in the pit of her stomach as they pulled down their bags from the overhead lockers. There was something near, an innate evil that taunted her on the periphery of her vampiric and witch senses. She said nothing of this to the others though. Instead she became quiet and serious which the vampires all thought was nothing more than her worry for Gabi.

Lilly looked the customs man in the eye and then released him before anyone noticed. Her passport was a fake, as was Chez's, but Anthony and Anja had real identities that they hadn't felt the need to change. Each of them was wearing the Kevlar suits beneath their regular clothing. They looked, for all intents and purposes, like tourists. The Kevlar should have given them problems, and so should the sword that Lilly carried in her hand luggage, but any incident that these might have caused had been quashed by Lilly before any alarm could be raised.

'You guys all related?' asked the customs officer looking them over in turn.

'Yes,' Lilly said meeting his eyes again. After that he only asked generic questions and the four vampires walked through passport control and out of the airport. They weren't even asked to give finger prints. Lilly thought this might be awkward so she hadn't allowed it.

'What just happened there?' asked Anthony as Chez hailed a taxi.

'He won't even remember us,' Lilly smiled. 'And technically we weren't even checked into the country.'

'Have you ever been to Las Vegas before?' Anja asked.

'No. Have you?' said Lilly.

Anja shook her head. 'I always wanted to come. They have some interesting digs out in the desert. Indian relics and remains. Fascinating stuff.'

Lilly smiled. Sometimes she forgot that the seemingly young Anja had once worked as a relic thief. It was an image that went against her young and sweet appearance.

'I just wondered because you seemed to know what would happen as we reached passport control,' Anja said. 'Those guys are intense aren't they?'

'Internet,' Lilly smiled. 'And yes, US Customs are notoriously strict.'

The white and blue cab drove away from the airport and the four immortals sat in silence, looking at the scenery. Ten minutes later, the driver took them down the main strip, while describing all of the sights they were seeing.

They had booked into the MGM Grand Hotel. It was like a mini city, with several restaurants and even a mall there. Anja's eyes were wide and curious as they walked into the reception, which also led directly into a large casino. Slot machines, poker and craps tables, were all within a few short feet of the entrance.

'Hi folks. Glad to have you here,' said the receptionist. 'Here's your key cards and I also have to give you this. It's a police flyer warning all visitors on how to stay safe in Vegas.'

'Why? What happened?' asked Chez.

The receptionist leaned forward over the desk and gave Chez a very white flirty smile. 'I'm not supposed to gossip but there was a murder at one of the other hotels last week. Woman murdered in her room and the freaky thing was there was hardly any blood. Well actually there was a lot of blood but not as much as you might expect to find in a body. She was, like, mutilated too. It was all kinda kinky.'

Lilly looked up at the girl. She was about to question her more but Chez placed his hand on her arm.

'Thanks. We'll be careful.' Chez smiled at the receptionist.

The girl blushed and pushed back her dark brown hair from her eyes. Then she gave Chez another dazzling smile.

'Let's check this place out,' Anja said as they walked towards the lift. Her eyes were dazzled by the lights and the gambling machines that lined every part of the casino main floor. She looked like a child in a sweet shop and her attraction to the fake glitz surprised Lilly.

'Later,' said Lilly. 'We need to get the lie of the land first.'

'What's she talking about?' asked Anja.

'She is going to look for ley lines,' Chez explained. 'And for that we need to go to our room and get some privacy.'

Anthony linked Anja's arm and pulled her towards the lift. 'Gambling is bad for the soul and the pocket anyway.'

'Aw you're just no fun,' Anja sulked.

'This is not a holiday, Anja,' Lilly commented as they entered the lift. 'We have to find Gabi.'

'Do you think I don't know that?' Anja said through gritted teeth. 'God I wish you'd all stop treating me like a child.'

'Fine. Then go and play with the machines, because that just seems like the grown-up thing to do right now, doesn't it?' Lilly said.

There was no anger in Lilly's voice though. She sounded tired and Anja instantly regretted her momentary tantrum. It was childish and she had allowed the lure of the casino to distract her from their task. As the lift doors closed Anja began to question herself on why she had been even slightly interested in the gaming floor. It seemed a bizarre reaction after all the stress of the last few days. She shook herself mentally. This was about Gabi. They had to find Gabi, how could she forget that even for a second? She felt incredibly guilty.

They had a suite of rooms on the top floor. A three bedroom apartment. The best the hotel had to offer. With three bathrooms between them, and a large private lounge-diner, there was ample space for the four immortals to spread out. Off the main room was a large balcony that not only contained a barbeque, but also had a fully stocked mini bar in a large American fridge that had its own ice dispenser. The balcony would afford them another exit and access point where they could come and go unobserved.

Chez poured them all a drink of Jack Daniels with ice and placed them on a low coffee table that sat between two wicker sofas. Lilly was the first to take her glass and she walked to the edge of the balcony and looked out over the desert.

'What did you make of the murder thing?' Anthony said.

Lilly shrugged. 'I don't know.'

'Whatever it is,' said Chez, 'we need to stay focused on the important things. We can't let something else distract us.'

'I've felt weird ever since we arrived,' Lilly said.

'You too?' asked Anthony. 'I thought it was just me.'

Lilly looked at Chez and he nodded, 'I feel something. I just don't know what it is. It's not … pleasant though.'

Anja stared at the others and shrugged, 'I thought it was just nerves. My stomach is churning.'

The four of them stood looking out over Vegas. The sounds - from the main strip, the hotels, the shows, the people - drifted faintly up to them. They could see the town spread out, but in the distance, the houses, shops and roads all abruptly stopped in an arc, beyond which was the golden desert of Nevada, stretching on to the horizon.

'Where is it coming from?' asked Anthony after a few moments.

'I don't know. I can't pinpoint it,' Lilly said.

Lilly sipped her whiskey and took a seat in one of the sun loungers.

'What now?' asked Chez.

The other vampires turned to Lilly and waited for her answer. They hung on her every word. She was their queen after all, their power source, and they felt awe mixed with respect whenever she made important decisions. Lilly was quiet for a time though. She wanted to think her choices through.

'We need to wait until nightfall,' she said. 'Then we will take a flight into the desert.'

'Which way?' Anthony asked.

Lilly didn't answer. Instead she picked up her glass and drank from it again. She gazed out over the horizon, her mind closed to them as she searched for the source. There was power here, a magic that was unfamiliar and she didn't like it. Although all magic had the same routes when it came down to it, didn't it? Maybe this one was just being wielded by the wrong hands.

Lilly recalled the power Caradien had used. If the Illuminati, or someone working for them, were involved in this, then there was a chance they could also manipulate ley lines and effectively block any attempt to use the portals.

A wind picked up and even at this height Lilly could smell the sand on the air. It gave her no comfort. Lilly sent her aura out on a search of the area. She felt for the positive force of ley and found … nothing. When she opened her eyes she found Chez sitting next to her.

The sun was going down over the city.

'Negative energy,' Lilly said eventually. 'It's like a void of nothingness. Some cities sit on it. Not usually harmful. It balances out the positive forces elsewhere on the planet. Unfortunately this is not something I can use or draw from.'

'What will we do then?' Chez asked.

'We'll use all the skills we have. We are immortal. We are vampires. The four of us could take on an army if we wanted to, ley power aside,' Anthony said.

'On a positive note. This means our enemies can't use it to their advantage either,' Anja said.

'Wise words. We have much to be thankful for on that score. But first we have to discover where Gabi is,' Lilly said.

Chez clasped Anthony in his arms, and Lilly embraced Anja, because neither of the younger vampires could fly. It would take a hundred kills before each of them would earn this power and, with Lilly's current rule of avoiding murder, this would be a long time in their future. They all took to the air and flew out over the desert, circling and doubling back as they traced the sense of danger that had been haunting them since their arrival.

By midnight they had found the army base and the source of dark power. It had been obvious from the air. A black cloud of energy which attracted them like moths to a flame. It hung over and around the low buildings like some sort of malignant invisible smog.

Five hundred yards away from the perimeter fence, the four immortals touched down and began to walk around the dust-filled circle of power.

They could each sense that something was there, that something was wrong, but the magic was so alien that none of them could appreciate just what awaited them within. Or what was buried deep beneath the sands underfoot.

Part Three

The Hungry Dead

1
Blood

Joe was tired and frayed but he entered Seventeen's room with confidence. He was becoming better at hiding the nervousness he felt around the vampire, and with Parker at his back he felt safe and secure in the knowledge that if Seventeen made one wrong move, Parker would put him to sleep with the tranquilliser.

Joe wheeled his trolley close to the bed. Seventeen was hunched up in the corner. He looked like a trauma victim and Joe immediately felt concerned that something had happened. Seventeen had been very quiet recently. He neither objected nor questioned for the need to take regular samples from his veins. Parker on the other hand did question him. The soldier was getting too nosey for his own good.

'The boss wants some more blood,' Joe said, not expecting a response but Gabi dutifully held out his arm and let Joe fill three syringes.

'Jeez, Doc. He ain't gonna have much left at this rate.'

'Then bring him some blood to drink.'

'He don't have that shit. He likes steak and wine. We got a fine dining vampire here don't ya know that?'

Joe glanced at Parker and then back at Gabi as he withdrew the last needle from his arm. There was no need to add pressure or apply a band aid, the vampire's skin healed instantly and Joe never wasted a drop. Joe placed the full phials on the medical trolley, and disposed of the needle in the yellow sharps bin he had with him. Then he backed away and out of the door. As he turned to walk down the corridor he heard Parker speak one more time.

'Sorry about that. These doctors are savages. I know you shouldn't be treated like a lab rat.'

Joe stopped and listened, but Parker said no more. In fact there was complete silence inside the cell. He turned and was about to make his way back to look inside when Parker came back out. Parker's gun was holstered and he was clutching his wrist. He began to lock the cell and a tingling sensation went up Joe's back. He felt suspicious of Parker. What had he been doing in the cell with Seventeen and why had he been holding his wrist? Their relationship seemed to be guard and prisoner, but what did Joe really understand about Seventeen's abilities? Was he the same as Lucy?

Joe knew that Lucy had bewitched him even though he was a willing victim. *Perhaps Parker is like me? Perhaps Parker is Seventeen's Renfield.* Joe stood upright, the word 'Renfield' had popped into his head from nowhere and he didn't understand the significance for a moment. He remembered *Dracula.* He hadn't read the book but knew of it. Literature never really appealed to him. Joe was a scientist and academic writing had been his only interest and source of study. Even so, he couldn't fail to know about the book, or the films that had spun off from it. It was a huge part of popular culture when he was growing up and some of his friends had even become Emos and Goths.

Parker looked down the corridor and saw Joe watching him. Frowning, the soldier took up his guard position at the door. Joe wheeled the trolley away resisting the urge to look back but he had already made his mind up that he would be watching Parker closely from now on.

Back at the lab, Joe could hear Lucy Collins and Preacher arguing again in the office. *Good,* he thought. *I can now stash the blood under a different name.* He wheeled the trolley in silently and set about hiding the samples with his other disguised blood. Joe was sure the regular doses of Seventeen's blood were making him feel strong and sane. He had noticed he was able to hear things around the base that he shouldn't have been able to, like now. Joe knew that under normal circumstances Lucy and Preacher's voices would not have carried beyond the walls of the small soundproofed office. Yet still he could hear them. The sound reached his ears on a level that Joe likened to dog hearing.

'You had no right to take him to One's cell,' Lucy said.

'I had every right, Doctor Collins. The creature wants to learn about the others. It was part of the bargain we made for his co-operation.'

'Not One. He didn't have to know about her.'

'Why not?' Preacher asked but Lucy wouldn't answer his question.

'I've reported your behaviour, Preacher. And I have permission from the top to have you removed from this facility.'

'Who gave you that permission?' Preacher laughed harshly. 'My clearance may not top yours, Collins, but it certainly matches it.'

'That was true, until you decided to be an ass and throw your superiority around a little too much. I'm in charge here and I say you leave.'

At that moment a group of soldiers entered the lab. Joe jumped. One of the samples slipped from his fingers. Joe reacted instantly, throwing himself downwards and managing to catch the phial seconds before it hit the floor. The glass would have shattered for certain. A bead of sweat slipped down his brow as Joe stood up to face the soldiers but by then they were heading towards Lucy's office. He clutched the sample to his chest. Fear gripped his soul.

They know what she is, he thought. *It's all over!*

The door of the office opened and Lucy stepped back to allow the soldiers to enter.

'Take Mr Preacher off the base. He no longer has clearance to be here,' Lucy said.

Joe heaved a sigh as he watched Preacher being led out by the six soldiers. He met Lucy's eyes briefly, then turned away and stashed the remaining blood sample securely in the fridge. When he turned back, Lucy was in her office and the door was closed.

After that, Joe worked silently. He was listening intently to the sound of Lucy's voice coming through the wall. She was on the telephone speaking to someone. Joe had no idea who, but her voice was hushed, as though she didn't want to be overheard.

'I don't know why he was sent here, but the man is unstable … I know he's a fixer … but he tried to undermine me …. Well, he went against the plan for a start … No. There isn't any evidence: I've made sure. All samples were destroyed.'

A few minutes later Lucy came out of the office.

'What was all that about?' Joe asked.

Lucy's eyes narrowed. 'All what?'

'Preacher being hauled outta here.'

'Oh. Him. His clearance was revoked from the top.'

'Ah. He must have pissed someone off,' Joe laughed.

Lucy said nothing.

'I have some new samples from the subjects who've been drinking blood. Shall I run the usual tests on them?' Joe asked.

'Yes. It will be interesting to see if there has been any impact… Joe?'

'Yes, Lucy?'

'You feeling okay?

'Bright as a button, why?'

Lucy came up to him, her hand slipped under his lab coat and around his waist. Joe fell into her arms willingly.

'I'm feeling a little frisky,' she said. 'The cameras are off again in the office, want to come in there and play?'

Joe's cock hardened at her touch. She was impossible to resist and he could think of nothing better at that moment than to service Lucy Collins over her desk. He let her lead him inside the room. She turned the privacy glass to black and the afternoon became a blur of pleasure and blood in which Joe fed from Lucy and she fed from him.

Maybe this is how you become a vampire, he thought.

Afterwards, he recalled the sick trade of blood with sexual perversity but he no longer forgot these exchanges. Lucy went back to work with enthusiasm and Joe went through the motions of being his own man. The truth lurked there, behind his eyes, in the darkest recesses of his memory. He was her Renfield, and despite his best efforts to be self-sufficient she could and would control him if she wished. Part of his mind applauded the thought, while the other part of him that was still Joe was horrified.

Joe glanced guiltily at the fridge. All he needed was there. He could stop taking from Lucy anytime he wanted. He could be in charge of his future. But did he really want to be?

Joe found his eyes lingering on Lucy's bowed head as she gazed down the microscope. She was the most desirable woman he had ever met. He wouldn't give her up, even if he could.

2
Goodbye Helaine

Paris 1740

'What are you doing here?' I asked Louis' lieutenant. It was around two in the morning and he and his six men stood inside the large hallway. Like most aristocrats of the time, I only rented rooms. Mine were in a large house close to the palace of Versailles.

'Count Caccini, we have orders to take you to the Bastille to be held there at the King's pleasure,' the lieutenant said.

He bowed, clicked his heels together and made his men do the same. I realised then that I was to be treated with respect at least, despite the fact that the men were there to arrest me.

'Can I have an explanation as to why I am under arrest?' I asked.

The lieutenant looked surprised. 'You don't know, Monsieur?'

'I wouldn't have asked if I did,' I said.

'His majesty is trying you for treason.'

'Treason? On what grounds?'

'His majesty feels that you are about to act in a way that could discredit the crown.'

I blinked in surprise. 'Act in what way? And, how can I be tried for treason on the basis of something I *might* do? That is ridiculous.'

'I'm sorry, Monsieur,' the lieutenant said. 'I have my orders.'

'I see. May I fetch some comforts from my room? I assume I will be treated in the way my wealth and station deserves?'

'Of course, Monsieur.'

My mind was all over the place but I was permitted to go to my room to gather some clothing. Of course two of the guards followed me and remained outside my open door while I retrieved my money and jewels as I had planned. I packed a small trunk, placing in some basic essentials and then I walked down the stairs, back to the soldiers. All this time I was planning my escape.

I had enjoyed my stay in Paris, but it was obviously time to leave. I nodded to my landlady, holding out a small purse of money.

'Please retain my rooms and keep my possessions safe for the length of time this money lasts. I am certain that this small misunderstanding will be quickly resolved,' I said.

The landlady took the purse and bowed, but I could see it in her eyes that she didn't believe I would return.

Outside I saw the carriage waiting for me. The streets were empty. I looked around, pulled out my handkerchief and drop it. As I bent to retrieve it, I let my fangs grow from my gums.

I stood, hand swinging with all the force of my supernatural strength and I sent the nearest soldier toppling backwards. He fell against his comrade and the two of them tumbled to the ground. The other guards were quicker than I expected. Drawing their swords, they ran at me as the lieutenant yelled orders to try and capture me alive.

I grabbed two of the soldiers by the throat, one in each hand, and raised them up above my head, while squeezing the life out of them.

The first two had recovered enough to stand and draw their weapons, but I threw their two dead colleagues against them.

'Stop him!' yelled the lieutenant. He was clearly brave, but not foolish, as he stepped back against the carriage and away from the danger as his men charged me.

I ripped the throat out of the first man, dragging him forward into my open mouth, fangs bared and hungry. Blood sprayed and I drank it down with pleasure, the life-fluid invigorating me and giving me more strength. The second soldier halted and backed away.

'Demon!' he yelled and I threw back my head and laughed at his superstition.

The lieutenant ran forward and collided with the retreating soldier.

'Kill him you coward,' said the lieutenant and I reached around the scared soldier and caught hold of the officer.

'Foolish mortal,' I said and then I buried my fangs in his face and ripped back, tearing away the skin on his cheek before bending down to his throat.

I felt a stab of pain rip through my back, narrowly missing my backbone. The other four soldiers had recovered and one of them was trying to wound me. I roared with fury, turning around on them as I threw the lieutenant away from me. The look of terror in their eyes was justification enough. They saw me covered in the blood of their colleagues and knew that I wouldn't stop until I had taken them all down.

I pulled the sword out of my back, then used it on the perpetrator as he turned and tried to run. I buried it in his spine. His legs gave under him and he collapsed to the floor, blood pouring from the protruding sword. Then I turned to the others, who foolishly still seemed to think they could rush me.

They fell. All of them. In a bloody heap. I punched a hole in the chest of the first one to come at me, ripping out his still beating heart, and the rest of the massacre became a blur of bone, sinew and gore as I let the fury take away all of my reserve.

I took to the air. Anger and blood lust raged in a red feverish mist as I flew back to Montmartre.

I cloaked myself as I flew to Helaine's. It was even more important that I got her away from Paris now. Her association with me could be her death warrant, but I knew that would depend on how much Louis really wanted her to entertain his expected guest. I suspected he didn't care who he gave to the Spaniard, but Helaine was to be taken from me because of his ultimate jealousy, though I wasn't sure why the King had become so obsessed when he had encouraged our romance in the first place. None of this made sense after the long friendship I had with him. I had known all along that Louis was mean-spirited, but even so this seemed a new low.

The house was in darkness as I landed on the balcony. I had expected Helaine to be packing, and at least to be able to hear Alice rushing around trying to prepare everything for their departure, but the silence was eerie. Something was wrong, terribly wrong.

I paused at the balcony door. The curtain was closed and I couldn't see inside but I concentrated my hearing on the interior. I should be able to hear Helaine or Alice if they were there, but I could hear nothing. Helaine often slept with the door open in summer and so I tried the door. The handle turned and the door opened. I stepped inside the dark room, and my eyes fell on the piles of clothes on the bed and the open cases. I sighed with relief; maybe they were both in another room.

Helaine's whole house had to be packed up, but I was certain that all she would bring was her personal possessions. She had no need of anything else as I could provide it all for her.

The bedroom door opened and Alice came in suddenly. She was carrying a candle and I saw instantly that she wasn't alone.

'Here are her things,' Alice said to the soldier that followed her into the room.

I stepped back onto the balcony, cloaking myself from them.

'Good,' said the soldier. He held out a purse to Alice and the girl took it. 'His majesty thanks you for exposing the traitors.'

I was stunned by Alice's betrayal and so I merely watched as she and the soldier packed up Helaine's clothing into a trunk. Where they had taken Helaine? I waited, hoping to learn more but the soldier said nothing and it was obvious that his presence made Alice nervous because the girl didn't speak again either. Several other soldiers came into the room and took away all of Helaine's personal possessions. This much care gave me hope. If they had killed her why bother to take her clothes and jewels?

I was torn between following the King's guard and killing our traitor, but I decided to come back to take care of Alice after I found and rescued Helaine. Her safety was more important to me then and so I followed the soldiers by air. They travelled at break-neck speed through the city and straight back to Versailles.

The palace was lit up and the King's guard were busy walking the grounds as though they expected an attack on the King. I thought then, that they probably did. I had after all murdered most of the King's soldiers who came to arrest me and try as I might I couldn't remember if I had left any of them alive or capable of speech. In my haste to get back to Helaine I had been careless. Not that it mattered by then as my position in the King's court was no longer viable. Louis had seen to that. There in lay the crux of the matter. The King. He had to die. Especially if he had hurt Helaine.

I looked over the palace from the air knowing that no one could see me and then I wondered where I could possibly find Helaine.

Ah. But of course ... the chambers of the King's mistress.

I landed on its balcony. Louis was not a faithful husband and although he frequented his marriage bed, he did not find pregnancy attractive. Once the queen was with child, he sought his pleasure elsewhere. This meant he had several mistresses and one in particular would be favoured enough to have her own chambers at court – making access to her easier. Currently though, the King had no mistress, but where better to keep mine but in the confines of the palace?

I listened at the door and heard nothing, but watched below as the King's guard emptied the carriage of Helaine's possessions. My lover had to be here. Why else would the soldiers unload her trunks? The room inside, however, appeared to be empty. I tried the door handle but found it was locked, and with the drapes closed I could see nothing inside. It felt exactly like the moment when I had found myself on Helaine's balcony earlier.

I took to the air again. I became light, allowed the wind to lift me of its own volition and I floated unseen around the palace walls looking for an entrance into the building. It wasn't long before I came across the King's chambers and discovered that

Louis had Helaine in his office. She was surrounded by soldiers while Louis sat pompously at his desk, just as he had when he received us earlier.

'You were about to leave Paris,' Louis insisted.

'No, Sire. You said we had a few days. A small trip is all we had planned and then we would have parted as you ordered.'

Helaine was good at manipulation. I could see that under normal circumstances she probably would have been able to convince Louis of our innocence. I knew of course that the time for such games was over. I wanted to save Helaine. I had to take her away from here. I couldn't allow her to be used in this fashion. I really loved her.

'We have been told otherwise,' Louis said harshly. 'Your maid servant informs us that you planned to leave with your lover and never return. We deem this to be treason, but still have need of your exceptional talents. My guest will arrive in two days and you will play the whore for him Helaine.'

'Your majesty, I will of course do all you command.'

'But your betrayal has changed the details of our personal offer,' Louis said. 'Now you will be doing this to spare your life, and to ensure your cooperation your lover will spend the next three months in the Bastille.'

'No! Please, Sire. I implore you.'

Louis stood up. His eyes were cold.

Helaine fell to the floor and grovelled at his feet. 'Please ... Let him go ... I will do anything you ask.'

'You will do anything we ask or you will die ...' Louis said.

Then Louis did something that I hadn't expected, he stood up, came around his desk and sent his guards out of the room. This gave me the perfect opportunity to break into the office and rescue Helaine but I held back because I wanted to know what his plan was. Why he wanted to be alone with her.

'The Spaniard is a man of certain tastes,' the King said quietly. 'You will give him all that he wishes.'

Helaine said nothing as she sobbed on the floor and then Louis grabbed her hair, pulling her face up so that he could gaze into her blue, tear-filled eyes.

'I still find you attractive,' Louis said. 'You will pleasure me tonight to show me your loyalty. Stand up.'

Helaine struggled to her feet, her gown catching under her made this difficult and Louis made no attempt to help her. I had seen enough. I reached for the door handle.

'What does your majesty require?' asked Helaine.

I was amazed by her sudden composure the way she went from tears to seductress but then I had observed that she was always a good actress.

The King reached for an apple from a bowl on the table and began to peel it with an ornate silver fruit knife. He ate a few pieces as though he was considering Helaine's question carefully. Then he placed the knife and the unfinished fruit back down on the desk. He began to unfasten his breeches and this I knew was the moment I would kill him. I began to squeeze the handle of the balcony door and I pressed my shoulder into the wood frame, to give it extra leverage. I would enter quietly if I could but I was prepared to do everything it took to get into the room and whisk Helaine away from the King.

Helaine began to bend once more as Louis opened his breeches and then a loud knock interrupted his sport and the soldiers re-entered, swords drawn.

'What is the meaning of this?' Louis demanded, holding together his clothing with one hand.

'Forgive me, Sire,' said one of the soldiers. 'We feared for your safety.'

'From a woman?'

'No. Her lover escaped the guard. He killed them all, your majesty, and the lieutenant said, before he died, that the man turned into a demon and drank their blood.'

'Preposterous!' Louis said, but even so he returned to his seat behind the desk and began to fasten his breeches.

Helaine collapsed down in the chair opposite, her face distraught.

Once his clothing was straightened Louis reached for a piece of parchment and dipped his quill in ink before rapidly beginning to write. Then he melted some wax onto the bottom of the page and pressed the royal seal onto the paper.

'Count Caccini's death warrant,' he said, holding the parchment out to the soldiers.

'No!' screamed Helaine and she hurled herself at the desk, grabbing hold of the fruit knife.

'Don't be foolish, Helaine. You are surrounded by my guard. I can order your death in an instant,' Louis said. He sat back in his chair and studied her. 'You really love him don't you?'

'Yes. And I won't be your whore anymore. Not with you or for you.'

Then Helaine raised the knife and plunged in down into her own chest. I screamed and burst into the room. The soldiers frantically surrounded the King but by then his death was the last thing on my mind. I wanted to save Helaine, and I had hesitated too long. I reached for her crumpled body, lifting her up into my arms before the guard could react, and ran back towards the balcony, leaping from it and into the air.

3
Red Alert

They saw a military vehicle leave the base at nine; a small truck with a green canvas canopy stretched over the back. It passed through the security barrier, churning up dust as it made its way along the highway towards the lights of Las Vegas. Lilly stared after the vehicle but her mind was far away. She was using both her witch and vampire senses to scan the base.

'I think ... I can sense Gabi,' Lilly said.

'You only think?' asked Chez.

'There's a residue of him, but it seems so far away. Perhaps ...'

'What?' asked Anja.

'Underground?'

'What do we do?' asked Chez.

'I could try opening a portal again, using witchcraft. I can't use ley magic obviously. It's a lot harder and involves a great deal of ritual,' Lilly said. 'Or we could just fight our way in there and hope we find him.'

Anthony shook his head. 'Let's try magic. It's not safe for any of us to go in there blind. It's obvious that they have the ability to incapacitate us if they were able to catch Gabi so easily.'

Lilly was thoughtful for a moment. 'I need to get closer. I might be able to establish where Gabi is then.'

At that moment the security lights burst on all over the base and an alarm went off somewhere in the centre. 'Cloak now!' Chez said as he saw the soldiers emerging from their barracks, fully dressed and armed to the teeth.

All four of them faded into invisibility. Lilly caught hold of

Anthony and lifted him off the ground as Chez reached for Anja. They passed over the perimeter fence then landed inside the compound just as the electric fence switched off and the soldiers passed through a gate at the back. They watched with amusement as the soldiers searched the area that they had just vacated.

'What happened there?' Anja whispered.

'Sensors buried in the ground,' Anthony said. 'I should have realised.'

'We're in now. And they are on a fool's errand. Maybe this is the perfect opportunity for us to enter the facility unnoticed and I might not have to resort to witchcraft.'

They walked past the barracks, certain that they wouldn't be seen, while taking in the direction from which the soldiers came.

'There is some kind of reception building there,' Anja said.

'Probably on lockdown,' Anthony said. 'That would be normal procedure on an intruder alert.'

'We should wait until they give up on the search,' said Lilly. 'Until then, let's look around.'

They passed through the base, examining the exterior of the warehouses and barracks – grey breeze-block buildings that lacked personality but which Lilly knew must contain the secrets of the base –discovering as much about the layout as possible.

Lilly's emotions were in turmoil, she felt fear for the first time since Gabi had disappeared. There was something else lurking below ground but she wasn't sure what it was and if it was any threat to them.

'He's definitely underground,' Lilly said and her voice trembled. 'I can feel him.'

'Lilly … you don't think my dream could be … real, do you? Gabi hasn't been pulled down into the sand, has he?' asked Anja. Her voice was little more than a breathless whisper.

Lilly was silent as she probed the ground with her mind. The lack of ley energy made her realise how much she had come to rely on this source of power. She was left now with only her vampiric wits and senses. Surely they should have been enough for her in any normal circumstances? But then – life had taught her that 'normal' wasn't something they could expect in their world.

It was more than likely that some supernatural force was at work here. She felt a whisper of magic floating around her, but wasn't sure what it was. It was nothing like any power she had felt before. It was neither evil nor good but she sensed intent nonetheless. *What is that,* she wondered.

'We need to find our way down there as soon as possible,' Lilly said finally.

'Why?' asked Chez.

'I have this feeling … I think we are running out of time.'

As they cornered the final warehouse Chez grabbed Lilly's arm and pulled her back. Without hesitation the four vampires ducked down behind a row of waste containers.

'Look,' Chez said.

Lilly followed his gaze and she saw a blonde woman in a white lab coat emerging from the back of the warehouse opposite. She quickly recognised Lucrezia Borgia beneath the disguise; after all she had spent many years in the woman's company. The memory of Lucrezia's corrupt behaviour floated behind Lilly's eyes. Once, Lilly had disguised herself as the gypsy Miranda in order to meet up with Lucy and to teach her a modicum of magic. Now, knowing what she did about the woman, she wished she hadn't given her any knowledge at all but it hadn't been her call at the time. Lilly had thought she was unable to escape destiny and she had tried to avert disaster when the lives of her vampire family had hung in the balance. She had done what she thought right, but later learned of Lucy's lies, and her decisions had been based on those false truths. The past was done though, and there was nothing she could do, but none of the vampires trusted Lucy now.

'Why am I not surprised that your sister has a hand in this?' Lilly said.

'Chez has a sister?' Anja said, leaning forward to see a woman.

'Shush. And stay back.' Lilly pushed Anja back behind the

bin.

'Why'd you do that?' mouthed Anja.

'Because she'll be able to see us even if no one else can,' Lilly whispered.

She glanced back around the bin and noticed that Lucy had stopped. She was talking to another man, also wearing a lab coat, and a soldier who was heavily armed. Lilly held her breath and on the exhale she tuned into their conversation.

'The Subjects are secure? Particularly Seventeen?' Lucy asked.

'Yes,' Joe said. 'We drugged him again just to be on the safe side. He's strapped back into the cuffs.'

'He won't be very happy about that when he wakes,' Lucy said.

'Well if you ask me he's been given way too much freedom as it is ...'

'No one is asking you Joe.'

Joe stiffened and stood upright and she followed his gaze as he looked towards the soldier standing by a door, apparently guarding it.

'I know which way is in ...' Lilly said quietly over her shoulder. When she glanced back she saw that Lucrezia was looking around her as though she sensed their presence. Lilly shrank back again and using all of her strength she gathered the shadows around them, creating a black void that she hoped Lucy would just glance over.

'What is it?' Joe asked.

'Nothing ...' Lucy said. 'Let's get below and check on the subjects again.'

Through the merest crack, Lilly watched as Lucy and Joe passed through the guarded door. It was in the back of one of the warehouses disguised as a food store.

'They even keep secrets from each other,' she observed. 'Let's go. It's time to find Gabi and get the fuck out of here.'

They moved forward like liquid night, swarming over the soldier before he could react. Chez bit into his throat, sucked him dry and dropped his body in one of the bins, before swooping back around. The dead soldier was soon forgotten as Chez followed Lilly, Anja and Anthony into the building.

Inside they found themselves in a huge warehouse. There was a pair of wide doors, and a lift that Lilly could see was still going down. They waited until it came to a complete stop at minus 20.

'Security cameras everywhere in here,' Anthony observed. 'Don't let your guard slip, even when we get into the lift.'

'My guess is that we'll find Gabi down there. I don't have to give you all the pep talk about being careful do I?' Lilly said.

The other three didn't answer but they each met Lilly's gaze and the resolve and determination she saw there led her to realise that this was going down, no matter how dangerous it might be. Anthony reached past her and pressed the lift call.

'Let's do this,' he said.

4
Darren's Death

The blood sharing had gone further than she had wanted it to but Lucy found herself unwilling to stop. Joe's blood interested her. It tasted like her blood and something else. It held more than a little of the vampire tang that was neither sweet nor bitter but had a sharp citric flavour that was utterly addictive.

This is stupid, she thought as they travelled down in the lift during the alert. She had to stay focused but all she could think about was fucking and feeding on Joe again.

In the lift Joe stayed beside her and said nothing but she knew all it would take was a small touch to encourage him.

I should just kill him and finish this. It's gone too far and I've learnt nothing that I didn't already know.

The lift came to a halt and Lucy automatically pushed aside the vertigo and sickness that tried to control her every time she reached the lowest level. The doors opened and she came face to face with Preacher.

'Why are you still here?' she demanded.

'Your soldiers had to leave me to deal with your emergency, but I'm hoping you'll reconsider your stance, doctor. I can be of great use to you and your experiments.'

'I doubt that,' Lucy said. Then she turned to Joe. 'Go and check on the subjects.'

'Okay,' Joe nodded and he went away.

'Come up to my office,' Lucy said. Then she turned to see the lift had already been called back. 'We'll take the stairs I could use the exercise.'

Preacher followed her down the corridor and through to the

stairwell. The lab was five floors up but Preacher didn't mind the walk either. There was something unpleasant about being so far underground that made him want to climb the stairs quickly to escape that nerve wracking feeling. He followed Lucy, wondering how long it would be before she tired from the climb. He wanted to see her sweat, particularly when he told her who he really was.

As Lucy climbed up ahead of him Preacher couldn't help notice the sensual sway of her hips; it reminded him of the attraction he had felt for her when he first arrived. That attraction had vanished soon after the tug of war between them started. He hated that Lucy wasn't intimidated by him when everyone else was. Plus his attraction now lay in a different area: Subject Seventeen. Although Preacher knew he would never act on that compulsion. Seventeen was far too dangerous despite his benign appearance.

Lucy swiped her security pass and led Preacher into the corridor on level minus fifteen. Preacher prided himself on his fitness but he had to take a breath once they left the stairs and he felt moisture pooling on his back and under arms. He felt flustered as he followed her back through the lab and into her office.

Lucy, however, looked cool and calm when she sat down in the chair behind her desk and Preacher marvelled at this.

'You are becoming a real problem for me,' she said.

'Of course I am. You didn't expect to get rid of me that easily did you, Collins?'

Lucy was intrigued by Preacher's confidence. She didn't state the obvious to Preacher, that he was on a military base and could, effectively be imprisoned and no one would know. She looked up at the cameras and narrowed her eyes. She sent an electric pulse through the air and the red light went out.

'Security watching you?' asked Preacher, noticing her stare. 'It's a bit like being in a goldfish bowl around here, isn't it?'

'Yes. You should know that everything is recorded in the labs and offices, sound and speech.'

'Who do you think looks at the footage?' Preacher asked.

'What do you mean? It's just a security thing. There are lots of secrets in this base including some germ warfare that should probably never get out.'

'Don't be naive, Collins. The big man at the top is watching: it's Nineteen Eighty Four all over again.'

'Big brother?' Lucy laughed. 'You're paranoid.'

'I identified myself to you when I arrived …' Preacher pointed out.

'You're Illuminati. So what?'

'So are you. You gave the response.'

Lucy's smile was slow. 'I'm not in any way connected to your organisation Preacher.'

Preacher's face dropped, 'You like to play games don't you, Collins? But only a member could know our responses. None of them would give that information. It would be signing their own death warrant.'

'I came to this base eighteen months ago. I had to find something I'd lost, you see, and I learnt that this organisation had found it.'

Preacher said nothing.

'I knew there were people like you out there.'

'People like me?'

'You call yourself a "fixer" don't you? A fixer and a finder. You find unusual things for your employees. Anyway, my history with blood led me here. The right whisper in the correct ear and I was employed. I also knew immediately that the American government wasn't solely behind this base.'

'How?'

'I've been around a long time. I know how governments form affiliations with groups such as yours. The Illuminati has been a pain in the arse for centuries. It wasn't hard to work out that the main money for these experiments was actually coming from them. These scientists, doctors and soldiers all think they work for their country, yet don't realise they are working for a power that would take over the world if it were strong enough. In some ways it already has. All that, and most people don't even believe the Illuminati exists.'

'That doesn't explain what you know, just your suspicions.' Preacher said. He sat down in the chair opposite Lucy. He felt relaxed. He had decided he would kill her once he learnt who had told her their secrets.

'True. But of course I'm not telling you anything you don't know. I know for example that your organisation has been controlling the rise of fuel prices, as well as feeding into the rumour that fuel is running out. At the same time they are buying stock in fuel companies. You manipulate the stock market to your own ends. Creating crashes whenever you need to destroy a rival company.'

'All conjecture. But who told you the passwords? Who gave you that information?'

Lucy smiled. 'You wish to kill him, is that it?'

'Yes.'

'But what if I told you that this person couldn't help himself? That he had to give me the information and that he doesn't even remember doing it?'

Preacher sat back in his chair and formed his hands into a pyramid under his chin, 'Go on … I suppose you used some kind of drug to extract the information?'

'You could say that. I started with Cameron first. He was the obvious choice. But I soon discovered that he was a pawn in someone else's game. He was also hopelessly loyal to the American Empire. He believed that the experiments with the revenants were for the good of his country.'

'Cameron is not one of us. I knew that,' Preacher said.

'Do you know everyone who is?'

Preacher remained silent and scrutinised her. He considered how much to say, Collins was trying to draw information from him by giving a little, wasn't she? But how much more would he learn if he told her something – and this was such a small question to answer.

'Not everyone. I only know some.'

'True answer. Perhaps we could learn to get along after all, Preacher. So. No one in the Illuminati knows all of the members, but you each know some. And you fell into my trap because you didn't know who the member was that worked here.'

'Yes. I was told it was a senior blood specialist.'

Lucy nodded and, as if on cue, Joe came back to the lab and walked to the doorway. 'All okay?' Lucy said.

Preacher turned around and glanced at Joe then back at Lucy.

'Thanks Joe that will be all. Please close this door before you go.'

'Him?' Preacher asked as the door closed.

Lucy smiled. 'I always knew you were smart.'

'It can't be him ...'

'Oh it certainly is.'

'I tried the phrase on him. He didn't give the right response. Instead he started to waffle about how he had never learnt Latin.'

'He's mine,' Lucy said and the tone of her voice made Preacher look at her sharply. 'By that I mean he's my servant. We like to call our servants Renfields – I'm sure you get the joke ...'

Preacher saw her fangs then. The sharp, long canines were identical to Subject Seventeen's. Preacher jumped up and his seat clattered away behind him.

'You can't be ...'

'I am. Why else would I do so much to infiltrate this base? They had something that was ours ... I had to be certain it belonged to us first, and now I am. Thanks to you.'

'W ... what do you mean?'

'You took Gabriele to see One. It confirmed to me that he had contact with the woman at least once before.'

'I don't understand ...'

'The revenants are our ... shall we say ... retarded offspring. They are mistakes that we didn't know about, or chose not to correct. I didn't understand why or how they had occurred until I took the blood samples. Their blood, you see, holds the key to the reproduction of our race. We have until now been a select group.'

Preacher edged back to the wall, then tried the door handle but it wouldn't open.

'It's locked,' Lucy stated. 'Won't you sit down again? I have no plans to kill you just now, Preacher. In fact if it makes you feel safer I'll call you Darren. That's far less formal isn't it?'

Preacher stared at her. She could smell the fear rushing through his veins and it excited her, but Lucy was an expert at self-control and so she tucked away her fangs and waited for Preacher to take his seat again.

'Why are you telling me all this?' Preacher said.

'I don't know. Maybe I just want to brag about my achievements to someone. You see my brothers and sisters would never approve of my pastime. They see my work as a waste of time when I could be living in luxury, feeding randomly on the blood of mortals. But blood fascinates me on so many levels, you understand.'

Preacher picked up his chair and sat down, placing his hands back under his chin in an attempt to look calm and appear confident. It didn't quite work but Lucy was too interested in talking now and Preacher realised that it didn't matter how he felt, the end result on this meeting would be whatever Lucy wanted it to be.

'The revenants have a similar DNA to us but it is somewhat retarded. Or at least something in it reacts to the change in a far less positive way than it does with the vampire gene carriers. They become devolved. Whereas we are evolved. The revenants have less brain capacity. We have more. But you know all this already from your studies of Gabriele.'

Preacher began to relax. It was clear she wanted to talk this through and he knew that to keep her talking would give him time to form a plan and perhaps even the opportunity to escape.

'Subject Seventeen … Gabriele … he knew One? He bit her?'

Lucy laughed. 'Oh good Lord no. He didn't bite that girl. That's what is so intriguing. She was his lover and I don't know the full facts, but I found out that she killed herself. You see. She must have still had some of him inside her when she died.'

'What do you mean?' asked Preacher.

'That's what is so amazing. I thought it was the blood … or perhaps saliva by which we passed on the … infection. Maybe he had blood shared with her? Don't look so shocked, Darren. How else are we to gain full control over a Renfield? But no. It can be any body fluid. That is, if the victim is susceptible. You see she died less than twelve hours after they had made love … she was carrying his semen inside her. Isn't that *incredible*? You know what else? And this is the real breakthrough … I had her drugged after you took Gabi to see her. Then I swabbed her. It was still there. Still inside her after all these years. Gabriele's sperm was still inside. Do you know what that means?'

Preacher thought that suddenly he was losing his mind. He didn't understand anything. All of this sounded impossible.

'You must be mistaken,' he said. 'The vampire bit her and she changed.'

Lucy stopped smiling and stared at Preacher. She was unhappy to be interrupted. 'I'm not mistaken, Darren Preacher, and you are beginning to bore me. I think for your sake you should respectfully listen.'

Lucy stood up and Preacher shrank back into the chair. He had nowhere to go and he knew that she had the strength to kill him anytime she wanted.

'I had Gabi drugged again and I took some of his sperm while he was sedated. The swab from One matched perfectly and it was still alive. It was feeding or being fed by One's blood. Our sperm is as infectious as our blood. She was turned because she died soon after he fucked her.'

Preacher didn't know how to answer but realised that Collins was waiting for some response from him.

'You are indeed an intelligent woman, Collins. It must have taken quite a brain to deduce that. Do you believe that all of these creatures were turned in this way?'

'The others were all bitten, I'm sure of it. That is why this is such a break through.'

'What now?' asked Preacher. 'Surely there is another direction we can take this investigation?'

Lucy reached for him. 'Oh there is, Darren. This is where we learn if you are a carrier of my gene, or of the revenants. But there is the almost certain possibility that you are neither and my bite will just kill you.'

'Please … I could help you.'

'Oh but you have helped me. You've made me realise that this base has to be destroyed and everything, every piece of information relating to me and my kind must burn with it. And you are just the first of many people here to reach the limit of your usefulness.'

'You're completely insane …' Preacher gasped.

'No. I'm merely a monster, Darren. And as such I must do what all monsters do: kill those who get in the way. Be they innocent or culpable, my hunger feels no guilt …'

Lucy pulled Preacher forward and though he kicked and screamed, no one came to help, he had forgotten that the little office was soundproofed. When her teeth penetrated the artery in his neck, his cock hardened in pleasure and he came. Sperm soaked his expensive chinos. By then, Preacher didn't care. All he wanted was to die in her arms and as she bled him he hoped that he would return her equal and not some retarded bastard child who craved flesh rather than blood.

The old scar itched on his wrist. It reminded him that one of these monsters still lay buried in concrete in his basement, and that the infection hadn't killed him last time. It gave him hope in those final moments.

Preacher died slowly as Lucy took her time. She enjoyed his blood, it was rich and sweet, just like Joe's. Then when his body died. She picked up the paperweight from her desk and bashed Preacher's brains out for good measure. This was one revenant that she didn't want to see coming back.

5
Vertigo

Lilly withdrew her sword from the sheath on her back and stood ready to fight as the doors opened. But thankfully the lift was empty. This did nothing to ease the unrest Lilly felt, however. Instead it added to her nervous tension and slight nausea as they stepped into the lift. She lowered the sword as Anthony pressed the minus 20 button and the lift doors closed and began its descent down into the bowels of the desert.

Halfway down, Anja staggered and stumbled against the wall of the lift. 'I feel dizzy,' she said.

'Yes,' Lilly answered. 'Me too. Hold on, we're almost there.'

At the same moment a black pain squeezed at Anthony's chest. He felt as though he couldn't breathe. It was as though something were draining the life and strength from him. Chez caught him as he fell backwards. Anthony's face was ashen and his eyes seemed to have sunk back into his head.

'What's happening?' Chez asked.

'I'm not sure but I don't think that being this far below ground agrees with us. It's worse for Anja and Anthony because they are both still young.'

'It feels like ...' Anja gasped. 'Something is choking me.'

'I'm sending you both back. Chez and I can do this. If we're not out within an hour, get off the base and don't come back,' Lilly said.

She caught hold of Anja and helped her stand upright as the lift continued to descend but both Anja and Anthony became sicker and more panicked the lower they went. Neither of the young vampires had the will or strength to argue with Lilly.

The lift came to a halt.

'Okay?' asked Lilly, and Chez nodded. She helped Anja over to Anthony and they clung to the handrail and to each other while Chez and Lilly stepped towards the lift doors.

The doors opened up onto an empty corridor. Lilly and Chez had managed to maintain their invisibility but Anja and Anthony couldn't sustain it with the pain and sickness they were experiencing. Lilly glanced over at the two before pressing the button that would send the lift back up to ground level.

'Remember. Get out of the base at the first sign of trouble. Until then, keep hidden.'

'I'm sorry,' Anthony gasped. 'I wanted to help …'

'In that condition both of you would be a burden to us. You understand that, don't you?'

They both nodded. Lilly stepped out of the lift with Chez and they watched the doors close before turning back to the corridor that would lead them, they hoped, straight to where Gabriele was being held.

It was colder below the ground, but not beyond human comfort. Even so, Lilly shivered from the tension she felt rather than the temperature. There was something strange and unpleasant down here and she almost dreaded finding out exactly what it was.

Chez took her arm when he noticed her pause.

'Are you okay?' he asked.

'I should be asking you that,' Lilly said.

'You were my maker, but you are barely older than me in real time,' Chez pointed out. 'I'm alright, but I can sense something. I don't like it at all.'

'Yes,' Lilly nodded. 'And it's evil.'

They moved between white-washed breeze-block walls. Strip lighting overhead lit their way, and as they reached the first set of double doors, Lilly felt an intense and overwhelming urge to scratch her skin. It was as though a plague of ants was crawling up her legs, arms and spine.

'Oh my God, what is that?' Chez asked and she knew he must be feeling it too.

'It's like a warning. Something is trying to scare us away, but why doesn't it affect Lucrezia?'

'How do we know it doesn't?' Chez said.

It was true that they were able to overcome the sensation by merely focusing on shutting it out. Lilly realised that Chez was right. Lucrezia, if she felt this thing, would no doubt do the same but she didn't understand why she would put herself through this intense discomfort in the first place.

They pulled one side of the double doors open and glanced through. They were weighted and automatically closed after people passed through. Lilly remembered these were safety doors and that they could hold back a fire if one ever started down here, giving the occupants an opportunity to escape. The corridor beyond was empty so Lilly and Chez stepped out into it. Chez noticed the security cameras but their invisibility was holding firm so they continued silently down the corridor towards another set of doors. On the other side the space widened into crossroads and, through windows across the corridor, they could see people working in a lab. They were faced with a choice of three corridors. One was open and seemed to lead to other labs, another had a set of doors closing it off like the one they had come through and the third one had doors that held the sign 'Restricted Access'.

Lilly nodded towards the sign and they walked directly towards the doors. They stood by them, and Lilly noted the pass-swipe mechanism which held them shut. At that moment one opened and the man called Joe, who they had seen talking to Lucrezia earlier, came through. Lilly and Chez both stepped back in time to avoid a collision, and Chez put his foot out to stop the door closing.

Lilly watched Joe walking back down the other corridor, the way they had come, but then he paused and entered a door that she hadn't noticed, just on the corner. Joe closed the door behind him, but not before Lilly noticed him shudder. Maybe everyone felt the effects of being underground like this, or maybe Joe had on some level sensed their presence.

Chez held the door open and they both walked through,

letting it shut behind them.

They found themselves in what appeared to be a corridor of cells. Each of the doors were firmly closed. Lilly paused by the first one. There was no obvious lock, but on the wall by the door was a keypad operated system. She looked at the door and noticed the sliding panel. Without thinking she reached up and opened the panel. Beyond was a dark and airless room, a gloomy concrete cell containing a small child strapped into a chair.

The child looked back at her with dead eyes and grinned hungrily with a mouthful of razor teeth that reminded Lilly of a shark.

'Jesus!' she gasped stepping back. 'I think we found one of those *things* that Anja told us about.'

Chez looked inside as Lilly stepped back. 'That is grotesque.'

Lilly looked around suddenly, 'Gabi. I can *sense* Gabi. He's nearby.'

They closed the panel and Lilly hurried ahead down the corridor as Chez followed. The corridor twisted right, then left then divided at a T-junction into two main passages.

'This way,' Lilly said and she led them down the right hand corridor. They passed several identical cell doors, and Lilly finally stopped when she reached the cell at the very end of the corridor. The passage ended in a blank wall here.

'Here?' Chez asked. He frowned. Then reached forward, pulling back the small panel and leaning forward to look inside.

An ugly, scrawny woman threw herself at the door like a rabid dog.

'What the fuck ...?' said Lilly.

'This is wrong. It's not Gabi's cell.'

'This place is confusing me,' said Lilly, frowning. 'I feel like I'm in some kind of maze and the sides have grown so tall that I can't work out my way home.'

'He is here somewhere. I can feel him,' Chez said.

They turned and looked at the cell door opposite. With more caution, Lilly opened the panel and they looked into the room to see a jumble of furniture, a flat screen television and a coffee table with a plate with the remains of a steak on. To one side was a bunk, and Gabi was stretched out on it, arms and legs pulled as though he were on a rack.

Gabriele groaned.

'We have to get him out of there!' Lilly said. 'What the hell have they done to him?'

Chez examined the panel beside the door but couldn't understand how to open it. He pressed several buttons but nothing happened.

'Parker ...' said Gabi under his breath.

'He knows we're here, he's trying to tell us something,' Lilly whispered. 'Gabi, how do we get you out?'

'Parker ...' he said again.

At that moment one of the soldiers turned into the corridor. He walked up to Gabi's door and began to key in the code. The soldier was in some kind of trance, as though he were sleep-walking. But Lilly and Chez soon realised that this man was under Gabi's spell.

The door opened and the locks holding Gabi automatically released. Parker walked into the room and knelt by Gabi's bed.

'Feed from me, master,' he said and Gabi sat up, dazed and confused, he reached for the proffered wrist and bit deeply into the man's vein. Parker groaned. His eyes rolled up and he sighed. He was like a junkie getting his fix.

6
Wa She Shu Magic

The former Private Elin was waiting at the perimeter when the monsters arrived. He saw them, but they could not see him. He hid himself well among the soldiers, running around, behaving like he too didn't know what had set off the alarms. But Little Bird knew that this meant the moment was finally here. He could end it all this day. Finish the evil that was contained in the base, and put all of the monsters to rest. The earth of his ancestors demanded it.

In his waking dreams Little Bird had seen the death of his people. A pestilence that had been brought by the white man had taken hold of many in the tribe. His blood line had survived because his ancestor, a shaman called Walking Spirit, had made a pact with the dead. Little Bird had seen it all. It was as though the tribe had returned to re-enact the final moments just for him. It helped him to understand what he had to do.

In his mind's eye he saw Walking Spirit, old and ravaged, his pock-marked face remaining blank throughout his spiritual trance, while the spirits of his ancestors danced around him. He felt as though he could conjure this image up at any time and so, standing at the perimeter, with his semi-automatic Beretta in his hands, Little Bird let the vision wash over him again.

Walking Spirit held up his hands. His ritual robes were so similar to Nonna's that Little Bird wondered if this had been passed down through the ages.

'Save our people,' Walking Spirit begged.

'Yes,' the spirits said, whirling around him. 'What do you offer us in return?'

'I offer my life for the future of my children's children,' Walking Spirit said.

'You are an old man. You have so little life left in you,' the spirits chanted.

'My blood then,' Walking Spirit said. 'All spirits crave the blood of a shaman.'

'Yesss …' hissed the spirits. 'We accept your blood for it will feed many.'

They used the sharpness of the sand to cut at Walking Spirit's arms and torso and legs and the old man bled down into the earth and the spirits continued to move around him.

'The dead shall rest again with your blood sacrifice,' they said.

Walking Spirit stood for as long as his strength allowed and then he fell forward onto the soil and bled until there was nothing left inside him. Still the spirits flew around his body and the wind whipped up until Little Bird felt that a tornado was building with the body of Walking Spirit in the centre. It ripped at the dead man's robes and hair and Little Bird felt it, as though it were him they surrounded.

They sang to him; a lyrical psalm, or hymn, that only the dead could know.

Walking Spirit rose from the ground and turned his dead, hungry eyes on Little Bird.

'Feed me,' he said, and his eyes burnt into Little Bird's until he felt the thoughts of Walking Spirit invade his mind.

'I don't know how,' said Little Bird. The part of him that still believed he was Pete Elin refused to accept the obvious but Little Bird knew deep down what he had to do. He had to feed the earth, just as his ancestor had done and then the circle around the base would close and it would trap the evil inside until …

Little Bird's mind stumbled. *Until what*, he thought and he heard Walking Spirit chuckle.

Until the dead rise again and take away the sins of the white man …

The vision fell away.

'Elin? You okay?' It was another soldier he knew, a female,

but her name wouldn't come to his mind. Little Bird was no longer part of the white man's world and its friendships and familiarities meant nothing to him. Still he had to play the part. Behave as though he was one of them until the time came and he could fulfil his destiny, just at Walking Spirit had.

'Yeah, sure. You find anything beyond the perimeter?'

'Nope. Probably an animal triggered the alarms,' said the soldier. She had warm brown eyes. Little Bird wondered which tribe she had come from and then he shook away the thought. She was white. They were all white on the base.

The soldiers began to head back inside the perimeter and the gates were locked. Soon the soldiers were returning to their duties or recreation activities. Little Bird, however, remained at the gate. He heard the sharp hum of electricity as the power returned to the fence

'I'll walk around a little longer. Just in case,' he told the female soldier.

'You do that. I on the other hand have a beer waiting for me in the mess.'

Little Bird watched her leave. His eyes were dull and he felt as though he were only half in this world. He squinted and could see the other world once again, the world that the spirits occupied. They waited. Endlessly patient. Their essence floated in and around the base like condensation. Among them, Little Bird could see Walking Spirit and Nonna but neither of these spirits acknowledged him as he walked the perimeter, chanting once more the song, or hymn, or psalm that gave power to the circle.

Soon …

7
Awakening

I could feel Lilly when she arrived on the base, but I had been rendered unconscious by that bitch Lucrezia. As always she had her own agenda, to which I was not privy, but as I come fully awake I remember this and try to explain it to Lilly.

Parker swoons in my arms.

'Lucrezia is here,' I say, pushing Parker aside. I pull myself up on trembling legs as the after-effect of the anaesthetic drug still shudders through my limbs. I bend down and unclip Parker's security card from the pocket of his khaki shirt.

'Can you cloak yourself?' Lilly asks.

'I think so …'

'Then hurry. We're getting you out of here.'

I stumble as I step away from the bed; the fresh blood in my system is fighting against the drug. Parker will revitalise me, but it is going to take more time. Chez takes my arm and I am grateful for his help.

'Anja's outside,' Chez tells me. 'She's been worried sick about you.'

'We've all been worried,' Lilly says a little sharply.

'True,' Chez answers. 'We've missed you, Gabi. Our family just wouldn't be the same without you.'

I see Lilly smile at him then and I know how much their love extends to all of us. We are a family and I have been foolish in my jealousy. It led me to this point, perhaps weakened me and I am relieved to see them, even though I have no idea how they found me.

'Explanations later,' Lilly says taking my other arm. They

lead me out of the cell and away down the corridor.

That strange and awful vertigo hits me as we reach the corridor intersection and I stumble over my feet again. Ahead I see the doors marked 'Restricted Access' and I recall that Helaine is down there. She is a monster and beyond my help but part of me, having remembered her so vividly, wants to go down and rescue her too.

'What is it?' Chez asks feeling my hesitation.

'I have to show you something before we leave. It's important to us all,' I say.

Lilly nods. She looks around and it is then I realise that she too is feeling that awful pressure of the earth around us. I straighten myself up and push my will into the discomfort, forcing it away with the last vestiges of the drug that is still trying to dampen my senses.

'It's like ants crawling over my skin,' Chez murmurs.

'You feel it too?' I ask.

'We all do. It made Anja and Anthony sick, which is why they are above ground. They could barely walk by the time we reached this level.'

'Let's hurry,' Chez says.

I lead them through the double doors, having lifted the pass code from Parker's brain as I sucked his blood. I had always been aware that I may need his information to escape this place. I swipe his security card, type in the code and then we pass through into the older part of the complex.

It looks no less deteriorated than it had on my previous visit. If anything it seems somehow worse. There is mould growing in the corners and one of the walls looks pitted. It is as though the insects we have been imaging have been picking their way through the concrete. We begin to walk down the corridor; there are patches here and there of what looks like earth and sand. Plus all of the cells, other than the one containing Helaine, are empty. I am sure that some of them were occupied a few days earlier. As we reach the end of the corridor I'm feeling much more myself and I'm able to stand without assistance.

'What is it?' Lilly asks as I stop in front of the cell.

'Helaine,' I explain. 'She was my lover.'

I flip back the cover and open the peep hole so that they can see what remains of the woman I once loved.

'Gabi, this isn't your fault ...' Lilly begins. 'Accidents happen.'

'I didn't bite her,' I say. I let my memories pour into them both and they see the scenario of my love and time spent with Helaine.

'I took her body that night and I buried her. Then I left France.'

'You were certain she was dead?' Lilly asks.

'I was certain. She was dead. There was no doubt in my mind.'

'Then ... what happened?'

A shudder wracks through my body and I feel the cold of the cell seeping out as though Helaine's deformed soul is reaching for me. I look in at her still form. She is too still. Perhaps she has given up her struggle to continue.

'I don't know. But now I have to lay her to rest.'

Chez and Lilly exchange a look that shows me they are confused.

I key in the pass code to the cell and the door springs open.

She is like a broken doll. She barely turns to look at us as we enter her cell. Even now I can see that she is unlike the others. The fire, the hunger and the violence seems to have burnt out. Maybe she is a tamed animal after all these years, or maybe she knows I have come to free her.

The cell reeks and I know already that the smell of decay emanates from this walking corpse. We approach her cautiously, ready to jump back should she suddenly decide to attack. I turn her over and stare down as the filth-caked face, the matted hair that still has hints of the glorious red it had once been. The blue eyes, red and blood-shot, like an alcoholic suffering from a serious hangover, stare back with a dull light and no recognition.

Then it occurs to me why she isn't moving.

'She's been drugged,' I frown. 'But why?'

'Because I wanted to learn how she had become what she is,' says a voice behind us.

We turn as one to stare at Lucrezia. She has rid herself of the contact lenses and spectacles and her blonde hair falls loose over her shoulders. She looks like our sister once again and I realise that she has finally decided to shed her disguise.

'What intrigues are you involved in here, sister?' Chez asks.

'Caesare. You never fail to surprise me with your capacity for survival,' Lucrezia sneers. 'You were the last face I expected to ever see again.'

'And why is it that you are always at the heart of something that causes harm to our kind, Lucrezia?' Lilly says.

'I have not harmed Gabriele,' Lucy replies. 'In fact I have ensured that all of his blood samples were destroyed before they were analysed. These fools know nothing about us that Gabi did not willingly show them. But even that I have taken care of.'

'What do you mean?' I ask.

'Preacher is dead.'

'I see. And I suppose drugging me was ensuring that I wasn't harmed?'

'I needed some samples from you that I knew you wouldn't willingly give,' Lucy says. 'It gave me the final answers I needed.'

'I didn't bite Helaine,' I say again.

'I know that. But nevertheless you did sire her.'

'How?' Lilly asks.

'I could show you. Back in my lab ...'

Lilly shakes her head. 'We're getting Gabi out of here. I suggest you make no attempt to stop us.'

'I have no intention of stopping you,' Lucy says. 'But if you want answers, a small delay will give you them.'

I meet Lilly's gaze. I don't trust Lucrezia, never have, but it is true that she didn't allow anyone to harm me. If anything she did all she could to protect me from Preacher's curiosity.'

'I want answers,' I say. 'But first ...'

I turn. I look down at Helaine and my heart hurts with grief to see her thus. It is as though I have been forced to open her grave after centuries of decay has corroded her beauty. I kneel beside her. Stroke her hair. She stares back at me blankly. And then, a horrible smile curves her lips. Hunger. Sickness. All of it illustrated by those awful pointed teeth. I pick Helaine's head up carefully and then without hesitation I dash her head hard against the concrete wall. Two sharp hard blows and her skull cracks open.

I lay her back down on the bunk. Bits of bone merge with the blood and brain tissue that seeps out from her crushed forehead. I stroke back the filthy hair, seeing again the face of my lover appearing briefly as the evil inside her dies.

'Rest now my beauty,' I tell her and I watch as her corpse finally falls into the decay her long buried body should have already endured. 'She is free now.'

Chez strokes my arm and I'm once again aware of his love and empathy. I turn and embrace him. I push back tears that fill my eyes because I refuse to show Lucrezia my pain. I turn and look at her. My eyes are cold and hard.

'You have some explaining to do,' I say.

Lucrezia smiles and I feel the urge to dash out her brains also.

'My office is this way,' she says, turning away from the door.

We follow her though I can see that Lilly is reluctant to do so. I need to have these answers though; it seems that this latest problem could affect all of our lives. Who knew how many more of my former lovers survive.

I look around at the empty cells as we pass them once more. *Who was in here? Perhaps* ... No. The thought was just too horrible to imagine.

8
Silent Sand

Little Bird felt a change in the air. There was sand moving on the wind and the earth shifted below his feet as he walked the perimeter. He paused during the second round of his walk. The time for the blood offering was almost here. Then nature would have its way and the natural balance between life and death would be restored.

The alarm had long since been switched off. The soldiers had relaxed back into their routines and those not currently on duty were enjoying themselves in the mess. Little Bird glanced over to the large social building. He could see lights on in the main bar area. The smokers of the group were loitering outside the open door in a cloud of stale smoke. Music picked up again and floated out into the warm night. Little Bird listened to the sound of relaxed laughter then turned and continued to walk.

Along the route the top soil had been churned up. It looked as though something had been burrowing under the surface. Little Bird watched as sand spilled out of a hole in the ground. He paused and examined it with curiosity. He took this as another sign that the land was ready.

A tremor rocked the ground under his feet. He staggered but managed to regain his balance. He looked around to see what impact the movement had on his colleagues. He saw a soldier standing by the reception door smoking a cigar and one of the germ scientists leaning against the wall. They didn't appear to be concerned about the sudden rumble beneath the earth. It was as though they couldn't even feel it.

Outside the perimeter Little Bird saw his tribe waiting.

Nonna was at its head with Walking Spirit by her side. He could see the scars covering the ancient shaman's arms and legs. The wounds gapped but they were devoid of blood.

'The land is barren,' Nonna said. 'Feed it Little Bird.'

But Little Bird wasn't ready. He wanted to walk the perimeter once more. He needed to be sure the circle would hold. So he turned his back on the tribe and continued to walk.

'Don't hold onto your white man's ways,' Nonna said.

Little Bird found her walking beside him.

'This is your destiny. Yet still you fight it.'

'I can feel the change in the air. But the time is not yet, Nonna,' Little Bird said. 'This will kill me won't it?'

Nonna continued walking beside him, 'Death is merely a transition. We all must travel it to reach the next plane.'

'I have no children,' said Little Bird. 'How can my blood-line continue?'

'These are the concerns of those who believe in nothing. Your blood will give life to the children once lost. The children buried under this earth. The white man has no respect for our traditions. They even poured their concrete over the remains of our ancestors.'

'This is a graveyard?' Little Bird said. 'That's what all this is about?'

'Not just a graveyard ...' Nonna said.

Little Bird paused and turned to Nonna but she had disappeared once more. He felt he needed answers. He was to sacrifice himself, yet why? Why was it so important to pour his blood into this sand? Why now? He had thought that Nonna had imparted all of her wisdom to him when she burned the white blood from his veins, but she hadn't told him everything. The lack of insight gave him severe doubts.

'Your white man's blood is filling you with doubt,' said Walking Spirit. 'We tried to burn it from you, but something still remains.'

'Yes I do have doubts,' Little Bird said. 'I need to know what will happen.'

'You will feed the earth,' said Walking Spirit. 'You will free our people.'

'How?'

'The dead will take back the land that has been stolen.'

Little Bird began to walk again. Faster this time. 'I don't like the sound of it. Yet I know this is my destiny because Nonna says it is.'

'I would never lie to you,' Nonna said, reappearing where Walking Spirit had been. She placed a calm hand on Little Bird's arm. He slowed his walk to an easier pace.

'I trust you Nonna. But I am afraid.'

'Then you are a truly brave warrior.'

'How can that be? My fear is all consuming.'

'Yes. But still you will do what needs to be done.'

Nonna left him then and Little Bird continued his walk until he had completed yet another circle. He thought about her words. The tribe would revere him. He would earn his place among the many spirits that guided the living ancestors.

He looked over at the barracks, then at the large warehouse and back to the reception building. The creatures were inside. He had to act before it was too late.

Little Bird rolled up the legs on his combat trousers exposing the bare skin to the warm evening air. Then he removed his jacket and tee-shirt, throwing them casually onto the sandy earth. He was now bare from the waist up. He bent down and collected two handfuls of sand. The grains seeped silently through his fingers but he managed to grip it tightly enough so that it did not all fall back to the ground.

Little Bird raised his arms and, fists clenched, began to sing. He felt the words of power burning his mouth and throat, yet still he chanted them. Behind and around him he could feel the presence of his ancestors and so the song continued to pour from his lips, growing stronger and more certain with every phrase. The hairs stood up on the back of his neck as he felt the circle close around the perimeter, locking in everyone on the base.

The spirits drew closer around him. They swirled like the

wind, faster and faster until the wind became as cold and sharp as steel.

The first cut across his breast shocked him. Little Bird almost released the sand from his hands and too much fell to the floor. He knew this didn't matter though, for as soon as the drops of blood from his wound dripped to the floor, he saw the sand rising up in a wave of golden grit. The wind and sand sliced at the exposed skin on his arms and legs. More blood fell. Little Bird felt strong. He knew he could remain standing for as long as needed and he knew that Nonna and Walking Spirit were right. He felt the dead beneath the earth. The old graves were shifting in the sand, rising to the surface from their deep, forgotten pit.

Another bubble of sand burst upwards and Little Bird saw the first skeletal hand reach up, pulling the ragged body with it. A splash of his blood fell on the rotted flesh and the creature began to flesh out, blossoming like a new flower growing from poisonous soil. It was a woman, someone Little Bird didn't recognise. She glanced at him then turned and shambled towards the base.

More of the dead pulled themselves from the ground around him. Each received a splash of blood, as though they were being anointed or receiving a holy sacrament. Although they reformed, in some part of his mind, Little Bird knew that the creatures weren't human. He watched them all stagger away as if they had forgotten how to use their limbs, or perhaps because they were reanimated corpses, the new spirit inside had trouble working the bodies. The thought brought a shudder from him. *New spirit*? Why had he even thought such a thing?

Despite the heat, as his blood dripped down to the earth, Little Bird began to feel cold. His arms cramped and dropped to his sides, but still he held onto the last grains of sand in his damp palms.

The corpse of a child heaved up from the ground and pulled itself towards Little Bird. He felt hypnotised by the small hands as they grappled at clumps of grass and earth, pulling one hand and then the other. When he looked at the figure's legs, he saw twisted and deformed bones. Despite the horror he felt at the sight of the creature, Little Bird held out his arm and watched as blood splashed on its face and chest.

Fresh skin began to grow from the blood spots and stretched over the face. Little Bird could see that the child was a boy of no more than eight or nine. A child much like he had once been when his mother died. The boy pressed skeletal hands against the new flesh. His fingers plumped out, perfect fingernails formed on pink, flushed skin. The boy pulled himself up, the deformed legs straightened as he turned and hobbled away towards the base.

The burial ground fanned out around him and over and over the sand gave birth to the dead. Each became reborn by the blood of Little Bird. Somewhere in the distance, Little Bird heard the alarms going off again. He turned his tired eyes to the base, but all he could see was the blurred naked shapes of his people as they shambled over to the buildings. He had no idea what would happen but he heard cries and shouts, followed by rapid gunfire.

At some point Little Bird's legs gave out. He slipped to his knees. His vision was fading, he was wracked with pain and the coldness had seeped deep into his bones, yet still they came – an army from an ancient graveyard – all demanding more of his blood to wake their limbs and consolidate their rebirth.

9
Lucy's Renfield

Joe was in the lab when Lucy brought the strangers in. He had just taken some of the blood from his hidden stash and it rested in a phial in his lab coat pocket. He stared at the four as they entered the room, his eyes blinking as he took in Lucy's new appearance and the fact that Seventeen was now roaming free around the building.

'Who's this?' asked Chez.

Joe's eyes fell on him, then passed to each of the vampires in turn.

'Nobody. He's just my Renfield. He'll do whatever I tell him to. Joe, go fetch the slides I took this morning.'

Joe reacted immediately and brought Lucy everything she asked for. Then he stepped back and watched her show the slides and explain her findings. This gave him ample opportunity to examine the four immortals. He knew Seventeen already but he had never really noticed the resemblance he had to Lucy before. They could be brother and sister; certainly they were from the same gene pool, with their pale blonde hair and green eyes. Joe noticed that Lucy had now discarded her contact lenses. He had known for some time that her eyes were different when they were alone and so he had taken careful note of her eyes during the day, when she barely noticed him around.

Then, of course, there was the other two. He hadn't seen them before but they interested him greatly. In appearance, the woman was in her early twenties – much like Lucy – but there was something about her … a feeling Joe had that made his head hurt and the limbs in his body ache. She was powerful and old.

Stronger than Lucy. He knew it. Lucy referred to the other man as Chez, and he was the closest to her in likeness. He noticed they had the same shape nose and the similarities between them went beyond the colouring. Joe knew there was more to their relationship but couldn't quite decide what. There was also tension between all of the vampires. Clearly, Lucy was the outcast, the black sheep.

Joe became aware that the four of them had rapidly dismissed his presence. It pleased and irritated him that the others treated him as though he was deaf, dumb and blind following Lucy's explanation. So he was her Renfield? That meant he belonged to her he supposed, but neither she nor the others knew that he had his own stash of blood now and he wasn't prepared to give up that source. He stared at Gabi again. His blood was rich and vibrant. Joe wasn't sure how he was going to keep his access to Seventeen but he knew he had to think of something.

'You are telling me you knocked me out to take some sperm?' Gabi said. 'I can't believe you.'

'You're missing the big picture here. I found out something important. We can reproduce via our body fluids as well as our bite. Although granted, I'm not sure if she would still have changed if you hadn't had sex prior to her death. But this is something we could experiment with in the future ...'

'Are you completely insane?' asked Lilly. 'There will be no more experiments on us or those creatures, Lucrezia.'

Lucy folded her arms and leaned back against the lab table. 'I don't think any of you are in a position to tell me what to do. You should know that I plan to shut this place down. But not because you want me to, it was always my plan.'

'How do you aim to do that?' asked Chez.

'Fire. It's the only way to ensure that everything is destroyed. As well as systematically taking down all those who have the knowledge to do this again elsewhere,' Lucy explained.

'You have a history of betrayal, so why should we believe you?' Lilly said.

Lucy unfolded her arms and turned to Joe. 'Joe, go in the office and fetch me the two gasoline cans I left there. I want you to sprinkle the gas all over this room. Then, take it down to minus 20. Once there you'll burn up the holding cells and the lab. If anyone gets in your way – kill them.'

Joe turned and walked into the office. He returned a few minutes later and began to slosh the liquid all over the floors and the equipment on the table.

'Joe. Here's my keys. Don't forget to burn all the records in the file cabinet.'

Joe took the keys from Lucy's hand and opened the files. He poured gasoline over the papers and the interior of the office.

'You might want to leave while I light this,' Joe said.

'Leave that for now. Start the fire downstairs. We'll be out of here before it arrives on this floor.'

Unable to disobey Joe took the gasoline cans and left the room. Outside the room he looked down the corridor at the lift and then turned in the opposite direction. Using his security pass he opened the door to the stairs. Most of the works at the base used the lifts, Joe knew there would be less chance of coming in contact with anyone else this way and he didn't want to come face to face with one of the armed soldiers.

When he reached minus 20 he realised that he had left most of his blood stash upstairs in the lab. A momentary panic overcame him. How was he to get it with Lucy and the others there? Going back now would show her that he wasn't completely her slave. Of course, he believed that he could disobey her if he wanted to. He still had free will and he was only following her instructions because it suited him. He stood at the bottom of the stairs, anxiety squeezing his chest. He wanted to go back, but found he couldn't.

I'll go back to light the room. They'll be gone then. I can take the blood before I strike a match, he decided. The pain of panic eased up as soon as he decided to continue Lucy's instructions, but Joe didn't worry too much about that. It was his needs and desires he was following, not hers. He swiped his security pass again and the stairwell door opened up onto minus 20.

Joe looked out. There was no one around. He quickly left the stairwell and hurried out into the holding cell corridor. At that moment alarms sounded and a red alert went up throughout the base. He had no idea what was happening but as the soldiers and scientists all ran to their emergency posts on the upper levels he realised this was a mixed blessing. No one would be around down here to question him and all cameras would be focused on where the emergency was. Not that it mattered. Some part of his brain knew that after this no one would be able to touch him. The alert worried him though and then he shrugged. It's probably another false alarm.

He went down the corridor and began to splash the gasoline over the walls and doors. He wondered if concrete could actually burn or be set on fire. He didn't think it could and wondered what the point of all of this really was? To destroy a few papers and chemicals is all that Lucy could hope to achieve. And *finish the revenants,* he thought, *which might be what she really wants to do.*

He opened the peephole of the nearest door, and found Cameron staring back at him.

'They're coming, Joe. They are coming to take us back …'

'What the fuck …?'

Cameron's eyes looked up. 'Can't you hear them? Tap. Tap. Tapping away at the walls, climbing up through the earth. They are around us, beneath us, and now some of them are above …'

Joe sloshed gasoline into the cell. 'Getting rid of you will be the best solution. You fucking freak.'

Joe pulled out a match and struck it against the wall. Then he threw the lit flame into Cameron's cell and closed the peephole.

'It's no use!' Cameron called. 'They are coming for us Joe. We don't belong here.'

Joe walked away as Cameron began to scream. He wasn't sure that the revenants felt pain, but the sounds of his former boss screaming grated on his nerves and made his stomach churn. He hurried away, hoping that the cries wouldn't bring anyone to investigate. He still had too much to do. As he passed the other cells, he opened the peepholes and emptied a small amount of the gas inside, lighting each one. He felt no remorse. The freaks had to die, there was no other solution.

He passed through the restricted area, noticing that the downstairs labs were now all deserted. Joe was glad of this because he didn't really want to kill any of his former colleagues directly. Even so, he knew he had to destroy all the evidence he could and so in the lab he sloshed a little of the gasoline on the floor and over the worktops, then he ran down the corridor that housed One.

Joe came to a halt. Someone had opened the cell. Probably moved the creature, but he was surprised that he hadn't known about it. He was about to turn away when he saw movement from inside. Surely they hadn't left the door open by accident? Joe backed away. He was afraid. He couldn't run forward to close the cell even though he knew One was probably still in there. The creatures, he knew, could move at lightning speed when they needed to. He threw some of the gasoline over the floor in front of himself instead. It was linoleum and he was certain it would catch. He emptied one of the containers completely, sloshing the contents over the walls and floor, before ditching the canister in the doorway of one of the other cells.

He looked up after he had completed his work. That was when he heard something moving in the cell. A scraping, shuffling sound that put his nerves on edge.

'What …?'

Joe backed away and fumbled in his pocket for another match. A tall male appeared at the door of the cell. He was naked and malformed. His skin hung from grey bones. He opened his mouth and Joe could see a set of broken and rotted teeth. By this, Joe could deduce that the thing was not a revenant. At least, not one of the ones he was familiar with. Still the creature moved towards him and behind he could see more of them coming through the cell door behind it.

There was a loud crack, and the wall at the end of the corridor in front of Joe split apart. As Joe watched, numerous pairs of hands emerged from the break and started pushing the wall into the corridor. There were skeletal creatures breaking into the base through the wall, and Joe couldn't believe what he was seeing.

Joe's clumsy fingers found a match. He turned to the wall and struck it. The flame flared briefly then went out. By then the first creature had reached the gasoline puddle on the floor. It kicked the empty can, sending it spinning across the corridor. Joe pulled another match free. His hands were trembling but he was more precise this time. He struck and threw it, while rapidly backing towards the double doors.

The gas caught with a whoosh and flames spread backwards towards the cell and the canister. Flames whipped around the metal container, briefly erupting in a burst of fire. The creature, standing in the gasoline, ignited. Dried flesh and old bone were perfect conductors for the flame and it went up with a whooshing sound.

Joe turned and ran through the doors. He saw the burning creature staggering forward holding out a pitiful hand to him as he pulled the double doors closed. Joe pressed the emergency key code that held the mechanism shut. He paused, breathing heavily.

It can't get out, his rational mind thought. But how had it – or them – got through the concrete in the first place? And what the hell were they?

At the lab Joe lit the gasoline pooled there, before turning back to the stairwell. His hands were shaking. He had never felt such fear in his life. He glanced briefly down the main holding cell corridor. He could feel the heat from the flames. Smoke was now filling the corridors despite the closed and locked fire doors. Joe glanced down at the remaining canister: only a quarter full. Then, placing the container down, he pulled his lab coat up over his mouth and nose. With his free hand he unclipped his security card and swiped it over the reader and tugged at the door.

Nothing happened. The door stayed shut. Joe scanned the card again. Nothing. Damn! He glanced down at the card and his hands. They reeked of gasoline, somehow he had managed to get fuel on his fingers.

The heat below intensified. Joe wiped the card down on his lab coat, and then swiped again to no avail. He shook the door but it was firmly shut.

'Shit!'

Panic overwhelmed him. He took a deep breath only to feel the smoke and fumes burn his lungs. He coughed and hacked, then lifted his coat over his face again. It was getting harder to breath and Joe was having a lot of difficulty concentrating. He tried to level his breathing, forcing himself to push back the fear which was causing his mind to blank. He wiped the card again against his clothing, this time taking more care.

The next swipe on the reader resulted in a satisfying clunk. The door sprang open. Joe inhaled sharply and only then did he realise he had been holding his breath. He pushed the door open and almost fell into the stairwell. Then he slammed the door shut behind him and began his ascent back to the main area.

He took a sip from the phial of blood that was still in his pocket. His hands stopped shaking. His heartbeat steadied. A surge of confidence flooded his body. His legs stopped trembling and he pulled himself up the first flight of stairs. By the time he reached the next level he was nimbly taking the stairs two at a time.

Three levels up Joe heard an explosion down below. He stumbled on the stairs. The whole building seemed to lurch but still he smiled. The containment cell level was as damaged as it could be now. All he had to do was get back upstairs and finish the task Lucy had set him. But first, he would retrieve the samples of Gabi's blood from their hiding place.

The stairwell above erupted into chaos. Joe paused, looking down at the gasoline container that would give away his part in the mess. He went back down another level. The door opened easily, but he couldn't risk being locked out of the stairs again and so he threw the container into the corridor and shut the door again. At that moment a group of soldiers came clattering down the stairs.

'What's happening?' Joe asked.

'Get up top!' ordered one of the men. 'We're being attacked. You need to find high ground.'

Joe pretended to obey and turned, running back up the stairs.

10
The Hungry Dead

Little Bird slumped. His head lolled on his chest, his once rich skin was stark white and marble cold. He looked worse than the souls that he had revived but still the blood kept coming. In his mind's eye he could see the battle that raged.

His people were taking back the land. The dead had risen to rid the *Wa She Shu* of the pestilence of the white man. Little Bird felt at peace with the fall-out and as his death rapidly approached he felt no remorse. Nonna had told him what to do and he had done it. He had been true to his heritage at last and his place in heaven was assured.

At some point he found himself floating above his body. He had no substance, yet his eyes could see clearer than they ever had and he could hear the roar of his ancestors all around him. He followed the last of them, a group of children that held each other's hands as they tottered on fragile bones towards the base and the massacre. There had barely been enough blood left inside him to give them skin and life, and yet they shared what was left and gleefully headed into the fray.

The soldiers were dying. Guns fired, but they were useless against the attacking tribe. Little Bird felt a momentary regret as he saw some of his former colleagues fall beneath the hungry mouths of the dead. The dead would feed and the souls of the enemy would be dragged down into the pit. Little Bird knew it had to happen but still he flew from one body to the next as he saw the soldiers die. Even if he had wanted to he had no power to stop it. It was too late, but his blood gave life to the creatures and his loyalty was torn between his heritage and his friends.

Little Bird found himself in the base and then he saw them. The real monsters. There were six of them here. As soon as he had shed his body he could sense them all. He saw the younger two first, fighting for their lives as his people caught at them, pulling them back towards the sandy earth. Their bodies were strong, and the hungry dead made no attempt to feed from them. But still they swarmed over them, like possessive parents trying to control wayward children.

The young female screamed. It was a fear-filled yell that tore at the other vampire's heart. She was fragile to look at, beautiful, pale with blonde hair and wide innocent eyes. Little Bird could see how she would fool the mortals, and he knew that she was one and the same with Seventeen. He had studied Seventeen long enough.

'Anja!' cried the male. He threw off the grasping hands and arms of the dead and reached for his companion. And then they did something Little Bird hadn't expected. They jumped. High. Grasping at the side of the nearest building. They climbed up and away from the eager horde. The risen dead scrabbled at the walls but were incapable of climbing. Little Bird watched, realising that each had come from the grave with only one purpose and they had little thought beyond that. They wanted to take back all that was theirs but they had little intelligence to overcome obstacles.

He saw the vampires reach the top of the building and there they waited, staring down at the dead, their faces blank and confused. Little Bird hovered closer to them. He felt the glow of their auras. He knew they were unnatural beings and had to die.

'What the hell are they?' asked Anja.

'Revenants. They must be,' Anthony said.

Anja stood on the roof and looked out towards the food store. Little Bird knew what was there. He could feel the other four making their way up the stairs and out of the complex. He glanced down at the dead, willing them forward towards the warehouse and they turned and headed away leaving Anthony and Anja staring after them.

A soldier ran out in front of the approaching army, a group of five dead fell upon the man, tearing at him with rotted teeth until clothing and flesh were consumed by stomachs that had starved for centuries. The blood of their victims did not give them new vigour though and the hungry dead looked around for more to fill the void in their bellies as well as their souls.

Little Bird turned away leaving Anja and Anthony behind on the roof. He knew the young immortals couldn't escape his circle of power and he wanted to guide the dead to the others. There was one among them that was strong enough to break them all free. Little Bird knew that she mustn't be given the opportunity.

'This place is fucked and my cover will be blown when the lab goes up in smoke. I've had enough of haematology. I think I've learnt all I can,' Lucy said when they felt the explosion on the lowest level rock the remainder of the underground base.

'What are you saying?' asked Gabi.

'Let's get the fuck out of here before it all goes up.'

Lilly and Chez exchanged a look. They didn't trust Lucy, but they wanted out of the base. The place gave them all such bad feelings that the sooner they left the better. Lilly was beginning to worry about Anja and Anthony outside alone, even though the fear was totally irrational. She knew that both of them could handle a few humans and, after careful probing of Lucy's knowledge, had discovered that there was nothing other than the sleeping drug that could harm any of the immortals. Lilly hadn't forgotten the toxic bullets that had torn into Gabi's spine in Stockholm. She had almost lost him then and didn't want to lose him or anyone else now.

'Okay. Let's go,' she said.

They left Lucy's lab and made their way back into the main corridor. Outside, the other occupants, soldiers and scientific staff were running around in response to the alarms and the explosion.

'Cloak,' murmured Lilly and she sank back into the shadows

just as a group of soldiers rounded the corner and headed towards the stairs.

All four of them watched as the soldiers herded the scientists up the stairwell and out towards the reception.

'We'll go the back way,' said Lucy.

They followed her along another corridor. She scanned her security pass and the doors opened immediately to let the immortals through.

Lucy led them towards a large lift at the end. She pressed the call button and waited.

'Is that a good idea?' Chez said. 'I think I'd rather take the stairs.'

The lift failed to come and after a few minutes Lucy shrugged. 'I think security has them on lockdown for everyone's safety. There are more stairs this way.'

She turned back down the corridor and the others followed until she halted at another door and swiped her card again. The door opened and the four vampires entered another stairwell.

They ran up the stairs at impossible speed.

'Where does this one lead?' asked Gabi.

'The back entrance. Basically a doorway in the food store.'

'That's the way we came in,' said Chez.

Lucy looked over at him sharply. 'Smart boy, I've been here months and only recently learnt of this access.'

They reached the top of the stairs in seconds and Lilly stepped forward before Lucy could swipe the key card.

'What exactly will we find beyond here?' Lilly asked.

'Just a warehouse with entrances that lead down into the main facility. There may be a few soldiers milling around, after all we are on red alert.'

Lilly pressed her ear to the door. She felt strangely disorientated and fear made her heart pound faster.

'It doesn't feel right.'

'What doesn't?' asked Lucy swiping the card.

The door opened and the hungry dead came forward.

'What the fuck …?' gasped Lilly.

The first line of naked, half-rotted, half-formed bodies

shambled into the stairwell. The immortals backed away. At the front of the line was an old woman with long white hair, she carried a stick, carved with faces of animals. Lilly thought it was like a mini totem pole. She realised the bodies – the walking dead – were reanimated corpses but didn't understand what motivated them.

Bony fingers with broken nails clawed at them, trying to get hold of their hair and clothing. Lucy yelped as one of them grabbed her and bit into her arm through the white lab coat. Blood pooled over the fabric, staining the cotton a deep dark red and the smell incensed the others. They pulled at her, tearing out chunks of hair and skin before the other vampires could reach her.

Gabi reacted first; he barged into the crowd, knocking away the creature that had bitten first. The vile thing still had strips of fabric caught in its sharp, broken teeth. He backhanded it, sending it smashing into a group of others. They fell back, not afraid but confused as they stumbled around. By this time Chez had hold of Lucy and he was pulling her away from the grasping hands of the others. There was a collection of men, women and children among the dead. All of whom had open hungry mouths that snapped and cracked as the immortals fought their way back outside.

Lilly leapt and kicked, punching back a crowd that tried to overwhelm her. The creatures didn't die when struck but they were slow to recover and so Lilly, Chez, Lucy and Gabi managed to physically fight their way out into the warehouse.

As they got through the initial horde, Lilly paused. She could see more of the creatures pouring into the room. There were thousands of them.

'This is like a nightmare ...' she gasped. Then, turning, she kicked out at yet another group that tried to reach for her.

Lilly leapt high above the crowd and hovered. She could see Chez and Gabi still fighting their way forward. The creatures were trying to bite and scratch the immortals. She flew forward, grabbed at Lucy from above and pulled her up, at the same time, sending the message 'Up!' to Chez and Gabi. Both of them immediately leapt up above the crowd.

'One of the benefits of being able to fly,' Lilly commented.

Lucy clasped her. She could fly herself but the bite of the creature had weakened her somehow and so she let herself be carried out of the warehouse, above the screaming, furious creatures as they roared their anger below them.

'Where's Anja?' yelled Gabi. 'She and Anthony can't fly!'

'I know,' Lilly said. 'Let's get the fuck away from here and find them.'

Outside they soared above the base, taking in what looked like the worst carnage from a war zone.

'They are fucking zombies,' Lilly said.

Lucrezia had recovered enough to fly herself, but her arm was aching and burning.

'I don't know what's going on,' she said. 'These creatures weren't part of anything we were doing here.'

'There! Anja and Anthony!' cried Gabi, and he flew directly over to the building where the two young vampires waited.

'What's going on?' asked Anthony.

'We don't know. It's like a George Romero movie down there,' Gabi said. 'I saw something like this in one of the Resident Evil films too.'

Lucy collapsed down onto the roof. 'Are you still into horror movies?'

'Yes,' said Anja. 'He is.'

The two women studied each other. Anja looked young and fresh and vibrant while Lucy looked grey and sick.

'Who the fuck are you?' asked Lucy.

'I'm Anja. I'm Gabi's lover. Who the fuck are *you*?'

'I'm Gabi's maker,' Lucy smirked at Anja's expression. Then she slumped, head lolling, bloody foam gurgling from her lips.

'Jesus!' said Anthony. 'What happened to her?'

'She was bitten by one of those things,' Lilly explained. 'This really doesn't look good.'

11
Renfield's Heart

Joe had his stash of blood packed into a small black rucksack which was thrown over his back. He scooped a wad of shredded paper up from the bin in Lucy's office and, stepping over the puddles of gasoline, he hurried back to the lab door. At the door he lit the paper in his hand and threw it into the office, then hurried across the lab to the corridor door. Once there, he lit another match and threw it into the nearest puddle of gas. He closed the lab door as he heard the familiar whoosh as the gasoline caught light.

Joe ran down the corridor. He knew there were several combustible components in the lab that would blow when a high temperature was reached. At the stairwell the fire extinguisher he had left propping open the door was still in place and Joe glanced back around at the deserted corridors and rooms. Everyone, fortunately, had evacuated the building it seemed. He pushed aside the extinguisher and entered the stairwell, slamming the door behind him.

Time to get out of here.

Joe began to climb the stairs up. He was on minus 5 when he heard a scream from below. Joe halted. He glanced down the stairwell but could see nothing but the rising plume of smoke from the furnace below. He turned back to the stairs and continued to climb. A few minutes later the lab blew. The ground shook so much that Joe was thrown against the wall and his skull cracked hard against the concrete. Somehow he managed to crawl to the top step then he slumped down, blood pooled in his left eye as it streamed down his forehead.

He pulled the rucksack from his back and removed one of the phials of blood. This would help him recover. This would give him the strength to get out of here. His hands trembled as he pulled at the stopper. It was airtight and Joe's hands felt weak. He was sure he had concussion. He placed the stopper in his mouth and twisted and pulled with his teeth until he heard the satisfying pop as the air broke through into the phial. He guzzled the blood carelessly, spilling some of it down his front. Then he lay back on the top step, eyes closed while the blood worked its magic.

He could smell the fumes and smoke even more now. The stairwell was full of it and Joe felt it burning his lungs, but for a while he didn't have the strength to stand.

Just need to get my breath back, he told himself.

The smoke thickened around him. He could taste the fire and ash in the air but his mind drifted, he remembered Lucy loving him. He imagined her in his arms. Only this time he was in charge and Lucy bowed to his will.

There was a scraping noise on the stairs below. Joe opened his eyes. He couldn't make out the bottom step but his heart lurched in fear. He cast aside the empty phial that was still gripped in his hand and staggered to his feet. Holding onto the wall, he looked down into the smoke. Another noise drew his attention. It was like nails on a chalk board, or bone scraping against bone.

Joe exhaled sharply as the creature came into view. The smoke seemed to clear around the thing. It was a charred and smoking bag of bones. Joe recognised this one. It was one of the revenants and it had somehow not only escaped its cell but had also managed to get past the security doors. Eighteen. That was it. Joe's foggy brain recalled that she had been brought in with Seventeen.

Eighteen took a step forward. Her bare, wasted feet stumbling onto the next step and then the next. Joe backed away. Then on instinct turned and ran upwards.

He was on minus three quickly and he didn't stop to catch his breath, just kept on going because he knew what would happen if Eighteen caught up with him and he really didn't want to die that way.

Minus two and Joe found the stairwell door open. He considered going onto that level but realised it would only be a matter of time before the fire reached there too. He pushed himself onwards. Minus one. Only one more flight and he would reach ground level.

Joe's lungs were bursting in his chest, every breath hurt as though he had swallowed glass. His heart bounced in his ribs like a trapped dog scratching at the door to his prison. He reached ground level, fumbled in his pocket for the security card. His fingers were damp and slick. He glanced down at the card. Blood dripped from his forehead onto the floor. He swiped the card. Nothing happened.

'Jesus. Fuck!'

He swiped again. Then he heard the scraping behind him. That secure slow walk, as though the creature felt no need to run. She knew she had him. Joe began to bang on the door. Surely someone would be on the other side making sure that all of the scientists and military staff got out safely.

'Help me! For fuck sake someone open this door!'

He turned around, staring at the smoke that seemed to precede her. The thing was definitely coming and she would eat him.

Joe slid to the floor. Panic made him feel momentarily blind and completely helpless. Despite the vampire blood he had consumed he knew he was no match for Eighteen. The revenants were strong and perpetually hungry. He banged his head back against the door as the smoke cleared again and Eighteen came into view.

She was grinning. That same moronic smile that Joe had seen so many times. This time though, there was intelligence lurking there too. She knew she had him. He would be her final meal no matter how this went down.

Then something extraordinary happened: the bare things, the monstrosities he had seen climbing from the walls on minus twenty, appeared from the smoke behind Eighteen and surrounded her. Her stupid evil smile finally dropped as the horde caught hold of her. They bit and tore at the ragged flesh. Eighteen screamed. Joe saw black blood splash from her poisoned veins. She struggled, a roar of anger and fear on her feral lips as the other creatures – and oh! Joe realised they were so much worse than her, for nothing could stop them until they had completed their awful task whatever that may be – dragged her back amongst them.

Joe imagined, but couldn't see, that they had taken her back, pulled her into the pit of hell from whence they came.

The horde turned to him. He opened his mouth to scream but no sound came out. A sharp pain gripped his chest and sent a tingling sensation down his arm. This was it. He was so scared, his heart was giving way. But no. Joe lived on. He saw their slow climb up, observed how they surrounded him, and didn't struggle when the first one bent and punched a hole straight through his chest. He was still alive when the creature pulled out his beating heart and held it up to the others like some sort of trophy.

12
Breaking the Circle

Lilly looked down at the silent group surrounding the building. It became obvious that the creatures knew the immortals were there as the horde, now thousands in number, gathered around below them. Some tried to scramble up the walls of the structure, only to slide down and be crushed by the next layer that pushed forward to touch the wall. While others just stared upwards at them, mouths open, hungry jaws snapping open and closed.

'How's Lucy?' she asked without turning round.

'If I didn't know better I would say she was dying,' Anthony said.

Anthony was kneeling beside her. He had removed her lab coat and tucked it under Lucy's head. He was now examining the bite on her arm.

'It looks infected,' Gabi said.

'Yes. And it's spreading.' Anthony pointed out.

Lilly turned around and looked down at the prone figure. Lucy's arm had turned a gangrenous green. Thin, black lines travelled the length of her arm and up towards her shoulder and a vile smell wafted up from the wound.

'Okay. So these things are dangerous to us. Anyone else been bitten or scratched?'

'They attacked us down below but they didn't ...' Anja said.

'I think we managed to get away in time,' Anthony said. 'Otherwise we'd be in the same mess.'

'Check anyway,' Lilly said, and Anja and Anthony began to check themselves over. Any normal wounds had healed almost immediately, and there was no sign of anything worse.

Chez came to the edge of the building and looked down. *What do we do*, he thought to Lilly. *We can't stay here indefinitely.*

'We could just fly away,' Lilly replied out loud. 'But then we wouldn't know anything about these things.'

'Who cares?' Gabi said. 'Let's get out of here. Maybe we can help Lucrezia then too.'

Lilly nodded, 'Okay. Escape now, observe later. It's as good a plan as any. Just one last look around though … Stay here. I'll be back soon.'

She took to the air and flew around the base. Below she saw a group of human soldiers die at the hands of inhuman dead and hungry children. The creatures swarmed over the men, biting and grabbing at their legs and ankles. One of the men fell over under the sheer weight of the onslaught. The soldier's blood spilt over the soil as they fell on him. Then, skeletal hands reached up from the dry sand, tearing at him from below. The ground opened up beneath him and the soldier was pulled back into the soil, screaming in terror as his mouth filled with sand.

The others began to shoot at the child monsters. But no matter what wounds they inflicted the horde continued to come until they had overwhelmed the humans by their mass and stamina.

Lilly flew on.

All around the base there were signs of devastation. Lilly noticed that a small group of scientists and soldiers were holding out in the reception building. So far the security doors had repelled the creatures that pressed against them. The building was surrounded however. She knew that they had no hope of escape if these monsters remained outside. The occupants would either die from starvation or they would become food for the fiends.

Near the food store warehouse Lilly saw a woman ripped in two as the creatures fought over her body. Her limbs tore away as though she were nothing more than a scarecrow stuffed with straw. One of the vile dead fell upon her remains and began to lap up her blood, while another ripped open her abdomen and lifted out her intestines and began to pass them out to the other creatures like rare delicacies. They fed each other the gore as though sharing a delicious feast. It was like a ritual and Lilly recalled that some ancient tribes had indulged in cannibalism as a way to take power from their enemies. They ate flesh in order to consume the soul of the person. It was a grotesque practice and one that she now felt resembled the behaviour of these monstrous things.

Lilly flew back to the others, the screams of the dying still ringing in her ears.

'Let's get out of here. This place is fucked,' she said.

'Thank God,' said Anja. 'I thought you might go all bleeding heart on us and try and rescue some of the humans.'

'Such an attempt would be suicide,' Lilly said. 'I'll take Lucy …' she said.

She bent to lift Lucrezia's unconscious body and the woman snapped awake. Turning her head towards Lilly. Lucy's eyes had changed. The once vibrant green was now a dark, bloody black.

Lilly jumped back as Lucy snapped at her; fangs drawn, her teeth dripping with vile green ichor.

'Don't let her bite you!' Gabi shouted. 'Lucy stop! We're trying to help you.'

Lucy was beyond help though. She raised herself up into a crouch, holding herself up by hooked, claw-like hands. Her demeanour was primitive. Her movements were reminiscent of a madwoman instead of the strong and fierce intelligence of an ancient vampire.

'Jesus! She's changing into one of them!' Anja said.

The five immortals surrounded Lucy. She snarled and snapped at them, teeth and fangs gnashing at her own lips until they were pouring black poisonous blood which she licked back up with obvious pleasure. Her eyes bled black pus, her teeth dripped blood and venom and her body became as twisted and monstrous as the dead things below.

'This isn't you!' Gabi said, trying to placate her. 'We need to get you out of here and get some help. You can see that can't you?'

Lucy dived for him, but Gabi leapt into the air and so she crashed past where he had stood, stumbling and falling onto the roof top. She roared with fury. Below, the crowd of naked creatures began to chant as though in response to her rage. She lifted herself up, took a tottering step and fell forward again.

She raised her head. She had transformed once more, back to her former self. She shook herself, her eyes had cleared and she stared back at the other vampires.

'What happened?' she said then slumped forward. 'Help me ...'

Lilly ran forward and turned her over. Lucy was once again unconscious.

'That's decided it. We're getting the fuck out now,' Lilly said.

'Anja,' Gabi said and she ran into his arms quickly.

'I'll take Lucy,' said Chez.

'No. I'll take her. Take Anthony for me, *please*?'

Lilly stood and embraced Chez. Her lips pressed against his throat. 'I love you. Please be careful. Whatever happens, promise me that you'll get away as fast as you can?'

Chez pushed back and looked into her eyes. 'What are you planning?'

Lilly shook her head. 'There's a circle around us.'

'What?'

'A circle of power. It's keeping us in, but more importantly it's keeping them in too.'

'Can you break through?' Chez asked.

'Yes. But I may not be able to restore it.'

Chez looked down at the chanting dead below. 'What will happen?'

'I don't know. They may follow us, killing everything and everyone in their wake.'

'Jesus,' said Anja. 'Not much of a choice.'

Lilly was silent for a moment, then she said, 'I'll stay behind with Lucy to distract them while I raise another circle.'

'I'm staying too. You can't do this alone,' Chez said.

'I need you to make sure everyone is safe ...'

'Lilly, what kind of man do you take me for? Do you think I can leave you in danger?'

'Chez, there's no time for chivalry. That's all bullshit anyway. Do you think it will help me if you or anyone else is injured?'

Gabi stepped forward, 'She's right Chez, and if anyone can survive this Lilly can. I have seen enough to know she could probably take on this entire horde and come out of it without a scratch.'

'If I had access to ley magic right now, that would probably be true. I'd just raise a door and we'd all be out of here,' Lilly smiled. 'Let them try and follow that.'

'We could try to raise a door,' Anthony said. 'I could help you.'

'I tried already,' Lilly said. 'It was no good. Nothing can get through this barrier. It's a strong and ancient magic. I've never felt anything like it before.'

'Then what makes you think you can break it?' asked Anthony.

'I can break a hole in it. But the magic will be crude and may not hold. Which is why you all need to be ready to fly when I do.'

They debated for a few moments how they would escape. Then Lilly withdrew her herb pouch from her jeans pocket and began to create another circle that filled a quarter of the roof. Inside this circle she added another one around Lucy.

'That will hold her if she decides to try and take a chunk out of me,' Lilly said.

Then she took Chez's arm again. 'Be ready.'

His eyes met hers. *I can't leave you!*

If all goes well I'll be right behind you, she thought.

Chez threw his arms around her then quickly turned back to Anthony, embracing him and lifting him up off the roof.

'Head towards the perimeter,' Lilly said and she watched as Gabi lifted Anja and followed Chez and Anthony.

Lilly turned back to the circle. Entering it, she closed the inner one, blocking Lucy off from the outer circle, then she raised her arms and began to chant her own words of power. The Latin fell naturally from her tongue and Lilly felt the hairs raise on the back of her neck as that old familiar power began to twist and turn around her, rapidly closing the bigger circle.

Sealed inside she heard the cries of the dead diminish as she turned around and around in the centre. She couldn't reach a ley line but she could access something else. She pulled all of the magic she could up through the manmade building, directly from the earth. She felt the shifting of the sand beneath the structure. Her mind's eye travelled down and down, passing more of the dead that were too far buried to raise themselves up above the ground. Still, they stirred as though they felt her essence touch them.

Lilly felt pain as the ancient dead railed against her psyche, but she pushed them aside, opening the channel all the way to the Earth's core.

The energy suddenly engulfed her, she threw back her head and let the magic explode through her body until she felt the current, like an electric charge, surging up through her feet and into her core. She joined with the power. She became its conductor and she let down the barrier of her outer circle as she lifted her face to stare at the point of origin, the thing that held the barrier in place.

It floated above her, watching the proceedings with interest. Lilly couldn't see a shape but she had the impression of heritage. Native American. It was using the strength of the dead to animate them, but how?

Lilly turned as the thing flitted around the smaller circle. She could see it now. Nothing more than a light but for all its brightness, a dark core lurked inside the illuminated centre. It smelt of vengeance and hatred: as though it had been hiding for years, waiting to avenge some ancient wrong.

'*Quisnam es vos?*' Lilly asked, still speaking Latin. *Who are you?*

The being didn't answer, but then it had no mouth, no form, no physical shape at all.

Energy crackled from Lilly's fingertips. It wanted to be used so that it could return once more to the earth. It stung to hold inside her, but still she hesitated. What would the thing do when she broke the circle? On impulse she projected some of the energy at the shape. It skittered away, but still she had the sense that it was watching her and would act when she did.

She turned then. Faced the barrier that held her family in and, closing her eyes, sent out a current of energy like a sharp lightning bolt right into the heart of the circle of power surrounding the base.

For a moment nothing happened. Then the sky flashed, the barrier imploded and the sparks sent Lilly tumbling backwards. There was a domino effect on the small circle. The magic dropped and Lilly fell through, right onto Lucrezia.

Lilly turned to see that Lucy was once more a creature of the dead. Her black eyes burned, and she sank her fangs deep into Lilly's hand. Lilly screamed. The bite burnt like nothing Lilly had ever felt. She pulled back, stumbling and fell from the roof of the building towards the waiting arms of the hungry dead.

It felt like everything happened in slow motion. She stared upwards at the staggering horror that had been Lucrezia. Lilly tried to lift herself out of the fall, calling on her vampiric nature and on the power she had borrowed from the Earth's core, but the energy had left her and so she fell, unable to stop herself.

The chanting continued as they caught her in their skeletal hands. She twisted and turned, but the strength had left her and she couldn't free herself. She was passed over the heads of the dead, onwards until they came to the point from which this horror had began. Lilly knew when she saw the bled corpse which had once been Private Elin, that this man had been the source of light and dark she had felt on the roof top. His dead soul was in some way controlling them.

The ground opened up under her. Dirt mixed with churning sand to reveal a golden grave. The chanting dead began to fall back into the ground around her.

This is it, she thought. Somehow by breaking the barrier I have made them return to their graves.

She saw Chez then, clasped and still and in the arms of a

group of female corpses.

'No!' Lilly screamed.

She managed to pull one arm free but was soon engulfed by more of the horde and found that she was helpless. She cried out as they pulled Chez down into the earth in front of her. Then came Anja, Anthony and Gabriele.

'Dear God no!' Lilly sobbed.

Somehow she had failed them. The barrier had brought them all crashing down to the ground: right into the arms of the corpses, or revenants. *No. The hungry dead, her mind corrected.* But what was their hunger really for? Flesh or revenge?

Gabi struggled as he was buried in the sand, the grains moving as he tried to escape the clutches of the dead who held him. But then they stilled.

They finally dragged Lilly into the sand. She felt the grains move as though each one had purpose and intent. The sand slid silently up and over her and she was pulled down into the cool grasp of the earth, held in the greedy hands of the dead. At some point she felt the presence of Lucy, burrowing down of her own accord. They were now in the earth and part of the dead. Just where they belonged.

The sands moved and curled above, smoothing over the place where an undead horde had just vanished. Then the movement stilled, and the sands were silent once more.

Epilogue
The Desolate Base

The viper arrived several seconds after the ground smoothed over the burial ground and the reanimated dead returned to their sandy graves. From the air the pilot could see a desolate landscape. What had once been the topside of a military base now revealed nothing more than broken and collapsed buildings, and burning piles of rubble.

'Washington, this is Zero Nine-a Six Seven. The buildings seem to be on fire. We can see no movement. No survivors. I repeat no survivors.'

'What the hell went on down there?' asked the co-pilot.

'Beats me,' said the pilot. 'I don't want to know either.'

'Zero Nine-a Six Seven, this is Washington. Destroy any structures remaining.'

'Napalm?' confirmed the pilot.

'That's an affirmative.'

The viper turned, making one more pass before completing its task on the third round. The napalm bomb dropped, free-falling into the centre of the base. The viper swooped up and back far enough away to watch the damage.

The bomb exploded about fifty feet above the base, showering it with the sticky, ignited chemical. What remained of the base exploded into intense flames.

'Washington: We have a clean sweep,' reported the pilot.

'Come on home,' came the response.

The pilot turned the viper back and away from the area of devastation.

'Jim,' said the co-pilot, 'we didn't land. What if there were survivors.'

'There were no survivors,' the pilot said firmly.

ABOUT THE AUTHOR

Award winning author Sam Stone began her professional writing career in 2007 when her first novel won the Silver Award for Best Novel with *ForeWord Magazine* Book of the Year Awards. Since then she has gone on to write several novels, three novellas and many short stories. She was the first woman in 31 years to win the British Fantasy Society Award for Best Novel. She also won the award for Best Short Fiction in the same year (2011).

Stone loves all genus fiction and enjoys mixing horror (her first passion) with a variety of different genres including science fiction, fantasy and steampunk.

Her works can be found in paperback, audio and e-book.

PRAISE FOR SAM STONE

'A deceptively readable date with darkness – watch your step! This book is lit for the much more discerning chick (and cock) who likes to walk in the shadows. Relax with it, but be prepared for sudden jewels and little masterpieces and the rug to be pulled from under your feet.' Tanith Lee on *Killing Kiss*

'Stone has such fun reinventing the material and running it through a horror-come-steampunk grinder that it works and marvellously well ... The obvious progenitor in this field is *Pride and Prejudice and Zombies* but Stone's work is far more engaging and less forced than that one-joke outing.' Peter Tennant on *Zombies at Tiffany's*

'Sam Stone without doubt is a mistress of the grisly and the glutinous. I believe that we can look forward to seeing Sam Stone develop into a major influence in the realm of blood and shadows and things that wake you up, wide-eyed, in the middle of the night.' Graham Masterton

'*Zombies at Tiffany's* reminds me a lot of Alan Moore's *League of Extraordinary Gentlemen* or the work of H G Wells ... this is a brilliantly authored piece of steampunk literature, and then some.' Jim Reader, *Exquisite Terror*

MORE TITLES BY SAM STONE

THE VAMPIRE GENE SERIES
Horror, thriller, time-travel series.
1: KILLING KISS
2: FUTILE FLAME
3: DEMON DANCE
4: HATEFUL HEART
5: SILENT SAND
6: JADED JEWEL (Forthcoming)

KAT LIGHTFOOT MYSTERIES
Steampunk, horror, adventure series
1: ZOMBIES AT TIFFANY'S
2: KAT ON A HOT TIN AIRSHIP
3: WHAT'S DEAD PUSSYKAT
4: KAT OF GREEN TENTACLES

JINX CHRONICLES
Hi–tech science fiction fantasy series
1: JINX TOWN
2: JINX MAGIC (Forthcoming)
3: JINX BOUND (Forthcoming)

THE DARKNESS WITHIN
Science Fiction Horror Short Novel

ZOMBIES IN NEW YORK AND OTHER BLOODY JOTTINGS
Thirteen stories of horror and passion, and six mythological and
erotic poems from the pen of the new Queen of Vampire fiction.

www.ingramcontent.com/pod-product-compliance
Lightning Source LLC
Chambersburg PA
CBHW070433170726
48291CB00002B/478